INFELICIA
AND OTHER WRITINGS

INFELICIA
AND OTHER WRITINGS

Adah Isaacs Menken

edited by Gregory Eiselein

broadview literary texts

National Library of Canada Cataloguing in Publication Data

Menken, Adah Isaacs, 1835–1868
    Infelicia and other writings

(Broadview literary texts)
Includes bibliographical references.
ISBN 1-55111-284-1

I. Eiselein, Gregory, 1965-   II. Title.   III. Series.

PS2389.M2415 2002   811'.4   C2002-900672-4

Broadview Press Ltd. is an independent, international publishing house, incorporated in 1985.

North America:
P.O. Box 1243, Peterborough, Ontario, Canada K9J 7H5
3576 California Road, Orchard Park, NY 14127
TEL: (705) 743-8990; FAX: (705) 743-8353;
E-MAIL: customerservice@broadviewpress.com

United Kingdom:
Thomas Lyster Ltd
Unit 9, Ormskirk Industrial Park
Old Boundary Way, Burscough Road
Ormskirk, Lancashire L39 2YW
TEL: (01695) 575112; FAX: (01695) 570120; E-mail: books@tlyster.co.uk

Australia:
St. Clair Press, P.O. Box 287, Rozelle, NSW 2039
TEL: (02) 818-1942; FAX: (02) 418-1923

www.broadviewpress.com

Broadview Press gratefully acknowledges the financial support of the Book Publishing Industry Development Program, Ministry of Canadian Heritage, Government of Canada.

Broadview Press is grateful to Professor Eugene Benson and Professor L. W. Conolly for advice on editorial matters for the Broadview Literary Texts series.

PRINTED IN CANADA

Contents

for Victor

Acknowledgements

In preparing this edition of Adah Isaacs Menken's *Infelicia and Other Writings* I have had help from many different colleagues, universities, libraries, and archives. I am very pleased to thank Renée Sentilles. She shared with me her sense of humor and her vast store of research and insight on Menken. She read my introduction. I am grateful too for copies of the Menken texts she discovered in *The Liberty Gazette*. Peter Dollard, another generous and intrepid Menken scholar, also shared his research. For listening to my ideas about Menken and offering helpful responses, I would like to thank Paula Bennett, Elizabeth Petrino, Janet Gray, Marianne Noble, Cheryl Torsney, and the anonymous readers for Broadview Press. The archivists at the Harvard Theatre Collection provided valuable assistance. So did the staffs at the Jacob Rader Marcus Center of the American Jewish Archives at Hebrew Union College (Cincinnati), the Department of Rare Books and Manuscripts at the Boston Public Library, the American Jewish Historical Society, and the Carl A. Kroch and John M. Olin Libraries at Cornell University, especially Nancy Skipper. For help in locating the German poems Menken translated, I thank Martha Hsu. I am grateful to Nilli Diengott for help with questions about Menken's Hebrew.

I would also like to thank my colleagues and students at Kansas State University, which has been a happy and productive place to work. Amy Grieshaber and the other students in my Nineteenth-Century American Poetry course first encouraged me to pursue this project. Larry Rodgers offered his enthusiasm and insight; he also found ways to fund editorial assistance and visits to libraries and archives in Ohio and New York. The Provost's Office provided much needed support in the form of a USRG grant that enabled me to spend time at Harvard, the Boston Public Library, and the American Jewish Historical Society. The always helpful staff of Kansas State's Interlibrary Loan department (Kathy Coleman, Sharon Van Rysselburghe, Lori Fenton, Bernie Randall, and Cherie Geise) managed to locate a number of difficult-to-find texts. Sara Wege provided valuable computer support and help with numerous details. For assistance with transcription, proofreading, and research, I want to thank Kyle Semmel, Audrea Suther, and especially Amy Mauton, whose year of work on this edition was consistently excellent. For reading Juan Clemente Zenea's poetry with me, my appreciation goes to Christina Hauck. For help with questions about Menken's translations from Latin and German, I thank Linda Brigham. And for their conversations with me about Menken, I am grateful to Linda Brigham, Melissa Divine, Michele Janette, Amy Mauton, Amy Grieshaber, and Victor Force.

Working with Broadview Press has been a pleasure, and I thank Don LePan, Julia Gaunce, Mical Moser, and Barbara Conolly for their support of this project.

For permission to publish letters by Menken from their manuscript collections, I thank the American Jewish Historical Society; the Boston Public Library/Rare Books Department, Courtesy of the Trustees; and the Harvard Theatre Collection, Houghton Library. For "The Menken" (from *Mark Twain of the Enterprise: Newspaper Articles and Other Documents, 1862–1864,* ed. Henry Nash Smith, copyright © 1957 Mark Twain Company), I gratefully acknowledge permission from the University of California Press.

Adah Isaacs Menken. Photograph courtesy of the Harvard Theatre Collection, Houghton Library.

Introduction

Learning about Adah Isaacs Menken's extraordinary life and writings is best done with an appreciation for questions and ambiguities rather than a need for definite or simple answers. When sorting through the facts about her life, an alert skepticism is also handy, though perhaps no amount of historical rigor could infallibly separate the facts from the legends that swirl around her.

The questions begin with her birth and the various, disputed stories about her parentage. In the version most common among her nineteenth-century biographers, Menken's father is James McCord, and she is born as Adelaide McCord on 15 June 1835 in Milneburg, Louisiana, near New Orleans. The original source for these details might be Menken herself, who seems to have given this or similar information to Thomas Allston Brown.[1]

Yet Menken's own personal narrative, the rather dramatic "Notes of My Life" (see Appendix A), claims she was born as Marie Rachel Adelaide de Vere Spenser on 11 December 1839 in New Orleans to a father named Richard Irving Spenser and a mother named Marie Josephine de Vere Laliette. Few biographers have ever accepted this version of her life story, in part because its narrative style makes extravagant use of formulas borrowed from popular fiction. At other times and places, Menken had different but equally romantic versions of her life story. In 1865 she revealed her real name as Dolores Adios Los Fiertes, the daughter of a French woman from New Orleans and a Jewish man from Spain, and moved the year of her birth to 1841. In an early encounter with the press about the details of her life, an 1860 series in the *New-York Illustrated News*, Menken said she was born in January 1839 and identified her father as Josiah Campbell. In addition to Adah, Adelaide, Ada, Marie

---

[1] In 1861 Menken sent Brown biographical notes that she insists were "strictly *true*," notes that he probably used in his sketch of her life. See Menken to Thomas Allston Brown in Appendix B; and Brown, 243-44. Most of the biographical information in this Introduction is from the nineteenth-century biographical sources in Appendix A, the correspondence in Appendix B, and the works by Lesser, Mankowitz, and Sentilles listed in the Bibliography at the end of this volume.

Rachel Adelaide, Dolores, and Dolo, she also went by the names Ada Bertha, Ada Bertha Theodore, and Rachel Adah Isaacs.

Other nineteenth-century accounts of her life would have different "facts." *The American Year Book and National Register*, for instance, records her birthplace as Chicago in 1832, as does the *New-York Tribune*. Joaquin Miller, on the other hand, insists it was Cincinnati. Because he seemed passionate about biographical inaccuracies and indicated first-hand knowledge about her life, one might be inclined to accept Miller's story as possibly more reliable; but, according to his biographer, Miller didn't really know Menken.[1]

Twentieth-century researchers would find evidence for still other renditions of Menken's parentage and birth. A current and often accepted scholarly account of her life argues that Menken was born Philomène Croi Théodore on 3 May 1839 in New Orleans. Her mixed race father, Auguste Théodore, is described as a "free man of color," while her French Creole mother is identified as Magdaleine Jean Louis Janneaux. With this understanding of her family history and cultural background, scholars began treating Menken as an African American author. Another version of her life insists that Menken was Jewish from birth, locates her birth in Milneburg on 15 June 1835, but then concedes her parents are not precisely identifiable. Some have been persuaded by evidence that suggests she was born Ada McCord on 15 June 1835 in Memphis, while still others have adopted the view that she was born "Ada Bertha Theodore near New Orleans to a Creole father and a Jewish-Irish mother" in 1835.[2]

Bewildering as this beginning might be, with its surfeit of

---

[1] "Menken, Adah Isaacs," *The American Year Book and National Register for 1869* (Hartford, 1869), 790–91; Obituary, *New-York Tribune* (12 Aug. 1868): 5; Miller in Appendix C. In *Splendid Poseur: Joaquin Miller—American Poet* (New York: Thomas Y. Crowell Company, 1953), M.M. Marberry points out that "Menken was not in San Francisco when Joaquin was there in 1862" (49).

[2] For respective instances of these twentieth-century versions of Menken's life, see Mankowitz, 34; Lesser, 248; Cofran, 54; Scharnhorst, 310. For examples of literary historians who have treated Menken as an African American writer, see Sherman; Gates and Sherman. For a critical examination of Menken's biographers, see Brooks. For the most insightful and reliable account of Menken's life and the complexities of her biography (and biographers), see Sentilles.

possible parents, birthdates, birthplaces, and ethnic identities (Irish, Jewish, Creole, African American, French, Spanish, British, and Scotch-Irish), Menken's later life is equally complex and often just as enigmatic. Wherever exactly she was born, New Orleans is the place Menken considered the hometown of her childhood. She had a sister who went by the name Josephine, Jo(e), or Annie (Campbell) Josephs and a brother called John Auguste, Augustus, or Gus. Her father died, it seems, in 1842, and her mother re-married a Josiah Campbell. As a child, she may have been a dancer and performer along with her sister.[1] Moreover, at some point in her life, Menken enjoyed an ample liberal education, particularly for a young woman. She was well read and knew several languages, not only the French and English of her hometown, but also Latin and German, Spanish probably, a little Hebrew, and purportedly even ancient Greek. Although she did not have the kind of comprehensive, systematic university education available to America's elite male authors, Menken's contemporaries often commented on her intelligence, wide reading, and her ability with languages. Her contemporaries described her as "well educated" and "very intelligent," and Adrian Marx took note of the breadth, if not depth, of her erudition: "she possessed a smattering of all human knowledge. She knew and talked on every subject with giddying facility, from the dialects of the New World to transcendental mathematics, from Latin to philosophy—from versification to theology."[2]

In 1855 Menken was living in East Texas, giving readings of Shakespeare, and writing poems and sketches for *The Liberty Gazette*. In February of that year in Galveston County, under the name Miss Adda Theodore, she married W.H. or Nelson Kneass (1823–68/69), the Philadelphia-born musician, composer (most famous for his music to the popular "Ben Bolt"), and founder of the Kneass Opera Troupe. Her marriage to Kneass might have

---

[1]   Little is known about her brother; and most biographers loose track of her sister after 1860 (see Lesser 251), though a letter at the AJHS indicates she died on 28 April 1862 in New Orleans. See Menken, to Henry Francis Keenan, 5 Sept. 1862, AJHS.

[2]   Obituary, *New-York Tribune* (12 Aug. 1868): 5; Charles Reade qtd. in Stoddard, 478; [Adrian Marx?], "Letter of Paris Correspondent," *New York World* (20 Aug. 1868?), from transcription at AJA.

been her first. It is the first documented. Yet there were also rumors about other early marriages—one about someone from Louisville, another about a man named "McA—" from New Orleans. Menken's own autobiography claims she wed Juan Clemente Zenea (1832-71), the Cuban poet and revolutionary, before seeing the marriage "legally dissolved" by the courts. Such a claim has seemed far-fetched to Menken biographers, but the exact mix of truth and legend in Menken biography has always been difficult to sort out. Zenea did remember Menken in his poetry; and José Lezama Lima, the great modern Cuban writer and one of the foremost authorities on Cuban literature, believes the teenage lovers had "una relación íntima" in Havana in 1850, one that Zenea recalled nostalgically for the rest of his life.[1]

Whether it was her first or second, her marriage to Kneass didn't last long. The following year, on 3 April 1856, in Livingston, Texas, she married Alexander Isaac Menken, another musician. Alexander was the son of Solomon Menken, a successful wholesale dry goods dealer and the head of a German Jewish family who had lived in Cincinnati since 1820. She took the last name, adopted Alexander's middle name and appended an "s," and added an "h" to her own first name, becoming and more or less remaining Adah Isaacs Menken. While married to Alexander, Adah began to develop a career as a professional actress, first on a New Orleans/ southern Louisiana/ eastern Texas circuit and later, after moving to Cincinnati in June 1857, through the Midwest. In Cincinnati, before Alexander's family and the Jewish community in general, Adah presented herself as Jewish from birth. She never converted in any formal or official manner, and there are reasons to doubt the view (promoted by Menken, some of her nineteenth-century contemporaries, and some twentieth-century

---

[1] Menken in Appendix A; José Lezama Lima, Prólogo, in Juan Clemente Zenea, *Poesía* (La Habana: Editorial Nacional de Cuba, 1966), 12. On the grounds of a chronological impossibility, Lesser and Mankowitz have each rejected Menken's claim that she married Zenea (Lesser, 247; Mankowitz, 31). But see Zenea, *Poesía*, especially Lezama Lima's introduction (11-12, 17 [7-19]) and Zenea's "Infelicia" (291-95), and "El Olvido Me Mató" ["The Forgetfulness Killed Me"] (37-38). Dollard also points to the Zenea-Menken connection, noting that Zenea's "biographers assert that the two met in Havana in 1850" (Dollard, 105n12).

scholars such as Allan Lesser) that she was born and raised Jewish. Nevertheless, she soon began writing exuberant, often serious Jewish-themed poems and essays for *The Israelite*, Cincinnati's Jewish newspaper, edited by the distinguished Rabbi Isaac Mayer Wise, the founder of organized Reform Judaism in the U.S. Moreover, the Menken family, Wise, and the Cincinnati Jewish community embraced Adah as Jewish. She studied Hebrew with Wise, applauded the admission of Baron Rothschild to the British Parliament, denounced the Catholic church's kidnapping of a six-year-old Jewish boy, delivered a lecture on Judaism at a Louisville synagogue, published poems and essays in *The Jewish Messenger* (a New York weekly), and began work on a book of "Tales and Poems on Judaism." Yet, as Adah actively pursued her career, becoming a successful actress and an increasingly well-known celebrity, and as Alexander took to drinking, their marriage slowly deteriorated, until July 1859 when they were granted a rabbinical divorce and Adah left Cincinnati for New York.[1]

By September, Menken was performing in Albany and had begun publishing poems in the *Sunday Mercury*. She had also married again, this time to a famous boxer named John Carmel Heenan—or, as he was known to prizefighting fans, the Benicia Boy. By the new year, however, Heenan had abandoned his new and now pregnant spouse, leaving for England on 5 January 1860 to fight in a match for the heavyweight championship of the world and denying through his press agents and associates his marriage to Menken. The couple soon thereafter became the focus of a scandal covered in various national newspapers—a scandal that included charges of bigamy and revelations about Menken's previous marriage to Alexander, public statements affirming and denying the marriage of Menken to the Benicia Boy, and reports about the death of their infant son in the summer of 1860. During this tumultuous year, Menken began socializing with Walt Whitman, Ada Clare, and the rest of a group of bohemian writers and critics who gathered at Pfaff's beer

---

[1]   About her lecture in Louisville, see *The Israelite*'s German-language supplement *Die Deborah* (24 Dec. 1858):149. About the proposed volume of "Tales and Poems on Judaism," see *The Israelite* (16 Oct. 1857): 118; and *Die Deborah* (20 Nov. 1857):109.

cellar in New York City. No doubt influenced by Whitman and this circle of bohemian friends, she wrote a series of rather unconventional poems and essays for the *Sunday Mercury*. The year and a half from March 1860 through the summer of 1861 would be the most creative and prolific period in Menken's career as a poet. It was also the most painful and depressing period of her personal life. Following Heenan's desertion, the ensuing financial difficulties, the newspaper scandals and public humiliation, the death of her son and later her mother, a desperate and dejected Menken contemplated suicide and penned at the end of the year a note that explained, "I have suffered so much, that there can not be any more for me" ("To the Public," 29 Dec. 1860, in Appendix B).

She didn't, however, take her own life, and in the new year Menken would find her acting career blossom as never before. In June 1861, in Albany, Menken took the stage for the first time as the male lead in the dramatic version of Byron's *Mazeppa*, a role that would make her a world-famous celebrity. She later married the *Sunday Mercury*'s literary editor, the humorist and pundit Robert Henry Newell, known to the public by his pen name "Orpheus C. Kerr," in September 1862. During the midst of the Civil War, in 1863-64, the couple relocated to the West where Menken performed to packed houses in San Francisco, Sacramento, and Virginia City, Nevada, and in the process became the most highly paid actress of her time. She also met a new circle of literary friends, including Mark Twain, Bret Harte, Ina Coolbrith, and Charles Warren Stoddard. She reunited with bohemian comrades from Pfaff's, Ada Clare and Charles F. Browne (better known as "Artemus Ward"), and began contributing to San Francisco's literary paper, the *Golden Era*. While her career prospered, her marriage failed; the modest, conventional, sometimes sullen, and often condescending Newell seems to have been a poor match for Menken. In 1864 she sailed to London after a brief stay in New York, and eventually the couple divorced.

Menken was a triumphant success in London, opening in *Mazeppa* on 3 October 1864. She also had a new boyfriend named Captain James Barkley, who was a gambler turned financier and, like Menken, a Southerner. Although she resisted marrying him for two years, the couple eventually wed, after learning of her pregnancy, in August of 1866. Three days later, Menken departed for Paris, never to see him again. In November, she gave birth to a son, Louis Dudevant Victor Emmanuel Barkley, who later died in the summer of 1867. Before his death, however, Menken became a star in Paris in a prosperous, long-running production called *Les Pirates de la Savane.*

During this period, Menken's celebrity and wealth permitted her to foster something of a literary salon in London composed of the bohemian writers, critics, artists, and intellectuals whose company she so enjoyed. There she mixed with critics like John Oxenford and writers such as Charles Dickens, Dante Gabriel Rossetti, and Algernon Charles Swinburne (with whom she allegedly had an affair in late 1867 and early 1868). In Paris as well, Menken loved socializing with writers like George Sand, Théophile Gautier, and Aléxandre Dumas. She enjoyed a close (some suggest erotic) relationship with Sand and an intimate (some suggest erotic) friendship with Dumas, which led to rumors of an affair following the public circulation of photographs of Menken and Dumas together. Although she wrote little poetry during the years she spent in London and Paris, she did begin to collect her poems for the volume that eventually became *Infelicia*. In May 1868, as the publication of her collection slowly moved forward, Menken grew ill, stopped performing, and drew up a will. Despite a period of convalescence and recuperation that summer and even some plans to return to the stage in *Les Pirates de la Savane*, Menken died in Paris on 10 August 1868 and was buried in the Jewish section of the Père la Chaise cemetery. The following week *Infelicia* was published.

In most of the biographies and criticism about Menken, her scandalous behavior and theatre career tend to overshadow how important literature was to her. Wherever she lived, she sought out writers. In New York, it was Whitman and the literati who frequented Pfaff's; in the West, it was Bret Harte and Mark Twain; in London, Swinburne and the Rossetti's; in Paris, Sand and Dumas. Although she knew acting paid far better than poetry, Menken thought of herself as a writer and saw writing as essential to her identity and survival: "I am writing again, which is my only salvation," she wrote to her friend Ed James (qtd. in Mankowitz, 112-113). Moreover, while not a prolific poet, she did produce a significant body of work between 1855 and 1868, publishing almost twenty essays, around 100 individual poems, and a book of collected poems.

Menken's earliest work appeared in *The Liberty Gazette*, while she was living in east Texas in 1855. During the mid-1850s, Menken allegedly published a volume of poems titled *Memories* under the pseudonym "Indigena," yet no copy has ever been located, and scholars now seriously doubt it ever existed.[1] Her earliest extant efforts are mostly poems of love and devotion addressed to her family (like "I Am Thine") and flirtatious light verse (such as "New Advertisement!!!"). In early pieces such as "Wounded" and "A Twilight Whisper," however, Menken also writes about death and experiments with poetic personas: the speaker of "Wounded," for example, is a male soldier at the moment of his death.

While married to Alexander Menken, the center of Adah's literary career was *The Israelite*. She kept authoring affectionate poems of admiration, now dedicating them either to members of the Menken family or to fellow writers for *The Israelite*. She also started sending essays and poems to *The Jewish Messenger* in New York. Unlike her early pieces, the poems from this period explore traditional Jewish themes such as the importance of reflection at Rosh Hashanah, God's presentation of the Law on Mount Sinai, and the death of Moses. With the exception of the republication of her essay on "Shylock," her work for the *Messenger* focused primarily on spiritual themes, in particular the immortality of the soul. In *The Israelite*, however, her poems and prose pieces addressed religious as well as contemporary Jewish political issues, including antisemitism, the admission of Rothschild to Parliament, and the Catholic church's kidnapping of a six-year-old Jewish boy named Edgardo Mortara.

Menken's Jewish-themed work continued into the 1860s, in

---

[1] Barclay provides two early poems he claims appeared in *Memories*, "Wounded" and "'Milton wrote a letter to his lady love.'" See Barclay, 30.

poems such as "Hear, O Israel!" and essays such as "Affinity of Poetry and Religion." Nevertheless, when Menken moved to New York, endured a distressing marriage to and divorce from Heenan, and began her association with the circle of writers who frequented Pfaff's, the form and content of Menken's verse changed. Her writings from the early 1860s, most of them appearing in the pages of the New York *Sunday Mercury*, tend to focus on love and lost love, sorrow and misfortune, intense unhappiness and despair. Some poems treat the agony of betrayal, the loss of hope, and the experience of death as a welcome release from the pain of life. Others represent an exhilarating return of courage, power, and even revenge. Still others are about the need to mask or hide one's identity in order to survive in a vicious world that has no place for women's passions or desires. The most striking aspects of these poems are the daring eroticism, the defiant declarations of female independence, and the thematizations of rage, vengeance, and wild despair. Formally, the poems range from the sentimental, to occasional poems and dedications, to what she called her "wild soul-poems" in free verse (see "Notes on My Life," in Appendix A). During these years, she also supplied the *Sunday Mercury* with translations of contemporary German and ancient and medieval Latin poetry as well as several prose pieces. The essays addressed topics ranging from Whitman's poetry (one of the first positive public assessments of his work), to the connection between creativity and Jewish spirituality, to the need for women's education and independence.

After she left New York for San Francisco in the summer of 1863, Menken wrote only about a half dozen new poems and revised some earlier work. In 1863 and 1864, she published three new poems and several revised or reprinted pieces in the San Francisco *Golden Era*. Later, she would publish a poem ("Reply to Dora Shaw") in the *New York Clipper* and write a couple of poems that were never published in her lifetime, "The Poet" and "Venetia." The last years of her career as a poet were dedicated to collecting and revising poems for publication in her only book, *Infelicia*. Dedicated to her London acquaintance Charles Dickens, *Infelicia* remained in print through several editions from

1868 to 1902. Most of the reviews were negative or condescending, which isn't surprising. As Marie Louise Hankins's article on "The Female Writer" (in Appendix D) illustrates, women writers in the nineteenth-century encountered fierce public censure for their work, and Menken's very public career and her unconventional life, ideas, and poetic style all served to exacerbate such disapproval. Her work did manage to find some admirers, however, including writers like Rossetti and Miller.

Menken is the first poet and the only woman poet before the twentieth century to follow the revolution in prosody started by Whitman's *Leaves of Grass* (1855). Her adoption of free verse—her avant-garde use of poetic forms dependent on neither regular rhyme nor regular meter for their rhythms and patterns of sound—is truly exceptional. Although the majority of her poems were composed in a conventional, rhyming, accentual-syllabic verse, two-thirds of the poems she selected for *Infelicia* were in free verse; of those, all but one was written during the 1860-61 period when she was mostly directly influenced by Whitman and the bohemian literati at Pfaff's. Clearly she valued these poems, perhaps more than any of her other writings. In "Notes of My Life" she both distanced herself from these "wild soul-poems" ("they were to me the deepest mystery.... I do not see in them a part of myself; they do not seem at all familiar to me") and then imagined their origins in the deepest and most spiritual part of herself ("the soul that prompted every word and line is somewhere within me, but not to be called at my bidding—only to wait the inspiration of God").

Like Whitman's *Leaves of Grass*, Menken's free verse poems use images and rhythms gleaned from Ossian, the Old Testament, and popular oratory, in particular the sermon and the campaign or reform speech. Relinquishing fixed meters and rhyme schemes meant finding other ways to pattern sounds and generate rhythms, new ways for creating lyric order. Following Whitman, Menken relied heavily on forms of repetition besides rhyme and meter. In "Where the Flocks Shall Be Led," for example, she deploys not only parallel sentence constructions, a series of interrogatives, but also anaphora, the repetition of the same word or words at the beginning of a line, to construct a rhythmic pattern:

Must I pine in bondage and drag these heavy chains
through the rocky path of my unrecompensed toll?

Must I, with these pale, feeble hands, still lift the
wreathed bowl for others to drink, while my lips are
parched and my soul unslaked?

Must I hold the light above my head that others may
find the green pastures as they march in advance, whilst I
moan and stumble with my bare feet tangled and clogged
with this load of chains?

Must I still supply the lamp with oil that gives no light
to me?

In this poem, like others in *Infelicia*, she also makes use of what
rhetoricians and literary critics call conduplicato, the repetition
of words in a successive line or clause for emotional emphasis:
"Answer me, ye who are ranged mockingly around me with
your unsheathed knives. Answer me." Moreover, it should be
noted, Menken sometimes incorporates conventional metered
lines into her free verse poems, as if to blend conventional with
unconventional rhythms or to mark her departure from them.
Just as "Song of Myself" begins with the most familiar meter in
English poetry, a line of iambic pentameter ("I celebrate myself,
and sing myself"), "Where the Flocks Shall Be Led" opens with
a four-beat line reminiscent of traditional English language
hymns ("Where shall I lead the flocks to-day?") before deviat-
ing from the familiar pattern to explore other kinds of rhythm.

Though they ditch set end rhyme patterns, her free verse
poems are nevertheless rich in prosodic techniques such as allit-
eration, assonance, and variations of conventional rhyme. In a pair
of lines from "Into the Depths," for example, Menken sings:

Fleet of foot, they front me with their daggers at my
breast.

All heedless of my tears and prayers, they tear the
white flowers from my brow, and the olive leaves from
my breast, and soil with their blood-marked hands the
broidered robes of purple beauty.

This short passage opens with a triplet of frame rhymes or what Wilfred Owen would later call pararhymes, words with differing vowel sounds but similar initial and final consonants (*fleet* / *foot* / *front*). But just as the alliteration of *f* sounds starts to sound overdone, the end of the line picks up on the pararhyme's less obvious *t* (a*t* / breas*t*), carries this emphasis over into the first part of second longer line (*t*ears / *t*ear / whi*t*e), and begins an alliteration of *s* sounds (dagger*s* / brea*s*t / heedle*ss* / tear*s* / prayer*s* / flower*s* / leave*s* / *s*oil / hand*s* / robe*s*). Yet, before that line becomes too thick with *t*'s and *s*'s, she slowly shifts again her emphasis to a clustering of plosive *b* and *d* sounds (*b*reast / *b*loo*d*-marke*d* / han*d*s / *b*roi*d*ere*d* / ro*b*es / *b*eauty) at the line's end. And in the clustering of "tears," "prayers," and "tear," each separated by a single unstressed syllable, she mingles consonant rhyme (tea*rs* / praye*rs*), assonant rhyme (pr*ay*ers / t*ea*r), and eye rhyme (tears/tear). In short, Menken does not so much dispense with meter and rhyme as make use of alternative patterns of sound and rhythm for the sonic textures and emphases of her free verse poems.

Such a free verse prosody is well suited to the extravagant representation of emotions, the most conspicuous feature of Menken's poetry. In "Judith," for example, Menken combines short and long lines with Old Testament diction and rhythms to create a strikingly unconventional and emotionally charged poem. The speaker of the poem is Judith, the heroine from Jewish legend who saves her people by slaying the Assyrian general Holofernes. Many nineteenth-century images of Judith portray her as strong-willed and courageous, but nothing like the powerful, blood-craving, boastful, and erotic persona that comes to life in *Infelicia*. She promises to "revel" in her "passion," a breathtaking mixture of love and hate, and hold up the severed head of Holofrenes for a kiss:

> My sensuous soul will quake with the burden of so much bliss.
> Oh, what wild passionate kisses will I draw up from that bleeding mouth!
> I will strangle this pallid throat of mine on the sweet blood!

....

I am starving for this feast.

Although Menken uses similarly lurid images of blood and violence in "The Autograph on the Soul," "A Fragment," and "Dying," the mixture of anger, threats, violence and blood, sadistic delight, and daring eroticism is quite unlike anything else in nineteenth-century women's poetry.

Although "Judith" is a highly unique poem, such affective intensity—which has been called "a torrent of force" and described as "hysterical," "spectacular," and most frequently "wild," "erratic," and "intense"—finds various forms throughout Menken's oeuvre. Indeed her exploration of emotional complexity and power is not limited to the free verse wild-soul poems, as perhaps her conventionally rhymed and metered "Passion" illustrates. This poem, like many of her poems, is about "the desire for bonding," which Joanne Dobson has called "[t]he principal theme of the sentimental text."[1] Yet the emotion in Menken's poetry does not always fit our customary understandings of sentimentalism. "Passion" begins with the language of sentimentality: the addressee was thought to be "true" and the speaker's love "pure"; the speaker (who is male in the Latin text upon which this poem is based) compares his love to the virtuous love parents feel for their children, and domestic affection is the sentimental affect par excellence. Yet from the very first troubling "*When* I believed thee true" (emphasis added), we know that this sentimental affection is set in the past. In the second stanza, the speaker borrows figures from sentimental discourse (such as knowing the other truly, concern for the heart) only to insist that "since all thy ways I know,/ Thy heart is worthless in my eyes." What's interesting and unsentimental about this poem is that the discovery that one's beloved is faithless does not lead to heartbreak, piety, and renunciation but to a rather cruel devaluation of the beloved and a frank

---

[1]   Joanne Dobson, "Reclaiming Sentimental Literature," *American Literature* 69 (1997): 267. The descriptions of Menken's poetry can be found in Appendix C, though the term "hysterical" is from Sherman (182) and "spectacular" from Louis Untermeyer, to Allan Lesser, 29 May 1933, AJA.

confession of heightened lust, now that the "chastening thought" that the beloved was "pure and good" no longer "represse[s]" the speaker's "high desires" and "fervent currents of the blood." The speaker admits that his formerly domestic affection for the beloved was based on repression, and now that the cause for that repression is gone, he admits to a rather dark, uncaring lust for the addressee. The poem is about the death of sentimental affection and, "in its seat," the triumph of audacious and cruel erotic passion. The speaker's view is pronouncedly pitiless, unsympathetic, and downright antisentimental.

Many of Menken's poems contemplate the difficulties of sexual/romantic relationships, but not all are so cruel as "Passion." In "A Memory," for example, the speaker recalls with sad affection the dark, beautiful eyes of a woman she loved: "The stars ... Are soft and beautiful, yet still / Not equal to her eyes of light." She remembers their meetings, kisses, but most of all her beloved's eyes:

> They may not seem to others sweet,
>   Nor radiant with the beams above,
> When first their soft, sad glances meet
>   The eyes of those not born for love;
> Yet when on me their tender beams
>   Are turned, beneath love's wide control,
> Each soft, sad orb of beauty seems
>   To look through mine into my soul.

Invoking central features of the discourse of romantic relationships, the poem depicts the women's wordless communication, which reaches past the eyes into the soul and confirms their unique, exclusive love for each other. According to G. Lippard Barclay, this poem was written for a young American Indian woman named Laulerack, whom Menken had met in Texas. This part of Barclay's biography has never been substantiated with any sort of reliable evidence; the story about Laurelack is almost certainly fictional. Still, the poem, whether based on a real encounter or not, exemplifies both Menken's handling of female-female romance and a far more tender form of erotic relation. Nevertheless, the poem is not a happy one, as it ends with their separation and its lingering pain.

Indeed, the most often represented emotion in Menken's work is melancholy or despair, though her handling of these feelings is not always conventional. "Saved," for example, a poem written in the summer of 1861 during the first year of the Civil War, portrays the death of a soldier. Yet the poem does not explicitly mourn his dying. Instead, in a kind of wild desperation, the speaker cradles his dead body, kisses "his pale, cold mouth," refuses to believe he has died, and promises in optimistic tones animated by a deranged denial that tomorrow the fallen soldier will "lead ye cheerily on to the attack!" "Into the Depths," on the other hand, represents a grief that leads the speaker to believe that "All life is bitter," everything that matters is lost, every effort in vain. The final two sections of the poem turn momentarily hopeful as the speaker yearns for Eros, the "unspeakable, passionate fire of love," to rescue her from the pit of languid hopelessness, but the poem ends ambiguously: Does Eros arrive in time to restore passion? Does Eros arrive at all? Or does Love return just in time to hold the speaker's cold body as she drifts into death? In a poem such as "Infelix," however, there is no release from despair, either through restored passion and life or the peacefulness of death. Instead, the despair is so thorough that it has transformed itself into a painful and seemingly endless regret:

> I stand a wreck on Error's shore,
> A spectre not within the door,
> A houseless shadow evermore,
> An exile lingering here.

Thus, whether stimulated by an encounter with death or the loss of a beloved or a sense of aching regret, profound unhappiness courses its way through Menken's poetry, particularly the poems from the early 1860s.

Such unhappiness both generates and destroys identity, as perhaps the reference to "exile" indicates. An exile is simultaneously a kind of identity and the label for someone without an identity, someone who's been separated from or banished from the community that provides one with an identity. As one can gather from studying Menken's life and writings, identity is one of the key themes in her work. Yet attempts to understand identity in Menken in terms of binary designations like real/not-real, true/fake, or authentic/inauthentic are likely to miss exactly what is most fascinating about Menken's work. As Renée Sentilles argues, Adah performs Menken and her identities. Moreover, in explicit and implicit ways, Menken's writing is about not only the constitution and defense of specific identities but also the dissolution and often ephemeral nature of identity.

In her poems from 1857-59, Menken reproduces elements of Jewish identity through exhortations to maintain hope in God, admonishments to defend Judaism against Gentiles, and a variety of references to tradition and history: the Law, the Patriarchs, Rosh Hashanah, etc. In phrases such as "our great and holy laws," "*our ancient race*," and "OUR FAITH," Menken clearly and vigorously presents herself with Jewish culture. For Menken-as-a-Jewish-poet, threats to identity—whether from Islamic and Christian oppressors, for example, or hardships, or feelings of hopelessness and doubt—can be overcome by waiting patiently and placing faith in God. When she felt the Jewish people were under attack following the Mortara abduction case (see Appendix D), Menken used her poem "To the Sons of Israel" to rouse her Jewish readers and to rail against "Popish rule."

However thunderous her declarations of Jewish identity, however passionate about her Jewish faith, Menken's publishing career also reveals a poet with doubts, or at least ambivalence, about her Jewishness. On more than a couple of occasions Menken plagiarized the work of her contemporaries. "Dying," for instance, borrows from Alice Cary's "Perversity," while "Spiritual Affinity" poaches a line from Whitman's "Song of Myself." Some of Menken's plagiarisms are not as easily detected. Sentilles has discovered Menken's copying of passages from Margaret J.M. Sweat's *Ethel's Love-Life* in a personal letter to a fellow poet, Hattie Tyng (see Appendix C), and portions of Rev. D.J. Pinckney's not especially well-known "Who Will Work?" make their way into Menken's essay titled "The Mightiness of the Pen." Menken's most egregious acts of plagiarism, however, involve a half dozen poems for *The Israelite*. One of them, "Dream of the Holy Land," is a reworking of John Greenleaf Whittier's

"The Holy Land," which happens to be a reworking of lines from Alphonse de Lamartine's *Voyage en Orient* (1835). The other five— "Queen of the Nations," "The Sacrifice," "The Hebrew's Prayer," "The Sabbath," and "Passover"— she stole from hymns by Penina Moïse, a Charleston poet whose work was rather beloved within nineteenth-century Jewish communities in the United States. Unlike Menken's other instances of plagiarism—many of which were incidental, private, or obscure—her copying of these poems for re-publication in *The Israelite* was flagrant. Her pirating of Moïse's hymns is not subtle (it's often verbatim), and Whittier and Moïse would have been among the most recognized nineteenth-century American poets by Cincinnati's Jewish community in the 1850s. Predictably enough, in a June 1859 letter to *The Jewish Messenger*, Menken's plagiarism of Moïse was made public.[1]

It is not clear whether the conspicuousness of these plagiarisms indicate a certain irrationality impelled by a desire to impress others, or deep-seated doubts about her place within the Jewish community, or an ambivalence about that community and a certain wish to be discovered. Was she so eager to be accepted and admired as a Jew that she ventriloquized the words she believed the community wanted to hear? If admiration and acceptance were what she sought, why would she plagiarize in such an outrageous fashion, in ways likely to be recognized, and risk public humiliation? Or did Menken the actress-performer regard poems as lines from a play, available for speaking by whomever is to play the role, by whomever speaks the words most convincingly?

After the revelations about her theft of Moïse's hymns, Menken published just one more piece in a Jewish periodical, "All is Beauty, All is Glory!" in *The Jewish Messenger* on 19 August 1859. About a month earlier, Menken had moved to New York, and gradually her public identity and voice would become less identified with Jewish politics and culture and more with women's issues. Although she did not devote time to women's organizations or work within the movement, as did writers such as Lillie Devereux Blake (see Appendix D), the New York press saw Menken as an advocate for women's rights:

---

[1] "The Plagiarisms of Ada Isaacs Menken," *The Jewish Messenger* (10 June 1859): 174.

At length, the hobby of Horace Greeley and Adah Isaacs Menken Heenan; of Wendell Phillips and Fanny Wright; of Adin Ballou and Mrs. Jones of Ohio; is a success. Yes, Woman's Rights are a fixed fact, and a big thing. Let the conservatives weep, the henpecked husbands howl, and the irreverent scoffers of the press dry up.[1]

Vanity Fair's 1860 mock concession to feminist progress overlooked Menken's awfully submissive poems of love and devotion, from "I Am Thine" for Kneass and "Karazah to Karl" for Menken to the "*Why do I love you?*" for Heenan. Instead what probably captured the gossipy column's attention was Menken's position as a *public* woman (in an age when femininity was allied in a powerfully ideological way with the *private* sphere), details about her personal behavior (she smoked in public, visited bohemian night spots, wore unconventional and un-ladylike clothes), and her rather bolder writing that was appearing on weekly or bi-weekly basis in the *Sunday Mercury*. Her earliest work in the *Sunday Mercury* was not explicitly feminist, however, although she champions reform in general in "Swimming Against the Current" and in "My Heritage" expresses dissatisfaction with the cultural valorization of self-sacrifice, with having "To think, and speak, and act, not for my pleasure, / But others'." Later, however, after *Vanity Fair* had named Menken to its list of women's rights activists, Menken's work turns even more decidedly feminist in tone and subject matter. She creates powerful and defiant female personas, such as Judith, and draws attention to the exploitation of working women in "Working and Waiting." In "Women of the World," she addresses classic themes in eighteenth- and nineteenth-century feminist thought. Unlike Dinah Maria Mulock Craik, whose discussion of "Women of the World" emphasizes "the universal law, that woman's proper place is home," (see Appendix D) but rather more like Blake's "The Social Condition of Woman," Menken advocates more serious educational opportunities for women and criticizes the oppressiveness of fashion for its role in stifling solidarity between women and enfeebling women's intellectual curiosity.

---

[1]   "The Result," *Vanity Fair* (7 July 1860): 21.

Moreover, Menken is forthright in her assertion that "There are other missions for woman than that of wife and mother." In other pieces, such as "Self Defence," Menken's use of feminist rhetoric ("This weak little hand will strike its meagre weight against sin and oppression, and lift up the down-trodden colors of *woman's rights!*—her birth-rights—her rights of intellect—her rights of honor ... ") is aimed at the hypocrisy of the Victorian era's sexual double standard and its devastating consequences for women. While some might see this essay's concerns as more personal than political, other readers might be more interested in the ways the personal and political come together in a piece like "Self Defence."

Although her representations of Jewish and feminist identities are certainly emphatic, Menken's work suggests that identity is not always secure or easily known. Her essay titled "Behind the Scenes," for instance, emphasizes the contrast between what appears to others in public and what forms of emotional agony remain unseen. In a poem such as "Myself," she takes this theme a bit further and contends that survival depends on assuming a mask, for the world "lash[es] with vengeance all who dared to be what their God had made them." Thus, with sadness and some yearning that she's not quite able to stifle, the speaker accepts her mask ("Now I gloss my pale face with laughter") and waits for a kind of Messianic release from role playing.

Menken's ideas about identity are not typically clarified by contextualizing them in terms of what we know about her life.[1] In fact, interpreting her work and its thinking about and perform- ance of identity with reference to her biography tends to compli- cate (rather than simplify or resolve) issues of identity and raise an array of interesting but difficult questions. What's the difference between assuming a public identity and creating a poetic persona, which some readers will understand to be the poet herself? If Menken is right about society's coercion of individuals, especially women, into wearing specific kinds of masks and assuming certain

---

[1]   This has not prevented a number of nineteenth- and twentieth-century critics from attempting to discover the meaning of her poems in her biography or looking for the truth about her life in the poems. See Appendix C. See also, for a twentieth- century example, Foster and Foster, 53.

roles, how would this change our notions about authenticity, writing, and identity? How does it change our thinking about the morality of passing, masking, role-playing, and/or plagiarism? To what extent is plagiarism the theft of someone else's identity, the destruction of identity, or the re-creation of a new identity? If Menken were born into a mixed-race family, why and how did she pass as white? If she were born a Gentile, why would she adopt a Jewish identity in her private life, public life, and poems and essays—an identity she would carry with her to her grave? What do Menken's writings—her cravenly submissive love poems, rebellious feminist pieces, erotic passages, and same-sex love letters and poems—tell us about sexual identity? Are celebrities who self-consciously dramatize various identities in their lyrics and life (celebrities such as Byron, Madonna, or Menken) to be understood as texts or persons? as both or not exactly either? To what extent are such celebrities not really "real" people (like you and me)? To what extent are all of us necessarily performers of an always-evolving repertoire of identities?

Literary scholars who examine now overlooked writers sometimes imagine that earlier disdain or neglect can be explained as a past failure to appreciate what we can now recognize as daring, masterful, or significant. Yet, the fact is that as brutal and predictable as the criticism of Menken often was, many in her own era found Menken and her work supremely mesmerizing. Miller called her "the most entirely poetical of all women that have yet found expression in America" and described her poetry as "grand, sublime, majestic" (see Appendix C). What made her a captivating, popular writer in her own era—her attempts to adopt a Whitmanesque prosody, her gothic morbidity, her lurid sensationalism, her "erratic" or over-the-top style, her defiance of convention and traditional moralities, her attempt to viscerally invoke something as elusive as emotion—were also precisely the aspects of her work that brought her censure. Likewise, it is unlikely that Menken will suit the tastes or compel the interests of all twenty-first-century readers. Some may see her poetry as dated, a relic of a past era; others will find their own late modern interests and concerns resonating with various aspects of Menken's work, including its avant-garde formal experiments, its powerful expression of women's rage and desire, its feminist politics, as well as its performances of multiple racial, sexual, and religious identities and its questioning of fixed identity in general. Some will probably dislike or disparage these poems for their strange, emotional, and theatrical quality, and others will find them absolutely fascinating for precisely the same reasons.

Adah Isaacs Menken: A Brief Chronology

1835(?) Menken born. Andrew Jackson is President.

1842 Father dies (?). Mother remarries Josiah Campbell.

1850 Performs in Cuba with her sister (?). Meets Juan
Clemente Zenea (?).

1855 Publishes poetry under the name Ada Bertha
(Theodore) in *The Liberty Gazette* (Liberty, Texas).
Marries W.H. or Nelson Kneass, a musician and
composer, in Galveston County, Texas. Whitman
publishes first edition of *Leaves of Grass*.

1856 Marries musician Alexander Isaac Menken. Begins
calling herself Adah Isaacs Menken.

1857 Appears on stage in Shreveport and New Orleans.
Publishes essay, "Shylock," in a New Orleans paper,
The Sunday Delta. Moves to Cincinnati. Begins
publishing essays and poems in *The Israelite* and *The
Jewish Messenger*.

1858 Performs in Louisiana, Kentucky, and Ohio. Continues
to write for *The Israelite* and *The Jewish Messenger*.

1859 Appears on stage in New York, New Jersey, and
Pennsylvania. Begins publishing poetry in the New
York City *Sunday Mercury*. Divorces Alexander Isaac
Menken. Moves to New York City. Marries boxer
John Carmel Heenan, who shortly thereafter leaves
for England.

1860 Performs at several theatres throughout the Northeast.
Marriage to Heenan becomes a public scandal. Begins
association with group of New York City bohemian
writers, artists, and intellectuals who meet at Pfaff's.
Begins publishing free verse poems in *Sunday Mercury*.
Writes defense of Walt Whitman's work ("Swimming
Against the Current"). Gives birth to a son who dies
just weeks later. Mother dies. Abraham Lincoln elected
President. Writes a suicide note from Jersey City.

1861 Appears on stage throughout the Midwest and
Northeast. Continues to publish poems and essays in

the *Sunday Mercury*. United States Civil War begins. Takes the stage in Albany, New York, in *Mazeppa* for the first time. Emily Dickinson begins the most creative and prolific phase of her writing career.

1862 As acting career becomes increasingly successful and busy, literary productivity slows. Divorces Heenan. Marries editor and satirist Robert Henry Newell. Sarah Bernhardt makes her debut.

1863 Performs in Baltimore. Moves to San Francisco with Newell. Begins publishing revised work and new material in the *Golden Era*. Begins association with group of California writers. Performs in San Francisco and Sacramento.

1864 Performs in San Francisco and Virginia City, Nevada. After brief stay in New York, sails for London without Newell. Begins relationship with financier James Barkley. Opens in *Mazeppa* at Astley's in London. Begins association with various writers and critics in London. Starts planning a collection of poems.

1865 Appears in various theatres in England and Scotland. Civil War ends. Lincoln assassinated. Returns to New York for short visit. Divorces Newell. Returns to London to perform again at Astley's in *Child of the Sun*.

1866 Returns to the United States and embarks on performance tour. Marries Barkley. Leaves for Paris without Barkley. Gives birth to a son, Louis Dudevant Victor Emmanuel Barkley. Performs in *Les Pirates de la Savane* in Paris.

1867 Works on collection of her poems. Release of photographs of Dumas with Menken spur a public scandal. Son dies. Appears on stage in Vienna, London, and Birmingham. Begins romantic relationship with Swinburne.

1868 Performs in London. Continues to make arrangements for the publication of volume of her selected poems. Grows increasingly ill. Returns to France to recuperate. Dies in Paris on August 10. Buried on August 13. *Infelicia* is published the following week.

A Note on the Text

This Broadview Literary Texts edition of Menken's writings presents the text of the first edition of *Infelicia* along with a generous selection of uncollected poems and essays.

In selecting uncollected writings, this volume has aimed for a representative selection of the range of Menken's work, in terms of subject and style, over the course of her career from 1855 through 1868. To provide examples of her first efforts, the earliest version of a text has sometimes been preferred: "The Angel's Whisper" as published in *The Liberty Gazette* in 1855, for instance, was selected over later revisions of the essay, "The Twilight Whisper" (*The Israelite*, 1858) and "Spiritual Affinity" (*Sunday Mercury*, 1860). For later works, the last published version over which the author had control has often been printed: for instance, "My Spirit Love" (*Golden Era*, 1863) appears here instead of "Lost Love" (*Sunday Mercury*, 1860). In the selection of uncollected pieces, plagiarized work has been avoided, but it is entirely possible that future research will reveal further instances of textual appropriation. Similarly, although the selection of texts for this volume were made after studying all of the known extant writings by Menken and their textual histories, it is possible that there are more Menken poems to be discovered.

In general, Menken's texts are presented here without change, although typographical and printer's errors have been corrected, and misspellings of proper names and non-English words have been corrected to avoid confusion. To illustrate the kinds of changes made, the following is a list of errors in the original text of *Infelicia* that have been corrected: world. (page 55, line 11); Garabaldi (page 66, line 62); Are (page 103, line 9); make (page 108, line 41); wise. (page 113, line 43).

Below is a list of the sources of the texts included in this volume.

Abbreviations: I = *The Israelite* [Cincinnati]; JM= *The Jewish Messenger* [New York]; LG = *The Liberty Gazette* [Liberty, Texas]; NYC = *New York Clipper*; SM = *Sunday Mercury* [New York].

Infelicia. Philadelphia: [J.B. Lippincott & Co.], 1868.
"To My Brother Gus." LG (8 Oct. 1855): 2.
"I am Thine—To W.H.K." LG (5 Nov. 1855): 2.
"The Bright and Beautiful." LG (12 Nov. 1855): 2.
"New Advertisement!!!" LG (3 Dec. 1855): 2.
"'Milton wrote a letter to his lady love.'" Barclay, 30.
"Wounded." Infelicia. London: Chatto & Windus, 1888. 123-24.
"Sinai." I (25 Sept. 1857): 93.
"Dum Spiro, Spero." I (23 Oct. 1857): 121.
"Moses." I (23 Oct. 1857): 121.
"Oppression of the Jews, Under the Turkish Empire." I (6 Nov. 1857): 137.
"Spring!" I (28 May 1858): 372.
"ר ו א . י ת י ." I (4 June1858): 377.
"To Nathan Mayer, M.D." I (6 Aug. 1858): 37
"Rosaline." I (20 Aug. 1858): 50.
"What an Angel Said to Me." I (10 Dec. 1858): 178.
"To the Sons of Israel." I (28 Jan. 1859): 236.
"A Heart-Wail." I (4 Feb. 1859): 241.
"ראש השנה." JM (23 Oct. 1857): 70.
"Spirit Sighs." JM (20 Nov. 1857): 81.
"My World of Thought." JM (8 Oct. 1858): 59.
"All is Beauty, All is Glory!" JM (19 Aug. 1859): 50.
"On the Death of Rufus Choate." SM (18 Sept. 1859): 2.
"The Dark Hour." SM (25 March 1860): 1.
"'Why do I love you?'" SM (29 April 1860): 5.
"Knocking at the Door." SM (1 July 1860): 2.
"Dream of the Alhambra." SM (8 July 1860): 1.
"Song." SM (15 July 1860): 1.
"Our Mother." SM (23 Sept. 1860): 6.
"The Last." SM (14 Oct. 1860): 1.
"Passion." SM (18 Nov. 1860): 3.
"Conscience." SM (25 Nov. 1860): 6.
"Gold." SM (2 Dec. 1860): 3.
"Farewell to Fanny." SM (9 Dec. 1860): 3.
"A Wish for Nellie." SM (17 Feb. 1861): 2.
"Louisiana." SM (31 Mar. 1861): 5.
"Lake Michigan." SM (25 Aug. 1861): 4.

"The Storm." SM (30 Mar. 1862): 1.

"A L'Outrance!" NYC (23 April 1859): [front page].

"My Spirit Love." *The Golden Era* [San Francisco] (15 Nov. 1863): 5.

"The Poet." Stoddard, 483.

"Reply to Dora Shaw." NYC (24 Sept. 1864): [front page].

"The Angel's Whisper." LG (29 Oct. 1855): 2.

"Shylock." *The Sunday Delta* [New Orleans] (6 Sept. 1857): [front page].

"Midnight in New-Orleans." I (21 May 1858): 362.

"Death and Eternity." JM (27 Aug. 1858): 38.

"The Jew in Parliament." I (3 Sept. 1858): 68–69.

"Swimming Against the Current." SM (10 June 1860): 1.

"Self Defence." *The New-York Times* (6 Sept. 1868): 8.

"Affinity of Poetry and Religion." SM (9 Sept. 1860): 1.

"Women of the World." SM (7 Oct. 1860): 6.

"Behind the Scenes." SM (14 Oct. 1860): 8.

"Lodgings to Let—References Exchanged." SM (9 Dec. 1860): 1.

INFELICIA
AND OTHER WRITINGS

"Leaves pallid and sombre and ruddy,
Dead fruits of the fugitive years;
Some stained as with wine and made bloody,
And some as with tears."[1]

TO
CHARLES DICKENS.

1   Algernon Charles Swinburne, "Dedication of *Poems and Ballads* (1865)," *Selected Poems*
    (London: Oxford University Press, 1939) 67. Lines 13-16.

Infelicia. [1]

Resurgam. [2]

I.

Yes, yes, dear love! I am dead!
Dead to you!
Dead to the world!
Dead for ever!
It was one young night in May.
The stars were strangled, and the moon was blind with the
flying clouds of a black despair.
Years and years the songless soul waited to drift out
beyond the sea of pain where the shapeless life was wrecked.
The red mouth closed down the breath that was hard and
fierce.
The mad pulse beat back the baffled life with a low sob.
And so the stark and naked soul unfolded its wings to the
dimness of Death!
A lonely, unknown Death.
A Death that left this dumb, living body as his endless mark.
And left these golden billows of hair to drown the
whiteness of my bosom.
Left these crimson roses gleaming on my forehead to hide
the dust of the grave.
And Death left an old light in my eyes, and old music for
my tongue, to deceive the crawling worms that would seek my
warm flesh.
But the purple wine that I quaff sends no thrill of Love
and Song through my empty veins.
Yet my red lips are not pallid and horrified.
Thy kisses are doubtless sweet that throb out an eternal
passion for me!

---

[1] Unfortunate, unhappy, miserable (from the Latin *infelix*).
[2] I will rise again (Latin).

But I feel neither pleasure, passion nor pain.
So I am certainly dead.
  Dead in this beauty!
  Dead in this velvet and lace!
  Dead in these jewels of light!
  Dead in the music!
  Dead in the dance!

II.

Why did I die?
  O love! I waited—I waited years and years ago.
  Once the blaze of a far-off edge of living Love crept up
my horizon and promised a new moon of Poesy.
  A soul's full life!
  A soul's full love!
  And promised that my voice should ring trancing shivers
of rapt melody down the grooves of this dumb earth.
  And promised that echoes should vibrate along the purple
spheres of unfathomable seas, to the soundless folds of the clouds.
  And promised that I should know the sweet sisterhood of
the stars.
  Promised that I should live with the crooked moon in her
eternal beauty.
  But a Midnight swooped down to bridegroom the Day.
  The blazing Sphynx of that far off, echoless promise,
shrank into a drowsy shroud that mocked the crying stars of
my soul's unuttered song.
  And so I died.
  Died this uncoffined and unburied Death.
  Died alone in the young May night.
  Died with my fingers grasping the white throat of many a
prayer.

III.

Yes, dear love, I died!
  You smile because you see no cold, damp cerements of a
lonely grave hiding the youth of my fair face.
  No head-stone marks the gold of my poor unburied head.

But the flaunting poppy covered her red heart in the sand.

Who can hear the slow drip of blood from a dead soul?

No Christ of the Past writes on my laughing brow His "Resurgam."

Resurgam.

What is that when I have been dead these long weary years!

IV.

Silver walls of Sea!

Gold and spice laden barges!

White-sailed ships from Indian seas, with costly pearls and tropic wines go by unheeding!

None pause to lay one token at my feet.

No mariner lifts his silken banner for my answering hail.

No messages from the living to the dead.

Must all lips fall out of sound as the soul dies to be heard?

Shall Love send back no revelation through this interminable distance of Death?

Can He who promised the ripe Harvest forget the weeping Sower?

How can I stand here so calm?

I hear the clods dosing down my coffin, and yet shriek not out like the pitiless wind, nor reach my wild arms after my dead soul!

Will no sun of fire again rise over the solemn East?

I am tired of the foolish moon showing only her haggard face above the rocks and chasms of my grave.

O Rocks! O Chasms! sink back to your black cradles in the West!

Leave me dead in the depths!

Leave me dead in the wine!

Leave me dead in the dance!

V.

How did I die?

The man I loved—he—he—ah, well!

There is no voice from the grave.

The ship that went down at sea, with seven times a

thousand souls for Death, sent back no answer.

The breeze is voiceless that saw the sails shattered in the mad tempest, and heard the cry for mercy as one frail arm clung to the last spar of the sinking wreck.

Fainting souls rung out their unuttered messages to the silent clouds.

Alas! I died not so!
I died not so!

VI.

How did I die?

No man has wrenched his shroud from his stiffened corpse to say:

"Ye murdered me!"

No woman has died with enough of Christ in her soul to tear the bandage from her glassy eyes and say:

"Ye crucified me!"

Resurgam! Resurgam!

Dreams of Beauty.

Visions of Beauty, of Light, and of Love,
    Born in the soul of a Dream,
Lost, like the phantom-bird under the dove,
    When she flies over a stream—

Come ye through portals where angel wings droop,
    Moved by the heaven of sleep?
Or, are ye mockeries, crazing a soul,
    Doomed with its waking to weep?

I could believe ye were shadows of earth,
    Echoes of hopes that are vain,
But for the music ye bring to my heart,
    Waking its sunshine again.

And ye are fleeting. All vainly I strive
    Beauties like thine to portray;

Forth from my pencil the bright picture starts,
And—ye have faded away.

Like to a bird that soars up from the spray,
    When we would fetter its wing;
Like to the song that spurns Memory's grasp
    When the voice yearneth to sing;

Like the cloud-glory that sunset lights up,
    When the storm bursts from its height;
Like the sheet-silver that rolls on the sea,
    When it is touched by the night—

Bright, evanescent, ye come and are gone,
    Visions of mystical birth;
Art that could paint you was never vouchsafed
    Unto the children of earth.

Yet in my soul there's a longing to tell
    All you have seemed unto me,
That unto others a glimpse of the skies
    You in their sorrow might be.

Vain is the wish. Better hope to describe
    All that the spirit desires,
When through a cloud of vague fancies and schemes
    Flash the Promethean fires.

Let me then think of ye, Visions of Light,
    Not as the tissue of dreams,
But as realities destined to be
    Bright in Futurity's beams.

Ideals formed by a standard of earth
    Sink at Reality's shrine
Into the human and weak like ourselves,
    Losing the essence divine;

But the fair pictures that fall from above
  On the heart's mirror sublime
Carry a signature written in tints,
  Bright with the future of time.

And the heart, catching them, yieldeth a spark
  Under each stroke of the rod—
Sparks that fly upward and light the New Life,
  Burning an incense to God!

My Heritage.[1]

"My heritage!" It is to live within
The marts of Pleasure and of Gain, yet be
No willing worshiper at either shrine;
To think, and speak, and act, not for my pleasure,
But others'. The veriest slave of time
And circumstances. Fortune's toy!
To hear of fraud, injustice, and oppression,
And feel who is the unshielded victim.
            Cold friends and causeless foes!
            Proud thoughts that rise to fall.
Bright stars that set in seas of blood;
Affections, which are passions, lava-like
Destroying what they rest upon. Love's
Fond and fervid tide preparing icebergs
That fragile bark, this loving human heart.
            O'ermastering Pride!
            Ruler of the Soul!
Life, with all its changes, cannot bow ye.
            Soul-subduing Poverty!
That lays his iron, cold grasp upon the high

---

[1] When first printed in the *Sunday Mercury* (3 June 1860), the epigraph to the poem
read: "*Extract from a letter dated New Orleans, April 17th.*—'Why are your letters so sad?
Forget the world—laugh at poverty. Be glad and happy with your heritage of
genius.'—*J. W. Overall.*" Overall was a poet and critic who wrote for the New Orleans
Sunday Delta and *Daily Delta*.

Free spirit: strength, sorrow-born, that bends
But breaks not in his clasp—all, all
These are "my heritage!"
And mine to know a reckless human love, all passion and
intensity, and see a mist come o'er the scene, a dimness steal
o'er the soul!
Mine to dream of joy and wake to wretchedness!
Mine to stand on the brink of life
One little moment where the fresh'ning breeze
Steals o'er the languid lip and brow, telling
Of forest leaf, and ocean wave, and happy
Homes, and cheerful toil; and bringing gently
To this wearied heart its long-forgotten
Dreams of gladness.
But turning the fevered cheek to meet the soft kiss of the
winds, my eyes look to the sky, where I send up my soul in
thanks. The sky is clouded—no stars—no music—the heavens
are hushed.
My poor soul comes back to me, weary and disappointed.
The very breath of heaven, that comes to all, comes not to
me.
Bound in iron gyves of unremitting toil, my vital air is
wretchedness—what need I any other?
"My heritage!" The shrouded eye, the trampled leaf, wind-
driven and soiled with dust—these tell the tale.
Mine to watch
The glorious light of intellect
Burn dimly, and expire; and mark the soul,
Though born in Heaven, pause in its high career,
Wave in its course, and fall to grovel in
The darkness of earth's contamination, till
Even Death shall scorn to give a thing
So low his welcome greeting!
Who would be that pale,
Blue mist, that hangs so low in air, like Hope
That has abandoned earth, yet reacheth
Not the stars in their proud homes?
A dying eagle, striving to reach the sun?

A little child talking to the gay clouds as they flaunt past in their purple and crimson robes?

A timid little flower singing to the grand old trees?

Foolish waves, leaping up and trying to kiss the moon?

A little bird mocking the stars?

Yet this is what men call Genius.

Judith.[1]

"Repent, or I will come unto thee quickly, and will fight thee with the sword of my mouth."—REVELATION ii. 16.

I.

Ashkelon[2] is not cut off with the remnant of a valley.

Baldness dwells not upon Gaza.

The field of the valley is mine, and it is clothed in verdure.

The steepness of Baal-perazim is mine;

And the Philistines spread themselves in the valley of Rephaim.[3]

They shall yet be delivered into my hands.

For the God of Battles has gone before me!

The sword of the mouth shall smite them to dust.

I have slept in the darkness—

But the seventh angel woke me, and giving me a sword of flame, points to the blood-ribbed cloud, that lifts his reeking head above the mountain.

Thus am I the prophet.

I see the dawn that heralds to my waiting soul the advent of power.

Power that will unseal the thunders!

Power that will give voice to graves!

---

[1] Judith is a heroine from Jewish legend. According to the Book of Judith, the Assyrians, led by their general Holofernes, attacked the people of Israel at Bethulia. Judith saved Israel by killing Holofernes: she plied him with food and wine and then "she struck his neck twice with all her might, and severed his head from his body" (Judith 13.8).

[2] An area in southwest Palestine. The other place names here refer to the Ashkelon area.

[3] Located west of Jerusalem.

Graves of the living;
Graves of the dying;
Graves of the sinning;
Graves of the loving;
Graves of despairing;
And oh! graves of the deserted!
These shall speak, each as their voices shall be loosed.
And the day is dawning.

II.

Stand back, ye Philistines!
Practice what ye preach to me;
I heed ye not, for I know ye all.
Ye are living burning lies, and profanation to the garments
which with stately steps ye sweep your marble palaces.
Your palaces of Sin, around which the damning evidence
of guilt hangs like a reeking vapor.
Stand back!
I would pass up the golden road of the world.
A place in the ranks awaits me.
I know that ye are hedged on the borders of my path.
Lie and tremble, for ye well know that I hold with iron
grasp the battle axe.
Creep back to your dark tents in the valley.
Slouch back to your haunts of crime.
Ye do not know me, neither do ye see me.
But the sword of the mouth is unsealed, and ye coil
yourselves in slime and bitterness at my feet.
I mix your jeweled heads, and your gleaming eyes, and
your hissing tongues with the dust.
My garments shall bear no mark of ye.
When I shall return this sword to the angel, your foul
blood will not stain its edge.
It will glimmer with the light of truth, and the strong arm
shall rest.

III.

Stand back!

I am no Magdalene[1] waiting to kiss the hem of your garment.

It is mid-day.

See ye not what is written on my forehead?

I am Judith!

I wait for the head of my Holofernes!

Ere the last tremble of the conscious death-agony shall have shuddered, I will show it to ye with the long black hair clinging to the glazed eyes, and the great mouth opened in search of voice, and the strong throat all hot and reeking with blood, that will thrill me with wild unspeakable joy as it courses down my bare body and dabbles my cold feet!

My sensuous soul will quake with the burden of so much bliss.

Oh, what wild passionate kisses will I draw up from that bleeding mouth!

I will strangle this pallid throat of mine on the sweet blood!

I will revel in my passion.

At midnight I will feast on it in the darkness.

For it was that which thrilled its crimson tides of reckless passion through the blue veins of my life, and made them leap up in the wild sweetness of Love and agony of Revenge!

I am starving for this feast.

Oh forget not that I am Judith!

And I know where sleeps Holofernes.

Working and Waiting.

Suggested by Carl Müller's Cast of the Seamstress, at the Dusseldorf Gallery.[2]

I.

Look on that form, once fit for the sculptor!

Look on that cheek, where the roses have died!

---

[1] A reformed and presumably grateful prostitute, from Mary Magdalene. Tradition has sometimes assumed that the woman who kisses Jesus's feet in Luke 7.36-50 is Mary Magdalene.

[2] Carl Müller was a German artist popular in mid-nineteenth-century America.

Working and waiting have robbed from the artist
All that his marble could show for its pride.
Statue-like sitting
Alone, in the flitting
And wind-haunted shadows that people her hearth.
God protect all of us—
God shelter all of us
From the reproach of such scenes upon earth!

II.
All the day long, and through the cold midnight,
Still the hot needle she wearily plies.
Haggard and white as the ghost of a Spurned One,
Sewing white robes for the Chosen One's eyes—
Lost in her sorrow,
But for the morrow
Phantom-like speaking in every stitch—
God protect all of us—
God shelter all of us
From the Curse, born with each sigh for the Rich!

III.
Low burns the lamp. Fly swifter, thou needle—
Swifter, thou asp for the breast of the poor![1]
Else the pale light will be stolen by Pity,
Ere of the vital part thou hast made sure.
Dying, yet living:
All the world's giving
Barely the life that runs out with her thread.
God protect all of us—
God shelter all of us
From her last glance, as she follows the Dead!

---

[1]   According to legend, made even more famous by Shakespeare's *Antony and Cleopatra*
5.2, Cleopatra committed suicide by holding a venomous asp to her breast.

IV.

What if the morning finds her still bearing
  All the soul's load of a merciless lot!
Fate will not lighten a grain of the burden
  While the poor bearer by man is forgot.
      Sewing and sighing!
      Sewing and dying!
What to such life is a day or two more?
      God protect all of us—
      God shelter all of us
From the new day's lease of woe to the Poor!

V.

Hasten, ye winds! and yield her the mercy
  Lying in sleep on your purified breath;
Yield her the mercy, enfolding a blessing,
  Yield her the mercy whose signet is Death.
      In her toil stopping,
      See her work dropping—
Fate, thou art merciful! Life, thou art done!
      God protect all of us—
      God shelter all of us
From the heart breaking, and yet living on!

VI.

Winds that have sainted her, tell ye the story
  Of the young life by the needle that bled;
Making its bridge over Death's soundless waters
  Out of a swaying and soul-cutting thread.
      Over it going,
      All the world knowing!
Thousands have trod it, foot-bleeding, before!
      God protect all of us—
      God shelter all of us,
Should she look back from the Opposite Shore!

The Release.

I.

"Carry me out of the host, for I am wounded."[1]

The battle waged strong.
A fainting soul was borne from the host.
The tears robed themselves in the scarlet of guilt, and crowned
    with iron of wrong, they trod heavily on the wounded soul,
Bound close to the dark prison-walls, with the clanking chains
    of old Error.
Malice and Envy crept up the slimy sides of the turrets to mark
    out with gore-stained fingers the slow hours of the night.
The remorseless Past stood ever near, breathing through the
    broken chords of life its never-ending dirge.
Yet, Ahab-like,[2] the poor soul lingered on, bleeding and
    pining, pleading and praying.
Only through its mournful windows did the yearning soul
    dare speak;
Still through the tears did it ever vainly reach outward some
    kindred soul to seek.
Unheeding did the ranks sweep by;
And the weary soul sank back with all its deep unuttered
    longings to the loneliness of its voiceless world,
Hearing only the measured tread of Guile and Deceit on their
    sentinel round.
Wherefore was that poor soul of all the host so wounded?
It struggled bravely.
Wherefore was it doomed and prisoned to pine and strive apart?
It battled to the last. Can it be that this captive soul was a
    changeling, and battled and struggled in a body not its own?
Must Error ever bind the fetters deep into the shrinking flesh?
Will there come no angel to loose them?

---

[1] 1 Kings 22.34.
[2] King of Israel, infamous for his wickedness and marriage to Jezebel. See 1 Kings
    21.12-27.

And will Truth lift up her lamp at the waking?
Shall the cold tomb of the body grow warm and voice forth
    all the speechless thought of the soul when the sleeping
    dead shall rise?
Will there be no uprising in this world?
O! impatient Soul, wait, wait, wait.

II.

"The Angel
Who driveth away the demon band
Bids the din of battle cease."[1]

O prisoned Soul, up in your turrets so high, look down from
    thy windows to-day!
Dash down the rusty chains of old Error, and unbar the iron doors,
Break the bonds of the Past on the anvil of the Present.
O give me some token for the music that I have sent through
    your lonely chambers!
Wave but the tip of your white wing in greeting to the Angel
    that I have sent you!
Look forth on thy fellow Soul pausing at the gate!
List to the sound of his voice that rushes past the red roof, and
    with unfurled wings, sweeps up its music through the ivory
    gates to thee!
No other song can thrill its echoes up to thy captive life.
For this Angel hath chilled the hot hand of Sin, and crushed
    down the grave of the crimson eyes of the Past.
The daylight looms up softly, and feathery Hope is on guard.
O waiting Soul, come forth from your turrets, so lone and high!
Listen to the low sweet music of promise, rushing wildly
    through floods of God-inspiration of love, up to Eternity.
Tremble not at the bars. Come forth!
The tongue you fear sleeps in frozen silence, and doth thy
    mighty secret keep.

---

[1] Adelaide Anne Procter, "Life and Death," *The Poems of Adelaide A. Procter: Complete
    Edition* (New York: Thomas Y. Crowell & Co., [1903]) 61. Lines 11, 13-14.

In Vain.

I.

O foolish tears, go back!

Learn to cover your jealous pride far down in the nerveless heart that ye are voices for.

Your sobbings mar the unfinished picture that my trembling life would fill up to greet its dawn.

I know, poor heart, that you are reaching up to a Love that finds not all its demands in thy weak pulse.

And I know that you sob up your red tears to my face, because—because—*others* who care less for his dear Love may, each day, open their glad eyes his lightest wish to bless.

But, jealous heart, *we* will not give him from drops that overflow thy rim.

We will fathom the mysteries of earth, of air and of sea, to fill thy broad life with beauty, and then empty all its very depths of light deep into his wide soul!

II.

Ah! When I am a cloud—a pliant, floating cloud—I will haunt the Sun-God for some eternal ray of Beauty.

I will wind my soft arms around the wheels of his blazing chariot, till he robes me in gorgeous trains of gold!

I will sing to the stars till they crown me with their richest jewels!

I will plead to the angels for the whitest, broadest wings that ever walled their glorious heights around a dying soul!

Then I will flaunt my light down the steep grooves of space into this dark, old world, until Eyes of Love will brighten for me!

III.

When I am a flower—a wild, sweet flower—I will open my glad blue eyes to one alone.

I will bloom in his footsteps, and muffle their echoes with my velvet lips.

So near him will I grow that his breath shall mark kisses on all my green leaves!

I will fill his deep soul with all the eternal fragrance of my love!

Yes, I will be a violet—a wild sweet violet—and sigh my very life away for him!

IV.

When I am a bird—a white-throated bird—all trimmed in plumage of crimson and gold, I will sing to one alone.

I will come from the sea—the broad blue sea—and fold my wings with olive-leaves to the glad tidings of his hopes!

I will come from the forest—the far old forest—where sighs and tears of reckless loves have never moaned away the morning of poor lives.

I will come from the sky, with songs of an angel, and flutter into his soul to see how I may be all melody to him!

Yes, I will be a bird—a loving, docile bird—and furl my wild wings, and shut my sad eyes in his breast!

V.

When I am a wave—a soft, white wave—I will run up from ocean's purple spheres, and murmur out my low sweet voice to one alone.

I will dash down to the cavern of gems and lift up to his eyes Beauty that will drink light from the Sun!

I will bring blue banners that angels have lost from the clouds.

Yes, I will be a wave—a happy, dancing wave—and leap up in the sunshine to lay my crown of spray-pearls at his feet.

VI.

Alas! poor heart, what am I now?

A weed—a frail, bitter weed—growing outside the garden wall.

All day straining my dull eyes to see the blossoms within, as they wave their crimson flags to the wind.

And yet my dark leaves pray to be as glorious as the rose.

My bitter stalks would be as sweet as the violet if they could.

I try to bloom up into the light.

My poor, yearning soul to Heaven would open its velvet eyes of fire.

Oh! the love of Beauty through every fibre of my lonely
life is trembling!
Every floating cloud and flying bird draws up jealous Envy
and bleeding Love!
So passionately wild in me is this burning unspeakable thirst
to grow all beauty, all grace, all melody to one—and to him alone!

Venetia.[1]

Bright as the light that burns at night,
    In the starry depths of Aiden,[2]
When star and moon in leafy June
    With love and joy are laden;
Bright as the light from moon and star,
    Stars in glorious cluster,
Be the lights that shine on this life of thine,
    Be the beauty of its lustre.

Beneath the moon in leafy June,
    Sweet vows are fondly spoken;
Beneath the stars, the silvery tune
    Of music floats unbroken.
Beneath the sky, and moon and stars,
    Come nestling birds of beauty,
And Love with Bliss, and Hope with Joy
    Troop down the path of duty.

Oh! ever may'st thou, bird of mine,
    Nestle to my bosom sweetly,
Birds of my soaring, feathery hope,
    That flyeth to me so fleetly.
Oh! ever thus may vows of love
    My yearning soul inherit—
Vows unbroken, as those spoken
    By celestial spirit.

---

[1] A region of northeastern Italy on the Adriatic.
[2] Poetic spelling of Eden.

And when the vow thou breathest now,
    For me, for mine and only,
Shall float to Aiden's starry land,
    Where none are lost or lonely,
Believe me, when the angel bends
    His loving ear to listen,
Radiant will be the smile that blends
    With the beauteous tears that glisten.

For darling, those who love us here
    With tender, sweet emotion,
With love that knows no stop or fear,
    But burneth with devotion;
'Tis only but another proof
    That something good is left us,
That we are not by Heaven forgot,
    That Heaven hath not bereft us.

The Ship That Went Down.

I.

Who hath not sent out ships to sea?
Who hath not toiled through light and darkness to make them
    strong for battle?
And how we freighted them with dust from the mountain
    mines!
And red gold, coined from the heart's blood, rich in Youth,
    Love and Beauty!
And we have fondly sent forth on their white decks seven
    times a hundred souls.
Sent them out like sea-girt worlds full of hope, love, care, and faith.
O mariners, mariners, watch and beware!

II.

See the Ship that I sent forth!
How proudly she nods her regal head to each saluting wave!
How defiantly she flaps her white sails at the sun, who, in envy

of her beauty, screens his face behind a passing cloud, yet never losing sight of her.

The ocean hath deck'd himself in robes of softest blue, and lifted his spray-flags to greet her.

The crimson sky hath swooped down from her Heaven-Palace, and sitteth with her white feet dabbling in the borders of the sea, while she sendeth sweet promises on the wings of the wind to my fair Ship.

O mariners, mariners, why did ye not watch and beware?

III.

The faithless sky is black.

The ocean howls on the Ship's rough track.

The strong wind, and the shouting rain swept by like an armed host whooping out their wild battle-cry.

The tall masts dip their heads down into the deep.

The wet shrouds rattle as they seem to whisper prayers to themselves;

But the waves leap over their pallid sails, and grapple and gnaw at their seams.

The poor Ship shrieks and groans out her despair.

She rises up to plead with the sky, and sinks down the deep valley of water to pray.

O God, make us strong for the battle!

IV.

What says the mariner so hurried and pale?

No need to whisper it, speak out, speak!

Danger and peril you say?

Does your quivering lip and white cheek mean that the good Ship must go down?

Why stand ye idle and silent?

O sailors, rouse your brave hearts!

Man the rocking masts, and reef the rattling sails!

Heed not the storm-fires that so terribly burn in the black sky!

Heed not the storm-mad sea below!

Heed not the death-cry of the waves!

Foot to foot, hand to hand! Toil on brave hearts!

Our good Ship must be saved!
Before us lies the goal!

V.

Too late, too late!

The life-boats are lost.

The rent spars have groaned out their lives, and the white sails
have shrouded them in their rough beds of Death.

Strong mariners have fainted and failed in the terror and strife.

White lips are grasping for breath, and trembling out prayers,
and waiting to die.

And the Ship, once so fair, lies a life-freighted wreck.

The Promises, Hopes, and Loves, are sinking, sinking away.

The winds shriek out their joy, and the waves shout out their
anthem of Death.

Pitiless wind!

Pitiless ocean!

VI.

O mariners, is there no help?

Is there no beacon-light in the distance?

Dash the tears of blood from your eyes, and look over these
Alps of water!

See ye no sail glittering through the darkness?

Is there no help?

Must they all die, all die?

So much of Youth, so much of Beauty, so much of Life?

The waves answer with ravenous roar;

They grapple like demons the trembling Ship!

Compassless, rudderless, the poor Ship pleads.

In vain! in vain!

With a struggling, shivering, dying grasp, my good Ship sank
down, down, down to the soundless folds of the fathomless
ocean.

Lost—lost—lost.

Battle of the Stars.

(*After Ossian.*)[1]

Alone on the hill of storms
The voice of the wind shrieks through the mountain.
The torrent rushes down the rocks.
Red are hundred streams of the light-covered paths of the dead.
Shield me in from the storm,
I that am a daughter of the stars, and wear the purple and gold
    of bards, with the badges of Love on my white bosom.
I heed not the battle-cry of souls!
I that am chained on this Ossa[2] of existence.
Sorrow hath bound her frozen chain about the wheels of my
    chariot of fire wherein my soul was wont to ride.
Stars, throw off your dark robes, and lead me to the palace
    where my Eros rests on his iron shield of war, his gleaming
    sword in the scabbard, his hounds haunting around him.
The water and the storm cry aloud.
I hear not the voice of my Love.
Why delays the chief of the stars his promise?
Here is the terrible cloud, and here the cloud of life with its
    many-colored sides.
Thou didst promise to be with me when night should trail her
    dusky skirts along the borders of my soul.
O wind! O thought! Stream and torrent, be ye silent!
Let the wanderer hear my voice.
Eros, I am waiting. Why delay thy coming? It is Atha[3] calls thee.
See the calm moon comes forth.

---

[1] The rhapsodic poems of Ossian were popular "translations" of ancient Scottish Gaelic epics. Scottish schoolteacher and poet James Macpherson (1736-96) was commissioned to research the story of the legendary hero Fingal, as told by his son Ossian. Macpherson eventually published *Temora, an Epic Poem, in Eight Books* (1763) and *Fingal: an Ancient Epic Poem in Six Books* (1762), which includes "The Songs of Selma," the piece most directly related to Menken's own poem. Although the poems of Ossian were widely read in the late eighteenth and nineteenth centuries and influenced American poets such as Emerson and Whitman, it was later discovered that most of the work was fabricated by Macpherson.

[2] Mountain in northeastern Greece.

[3] This character appears to be Menken's invention. In Ossian's *Temora*, Atha is the name of a place in Connaught, over which Cairbar is lord.

The flood is silver in the vale.

The rocks are gray on the steep.

I see him not on the mountain brow;

The hounds come not with the glad tidings of his approach.

I wait for morning in my tears.

Rear the tomb, but close it not till Eros comes:

Not unharmed will return the eagle from the field of foes.

But Atha will not mark thy wounds, she will be silent in her
blood.

Love, the great Dreamer, will listen to her voice, and she will
sleep on the soft bosom of the hills.

O Love! though Mighty Leveler,

Thou alone canst lay the shepherd's crook beside the sceptre,

Thou art the King of the Stars.

Music floats up to thee, receives thy breath, thy burning kisses,
and comes back with messages to children of earth.

Thou art pitiful and bountiful.

Although housed with the golden-haired Son of the Sky, with
stars for thy children, dwelling in the warm clouds, and
sleeping on the silver shields of War, yet ye do not disdain
the lonely Atha that hovers round the horizon of your
Grand Home. You awake and come forth arrayed in trailing
robes of glory, with blessing and with song to greet her
that seeketh thy mighty presence.

Thy hand giveth Morn her power;

Thy hand lifteth the mist from the hills;

Thy hand createth all of Beauty;

Thy hand giveth Morn her rosy robes;

Thy hands bound up the wounds of Eros after the battle:

Thy hands lifted him to the skirts of the wind, like the eagle of
the forest.

Thy hands have bound his brow with the spoils of the foe.

Thy hands have given to me the glittering spear, and helmet of
power and might;

Nor settles the darkness on me.

The fields of Heaven are mine.

I will hush the sullen roar of the enemy.

Warriors shall lift their shields to me.

My arm is strong, my sword defends the weak.

I will loose the thong of the Oppressed, and dash to hell the Oppressor.

A thousand warriors stretch their spears around me.

I battle for the stars.

It was thy hands, O Love, that loosed my golden tresses, and girded my white limbs in armor, and made me leader of the armies of Heaven.

Thy voice aroused the sluggard soul.

Thy voice calleth back the sleeping dead.

Thou alone, O Mighty Ruler, canst annihilate space, hush the shrieking wind, hide the white-haired waves, and bear me to the arms and burning kisses of my Eros.

And it is thou who makest beautiful the prison-houses of earth.

I once was chained to their darkness, but thou, O Love, brought crimson roses to lay on my pale bosom, and covered the cold damp walls with the golden shields of the sun, and left thy purple garments whereon my weary bleeding feet might rest.

And when black-winged night rolled along the sky, thy shield covered the moon, and thy hands threw back the prison-roof, and unfolded the gates of the clouds, and I slept in the white arms of the stars.

And thou, O Beam of Life! didst thou not forget the lonely prisoner of Chillon[1] in his gloomy vault? thy blessed ray of Heaven-light stole in and made glad his dreams.

Thou hast lifted the deep-gathered mist from the dungeons of Spielberg;[2]

Ugolino[3] heard thy voice in his hopeless cell:

Thy blessed hand soothed Damiens on his bed of steel;[4]

---

[1] In Byron's verse tale *The Prisoner of Chillon* (1816), the title character is incarcerated in a castle dungeon for his republican ideas.

[2] In the eighteenth and nineteenth centuries, the Spielberg castle (located in present day Brno, Czech Republic) was an infamous political prison.

[3] In 1288, after earlier deserting the Pisans in their war against Genoa, Count Ugolino was cast into prison with his two grandsons, where they were all starved to death. Dante tells his story in *The Inferno*, canto 33.

[4] In 1757, following a failed attempt on the life of King Louis XV of France, R. F. Damiens was chained to a metal bed, tortured, and eventually torn to pieces by horses.

It is thy powerful hand that lights up to Heaven the inspired
life of Garibaldi.[1]

And it is thy undying power that will clothe Italy in the folds
of thy wings, and rend the helmet from the dark brow of
old Austria, and bury her in the eternal tomb of darkness.

Thou didst not forget children of earth, who roll the waves of
their souls to our ship of the sky.

But men are leagued against us—strong mailed men of earth,
Around the dwellers in the clouds they rise in wrath.

No words come forth, they seize their blood-stained daggers.

Each takes his hill by night, at intervals they darkly stand
counting the power and host of Heaven.

Their black unmuzzled hounds howl their impatience as we
come on watch in our glittering armor.

The hills no longer smile up to greet us, they are covered with
these tribes of earth leading their war-dogs, and leaving
their footprints of blood.

Unequal bursts the hum of voices, and the clang of arms
between the roaring wind.

And they dare to blaspheme the very stars, and even God on
His high throne in the Heaven of Heavens, by pleading
for Love.

Love sacrifices all things to bless the thing it loves, not destroy.

Go back to your scorching homes;

Go back to your frozen souls;

Go back to your seas of blood;

Go back to your chains, your loathsome charnel houses;

Give us the green bosom of the hills to rest upon;

Broad over them rose the moon.

O Love, Great Ruler, call upon thy children to buckle on the
armor of war, for behold the enemy blackens all earth in
waiting for us.

See the glittering of their unsheathed swords.

They bear blood-stained banners of death and destruction.

And, lo, their Leader comes forth on the Pale Horse.

His sword is a green meteor half-extinguished.

---

[1]   Italian patriot (1807–82) who led the fight for Italy's reunification.

His face is without form, and dark withal, dark as the tales of other times, before the light of song arose.

Mothers, clasp your new-born children close to your white bosoms!

Daughters of the stars, sleep no more, the enemy approacheth!

Look to your white shields!

Bind up your golden tresses!

See the blood upon the pale breasts of your sisters.

Where are your banners?

O sluggards, awake to the call of the Mighty Ruler!

Hear ye not the clash of arms? Arise around me, children of the Land Unknown.

Up, up, grasp your helmet and your spear!

Let each one look upon her shield as the ruler of War.

Come forth in your purple robes, sound your silver-tongue trumpets;

Rush upon the enemy with your thousand and thousands of burnished spears!

Let your voices ring through the Universe, "Liberty, liberty for the stars." Thunder it on the ears of the guilty and the doomed!

Sound it with the crash of Heaven's wrath to the hearts of branded—God-cursed things who have stood up and scorned their Maker with laughing curses, as they dashed the crown from her brow, and hurled her into Hell.

Pray ye not for them, hills! Heed ye not, O winds, their penitence is feigned!

Let your voices, O floods, be hushed! stars, close your mighty flanks, and battle on them!

Chain them down close to the fire!

They were merciless, bind their blood-stained hands.

They are fiends, and if ye loose them they will tear children from their mothers, wives from their husbands, sisters from their brothers, daughters from their fathers.

And these fiends, these children of eternal damnation, these men will tear souls from bodies, and then smear their hands with blood, and laugh as they sprinkle it in the dead up-turned faces of their victims.

It is Atha thy leader that calls to you.

Beat them down, beat them down.
I know these war-dogs.
They strangled my warrior, Eros!
Warrior of my soul;
Warrior of the strong race of Eagles!
His crimson life crushed out on the white sails of a ship.
Battle them down to dust.
Battle them back into their own slimy souls;
Battle them, ye starry armies of Heaven, down into the silent
    sea of their own blood;
Battle on, the wind is with ye;
Battle on, the sun is with ye;
Battle on, the waves are with ye;
The Angels are with ye;
God is with us!

Myself.

"La patience est amère; mais le fruit en est doux!"[1]

I.

Away down into the shadowy depths of the Real I once
lived.
I thought that to seem was to be.
But the waters of Marah[2] were beautiful, yet they were bitter.
I waited, and hoped, and prayed;
Counting the heart-throbs and the tears that answered them.
Through my earnest pleadings for the True, I learned that
the mildest mercy of life was a smiling sneer;
And that the business of the world was to lash with
vengeance all who dared to be what their God had made them.
Smother back tears to the red blood of the heart!
Crush out things called souls!
No room for them here!

---

[1] Patience is bitter, but its fruit is sweet! (French proverb).
[2] Hebrew word for bitterness, a fountain the Israelites encountered. See Exodus 15.23–
   24; Numbers 33.8.

II.

Now I gloss my pale face with laughter, and sail my voice
on with the tide.

Decked in jewels and lace, I laugh beneath the gaslight's
glare, and quaff the purple wine.

But the minor-keyed soul is standing naked and hungry
upon one of Heaven's high hills of light.

Standing and waiting for the blood of the feast!

Starving for one poor word!

Waiting for God to launch out some beacon on the
boundless shores of this Night.

Shivering for the uprising of some soft wing under which
it may creep, lizard-like, to warmth and rest.

Waiting! Starving and shivering!

III.

Still I trim my white bosom with crimson roses; for none
shall see the thorns.

I bind my aching brow with a jeweled crown, that none
shall see the iron one beneath.

My silver-sandaled feet keep impatient time to the music,
because I cannot be calm.

I laugh at earth's passion-fever of Love; yet I know that
God is near to the soul on the hill, and hears the ceaseless ebb
and flow of a hopeless love, through all my laughter.

But if I can cheat my heart with the old comfort, that love
can be forgotten, is it not better?

After all, living is but to play a part!

The poorest worm would be a jewel-headed snake if she
could!

IV.

All this grandeur of glare and glitter has its night-time.

The pallid eyelids must shut out smiles and daylight.

Then I fold my cold hands, and look down at the restless
rivers of a love that rushes through my life.

Unseen and unknown they tide on over black rocks and
chasms of Death.

Oh, for one sweet word to bridge their terrible depths!

O jealous soul! why wilt thou crave and yearn for what thou canst not have?

And life is so long—so long.

V.

With the daylight comes the business of living.

The prayers that I sent trembling up the golden thread of hope all come back to me.

I lock them close in my bosom, far under the velvet and roses of the world.

For I know that stronger than these torrents of passion is the soul that hath lifted itself up to the hill.

What care I for his careless laugh?

I do not sigh; but I know that God hears the life-blood dripping as I, too, laugh.

I would not be thought a foolish rose, that flaunts her red heart out to the sun.

Loving is not living!

VI.

Yet through all this I know that night will roll back from the still, gray plain of heaven, and that my triumph shall rise sweet with the dawn!

When these mortal mists shall unclothe the world, then shall I be known as I am!

When I dare be dead and buried behind a wall of wings, then shall he know me!

When this world shall fall, like some old ghost, wrapped in the black skirts of the wind, down into the fathomless eternity of fire, then shall souls uprise!

When God shall lift the frozen seal from struggling voices, then shall we speak!

When the purple-and-gold of our inner natures shall be lighted up in the Eternity of Truth, then will love be mine!

I can wait.

Into the Depths.

I.

Lost—lost—lost!

To me, for ever, the seat near the blood of the feast.

To me, for ever, the station near the Throne of Love!

To me, for ever, the Kingdom of Heaven—and I the least.

Oh, the least in love—
The least in joy—
The least in life—
The least in death—
The least in beauty—
The least in eternity.

So much of rich, foaming, bubbling human blood drank down into the everlasting sea of Sin.

The jasper gates are closed on the crimson highway of the clouds.

The Seven Angels stand on guard.

Seven thunders utter their voices.

And the angels have not sealed up those things which the seven thunders have uttered.

I have pleaded to the seventh angel for the little book.

But he heedeth me not.

All life is bitter, not one drop as sweet as honey.

And yet I prophesy before many people, and nations, and tongues, and kings!

II.

Lost—lost—lost!

The little golden key which the first angel entrusted to me.

The gates are closed, and I may not enter.

Yet arrayed in folds of white, these angels are more terrible to me than the fabled watcher of the Hesperides golden treasures.[1]

Because it is I alone of all God's creatures that am shut out.

---

[1] The Hesperides were the guardians of a tree of golden apples, a gift from Gaia to Hera. Ladon, a dragon, was also a guardian of this garden of the Hesperides and the golden apples.

For others the bolts are withdrawn, and the little book unsealed.

With wistful eyes, and longing heart, I wander in the distance, waiting for the angels to sleep.

Tremblingly I peer through the gloaming of horrid shadows, and visions of wasted moments.

But the white eyelids of the angels never droop.

In vain I plead to them that it was I who built the throne.

In vain do I tell them that it was I who gemmed it with Faith and Truth, and the dews of my life's morn.

In vain do I tell them that they are my hopes which they stand in solemn guard to watch.

In vain do I plead my right as queen of the starry highway.

In vain do I bind my golden tresses with the pale lilies of the valley.

In vain do I display to them my purple broidered robes, and the silver badge of God's eternal bards that I wear on my white bosom.

In vain do I wind my soft arms around their silver-sandaled feet.

They heed me not.

But point to the whirlpool called the world.

Must the warm, living, loving soul a wanderer be?

Are all its yearnings vain?

Are all its prayings vain?

Will there be no light to guide me?

Will there be strong arm at the helm?

Must the full lamp of life wane so early?

Ah, I see, all is lost—lost—lost!

III.

Deep into the depths!

Struggling all the day-time—weeping all the night-time!

Writing away all vitality.

Talking to people, nations, tongues, and kings that heed me not.

Cast out of my own kingdom on to the barren battle-plain of bloodless life.

A thousand foes advancing?
A thousand weapons glancing!
And I in the sternest scene of strife.
Panting wildly in the race.
Malice and Envy on the track.
Fleet of foot, they front me with their daggers at my breast.

All heedless of my tears and prayers, they tear the white flow-
ers from my brow, and the olive leaves from my breast, and soil
with their blood-marked hands the broidered robes of purple
beauty.

Life's gems are torn from me, and in scattered fragments
around me lie.

All lost—lost—lost!

IV.

Out of the depths have I cried unto thee, O Lord!
Weeping all the night-time.
Weeping sad and chill through the lone woods.
Straying 'mong the ghostly trees.
Wandering through the rustling leaves.
Sobbing to the moon, whose icy light wraps me like a shroud.
Leaning on a hoary rock, praying to the mocking stars.

With Love's o'erwhelming power startling my soul like an
earthquake shock.

I lift my voice above the low howl of the winds to call my
Eros to come and give me light and life once more.

His broad arms can raise me up to the light, and his red lips
can kiss me back to life.

I heed not the storm of the world, nor the clashing of its steel.

I wait—wait—wait!

V.

How can I live so deep into the depths with all this wealth of
love?

Oh, unspeakable, passionate fire of love!

Cold blood heedeth ye not.

Cold eyes know ye not.

But in this wild soul of seething passion we have warmed
together.

I feel thy lava tide dashing recklessly through every blue course!

Grand, beauteous Love!

Let us live alone, far from the world of battle and pain, where we can forget this grief that has plunged me into the depths.

We will revel in ourselves.

Come, Eros, thou creator of this divine passion, come and lay my weary head on your bosom.

Draw me close up to your white breast and lull me to sleep.

Smooth back the damp, tangled mass from my pale brow.

        I am so weary of battle—
        Take this heavy shield.
        I am so weary of toil—
        Loosen my garments.

Now, wrap me close in your bosom to rest.

Closer—closer still!

Let your breath warm my cold face.

This is life—this is love!

Oh, kiss me till I sleep—till I sleep—I sleep.

Sale of Souls.

I.

Oh, I am wild—wild!

Angels of the weary-hearted, come to thy child.

Spread your white wings over me!

        Tenderly, tenderly,
        Lovingly, lovingly,
        Plead for me, plead for me!

II.

Souls for sale! souls for sale!

Souls for gold! who'll buy?

In the pent-up city, through the wild rush and beat of human
    hearts, I hear this unceasing, haunting cry:

        Souls for sale! souls for sale!
        Through mist and gloom,
        Through hate and love,

Through peace and strife,
Through wrong and right,
Through life and death,
The hoarse voice of the world echoes up the cold gray sullen
   river of life.
On, on, on!
No silence until it shall have reached the solemn sea of God's
   for ever;
No rest, no sleep;
Waking through the thick gloom of midnight, to hear the
   damning cry as it mingles and clashes with the rough clang
   of gold.
Poor Heart, poor Heart,
Alas! I know thy fears.

III.

The hollow echoes that the iron-shod feet of the years throw
   back on the sea of change still vibrate through the grave-
   yard of prayers and tears;—
Prayers that fell unanswered,
Tears that followed hopelessly.
But pale Memory comes back through woe and shame and
   strife, bearing on her dark wings their buried voices;
Like frail helpless barks, they wail through the black sea of the
   crowded city,
Mournfully, mournfully.

IV.

Poor Heart, what do the waves say to thee?
The sunshine laughed on the hill sides.
The link of years that wore a golden look bound me to
   woman-life by the sweet love of my Eros, and the voice of
   one who made music to call me mother.
Weak Heart, weak Heart!
Oh, now I reel madly on through clouds and storms and night.
The hills have grown dark,
They lack the grace of my golden-haired child, to climb their
   steep sides, and bear me their smiles in the blue-eyed

violets of our spring-time.

Sad Heart, what do the hills say to thee?

They speak of my Eros, and how happily in the dim discolored
hours we dreamed away the glad light, and watched the
gray robes of night as she came through the valley, and
ascended on her way to the clouds.

Kisses of joy, and kisses of life,
Kisses of heaven, and kisses of earth,

Clinging and clasping white hands;

Mingling of soft tresses;

Murmurings of love, and murmurings of life,

With the warm blood leaping up in joy to answer its music;

The broad shelter of arms wherein dwelt peace and content, so
sweet to love.

All, all were mine.

Loving Heart, loving Heart,

Hush the wailing and sobbing voice of the past;

Sleep in thy rivers of the soul,

Poor Heart.

V.

Souls for sale!

The wild cry awoke the god of ambition, that slumbered in
the bosom of Eros;

From out the tents he brought forth his shield and spear, to see
them smile back at the sun;

Clad in armor, he went forth to the cities of the world, where
brave men battle for glory, and souls are bartered for gold.

Weeping and fearing, haggard and barefoot, I clung to him
with my fainting child.

Weary miles of land and water lay in their waste around us.

We reached the sea of the city.

Marble towers lifted their proud heads beyond the scope of vision.

Wild music mingled with laughter.

The tramp of hoofs on the iron streets, and the cries of the
drowning, and the curses of the damned were all heard in
that Babel, where the souls of men can be bought for gold.

All the air seemed dark with evil wings.

And all that was unholy threw their shadows everywhere,
  Shadows on the good,
  Shadows on the bad,
  Shadows on the lowly,
  Shadows on the lost!
All tossing upon the tide of rushing, restless destiny;
Upon all things written:
  Souls for sale!
  Lost Heart, lost Heart!

VI.

A soul mantled in glory, and sold to the world;
  O horrible sale!
  O seal of blood!
  Give back my Eros.
His bowstring still sounds on the blast, yet his arrow was
  broken in the fall.
Oh leave me not on the wreck of this dark-bosomed ship
  while Eros lies pale on the rocks of the world.
Driven before the furious gale by the surging ocean's strife;
The strong wind lifting up the sounding sail, and whistling
  through the ropes and masts; waves lash the many-colored
  sides of the ship, dash her against the oozy rocks.
The strength of old ocean roars.
The low booming of the signal gun is heard above the tempest.
Oh how many years must roll their slow length along my life,
  ere the land be in sight!
When will the morning dawn?
When will the clouds be light?
When will the storm be hushed?
It is so dark and cold.
Angels of the weary-hearted, come to your child!
Build your white wings around me.
  Tenderly, tenderly,
  Pity me, pity me.

One Year Ago.

In feeling I was but a child,
    When first we met—one year ago,
As free and guileless as the bird,
    That roams the dreary woodland through.

My heart was all a pleasant world
    Of sunbeams dewed with April tears:
Life's brightest page was turned to me,
    And naught I read of doubts or fears.

We met—we loved—one year ago,
    Beneath the stars of summer skies;
Alas! I knew not then, as now,
    The darkness of life's mysteries.

You took my hand—one year ago,
    Beneath the azure dome above,
And gazing on the stars you told
    The trembling story of your love.

I gave to you—one year ago,
    The only jewel that was mine;
My heart took off her lonely crown,
    And all her riches gave to thine.

You loved me, too, when first we met,
    Your tender kisses told me so.
How changed you are from what you were
    In life and love—one year ago.

With mocking words and cold neglect,
    My truth and passion are repaid,
And of a soul, once fresh with love,
    A dreary desert you have made.

Why did you fill my youthful life
With such wild dreams of hope and bliss?
Why did you say you loved me then,
If it were all to end in this?

You robbed me of my faith and trust
In all Life's beauty—Love and Truth,
You left me nothing—nothing save
A hopeless, blighted, dreamless youth.

Strike if you will, and let the stroke
Be heavy as my weight of woe;
I shall not shrink, my heart is cold,
'Tis broken since one year ago.

Genius.

"Where'er there's a life to be kindled by love,
Wherever a soul to inspire,
Strike this key-note of God that trembles above
Night's silver-tongued voices of fire."[1]

Genius is power.

The power that grasps in the universe, that dives out beyond space, and grapples with the starry worlds of heaven.

If genius achieves nothing, shows us no results, it is so much the less genius.

The man who is constantly fearing a lion in his path is a coward.

The man or woman whom excessive caution holds back from striking the anvil with earnest endeavor, is poor and cowardly of purpose.

The required step must be taken to reach the goal, though a precipice be the result.

---

[1] When she first published this poem in the *Sunday Mercury* (11 Nov. 1860), Menken attributed these lines to John R. Walker.

Work must be done, and the result left to God.

The soul that is in earnest, will not stop to count the cost.

Circumstances cannot control genius: it will nestle with them: its power will bend and break them to its path.

This very audacity is divine.

Jesus of Nazareth did not ask the consent of the high priests in the temple when he drove out the "money-changers;" but, impelled by inspiration, he knotted the cords and drove them hence.[1]

Genius will find room for itself, or it is none.

Men and women, in all grades of life, do their utmost.

If they do little, it is because they have no capacity to do more.

I hear people speak of "unfortunate genius," of "poets who never penned their inspirations;" that

"Some mute inglorious Milton here may rest;"[2]

of "unappreciated talent," and "malignant stars," and other contradictory things.

It is all nonsense.

Where power exists, it cannot be suppressed any more than the earthquake can be smothered.

As well attempt to seal up the crater of Vesuvius as to hide God's given power of the soul.

"You may as well forbid the mountain pines
To wag their high tops, and to make no noise
When they are fretten with the gusts of heaven,"[3]

as to hush the voice of genius.

There is no such thing as unfortunate genius.

If a man or woman is fit for work, God appoints the field.

He does more; He points to the earth with her mountains, oceans, and cataracts, and says to man, *"Be great!"*

---

[1]   Matthew 21.12-17, Mark 11.15-19, Luke 19.45-48, John 2.13-17.
[2]   Thomas Gray, "Elegy Written in a Country Churchyard," line 59.
[3]   *The Merchant of Venice* 4.1.76-78.

He points to the eternal dome of heaven and its blazing worlds, and says: "Bound out thy life with beauty."

He points to the myriads of down-trodden, suffering men and women, and says: "Work with me for the redemption of these, my children."

He lures, and incites, and thrusts greatness upon men, and they will not take the gift.

Genius, on the Contrary, loves toil, impediment, and poverty; for from these it gains its strength, throws off the shadows, and lifts its proud head to immortality.

Neglect is but the fiat to an undying future.

To be popular is to be endorsed in the To-day and forgotten in the To-morrow.

It is the mess of pottage that alienates the birthright.[1]

Genius that succumbs to misfortune, that allows itself to be blotted by the slime of slander—and other serpents that infest society—is so much the less genius.

The weak man or woman who stoops to whine over neglect, and poverty, and the snarls of the world, gives the sign of his or her own littleness.

Genius is power.

The eternal power that can silence worlds with its voice, and battle to the death ten thousand arméd Hercules.

Then make way for this God-crowned Spirit of Night, that was born in that Continuing City, but lives in lowly and down-trodden souls!

Fling out the banner!

Its broad folds of sunshine will wave over turret and dome, and over the thunder of oceans on to eternity.

"Fling it out, fling it out o'er the din of the world!
    Make way for this banner of flame,
That streams from the mast-head of ages unfurled,
    And inscribed by the deathless in name.
And thus through the years of eternity's flight,
    This insignia of soul shall prevail,

---

[1]   In Genesis 25.29-34, Esau sells his birthright to Jacob for some red pottage.

The centre of glory, the focus of light;
O Genius! proud Genius, all hail!"

Drifts That Bar My Door.

I.

O Angels! will ye never sweep the drifts from my door?
Will ye never wipe the gathering rust from the hinges?
How long must I plead and cry in vain?
Lift back the iron bars, and lead me hence.
Is there not a land of peace beyond my door?
Oh, lead me to it—give me rest—release me from this unequal strife.
Heaven can attest that I fought bravely when the heavy blows fell fast.
Was it my sin that strength failed?
Was it my sin that the battle was in vain?
Was it my sin that I lost the prize? I do not sorrow for all the bitter pain and blood it cost me.
Why do ye stand sobbing in the sunshine?
I cannot weep.
There is no sunlight in this dark cell. I am starving for light.
O angels! sweep the drifts away—unbar my door!

II.

Oh, is this all?
Is there nothing more of life?
See how dark and cold my cell.
The pictures on the walls are covered with mould.
The earth-floor is slimy with my wasting blood.
The embers are smouldering in the ashes.
The lamp is dimly flickering, and will soon starve for oil in this horrid gloom.
My wild eyes paint shadows on the walls.
And I hear the poor ghost of my lost love moaning and sobbing without.
Shrieks of my unhappiness are borne to me on the wings of the wind.

I sit cowering in fear, with my tattered garments close around my choking throat.

I move my pale lips to pray; but my soul has lost her wonted power.

Faith is weak.

Hope has laid her whitened corse upon my bosom.

The lamp sinks lower and lower. O angels! sweep the drifts away—unbar my door!

III.

Angels, is this my reward?

Is this the crown ye promised to set down on the foreheads of the loving—the suffering—the deserted?

Where are the sheaves I toiled for?

Where the golden grain ye promised?

These are but withered leaves.

Oh, is this all?

Meekly I have toiled and spun the fleece.

All the work ye assigned, my willing hands have accomplished.

See how thin they are, and how they bleed.

Ah me! what meagre pay, e'en when the task is over!

My fainting child, whose golden head graces e'en this dungeon, looks up to me and pleads for life.

O God! my heart is breaking!

Despair and Death have forced their skeleton forms through the grated window of my cell, and stand clamoring for their prey.

The lamp is almost burnt out.

Angels, sweep the drifts away—unbar my door!

IV.

Life is a lie, and Love a cheat.

There is a graveyard in my poor heart—dark, heaped-up graves, from which no flowers spring.

The walls are so high, that the trembling wings of birds do break ere they reach the summit, and they fall, wounded, and die in my bosom.

I wander 'mid the gray old tombs, and talk with the ghosts of my buried hopes.

They tell me of my Eros, and how they fluttered around him, bearing sweet messages of my love, until one day, with his strong arm, he struck them dead at his feet.

Since then, these poor lonely ghosts have haunted me night and day, for it was I who decked them in my crimson heart-tides, and sent them forth in chariots of fire.

Every breath of wind bears me their shrieks and groans.

I hasten to their graves, and tear back folds and folds of their shrouds, and try to pour into their cold, nerveless veins the quickening tide of life once more.

Too late—too late!

Despair hath driven back Death, and clasps me in his black arms.

And the lamp! See, the lamp is dying out!

O angels! sweep the drifts from my door!—lift up the bars!

V.

Oh, let me sleep.

I close my weary eyes to think—to dream.

Is this what dreams are woven of?

I stand on the brink of a precipice, with my shivering child strained to my bare bosom.

A yawning chasm lies below. My trembling feet are on the brink.

I hear again *his* voice; but he reacheth not out his hand to save me.

Why can I not move my lips to pray?

They are cold.

My soul is dumb, too.

Death hath conquered!

I feel his icy fingers moving slowly along my heart-strings.

How cold and stiff!

The ghosts of my dead hopes are closing around me.

They stifle me.

They whisper that Eros has come back to me.

But I only see a skeleton wrapped in blood-stained cerements.

There are no lips to kiss me back to life.

O ghosts of Love, move back—give me air!

Ye smell of the dusty grave.

Ye have pressed your cold hands upon my eyes until they are eclipsed.

The lamp has burnt out.

O angels! be quick! Sweep the drifts away!—unbar my door! Oh, light! light!

Aspiration.

Poor, impious Soul! that fixes its high hopes
 In the dim distance, on a throne of clouds,
And from the morning's mist would make the ropes
 To draw it up amid acclaim of crowds—
Beware! That soaring path is lined with shrouds;
 And he who braves it, though of sturdy breath,
May meet, half way, the avalanche and death!

O poor young Soul!—whose year-devouring glance
 Fixes in ecstasy upon a star,
Whose feverish brilliance looks a part of earth,
 Yet quivers where the feet of angels are,
And seems the future crown in realms afar—
 Beware! A spark *thou* art, and dost but see
Thine own reflection in Eternity!

Miserimus.[1]

"Sounding through the silent dimness
 Where I faint and weary lay,
Spake a poet:'I will lead thee
 To the land of song to-day.'"[2]

I.

O Bards! weak heritors of passion and of pain!

---

[1] Menken may simply be attempting to Latinize the English word misery, but "*miserimus*" is first-person plural perfect subjunctive form of the Latin verb *mitto* (to send, to dispatch): it means "we would have sent."

[2] Emily S. Brown, "Songland," *The Ladies Repository* (Oct. 1851): 364. Lines 1-4.

Dwellers in the shadowy Palace of Dreams!

With your unmated souls flying insanely at the stars!

Why have you led me lonely and desolate to the Deathless Hill of Song?

You promised that I should ring trancing shivers of rapt melody down to the dumb earth.

You promised that its echoes should vibrate till Time's circles met in old Eternity.

You promised that I should gather the stars like blossoms to my white bosom.

You promised that I should create a new moon of Poesy.

You promised that the wild wings of my soul should shimmer through the dusky locks of the clouds, like burning arrows, down into the deep heart of the dim world.

But, O Bards! sentinels on the Lonely Hill, why breaks there yet no Day to me?

II.

O lonely watchers for the Light! how long must I grope with my dead eyes in the sand?

Only the red fire of Genius, that narrows up life's chances to the black path that crawls on to the dizzy clouds.

The wailing music that spreads its pinions to the tremble of the wind, has crumbled off to silence.

From the steep ideal the quivering soul falls in its lonely sorrow like an unmated star from the blue heights of Heaven into the dark sea.

O Genius! is this thy promise?

O Bards! is this all?

A Memory.[1]

I see her yet, that dark-eyed one,
    Whose bounding heart God folded up

---

[1] Purportedly written in memory of an "Indian maiden" of the same name, this poem was first titled "Laulerack." See Barclay, *The Life and Remarkable Career of Adah Isaacs Menken*, in Appendix A.

In His, as shuts when day is done,
   Upon the elf the blossom's cup.
On many an hour like this we met,
   And as my lips did fondly greet her,
I blessed her as love's amulet:
   Earth hath no treasure, dearer, sweeter.

The stars that look upon the hill,
   And beckon from their homes at night,
Are soft and beautiful, yet still
   Not equal to her eyes of light.
They have the liquid glow of earth,
   The sweetness of a summer even,
As if some Angel at their birth
   Had dipped them in the hues of Heaven.

They may not seem to others sweet,
   Nor radiant with the beams above,
When first their soft, sad glances meet
   The eyes of those not born for love;
Yet when on me their tender beams
   Are turned, beneath love's wide control,
Each soft, sad orb of beauty seems
   To look through mine into my soul.

I see her now that dark-eyed one,
   Whose bounding heart God folded up
In His, as shuts when day is done,
   Upon the elf the blossom's cup.
Too late we met, the burning brain,
   The aching heart alone can tell,
How filled our souls of death and pain
   When came the last, sad word, *Farewell!*

Hemlock in the Furrows.

I.

O Crownless soul of Ishmael![1]

Uplifting and unfolding the white tent of dreams against the sunless base of eternity!

Looking up through thy dumb desolation for white hands to reach out over the shadows, downward, from the golden bastions of God's eternal Citadel!

Praying for Love to unloose the blushing bindings of his nimble shaft and take thee up to his fullest fruition!

Poor Soul! hast thou no prophecy to gauge the distance betwixt thee and thy crown?

Thy crown?

Alas! there is none.

Only a golden-rimmed shadow that went before thee, marking in its tide barren shoals and dust.

At last resting its bright length down in the valley of tears.

Foolish soul! let slip the dusty leash.

Cease listening along the borders of a wilderness for the lost echoes of life.

Drift back through the scarlet light of Memory into the darkness once more.

A corpse hath not power to feel the tying of its hands.

II.

To-night, O Soul! shut off thy little rimmings of Hope, and let us go back to our hemlock that sprang up in the furrows.

Let us go back with bleeding feet and try to break up the harvestless ridges where we starved.

Let us go down to the black sunset whose wings of fire burnt out thy flowery thickets of Day, and left a Night to swoop down the lonesome clouds to thee.

---

[1] The outcast son of Abraham and Hagar. See Genesis 16-17, 21, and 25.

Go back to the desolate time when the dim stars looked out from Heaven, filmy and blank, like eyes in the wide front of some dead beast.

Go, press thy nakedness to the burnt, bare rocks, under whose hot, bloodless ribs the River of Death runs black with human sorrow.

To-night, O Soul! fly back through all the grave-yards of thy Past.

Fly back to them this night with thy fretful wings, even though their bloody breadth must wrestle long against Hell's hollow bosom!

III.

Jealous Soul!

The stars that are trembling forth their silent messages to the hills have none for thee!

The mother-moon that so lovingly reacheth down her arms of light heedeth not thy Love!

See, the pale pinions that thou hast pleaded for gather themselves up into rings and then slant out to the dust!

The passion-flowers lift up their loving faces and open their velvet lips to the baptism of Love, but heed not thy warm kisses!

Shut out all this brightness that hath God's Beauty and liveth back the silence of His Rest.

Cease knocking at the starry gate of the wondrous realm of Song.

Hush away this pleading and this praying.

Go back to thy wail of fetter and chain!

Go back to thy night of loving in vain!

IV.

O weak Soul! let us follow the heavy hearse that bore our old Dream out past the white-horned Daylight of Love.

Let thy pale Dead come up from their furrows of winding-sheets to mock thy prayers with what thy days might have been.

Let the Living come back and point out the shadows they swept o'er the disk of thy morning star.

Have thou speech with them for the story of its swimming down in tremulous nakedness to the Red Sea[1] of the Past.

Go back and grapple with thy lost Angels that stand in terrible judgment against thee.

Seek thou the bloodless skeleton once hugged to thy depths.

Hath it grown warmer under thy passionate kissings?

Or, hath it closed its seeming wings and shrunk its white body down to a glistening coil?

Didst thou wait the growth of fangs to front the arrows of Love's latest peril?

Didst thou not see a black, hungry vulture wheeling down low to the white-bellied coil where thy Heaven had once based itself?

O blind Soul of mine!

V.

Blind, blind with tears!

Not for thee shall Love climb the Heaven of thy columned Hopes to Eternity!

Under the silver shadow of the cloud waits no blushing star thy tryst.

Didst thou not see the pale, widowed West loose her warm arms and slide the cold burial earth down upon the bare face of thy sun?

Gazing upon a shoal of ashes, thou hast lost the way that struck upon the heavy, obstructive valves of the grave to thy Heaven.

Mateless thou needs must vaguely feel along the dark, cold steeps of Night.

Hath not suffering made thee wise?

When, oh when?

---

[1] The body of water through which the Israelites made their escape from Egypt. See Exodus 13-14.

VI.

Go down to the black brink of Death and let its cool waters press up to thy weary feet.

See if its trembling waves will shatter the grand repeating of thy earth-star.

See if the eyes that said to thee their speechless Love so close will reach thee from this sorrowful continent of Life.

See if the red hands that seamed thy shroud will come around thy grave.

Then, O Soul! thou mayst drag them to the very edges of the Death-pit, and shake off their red shadows!

Thy strong vengeance may then bind the black-winged crew down level with their beds of fire!

VII.

But wait, wait!

Take up the ruined cup of Life that struck like a planet through the dark, and shone clear and full as we starved for the feast within.

Go down to the black offings of the Noiseless Sea, and wait, poor Soul!

Measure down the depth of thy bitterness and wait!

Bandage down with the grave-clothes the pulses of thy dying life and wait!

Wail up thy wild, desolate echoes to the pitying arms of God and wait!

Wait, wait!

Hear, O Israel!

(From the Hebrew.)[1]

"And they shall be my people, and I will be their God."
— Jeremiah ii. 38.

I.

Hear, O Israel! and plead my cause against the ungodly nation!

'Midst the terrible conflict of Love and Peace, I departed from thee, my people, and spread my tent of many colors in the land of Egypt.

In their crimson and fine linen I girded my white form.

Sapphires gleamed their purple light from out the darkness of my hair.

The silver folds of their temple foot-cloth was spread beneath my sandaled feet.

Thus I slumbered through the daylight.

Slumbered 'midst the vapor of sin,
Slumbered 'midst the battle and din,
Wakened 'midst the strangle of breath,
Wakened 'midst the struggle of death!

II.

Hear, O Israel! my people—to thy goodly tents do I return with unstained hands.

Like as the harts for the water-brooks, in thirst, do pant and bray, so pants and cries my longing soul for the house of Jacob.

---

[1] This poem contains several references to and borrowings from Jewish scripture. The title is from the opening of the *Shema*, the central prayer of the Jewish faith (see Deuteronomy 6.4). The poem mentions Old Testament characters (Jacob, the tribe of Judah, the Philistines, for example) and places (Egypt, the Red Sea, Jerusalem). The poem is also filled with a variety of allusions to or quotations from the Hebrew scriptures. Some examples include: line 1 alludes to Psalm 43.1; line 2 to Genesis 37.3; line 3 to 2 Chronicles 3.14; line 22 to Deuteronomy 22-24; line 24 to Daniel 3; line 25 to Exodus 14-15; line 36 to Genesis 4.15; line 37 to Exodus 21.23; line 49 to Exodus 7.3. This list is not exhaustive, but should provide a sense of Menken's borrowing from Hebrew scripture to piece together this poem.

My tears have unto me been meat, both in night and day:
And the crimson and fine linen moulders in the dark tents
of the enemy.
With bare feet and covered head do I return to thee, O Israel!
With sackcloth have I bound the hem of my garments.
With olive leaves have I trimmed the border of my bosom.
The breaking waves did pass o'er me; yea, were mighty in
their strength—
Strength of the foe's oppression.
My soul was cast out upon the waters of Sin: but it has
come back to me.
My transgressions have vanished like a cloud.
The curse of Balaam hath turned to a blessing;
And the doors of Jacob turn not on their hinges against me.
Rise up, O Israel! for it is I who passed through the fiery
furnace seven times, and come forth unscathed to redeem thee
from slavery, O my nation! and lead thee back to God.

III.

Brothers mine, fling out your white banners over this Red
Sea of wrath!
Hear ye not the Death-cry of a thousand burning,
bleeding wrongs?
Against the enemy lift thy sword of fire, even thou, O
Israel! whose prophet I am.
For I, of all thy race, with these tear-blinded eyes, still see
the watch-fire leaping up its blood-red flame from the
ramparts of our Jerusalem!
And my heart alone beats and palpitates, rises and falls with
the glimmering and the gleaming of the golden beacon flame,
by whose light I shall lead thee, O my people! back to freedom!
Give me time—oh give me time to strike from your
brows the shadow-crowns of Wrong!
On the anvil of my heart will I rend the chains that bind ye.
Look upon me—oh look upon me, as I turn from the
world—from love, and passion, to lead thee, thou Chosen of
God, back to the pastures of Right and Life!

Fear me not; for the best blood that heaves this heart now runs for thee, thou Lonely Nation!

Why wear ye not the crown of eternal royalty, that God set down upon your heads?

Back, tyrants of the red hands!

Slouch back to your ungodly tents, and hide the Cain-brand on your foreheads!

Life for life, blood for blood, is the lesson ye teach us.

We, the Children of Israel, will not creep to the kennel graves ye are scooping out with iron hands, like scourged hounds!

Israel! rouse ye from the slumber of ages, and, though Hell welters at your feet, carve a road through these tyrants!

The promised dawn-light is here; and God—O the God of our nation is calling!

Press on—press on!

IV.

Ye, who are kings, princes, priests, and prophets. Ye men of Judah and bards of Jerusalem, hearken unto my voice, and I will speak thy name, O Israel!

Fear not; for God hath at last let loose His thinkers, and their voices now tremble in the mighty depths of this old world!

Rise up from thy blood-stained pillows!

Cast down to dust the hideous, galling chains that bind thy strong hearts down to silence!

Wear ye the badge of slaves?

See ye not the watch-fire?

Look aloft, from thy wilderness of thought!

Come forth with the signs and wonders, and thy strong hands, and stretched-out arms, even as thou didst from Egypt!

Courage, courage! trampled hearts!

Look at these pale hands and frail arms, that have rent asunder the welded chains that an army of the Philistines bound about me!

But the God of all Israel set His seal of fire on my breast, and lighted up, with inspiration, the soul that pants for the Freedom of a nation!

With eager wings she fluttered above the blood-stained

bayonet-points of the millions, who are trampling upon the
strong throats of God's people.

Rise up, brave hearts!
The sentry cries: "All's well!" from Hope's tower!
Fling out your banners of Right!
The watch fire grows brighter!
All's well! All's well!
Courage! Courage!
The Lord of Hosts is in the field,
The God of Jacob is our shield!

Where the Flocks Shall Be Led.[1]

Where shall I lead the flocks to-day?

Is there no Horeb for me beyond this desert?

Is there no rod with which I can divide this sea of blood
to escape mine enemies?

Must I pine in bondage and drag these heavy chains
through the rocky path of my unrecompensed toll?

Must I, with these pale, feeble hands, still lift the wreathed
bowl for others to drink, while my lips are parched and my
soul unslaked?

Must I hold the light above my head that others may find
the green pastures as they march in advance, whilst I moan and
stumble with my bare feet tangled and clogged with this load
of chains?

Must I still supply the lamp with oil that gives no light to me?

Shall I reck not my being's wane in these long days of
bondage and struggle?

Is there no time for me to pray?

Others are climbing the hill-side of glory whilst I am left
to wrestle with darkness in the valley below.

---

[1] Like "Hear, O Israel," this poem contains a variety of allusions to Hebrew scriptures.
It refers to Biblical characters (Aaron, the high priest of the Israelites and brother of
Moses) and places (Hebron). Line 2 and 42 mention Horeb, the mountain where
God appeared to Moses as a burning bush (Exodus 3.1-3). Line 3 alludes to Exodus
14; line 8 to Daniel 3; and line 41 to the pillar of cloud in which the Lord appeared
before the people of Israel to lead them out of Egypt (Exodus 13.21-22).

Oh where shall I lead the flocks to-day?

Once the soft white flowers of love bloomed upon my bosom.

But, oh! see this iron crown hath crushed the purple blood from my temples until the roses are drowned in it and 'tis withered and weeping on my breast.

The dear hands that planted the sweet flowers should not have been the ones to clasp this heavy iron band round my aching head.

Oh why is it that those we love and cling to with the deepest adoration of our unschooled natures should be the first to whet the steel and bury it in the warm blood that passionate love had created?

Answer me, ye who are ranged mockingly around me with your unsheathed knives. Answer me.

I know that ye are waiting to strike, but answer me first.

I know that if my tearful eyes do but wander from ye one moment, your trembling cowardly hands will strike the blow that your black souls are crying out for.

But let your haggard lips speak to give me warning.

Ye wait to see if these tears will blind me.

But I shall not plead for mercy.

Weak and fainting as I am, I fear you not.

For, lo! behold!

I bare to you my white mother bosom!

See, I draw from my heart a dagger whose blade is keener than any ye can hold against me.

The hands I loved most whetted it, and struck with fatal precision ye never can, for he knew where the heart lay.

No one else can ever know.

Look how the thick blood slowly drips from the point of the blade and sinks into the sand at my feet.

The white sand rolls over and covers the stains.

Flowers will spring up even there.

One day the sands will loose their seal, and they will speak.

The first shall be last and the last shall be first.[1]

The first is my own life and the last my child.

---

[1] Matthew 20.16.

That one will bloom eternally.

And together we will sound the horn that shall herd the flocks and lead them up to the Father's pastures.

For I know that somewhere there grows a green bush in the crevice of a rock, and that the enemy's foot may not crush it nor his hand uproot it.

A golden gate shall be unloosed, and we shall feed upon the freshness of the mountains.

But, see, the furnace has been heated seven times.

I still stand barefoot and bondage-bound, girt around my warriors, and chained and down-trodden upon these burning sands.

And yet I will escape.

Look, the pillar of cloud is over my head.

He who saved the bush on Horeb from the flames can lead me through the Red Sea, beyond the reach of these Egyptians with their rumbling chariots, tramping steeds, clashing weapons, and thunders of war.

Above the tumult I hear the voice of Aaron.

When the sun rises the chains shall be unsealed.

The blood shall be lifted from the earth and will speak.

The task-masters shall perish.

The white flocks shall be led back to the broad plains of Hebron.

I still see the pillar of cloud.

God is in the midst of us!

Pro Patria.[1]

America, 1861.

God's armies of Heaven, with pinions extended,
    Spread wide their white arms to the standard of Light;
And bending far down to the great Heart of Nature,
    With kisses of Love drew us up from the Night.

---

[1]   For one's native country, on behalf of one's homeland/fatherland (Latin). The poem is an expression of support for the Union at the beginning of the Civil War.

Proud soul of the Bondless! whose stars fleck with crimson,
    And warm dreams of gold ev'ry pillar and dome,
That strengthens and crowns the fair temples upswelling
    To glitter, far-seen, in our Liberty's home—

The spirits of Heroes and Sires of the People,
    Leaned down from the battlements guarding the world;
To breathe for your Destiny omens of glory
    And freedom eternal, in Honor impearled.

The storm-goaded mountains, and trees that had battled
    With winds sweeping angrily down through the years,
Turned red in the blood of the roses of Heaven,
    'Neath fires lit by sunset on vanishing spears.

The soft Beam of Peace bronzed the rocks of stern ages,
    And crept from the valley to burn on the spire;
And stooped from the glimmer of gems in the palace,
    To glow in the hovel a soul-heating fire.

Each turret, and terrace, and archway of grandeur,
    Its beauty up-rounded through laughs of the light;
And world-crown'd America chose for her standard
    The blush of the Day and the eyes of the Night.

Then Liberty's sceptre, its last jewel finding,
    Was waved by a God o'er the years to be born,
And far in the future there rusted and crumbled
    The chains of the centuries, ne'er to be worn.

The wave-hosts patrolling the sullen Atlantic,
    With helmets of snow, and broad silvery shields,
Ran clamoring up to the seed-sown embrasures,
    And fashioned new dews for the buds of the fields:

They spread their scroll shields for the breast of Columbia,
    And turned their storm-swords to the enemy's fleet;

Their glory to humble the tyrant that braved them,
  Their honor to lave fair America's feet!

No hot hand of Mars scattered red bolts of thunder
  From out the blest land on their message-wind's breath;
But softly the murmur of Peace wantoned o'er them,
  And soothed War to sleep in the Cradle of Death,

Then hiding their snow plumes, they slept in their armor,
  And as the sun shone on their crystalline mail;
Lo! Freedom beheld, from her mountains, a mirror,
  And caught her own image spread under a sail!

So, blest was Columbia; the focus of Nature's
  Best gifts, and the dimple where rested God's smile;
The Queen of the World in her young strength and beauty,
  The pride of the skies in her freedom from guile.

Aloft on the mount of God's liberty endless,
  Half-veiled by the clouds of His temple she stood,
Arrayed in the glory of Heaven, the mortal,
  With vigor Immortal unchained in her blood.

A bright helm of stars on her white brow was seated,
  And gold were the plumes from its clusters that fell
To light the gaunt faces of slaves in old kingdoms,
  And show them the way to the hand they loved well.

No gorget of steel rested on her bare bosom,
  Where glittered a necklace of gems from the skies;
And girding her waist was the red band of sunset,
  With light intertwined 'neath the glance of her eyes.

The sword that had bridged in the dark time of trouble,
  Her heart's grand Niagara rolling in blood;
Still sheathless she held; but it turned to a sunbeam.
  And blessed what it touched, like a finger of God!

The robes of her guardian Angels swept round her,
  And flashed through the leaves of the grand Tree of Life,
Till all the sweet birds in its depths woke to music,
  And e'en the bruised limbs with new being were rife.

The Eagle's gray eyes, from the crag by the ocean,
  Undazed by the sun, saw the vision of love,
And swift on the rim of the shield of Columbia,
  The bold Eagle fell from the white throne of Jove!

Columbia! My Country! My Mother! thy glory
  Was born in a spirit Immortal, divine;
And when from God's lips passed the nectar of heaven,
  Thy current baptismal was deified wine!

Thou born of Eternal! the hand that would harm thee
  Must wither to dust, and in dust be abhorred,
For thine is the throne whose blue canopy muffles
  The footfalls of angels, the steps of the Lord!

But hush! 'Twas the flap of the raven's dark pinions
  That sounded in woe on the breeze as it passed;
There cometh a hum, as of distance-veiled battle,
  From out the deep throat of the quivering blast;

There cometh a sound like the moan of a lost one
  From out the red jaws of Hell's cavern of Death;
The Eagle's strong wing feels the talon of Discord,
  And all the fair sunlight goes out with a breath!

And see how the purple-hued hills and the valleys
  Are dark with bent necks and with arms all unnerved;
And black, yelling hounds bay the soul into madness—
  The Huntsman of Hell drives the pack that has swerved!

The pale steeds of Death shake the palls of their saddles,
  And spread their black manes, wrought of shrouds, to
    the wind,

The curst sons of Discord each courser bestriding,
　　To guide the Arch-Demon, who lingers behind.

They thunder in rage, o'er the red path of Battle,
　　Far up the steep mount where fair Liberty keeps
The soul of a Tyrant in parchment imprisoned;
　　God pity us all, if her Sentinel sleeps!

Our Father in Heaven! the shadow of fetters
　　Is held in the shade of the Dove's little wing;
And must it again on our smothered hearts settle?
　　Peace slain—and the knell of our Honor they ring!

Behold! from the night-checkered edge of the woodland
　　A wall of red shields crowdeth into the land,
Their rims shooting horror and bloody confusion,
　　Their fields spreading darkness on every hand.

A forest of morions[1] utter grim murder—
　　Threats kissed by the sun from their long tongues of steel;
Lo, forests of spears hedge the heart of Columbia,
　　And soon their keen points her fair bosom may feel!

Her Cain-branded foes! How they crawl in the valley,
　　And creep o'er the hills, in their dastardly fear!
Afraid, lest their victim should suddenly waken
　　And blast them for e'er with a womanly tear!

Like hunters who compass the African jungle,
　　Where slumbers Numidia's lion by day,
They falter and pale, looking back at each other,
　　And some, in their falsehood, to Providence pray!

Assassins of Liberty! comes there not o'er you
　　A thought of the time, when the land you would blight,

---

[1] Helmet with a visor.

Though slumbering 'mid tombs of a hundred dead nations,
   Though Britain's steel bulwarks broke into the light?

And can ye forget the hot blood-rain that deluged
   The Hearts of the Fathers, who left to your care
The beautiful Trust now in slumber before you,
   They starved, fought, and fell to preserve from a snare?

Would ye splash, in your madness, the blood of the children,
   With merciless blows, in the poor mother's face?
Turn back, ye Assassins! or wear on your foreheads
   For ever the brand of a God-hated race!

Down, down to the dust with ye, cowards inhuman!
   And learn, as ye grovel, for mercy to live,
That Love is the Sceptre and Throne of the Nation,
   And Freedom the Crown that the centuries give!

Unrighteous Ambition has slept in our limits
   Since fearless Columbia sheathed her bright blade:
And at her dread Vengeance on those who awake it,
   The soul of the stoutest might well be dismayed.

Beware! for the spirit of God's Retribution
   Will make a red sunrise when Liberty dies;
The Traitors shall writhe in the glow of a morning,
   And drown in the blood that is filling their eyes!

The bright blade of old, when it leaps from the scabbard
   Like Lightning shall fall on the traitorous head,
And hurl with each stroke, in its world-shock of thunder,
   A thrice cursed soul to the deeps of the Dead!

Beware! for when once ye have made your Red Ocean,
   Its waves shall rise up with tempestuous swell,
And hurl your stained souls, like impurities, from them
   Up death's dark slope, to the skull beach of Hell!

Karazah to Karl.[1]

Come back to me! my life is young,
  My soul is scarcely on her way,
And all the starry songs she's sung,
  Are prelude to a grander lay.
          Come back to me!

Let this song-born soul receive thee,
  Glowing its fondest truth to prove;
Why so early did'st thou leave me,
  In our heaven-grand life of love?[2]
          Come back to me!

My burning lips shall set their seal
  On our betrothal bond to-night,
While whispering murmurs will reveal
  How souls can love in God's own light.
          Come back to me!

Come back to me! The stars will be
  Silent witnesses of our bliss,
And all the past shall seem to thee
  But a sweet dream to herald this!
          Come back to me!

A Fragment.

"Oh! I am sick of what I am. Of all
Which I in life can ever hope to be.
Angels of light be pitiful to me."[3]

---

1   First published in *The Israelite* on 3 September 1858, this poem is a personal one, a
    plea to her husband at the time, Alexander Menken, to return to her.
2   In various printings of *Infelicia*, this line reads: "Are our heaven-grand life of love?"
    It has been been restored to its original form, as it appeared in *The Israelite*, to clar-
    ify the sense of the sentence.
3   This epigraph and the other quotations in the poem are from Alice Cary, "Penitence."
    See *The Poets and Poetry of The West*, ed. William T. Coggeshall (Columbus, 1860) 354–55.

The cold chain of life presseth heavily on me to-night

The thundering pace of thought is curbed, and, like a fiery steed, dasheth against the gloomy walls of my prisoned soul.

Oh! how long will my poor thoughts lament their narrow faculty? When will the rein be loosed from my impatient soul?

Ah! then I will climb the blue clouds and dash down to dust those jeweled stars, whose silent light wafts a mocking laugh to the poor musician who sitteth before the muffled organ of my great hopes. With a hand of fire he toucheth the golden keys. All breathless and rapt I list for an answer to his sweet meaning, but the glittering keys give back only a faint hollow sound—the echo of a sigh!

Cruel stars to mock me with your laughing light!

Oh! see ye not the purple life-blood ebbing from my side? But ye heed it not—and I scorn ye all.

Foolish stars! Ye forget that this strong soul will one day be loosed.

I will have ye in my power yet, I'll meet ye on the grand door of old eternity.

Ah! then ye will not laugh, but shrink before me like very beggars of light that ye are, and I will grasp from your gleaming brows the jeweled crown, rend away your glistening garments, and hold ye up blackened skeletons for the laugh and scorn of all angels, and then drive ye out to fill this horrid space of darkness that I now grovel in.

But, alas! I am weary, sick, and faint.

The chains do bind the shrinking flesh too close.

"Angels of light, be pitiful to me."

Oh! this life, after all, is but a promise—a poor promise, that is too heavy to bear—heavy with blood, reeking human blood. The atmosphere is laden with it. When I shut my eyes it presses so close to their lids that I must gasp and struggle to open them.

I know that the sins of untrue hearts are clogging up the air-passages of the world, and that we, who love and suffer, will soon be smothered, and in this terrible darkness too.

For me—my poor lone, deserted body—I care not. I am not in favor of men's eyes.

> "Nor am I skilled immortal stuff to weave.
> No rose of honor wear I on my sleeve."

But the soft silver hand of death will unbind the galling bands that clasp the fretting soul in her narrow prison-house, and she may then escape the iron hands that would crush the delicate fibres to dust.

O soul, where are thy wings? Have they with their rude hands torn them from thy mutilated form? We must creep slowly and silently away through the midnight darkness. But we are strong yet, and can battle with the fiends who seek to drive us back to the river of blood.

But, alas! it is so late, and I am alone—alone listening to the gasps and sighs of a weary soul beating her broken wing against the darkened walls of her lonely cell.

> "My labor is a vain and empty strife,
> A useless tugging at the wheels of life."

Shall I still live—filling no heart, working no good, and the cries of my holy down-trodden race haunting me? Beseeching me—me, with these frail arms and this poor chained soul, to lift them back to their birthright of glory.

> "Angels of light, be pitiful to me."

I have wearied Heaven with my tears and prayers till I have grown pale and old, but a shadow of my former self, and all for power, blessed power! Not for myself—but for those dearer and worthier than I—those from out whose hearts my memory has died for ever.

But, alas! it is vain.

Prayers and tears will not bring back sweet hope and love.

I may still sigh and weep for these soft-winged nestling angels of my lost dreams till I am free to seek them in the grand homes where I have housed them with the golden-haired son of the sky.

It is midnight, and the world is still battling—the weak are falling, the strong and the wrong are exulting.

And I, like the dying stag, am hunted down to the ocean border, still asking for peace and rest of the great gleaming eyes that pierce the atmosphere of blood and haunt me with their pleading looks. Whispers are there—low, wailing whispers from white-browed children as though I could bear their chained souls o'er Charon's mystic river of their purple blood.

Alas! star after star has gone down till not one is in sight. How dark and cold it is growing!

Oh, light! why have you fled to a fairer land and left

> "An unrigged hulk, to rot upon life's ford—
> The crew of mutinous senses overboard?"

It is too late. I faint with fear of these atom-fiends that do cling to my garments in this darkness.

> Oh! rest for thee, my weary soul,
>   The coil is round thee all too fast.
> Too close to earth thy pinions clasp:
>   A trance-like death hath o'er thee past.

> Oh, soul! oh, broken soul, arise,
>   And plume thee for a prouder flight.
> In vain, in vain—'tis sinking now
>   And dying in eternal night.

> "Suffer and be still."

Death will bind up thy powerful wings, and to the organ music of my great hopes thou shalt beat sublimer airs.

Wait until eternity.

The Autograph on the Soul.

In the Beginning, God, the great Schoolmaster, wrote upon the white leaves of our souls the text of life, in His own autograph. Upon all souls it has been written alike.

We set forth with the broad, fair characters penned in smoothness and beauty, and promise to bear them back so, to the Master, who will endorse them with eternal life.

But, alas! how few of us can return with these copy-books unstained and unblotted?

Man—the school-boy Man—takes a jagged pen and dips it in blood, and scrawls line after line of his hopeless, shaky, weak-backed, spattering imitation of the unattainable flourish and vigor of the autograph at the top of our souls.

And thus they go on, in unweary reiteration, until the fair leaves are covered with unseemly blots, and the Schoolmaster's copy is no longer visible.

No wonder, then, that we shrink and hide, and play truant as long as we possibly can, before handing in to the Master our copy-books for examination.

How soiled with the dust of men, and stained with the blood of the innocent, some of these books are!

Surely, some will look fairer than others.

Those of the lowly and despised of men;

The wronged and the persecuted;

The loving and the deserted;

The suffering and the despairing;

The weak and the struggling;

The desolate and the oppressed;

The authors of good books;

The defenders of women;

The mothers of new-born children;

The loving wives of cruel husbands;

The strong throats that are choked with their own blood, and cannot cry out the oppressor's wrong.

On the souls of these of God's children of inspiration, His autograph will be handed up to the judgment-seat, on the Day of Examination, pure and unsoiled.

The leaf may be torn, and traces of tears, that fell as prayers went up, may dim the holy copy, but its fair, sharp, and delicate outlines will only gleam the stronger, and prove the lesson of life, that poor, down-trodden humanity has been studying for ages and ages—the eternal triumph of mind over matter!

What grand poems these starving souls will be, after they are signed and sealed by the Master-hand!

But what of the oppressor?

What of the betrayer?

What of him that holds a deadly cup, that the pure of heart may drink?

What of fallen women, who are covered with paint and sin, and flaunt in gaudy satins, never heeding the black stains within their own breasts?—lost to honor, lost to themselves; glittering in jewels and gold; mingling with sinful men, who, with sneering looks and scoffing laughs, drink wine beneath the gas-light's glare.

Wrecks of womanly honor!

Wrecks of womanly souls!

Wrecks of life and love!

Blots that deface the fair earth with crime and sin!

Fallen—fallen so low that the cries and groans of the damned must sometimes startle their death-signed hearts, as they flaunt through the world, with God's curse upon them!

What of the money-makers, with their scorching days and icy nights?

Their hollow words and ghastly smiles?

Their trifling deceits?

Their shameless lives?

Their starving menials?

Their iron hands, that grasp the throats of weary, white-haired men?

Will their coffins be black?

They should be red—stained with the blood of their victims!

Their shrouds should be made with pockets; and all their gold should be placed therein, to drag them deeper down than the sexton dug the grave!

How will it be with him who deceives and betrays women?

Answer me this, ye men who have brought woe and desolation to the heart of woman; and, by your fond lips, breathing sighs, and vows of truth and constancy—your deceit and desertion, destroyed her, body and soul!

There are more roads to the heart than by cold steel.

You drew her life and soul after you by your pretended love. Perhaps she sacrificed her home, her father and her mother—her God and her religion for you!

Perhaps for you she has endured pain and penury!

Perhaps she is the mother of your child, living and praying for you!

And how do you repay this devotion?

By entering the Eden of her soul, and leaving the trail of the serpent, that can never be erased from its flowers; for the best you trample beneath your feet, while the fairest you pluck as a toy to while away an idle hour, then dash aside for another of a fairer cast.

Then, if she plead with her tears, and her pure hands, to Heaven, that you come back to your lost honor, and to her heart, you do not hesitate to tear that suffering heart with a shameless word, that cuts like a jagged knife, and add your curse to crush her light of life!

Have ye seen the blood-stained steel, dimmed with the heart's warm blood of the suicide?

Have ye seen the pallid lips, the staring eyes, the unclosed, red-roofed mouth—the bubbling gore, welling up from a woman's breast?

Have ye seen her dying in shivering dread, with the blood dabbled o'er her bosom?

Have ye heard her choked voice rise in prayer—her pale lips breathing his name—the name of him who deceived her? Yes! a prayer coming up with the bubbling blood—a blessing on him for whom she died!

Why did she not pray for her despairing self?

O God! have mercy on the souls of men who are false to their earthly love and trust!

But the interest will come round—all will come round!

Nothing will escape the Schoolmaster's sleepless eye!

The indirect is always as great and real as the direct.
Not one word or deed—
Not one look or thought—
Not a motive but will be stamped on the programme of
our lives, and duly realized by us, and returned, and held up to
light heaven or flood hell with.
All the best actions of war or peace—
All the help given to strangers—
Cheering words to the despairing—
Open hands to the shunned—
Lifting of lowly hearts—
Teaching children of God—
Helping the widow and the fatherless—
Giving light to some desolate home—
Reading the Bible to the blind—
Protecting the defenceless—
Praying with the dying.
These are acts that need no Poet to make poems of them;
for they will live through ages and ages, on to Eternity. And
when God opens the sealed book on the Day of Judgment,
these poems of the history of lives will be traced in letters of
purple and gold, beneath the Master's Autograph.

Adelina Patti.[1]

Thou Pleiad of the lyric world
Where Pasta, Garcia shone,[2]

---

[1]   A famous Italian opera soprano (1843-1919). Patti made her debut in New York in 1859
      as Lucia in Donizetti's *Lucia di Lammermoor* and her European debut in 1861 as Amina
      in Bellini's *La sonnambula*. She was also known for playing Marie in Donizetti's *La figlia
      del reggimento*. See Hermann Klein, *The Reign of Patti* (New York: Century Co., 1920).
          This poem is a revision, abridgement, and rearrangement of "La Signora Vestvali"
      by "Cinna Beverley," a poem that appeared in *The Sunday Delta* (24 May 1857): 1.
      During 1857, Menken lived in New Orleans and contributed to *The Sunday Delta*.
      She first published "Adelina Patti" in the New York *Sunday Mercury* on 30 June 1861.
[2]   Pleiad is the name given to one of the tragic poets from Alexandria. It comes from the
      Greek mythological Pleiades, the attendants of Artemis who were changed into stars
      by the gods when they were pursued by Orion. Giuditta Pasta (1797-1865) was consid-
      ered the greatest European soprano of the 1820s and 30s. Garcia is Manuel del Pópolo
      Vicente Rodríquez García (1775–1832), a world famous Spanish tenor and composer.

Come back with thy sweet voice again,
And gem the starry zone.

Though faded, still the vision sees
The loveliest child of night,
The fairest of the Pleiades,
Its glory and its light.

How fell with music from thy tongue
The picture which it drew
Of Lucia, radiant, warm, and young—
Amina, fond and true.

Or the young Marie's grace and art,
So free from earthly strife,
Beating upon the sounding heart,
The gay tattoo of life!

Fair Florence! home of glorious Art,
And mistress of its sphere,
Clasp fast thy beauties to thy heart—
Behold thy rival here!

Dying.

I.

Leave me; oh! leave me,
Lest I find this low earth sweeter than the skies.

Leave me lest I deem Faith's white bosom bared to the
betraying arms of Death.

Hush your fond voice, lest it shut out the angel trumpet-call!

See my o'erwearied feet bleed for rest.

Loose the clinging and the clasping of my clammy fingers.

Your soft hand of Love may press back the dark, awful
shadows of Death, but the soul faints in the strife and struggles
of nights that have no days.

I am so weary with this climbing up the smooth steep
sides of the grave wall.

My dimmed eyes can no longer strain up through the darkness to the temples and palaces that you have built for me upon Life's summit.

God is folding up the white tent of my youth.

My name is enrolled for the pallid army of the dead.

II.

It is too late, too late!

You may not kiss back my breath to the sunshine.

How can these trembling hands of dust reach up to bend the untempered iron of Destiny down to my woman-forehead?

Where is the wedge to split its knotty way between the Past and the Future?

The soaring bird that would sing its life out to the stars, may not leave its own atmosphere;

For, in the long dead reaches of blank space in the Beyond, its free wings fall back to earth baffled.

Once gathering all my sorrows up to one purpose—rebel-like—I dared step out into Light, when, lo! Death tied my unwilling feet, and with hands of ice, bandaged my burning lips, and set up, between my eyes and the Future, the great Infinite of Eternity, full in the blazing sun of my Hope!

From the red round life of Love I have gone down to the naked house of Fear.

Drowned in a storm of tears.

My wild wings of thought drenched from beauty to the color of the ground.

Going out at the hueless gates of day.

Dying, dying.

III.

Oh! is there no strength in sorrow, or in prayers?

Is there no power in the untried wings of the soul, to smite the brazen portals of the sun?

Must the black-sandaled foot of Night tramp out the one star that throbs through the darkness of my waning life?

May not the strong arm of "I will," bring some beam to lead me into my sweet Hope again?

Alas, too late! too late!
The power of these blood-dripping cerements sweeps
back the audacious thought to emptiness.
Hungry Death will not heed the poor bird that has
tangled its bright wing through my deep-heart pulses.
Moaning and living.
Dying and loving.

IV.

See the poor wounded snake; how burdened to the
ground;
How it lengthens limberly along the dust.
Now palpitates into bright rings only to unwind, and
reach its bleeding head up the steep high walls around us.
Now, alas! falling heavily back into itself, quivering with
unuttered pain;
Choking with its own blood it dies in the dust.
So we are crippled ever;
Reaching and falling,
Silent and dying.

V.

Gold and gleaming jewel shatter off their glory well in the
robes of royalty, but when we strain against the whelming
waves, the water gurgling down our drowning throats, we
shred them off, and hug the wet, cold rocks lovingly.
Then old death goes moaning back from the steady
footing of Life baffled.
Ah! is it too late for me to be wise?
Will my feeble hands fail me in the moveless steppings
back to the world?
Oh! if youth were only back!
Oh! if the years would only empty back their ruined days
into the lap of the Present!
Oh! if yesterday would only unravel the light it wove into
the purple of the Past!
Ah! then might I be vigilant!
Then might the battle be mine!

Nor should my sluggish blood drip down the rocks till the noon-tide sun should draw it up mistily in smoke.

Then should the heaviness of soul have dropped as trees do their weight of rainy leaves.

Nor should the sweet leash of Love have slipped from my hungry life, and left me pining, dying for his strength.

I should have wrapt up my breathing in the naked bosom of Nature, and she would have kissed me back to sweetest comfort, and I would have drawn up from her heart draughts of crusted nectar and promises of eternal joys.

Oh! it is not the glittering garniture of God's things that come quivering into the senses, that makes our lives look white through the windings of the wilderness.

It is the soul's outflow of purple light that clashes up a music with the golden blood of strong hearts.

Souls with God's breath upon them,
Hearts with Love's light upon them.

VI.[1]

If my weak puny hand could reach up and rend the sun from his throne to-day, then were the same but a little thing for me to do.

It is the Far Off, the great Unattainable, that feeds the passion we feel for a star.

Looking up so high, worshipping so silently, we tramp out the hearts of flowers that lift their bright heads for us and die alone.

If only the black, steep grave gaped between us, I feel that I could over-sweep all its gulfs.

I believe that Love may unfold its white wings even in the red bosom of Hell.

I know that its truth can measure the distance to Heaven with one thought.

Then be content to let me go, for these pale hands shall reach up from the grave, and still draw the living waters of Love's well.

---

[1] Section VI incorporates phrases from Alice Carey [Cary], "Perversity," *Lyra and Other Poems* (New York, 1852) 41–42.

That is better, surer than climbing with bruised feet and bleeding hands to plead with the world for what is mine own.

Then straighten out the crumpled length of my hair, and loose all the flowers one by one.

God is not unjust.

VII.

Oh! in the great strength of thy unhooded soul, pray for my weakness.

Let me go! See the pale and solemn army of the night is on the march.

Do not let my shivering soul go wailing up for a human love to the throne of the Eternal.

Have we not watched the large setting sun drive a column of light through the horizon down into the darkness?

So within the grave's night, O my beloved! shall my love burn on to eternity.

O Death! Death! loose out thy cold, stiff fingers from my quivering heart!

Let the warm blood rush back to gasp up but one more word!

O Love! thou art stronger, mightier than all!

O Death! thou hast but wedded me to Life!

Life is Love, and Love is Eternity.

Saved.

I.

O soldiers, soldiers, get ye back, I pray!

Hush out of sound your trampings so near his lowly head!

Hush back the echoes of your footfalls to the muffling distance!

O soldiers, wake not my sleeping love!

Get ye back, I pray!

To-morrow will he wake, and lead ye on as bravely as before.

To-morrow will he lift the blazing sword above a crimson flood of victory.

Get ye back and wait.
He is weary, and would sleep.

II.
Soft, soft, he sleepeth well.
Why stand ye all so stern and sad?
So garmented in the dust and blood of battle?
Why linger on the field to-day? See how the dark locks
hang in bloody tangles about your glaring eyes!
Get ye to your silent tents, I pray!
See ye not your soldier-chief sleeps safe and well?
What say ye?
"Dead!"
O blind, blind soldiers! Should I not know?
Have I not watched him all the long, long battle?
On this cold and sunless plain my tottering feet struck the
pathway to my soldier.
My loving arms have clasped him from the black, hungry
jaws of Death.
With the neglected sunshine of my hair I shielded his pale
face from the cannon-glare.
On my breast, as on a wave of heaven-light, have I lulled
him to the soft beauty of dreams.
He has been yours to-day; he is mine now.
He has fought bravely, and would sleep.
I know, I know.

III.
O soldiers, soldiers, take him not hence!
Do not press tears back into your pitiful eyes, and say: "His
soul hath found its rest."
Why lean ye on your blood-stained spears, and point to
that dark wound upon his throat?
I can kiss its pain and terror out.
Leave him, I pray ye!
He will wake to-morrow, and cheer ye in your tents at dawn.
And ye shall see him smile on her who soothes his weary
head to sleep through this long night.

It was I who found him at the battle's dreadful close.
Weary and wounded, he sank to rest upon the field.
Murmuring out his tender voice, he called my name, and
whispered of our love, and its sweet eternity.
'Mid brooding love and clinging kisses, his tender eyes let
down their silken barriers to the day.
Their pale roofs close out the defeat, and in my arms he
finds the joy of glorious victory.

IV.

O soldiers, leave him to me!
The morning, bridegroomed by the sun, cannot look
down to the midnight for comfort.
In the thick front of battle I claimed what is mine own.
I saw the Grim Foe open wide his red-leafed book, but he
wrote not therein the name of my brave love.
Life hath no chance that he cannot combat with a single hand.
Now he wearies from the struggling grace of a brave
surrendering.
He sleeps, he sleeps.

V.

Go, soldiers, go!
I pray ye wake him not.
I have kissed his pale, cold mouth, and staunched the
crimson wound upon his throat.
The mournful moon has seen my silent watch above his
lonely bed.
Her pitying eyes reproached me not.
How durst yours?
Go, soldiers, go!

VI.

I charge ye by the love ye bear your sleeping chieftain,
wake him not!
To-morrow he will wake, eager to wheel into battle-line.
To-morrow he will rise, and mount the steed he loveth
well, and lead ye cheerily on to the attack!

To-morrow his voice will ring its Hope along your tramping troops!
But oh! wait, wait!
He is weary, and must sleep!
Go, soldiers, go!

Answer Me.

I.

In from the night.
The storm is lifting his black arms up to the sky.
Friend of my heart, who so gently marks out the life-track for me, draw near to-night;
Forget the wailing of the low-voiced wind:
Shut out the moanings of the freezing, and the starving, and the dying, and bend your head low to me:
Clasp my cold, cold hands in yours;
Think of me tenderly and lovingly:
Look down into my eyes the while I question you, and if you love me, answer me—
Oh, answer me!

II.

Is there not a gleam of Peace on all this tiresome earth?
Does not one oasis cheer all this desert-world?
When will all this toil and pain bring me the blessing?
Must I ever plead for help to do the work before me set?
Must I ever stumble and faint by the dark wayside?
Oh the dark, lonely wayside, with its dim-sheeted ghosts peering up through their shallow graves!
Must I ever tremble and pale at the great Beyond?
Must I find Rest only in your bosom, as now I do?
Answer me—
Oh, answer me!

III.

Speak to me tenderly.
Think of me lovingly.

Let your soft hands smooth back my hair.

Take my cold, tear-stained face up to yours.

Let my lonely life creep into your warm bosom, knowing no other rest but this.

Let me question you, while sweet Faith and Trust are folding their white robes around me.

Thus am I purified, even to your love, that came like John the Baptist in the Wilderness of Sin.

You read the starry heavens, and lead me forth.

But tell me if, in this world's Judea, there comes never quiet when once the heart awakes?

Why must it ever hush Love back?

Must it only labor, strive, and ache?

Has it no reward but this?

Has it no inheritance but to bear—and break?

Answer me—
Oh, answer me!

IV.

The Storm struggles with the Darkness.

Folded away in your arms, how little do I heed their battle!

The trees clash in vain their naked swords against the door.

I go not forth while the low murmur of your voice is drifting all else back to silence.

The darkness presses his black forehead close to the window pane, and beckons me without.

Love holds a lamp in this little room that hath power to blot back Fear.

But will the lamp ever starve for oil?

Will its blood-red flame ever grow faint and blue?

Will it uprear itself to a slender line of light?

Will it grow pallid and motionless?

Will it sink rayless to everlasting death?

Answer me—
Oh, answer me!

V.

Look at these tear-drops.

See how they quiver and die on your open hands.

Fold these white garments close to my breast, while I
question you.

Would you have me think that from the warm shelter of
your heart I must go to the grave?

And when I am lying in my silent shroud, will you love me?

When I am buried down in the cold, wet earth, will you
grieve that you did not save me?

Will your tears reach my pale face through all the
withered leaves that will heap themselves upon my grave?

Will you repent that you loosened your arms to let me fall
so deep, and so far out of sight?

Will you come and tell me so, when the coffin has shut
out the storm?

Answer me—

Oh, answer me!

Infelix. [1]

Where is the promise of my years;
　　　Once written on my brow?
Ere errors, agonies and fears
Brought with them all that speaks in tears,
Ere I had sunk beneath my peers;
　　　Where sleeps that promise now?

Naught lingers to redeem those hours,
　　　Still, still to memory sweet!
The flowers that bloomed in sunny bowers
Are withered all; and Evil towers
Supreme above her sister powers
　　　Of Sorrow and Deceit.

---

[1]　Unfortunate, unhappy, miserable (Latin).

I look along the columned years,
    And see Life's riven fane,
Just where it fell, amid the jeers
Of scornful lips, whose mocking sneers,
For ever hiss within mine ears
    To break the sleep of pain.

I can but own my life is vain
    A desert void of peace;
I missed the goal I sought to gain,
I missed the measure of the strain
That lulls Fame's fever in the brain,
    And bids Earth's tumult cease.

Myself! alas for theme so poor
    A theme but rich in Fear;
I stand a wreck on Error's shore,
A spectre not within the door,
A houseless shadow evermore,
    An exile lingering here.

To My Brother Gus.

How many lovely things we find
    In earth, and air, and sea—
The chime of bells upon the wind,
    The blossom on the tree;
But lovelier far than chime or flower,
A Brother's love in sorrow's hour.

Sweet is the carol of a bird,
    When warbling on the spray,
And beautiful the moon's pale beams
    That light us on our way:
Yet dearer is Gus' look and word
    Than moonlight or than warbling bird.

How prized the coral and the shell
    And valued, too, the pearl;
Who can the hidden treasures tell
O'er which the soft waves curl?
    Yet dearer still my brother to me
Than all in the earth, the air, or sea.

ADA BERTHA.
WASHINGTON, TEXAS, *October*, 1855.

I am Thine—To W.H.K. [1]

I am thine in thy gladness,
    I am thine in thy woe;
My spirit is with thee,
    Wherever thou go!

---

[1]   W.H. or Nelson Kneass, Menken's husband at the time.

No matter how distant
   Thy form is from me,
If you dwell with the stranger
   Far over the sea.

In poverty's hamlet,
   Or garlanded halls,
Your kindness and love
   My spirit recalls.

My heart bears thy image,
   Forever impressed,
Like the beautiful bow
   On the thunder cloud's breast.

Were a dungeon thy dwelling,
   I yet would be there,
To sooth thee and bless thee,
   And lessen thy care.

The throne of a monarch
   Were worthless to me
Could I never share it
   Willie, with thee!

In the breeze there's no freshness,
   No tints in the flower,
Unless thy dear presence
   Give light to each hour.

I am thine in thy gladness,
   I am thine in thy woe,
My spirit is with thee
   Wherever thou go!

                    ADA BERTHA.
WASHINGTON, TEXAS, *Oct.* 1855.

The Bright and Beautiful;
To Josephine[1]

The bright and beautiful are everywhere
    For those whose souls are filled with beauty.
To cheer with loving smiles [illegible] of care,
    And bless it in life's earnest duty.

For tis the soul gives coloring to life—
    Dyes it in gloom or Heavenly splendor,
As we, in all earth's varied scenes of life,
    To ill or good our hearts surrendered.

               ADA BERTHA.
WASHINGTON, TEXAS, *Oct.* 1855.

New Advertisement!!!
To R.M.T★★★★.[2]

I'm young and free, the pride of girls,
With hazel eyes and "nut brown curls;"
They say I am not void of beauty—
I love my friends, respect my duty—
I've had full many a BEAU IDEAL,
Yet never—never—found one *real*—
There must be one I know somewhere,
In all this circumambient air;
And I should dearly love to see him!
Now what if *you* should chance to be him?

        ADA BERTHA T———E.
AUSTIN CITY, *November* 23, 1855.

---

[1]   Menken's sister.
[2]   R.M.T. has not been identified.

"Milton wrote a letter to his lady love"[1]

Milton wrote a letter to his lady love,
    Filled with warm and keen desire—
He sought to raise a flame, and so he did,
    The lady cast his nonsense in the fire.

Wounded.[2]

Let me lie down!
Just here in the shade of this cannon-torn tree—
Here, low in this trampled grass, where I may see
The surge of the combat, and where I may hear
The glad cry of victory, cheer upon cheer,
    Let me lie down.

    Oh, it was grand!
Like the tempest we charged, in the triumph to share;
The tempest—its fury and thunder were there,
On, on o'er intrenchments, o'er living and dead,
With the foe underfoot and the flag overhead.
    Oh, it was grand!

    Weary and faint,
Prone on the soldier's couch, ah! how can I rest
With this shot-shattered head and sabre-pierced breast?
Comrades, at roll-call, when I shall be sought,
Say I fought where I fell, and fell where I fought,
    Wounded and faint.

    Oh, that last charge!
Right through the dread host tore the shrapnel and shell,
Through, without faltering—clear through with a yell—

---

[1]   This poem appears in Barclay's *Life of Adah Isaacs Menken* (see Appendix A). According to Barclay, it was included in a volume by Menken titled *Memories*, published in the South during the 1850s, though no such book has ever been located.

[2]   Not in the first edition, this poem was added to the 1888 edition of *Infelicia*. Barclay claims this poem appeared in the never located *Memories*.

Right in their midst, in the turmoil and gloom
Like heroes we dashed, at the mandate of doom.
   Oh, that last charge!

   But I am dying at last!
My mother, dear mother, with meek, tearful eye,
Farewell! and God bless you, forever and aye!
Oh, that I now lie on your pillowing breast,
To breathe my last sigh on the bosom first prest!
   I am dying, dying at last.

Uncollected Poems from The Israelite

Sinai.

Affectionately inscribed to brother Jacob.[1]

On that appalling morn, when Israel woke,
  To heap her Lord's omniscient decree;
When, as though Heaven's loud thunder broke,
  The very air grew rife with mystery;
When Sinai's Mount, involved in fire and smoke,
  Outswelled the aspiring eager of the sea;
This be my theme: presuming task! to sing
The praise of Israel's God, her everlasting King!

Oh! for a seraph's tongue or prophet's pen,
  My glorious song, enraptur'd to exalt!
Oh! to have heard Him, "with an angel's ken,"
  From yon triumphal wonder-paven vault,
Come clothed in wisdom to commune with men,
  And bid so near their tents His hierarchs halt!
O'er sapphire floods, the burning escort rolled
Through clouds of roseate fire and molten gold.

Soon from the hill's crest, fearful sounds began
  To radiate slowly to its hallowed base;
Through all the mustering tribes one impulse ran,
  One thrill of joy and fear: o'er shivering space
Pealed the celestial trump, and awe-struck man,
  With suppliant eyes, beheld the wondrous place,
Where eddying mist and lightning's livid stream,
Confest the Lord of Hosts—the Invisible Supreme!

Pillars of smoke, thick-falling, caught the eye;
  Dense but a moment; for the reddening blaze

---

[1]   Jacob S. Menken, the brother of her husband.

Gushed forth in plunging volleys to the sky,
    Fierce thunders roared, and meteors flashed amaze;
The unfathomed empyrean gleamed on high,
    With hues of amber, dazzling to the gaze,
And peal on peal, with wild tumultuous din,
Rolled on, far-echoing o'er the wilderness of sin.

In awful glory shone the firmament,
    Save where the vapor stained its glowing form:
Grey Sinai, with mighty earthquake rent,
    Upheaved its surging breast, as in a storm,
Shapeless, from side to side, the waves were sent,
    Toss'd by the power of an Almighty arm:
And Israel knelt, with hands and eyes upraised,
    While down the dusky hills, JEHOVAH's lightning blazed.

Then lo! the archangel's summons, loud and shrill,
    Shot terror and dismay through all their bands,
And, waxing longer, louder, louder still,
    Reverberating, o'er the desert sands,
Bidding God's seer ascend the flaming hill,
    From which He issued His divine commands,
And gave them statutes for the Promised Home,
    And lighted Heaven with love, through the ethereal dome!

NEW ORLEANS, September 7, 1857.

Dum Spiro, Spero.[1]
Inscribed to the author of The Last Struggle of the Nation.[2]

"In that hope, I throw mine eyes to heaven, scorning
whate'er you can afflict me with."[3]

---

[1] While I breathe, I hope (Latin). See H.T. Riley, ed., *Dictionary of Latin Quotations, Proverbs, Maxims, and Mottos* (London, 1856) 94.
[2] Isaac M.Wise published his historical novel, *The Last Struggle of the Nation, Or Rabbi Akiba and His Time,* in *The Israelite* in serialized installments from August 1856 to January 1858.
[3] *Henry 6, Part 3* 1.4.37–38.

Hope on, brave Heart, though friends forsake,
  Though Slander hurl her dart—
Do thou a firmer purpose take,
  To keep thee pure in heart.

Dark calumny and envy dare
  Assail, with Upas-tongue,
But innocence is strong to bear
  The weight against it flung.

Through pain and penury—toil and care—
  Bear up thy heart 'gainst dark despair;
And in OUR FAITH—through every ill—
  Learn thou to "suffer and be still!"

Hope on! it is not *always* night—
  The morn *must* break at last;
When thou shalt hail as clear a light,
  As o'er thy youth was cast.

Thou hast the *promise* still—O, then,
  Brave struggling heart, hope on!
And, for the sake of what *hath* been,
  Thy *rest* shall yet be won.

Though clouds are dark above thy head,
  Drear disappointment round thee spread—
But Truth's undimmed within thy breast,—
  Oh! bear on—leave to GOD the rest!

NEW-ORLEANS, Tishri 11, 5618.

Moses.

He who, for forty years, had led
  The wandering hosts of Israel,
At last was numbered with the dead;
  None could his place of burial tell.

High up the mount of God he trod,
  Where He on whom his love relied,
Waiting, the faithful servant stood,
  And his desire was satisfied.

Yea, though the promised land outspread,
  So far and vast before his eye,
Though Death the Jordan he must tread,
  He was content to know and die.

New-Orleans, Tishri, 5618.

Oppression of the Jews, Under the Turkish Empire. [1]

At spes non fracta. [2]

Will HE *never come?* Will the Jew,
  In exile eternally pine?
By the idolaters scorned, pitied only by few,
Will he never his vows to JEHOVAH renew,
  Beneath his own olive and vine?

Will he dwell with the Gentiles, who slight
  His shrine, and who make gold their god?
Must he slink in lone avenues, where the dark rite
Of cities is offered to Mammon? He of right,
  Whose fathers Jerusalem trod?

Why should he yield up his treasures of wealth,
  On the rack, at the gibbet or stake?
Shall his wife, daughter, son—shall his case and his health,
Aye, and life be cut off, or enjoyed but in stealth?
  Shall he not from such tyranny break?

---

[1] In 1840 the Muslim Turks regained control of Jerusalem and returned to Palestine.
Ottoman authorities ruled Jerusalem at the time this poem was written.
[2] Hope has not been broken (Latin). A commonly quoted motto found in *Roget's
Thesaurus* among other places.

Will he crouch 'neath Mohammed's control,
  In suburbs pent up like a thief?
And drink of contempt and reproaching the bowl,
Who, of chivalry, once, and of honor, was soul—
  Whose nation, of nations, was chief?

Shall his wine and his oil ne'er be reapt?
  Shall his harp hang by Euphrates' tide?
Whose music of sweetness, for ages, has slept,
O'er whose strings hath no finger of cheerfulness swept,
  In songs of deliv'rance and pride.

Shall he ne'er at the Festival's sheen,
  The New Moon nor Sabbath attend?
Where Israel, in beauty and glory, was seen;
Where shoutings went up, trumpets calling between,
  While praises were wont to ascend?

Where the censer gave od'rous perfume,
  Where the *Holy of Holies* had place,
Where the Almond of Aaron was laid up in bloom,
Where the *Ark of the Covenant* had resting and room,
  Where Shechinah gave token of grace!¹

ISRAEL! name that brings freshly the sigh—
  ISRAEL! name at which tears freely fall;
Even there, where mosques of Mohammed peer proudly on high,
Whence the Muzzein at noon sends idolatrous cry,
  Where Allah is worshipped of all!

---

¹ The Holy of Holies is the interior portion of the tabernacle which God instructed
the Israelites to build (Exodus 26.31-34). It contained the ark of the covenant (Exodus
25.10-16), the chest containing the tablets that recorded the written law God gave to
Moses. The Almond of Aaron refers to a story in Numbers 17, in which Aaron's rod
blossoms and bears almonds, a sign of God's choice of Aaron to be the leader of the
priestly tribe of Levi. Shechinah is a visible sign of God's presence with his people,
as a pillar of cloud leading the people of Israel through the wilderness and later in
the tabernacle.

'Tis ISRAEL, oh GOD! which Thy arm
    Still embraces! For Israel is set
Most safe in Thy love, deeply graved on Thy palm,
Secure from destruction, and terror and harm—
    Her bulwarks before Thee are yet!

And Thy oath was to Abraham given,
    Thy servant devoted to Thee—
As the sands on the shore, as the leaves by the wind driven,
As the hosts that then studded the Syrian heaven,
    To his children uncounted should be!

Like kings on their conquering car,
    They shall return! their bondage will burst!
"My sons shall be gather'd, my daughters from far,
To bear them where shines Jacob's beautiful star,
    To Tarshish, with ships shall be first." [1]

I see them! I see them! behold!
    Every stream, sea and ocean is white,
Where their canvass points home, where their standard broad fold
Waves on to the East, as it waved once of old,
    When the Ark moved, enveloped in light!

I see them! How wondrous the crowd!
    From Ganges, from Humber, from Nile—
As doves to their windows, they fly as a cloud;
How roll their Hosannas! how lordly and loud,
    Harp and timbrel give answer the while!

Who is HE, that of glory is King?
    To whom shall be lifted the gates?
Shout thousands of Israel! Ye worshippers bring
Oblation! Let Earth with her jubilee ring,
    Messiah! for thee, Israel waits!

NEW ORLEANS, Tishri 21, 5618.

---

[1] See Isaiah 60.9, Isaiah 43.6, and Numbers 24.17.

Spring!

The Spring is here again,
And over hill and plain,
    She hath flung
The magic of her smile,
And the world looks glad the while,
    As when young.

And hearts, long worn with care,
That heavy burdens bear,
    Towards the tomb,
Are now as light and free,
As they were wont to be,
    In Life's bloom.

But, ere another comes,
The hearth-stones of their homes
    May be left
Sad, desolate, and cold,—
Of their cheerfulness of old,
    All bereft.

For myriad years gone by,
With as bright and pure a sky,
    Hath the Spring
Succeeded to the blast
Of winter—binding fast
    Everything.

And, hearts that are to be,
In dim futurity,
    Will, like ours,
With joyous rapture burn,
At her annual return,
    With flowers.

Oh! THE SPRING—it makes me sad,
Though every thing looks glad,
    Round me here;
For the future, like the past,
Will be borne away at last,
    On its bier.

Yet, I love the Spring to come,
Driving winter from the home,
    Where I dwell;
Though its bursts of revelry,
Of passing time, to me,
    Sounds the knell.

יתי אור [1]

Inscribed to the Contributors to THE ISRAELITE.

Falter not, brothers, in the cause,
    So gloriously begun,
Until our great and holy laws
    Shall gladden every one;
Until JEHOVAH'S banners wave
    O'er every hill and plain,
And Israel looks up free and brave,
    Oh, "Let there be light," again!

What though our progress sometimes be
    But difficult and slow,
And hearts that beat most fervently,
    At times beat faint and low;
Though some grow weary by the way,
    And wander from the light,
And to the tempter fall a prey,
    O'ershadowed by the night;

---

[1] Let there be light (Hebrew). These words from Genesis 1.3 were the motto of *The Israelite*.

These are the clouds which will appear
Upon a summer's sky,
And shroud, with blacken'd forms and drear,
Awhile, the sun's bright eye;
His rays shall pierce the stormy cloud,
Till all its folds are riven,
And he shines forth undimmed and proud,
Through all the vault of Heaven!

And thus, if we but true remain,
Through every trying hour,
Our sun will yet arise again,
With all reviving power.
By labor we shall pierce the gloom,
Dispel the dark'ning night,
And cold, despairing hearts illume,
With prayer, "LET THERE BE LIGHT!"

To Nathan Mayer, M.D.[1]
Artes Honorabit.[2]

Blest be thy young, creative muse,
Genius of "THE ISRAELITE!"
Who, at thy call, did not refuse
"*Esther's Love*," to picture bright.

"Count Hohenfels,"[3] of love did dream,
Beyond this world of art;
And sweet Esther first glanced the gleam
Of Truth upon his heart.

---

[1] Mayer was a regular contributor to *The Israelite*.

[2] He will honor the arts (Latin). A commonly quoted motto for talent found in *Roget's Thesaurus*.

[3] Esther and Count Hohenfels are characters from Mayer's historical novel, *The Count and the Jewess, Or The Magic Cave of Wibulka. A Tale of the Sixteenth Century*, serialized in *The Israelite* in 1856.

She, so gifted, so young and fair,
   And yet, how sad the thought,
With all her Faith, pure and rare,
   On her was woman's lot—

To endure, to suffer, to weep;
   Neglect and coldness prove;
And yet, through all her Faith, to keep
   Through all, through all, *to love.*

Who taught thy firm—thy Eagle gaze,
   To fasten on the sun;
And turned thy bright and beaming face
   From prospects dim and dun?

And they are blessed that blesseth thee!
   Thy poet-thoughts expressed,
In lispings at parental knee,
   The world hath heard and blessed!

O, highly favored in thy birth,
   And highly favored in thy rearing;
The halls of science sent thee forth,
   With plaudits, animating, cheering!

And that well-merited applause,
   Inciting but to new endeavor;
Imparting to thy soul fresh cause,
   For honoring, with thy gifts, *the Giver!*

Bring thy soul of genius, at His feet
   Thy honors cast—thy golden floral;
He will raise thee to a higher seat,
   And give thee more than crown of laurel.

Thou'lt enter Heaven's eternal portal,
   And there thy thought-bound brow will grace

A fadeless wreath, a crown immortal,
Young Genius of our ancient race!

DAYTON, Ohio, July, 1858.

Rosaline.

In a bright city near a lake,
    With beauty's sheen,
Where steeples try to kiss the sky!
    There, without sin,
Dwells the fair and gentle maiden—
    My Rosaline!

Had I been a lovely violet,
    On banks of green,
Then, how happy, joyous, gladdened,
    I would have been,
Hadst thou chosen me for thy bosom,
    Sweet Rosaline!

If thou wert a star in Heaven,
    And I had been
Buried in the dark, deep ocean,
    There I'd have seen
Thy sweet beauty in my slumber,—
    Dear Rosaline!

What An Angel Said to Me!

Beside the toilsome way,
Lowly and sad, by fruits and flowers unblest,
Which my worn feet tread sadly, day by day,
    Longing in vain for rest.

An angel softly walks,
With pale, sweet face, and eyes cast meekly down,

The while with iron bands, and flowerless stalks,
    She weaves my fitting crown.

A sweet and patient grace,
A look of firm endurance—true and tried—
Of suffering meekly borne, rests on her face,
    So pure, so glorified!

And when my fainting heart
Desponds and murmurs at its adverse fate,
Then quietly the angel's bright lips part,
    Murmuring softly, "*Wait!*"

"*Patience!*" she sweetly saith—
"*The Father's mercies never come too late:*
Gird thee with Israel's strength and trusting faith,
    And firm endurance. Wait!"

Angel! behold, I wait;
Wearing the iron crown through all life's hours—
Waiting till thy hand shall ope the eternal gate,
    And change the iron to flowers!

To the Sons of Israel.
Written after reflecting on THE MORTARA CASE. [1]

Awake! ye souls of Israel's land,
    Your drowsy slumbers break;
Rise! heart with heart—Rise! hand in hand!
    All idle strife forsake!

For, see ye not tokens of a storm,
    Gathering o'er our hearts and homes?
Then, nerve each soul and every arm,
    To *conquer* when it comes!

---

[1] The Catholic church's kidnapping of a six-year-old Jewish boy inspired this protest
poem. See Guinzburg, "The Mortara Abduction Case Illustrated," Appendix D.

Already has a sacred home
　　Been trodden by the foe,
And loving hearts are crush'd to earth,
　　And in the grave lie low.

The barbarous fiends of priest-hood,
　　Are gathering fast and strong;
But be it ours to strike a blow,
　　They will remember long!

A dying mother's heart-shrieks,
　　Are sweeping o'er the wave,—
How can ye sleep, with that haunting cry,
　　Praying for her child to save?

Brothers, awake! strike high and strong,
　　For danger that may come;
Strike high for Israel's holy right—
　　And *strong for hearts and home!*

Rise! ye brave souls of freedom's land,
　　From every hill and every glade,—
Rise up! one strong and gallant band,
　　And draw the battle blade!

Lift the white flag that was unfurled
　　O'er Israel of yore—
Let the cry of "GOD AND OUR RIGHT!"
　　Echo from shore to shore!

Stand up in your glorious right,
　　And do what *men* may do—
Men that know not how to yield—
　　Men of *souls* firm and true.

With bleeding hearts and strong arms
　　Oh! charge upon the foe!

And down with Popish rule and power,
    At every freeman's blow!

Heed not the dark cathedral walls
    That frown above ye there,—
Nor *priestly* showers of hissing threats
    That fill the venomed air.

Israel's flag ye bravely bear!
    Shake off the chains that gall,
And lift that flag in triumph o'er
    Their blood-stained prison wall!

And curses rest upon ye all,
    If, when that flag's on high,
Ye are not with the glorious brave,
    To struggle or to die!

A Heart-Wail.

Roll back ye torrents of the soul—
    Who gave ye all this smart,
To touch with thy deep, dark control,
    The gushings of my heart?

I know that I am faint and weak,
    Scarce fit for the long strife,
Of those who would with honor fill
    The stern demands of life.

If for my failings and misdeeds,
    This crushing weight must fall;
I can spare many of hope's seeds,
    But oh, take not them *all*.

Ye may send that riches, fame nor power,
    Ne'er at my bidding come,
But spare, oh God! in its purity,
    My peace and love at home!

Uncollected Poems from The Jewish Messenger

ראש השנה [1]

Affectionately Inscribed to the "DEAR ONES AT HOME."

The knell
Of the Old Year hath sounded, and its days
Are numbered with the past. Say ye, who now
With merry voices greet the new-born year,
Are ye grown wiser, better than ye were
When last the New Year's day was here? If not
The mission of your lives is unfulfilled,
And life's great moral lesson yet unlearned.
How many thousands on this festive day
In thoughtless gaiety forget the past;
And yet, with equal thoughtlessness regard
The untried future? It is well to hold
The present good, nor dwell too moodily
On things that are no more, nor borrow pain
From hours that are not come. But yet this day,
This marker of the flight of time, were not
Unfitly passed, if to reflection given.
Let memory from her store-house bring the thoughts,
The actions, and the motives which filled up
The measure of the by-gone year; and if they
Yield unto the heart a soothing, sweet,
And kindly fragrance, truly ye are blest;
Your future shadows forth no forms of dread.
But if the conscience fain would whelm the past
In the silent sea of forgetfulness,
Or seek ingenious arguments to still
The workings of remorse, to justify
Itself unto its secret self, against

---

1   Rosh Hashanah or head of the year (Hebrew), the Jewish New Year. Rosh Hashanah
     is the beginning of a ten day period of penitence that culminates in Yom Kippur, the
     Day of Atonement.

Conviction. Oh, then, no pleasant memories
For thee, are blending with the knell of time,
Clanging its harsh, reproving tones, with low
Sweet-breathing harmonies. The future may,
All radiant with the smiles of hope, appear;
But if we draw no lesson from the past,
Nor learn this truth, that man lives not for self,
And self alone, those smiles will phantoms prove,
Alluring, yet eluding our pursuit.
If we would take the unembittered cup
Of human happiness, *we must be strong of heart,*
And our purpose good, and all of joy
That fall to human lot is within our reach.
It is that holy love for all the good
And beautiful of life, which gives to man,
Weal and degraded though he be, the power
To rise above the chain which, for awhile,
In bondage holds the immortal soul. It is
The purity of feeling that, amid
The cold and selfish world, remains untouched
And unpolluted—that assimilates
Degenerate man to those bright angels
Who sing praises round the throne of Him,
The Most High, the *Great Jehovah!*

New Orleans, Tishri, 5618.

Spirit Sighs.

Oh! Soul of Light! infinite love,
    Descend to earth from holy skies,
    And teach my weary heart to rise,
On Truth that has its source above.

Give me a refuge from all tears,
    To Thee I cry with feeble heart,
    Oh! bid the gloomy thoughts depart
Which cling around the rolling years—

And let me see the living grace
    Of holiest truth, and scorn the words
    Of that dark spirit which affords
No consolation in the race

Of life, but draws the glittering sword
    Against all high and holy things,
    That time my soul should mount on wings
And clasp thy ever-loving word

Made visible here—and strive to see
    The soft light o'er my path-way shed,
    That beams from blessings round me spread,
And raise my soul in prayer to Thee!

NEW ORLEANS, *Tishri* 11, 5618.

My World of Thought.

As the stars in their grandest glory run,
And rise and float around our heaven-sun;
As comets wild in wand'ring beauty stream
Erratic like the vivid lightning's gleam;
Now bathed in heat intense of solar ray,
Then flying out beyond the breath of day:
So I, through purple clouds, the light pursue,
Of faith that tints the earth a golden hue;
Now soaring o'er the star-tracks, then away
Where moon ne'er blushes in to beauty of day!

Israel's Light, is the badge of my soul,
That soars aloft and seeks a God-like goal,
Where our faith in immortality gleams
O'er the morning of Life's eternal streams,
This glorious love an ardent soul,
These fiery flashings that intensely roll
In thoughts that burn, erratic and sublime,
With thundering echoes tell of that clime

Where MIND upon its high altar and shine
Shall live in grand immortality divine!

All is Beauty, All is Glory!

The sun is sinking!—golden gleamings
    Follow in his rapid flight;
Hues and forms, like angel's dreamings
    Welcome the return of night.

Balmy winds are softly stealing
    Sweetest perfume from the rose;
Warbling birds are homeward wheeling,
    Ere the day shall reach its close.

See! Beyond those mystic mountains,
    In those fields of purest blue,
Fairy islands, sparkling fountains,
    Spirit forms of heavenly hue!

And far beyond, a rolling ocean,
    Tinted o'er with rosy light—
See!—its waves are all in motion,
    Foaming in ethereal might!

Oh, if death, when he shall sever
    Spirits from their homes of clay,
Will give life and rest forever,
    In those realms, *let mine away*!

For those bright and sunny regions,
    Do cause this restless soul to long
For a home, among the legions
    Crowding in that vapor throng.

New Orleans.

Uncollected Poems from the Sunday Mercury

On the Death of Rufus Choate.[1]

A solemn thing is death. Its ghastly form,
   Its dull and glassy eye, whose light is fled,
Its cold and stiffened limbs, that late were warm,
   Its very silence strikes the soul with dread.
We may look, unmoved, upon the dead,
   Though neither pomp nor power were theirs in life,
But, oh! what homilies to us are read,
   When sleeps a mighty one, and ends the strife,
Of his long, bright career, with fame and honor rife!

And such a one hath sunk in peace to rest,
   Whose clarion voice hath oftentimes been heard
Ringing throughout the land, and in each breast
   Emotions lasting strong and deep were stirred,
And listening millions hung upon his word;
   Whose mind expansive was as is the sea
That compasses the earth; whose heart ne'er erred,
   For 'twas as pure as ever man's may be.
And full of holy love for freedom and the free.

Now his career is ended, even his foes
   Must grant that he was brave, and pure, and kind:
That genius did unto his mind disclose
   Her rarest gems, so dazzling, yet refined,
That patriotism, in his thoughts enshrined,
   Was worshiped with a love that few may feel;
That in his country's councils, heart and mind,
   Were brought to act with energy and zeal,
To shield his country's rights, advance his country's weal.

---

[1] Rufus Choate (1799–1859), a lawyer and Congressman renowned for his oratory.

Whate'er his mind conceived, his tongue proclaimed,
    Regardless of what men might think or say;
The first approach of wrong his soul inflamed,
    With burning eloquence that none might stay,
But on it swept in its terrific sway.
    Tornado-like, throughout his native land,
And men of power unto his thoughts gave way,
    And even opponents, who fain would brand
That poet-patriot with shame, might not his words withstand.

All men must give thee praise; and I who sing
    This feeble tribute to thy virtue's worth,
Would to thy grave one laurel gladly bring,
    Though ne'er a partisan of thine. The earth
Hath claimed the manly form it once gave birth,
    And over all the land there rests a gloom,
And sorrow fills all hearts where late was mirth,
    For freedom's favored land must, in thy doom,
One of her jewels bright see mouldering in the tomb.

Peace and rest, glorious Choate, in thy narrow bed,
    Thy years were full of honor; greenest bays
Shall mark the spot where sleeps the patriot dead,
    And pilgrims from far climes, in future days,
Will journey to thy tomb, and bring thee praise;
    And gifted bards, in ages yet unborn,
Will sing thy fame in poetic lays,
    Thy name, thy nation's history will adorn,
And millions celebrate thy hallowed natal morn.

New York, September 2d, 1859.

The Dark Hour.

Hast thou e'er marked, just when the day was closing,
    How all west-heaven seemed hung with vapors white;
Red mingled hills, and yellow lakes reposing,

A wreathy billow here, and there a light
Gleaming up, golden mountain clouds disclosing,
    Folded o'er with white wings of seraphs bright?
Have ye ne'er watched them, too, minutely fade,
And all give place to black and sullen shade?

Even so have all the orient hues departed
    That tinged th' horizon of my opening years;
I, joyous, volatile, and sanguine-hearted,
    Deemed my sun rising, and repelled my fears;
Bright from the vale of Hope its splendors darted—
    It rose on misery, and set in tears,
Night, grisly night, upon my path rushed on!
A night to which I spy no earthly dawn.

For still it glooms, and still it deepens round me,
    And scatters baleful mists athwart the scene—
Now floods beset—now thunders deep astound me—
    Now rude winds buffet, bitter, cold, and keen.
To-day success, perhaps, with glee hath crowned me;
    To-morrow, disappointments intervene—
One moment sees me on my course advanced,
Another hurls me back with grief entranced.

And Pleasure, if I seek her, seems to fly me,
    Or, caught, proves barren of her native grace;
Though if I spurn her, and to distance hie me,
    A thousand joys pursue in elfin chase,
And warble on the gale that rushes by me,
    And flash their sun bright tresses in my face;
Shunted visions court me—treasured hope recede—
And where I trust to conquer, there I bleed.

★　★　★　★　★　★　★　★　★

Farewell!— I raise my lattice as it's spoken,
    And gaze out sadly on the vacant sky,
No pallid moon or shimmering stars foretoken

A sun to cheer my darkness-weary eye.
Farewell!—like dying dove-notes, faint and broken,
The mists around seems echoing in reply.
Leave me! I'll battle on amid the crowd.
Girded with patience, like an iron shroud.

"Why do I love you?" [1]

"Why do I love you?" Ask the poet
    Why he loves the soft twilight hour;
And ask the wild bird why it so loves
    To dwell in the woodland bower.
              I love you!

"Why do I love you?" Ask the streamlet
    Why it loves to wander away;
Ask the sweet flowers why they love
    The golden sunset's summer ray.
              I love you!

"Why do I love you?" Why do the waves
    Leap up to kiss the starlight tide?
Why does the eagle aloft to the sky
    Spread his airy pinions so wide?
              I love you!

"Why do I love you?" Ask the exile
    Why he clings to his native land;
Why do the wavelets love to kiss
    So sweetly on the pebbled strand?
              I love you!

"Why do I love you?" Why do the stars
    Stoop to kiss the lilies so white,

---

[1]   Menken wrote this untitled poem for her husband at the time, John Carmel Heenan,
a champion boxer, also known as "the Benicia Boy."

When the silver robe has fallen
O'er the reigning Queen of Night?
I love you!

Knocking at the Door.
From the German of Rückert.[1]

I sought Love's abode, and I knocked at the door;
But thousands, unanswered, had knocked there before.

I knocked at the golden-domed Temple of Fame,
And waited in vain; for no trumpeter came.

I knocked at the proud Honor's iron-bound castle-gate;
But Honor is only for lordly estate.

I knocked at the portals where Luxury reigns—
They threw me a penny to pay for my pains.

I knocked at the door of rude Labor's abode,
And a broken-heart wailed under poverty's load.

I asked, where the home of Contentment could be!
And none in the land could give answer to me.

No portal is open on all the long way;
My feet print with blood, weary day after day.

But I know there's a house at the foot of the hill,
Whose chambers, all open, are peaceful and still.

Its silence yields slumber to many a guest;
I'll knock at the door and go in to my rest.

---

[1] A translation of Friedrich Rückert's "Vor den Thüren." See Rückert's *Gesammelte Poetische Werke*, 12 vols. (Frankfurt, 1868-69) 2:119-20.

Dream of the Alhambra.[1]

Respectfully inscribed to Madame F. Lewellen Young.[2]

The golden sun of beauteous Spain,
  Now pours its light on ruined towers,
Where once Granada's monarchs reigned,
  In marble halls and glided bowers.

The sculptured fountains are defaced,
  And broken, pillared arch and gate;
The arcade and its columns razed—
  And all is sad and desolate.

Not so when smiling stars are bright,
  And dreamy moonshine fills the air—
A silver sea with waves of light,
  That wash e'en sable midnight fair.

Not so when tiny fairy bands,
  Descend from fragrant leaf and flower,
To tread the merry fairy dance;
  Not so when strikes the midnight hour.

Then rides along the winding way,
  A brilliant train of horsemen bold;
The radiant moonbeams dart and play,
  On flashing gems and burnished gold.

Ten thousand knights in armor ride,
  With waving plumes and flags displayed;
A thousand nobles, side by side,
  In jewels, silks and gold brocade.

---

[1]   The Alhambra is a palace in Granada, a medieval kingdom in Muslim Spain.
[2]   Peter Dollard has identified Madame Young and her husband, Col. W.H. Young, as
    the editors and proprietors of *Young's Spirit of the South*.

The moonbeams glint upon their mail;
But, oh! 'tis horrible to see!
Their faces are like corses pale,
Their horses step so noiselessly.

The knights a stately king surround
With flashing crown and golden beard;
His jeweled foot-cloth sweeps the ground,
His horses' steps can not be heard.

They enter the Alhambra's gate—
The walls are whole, the gardens bright;
The palace wakes to former state,
The gorgeous windows blaze with light!

The crescent shines on turrets tall,
The sounds of revelry arise,
And guests are in each gilded hall,
With rosy cheeks and diamond eyes.

With splendor round him like the sun,
The king doth sit in royal state;
While grouped before the dazzling throne,
The courtiers his commands await.

The fountains throw their spray aloft,
The birds sing in the myrtle grove;
From balconies fall whispers soft,
From orange-trees rise songs of love.

The moon is up! Her light has shone!
And all has vanished with the dream—
The knights, the monarch and the throne,
Which did but now so gorgeous seem.

'Tis thus the last of Moorish kings,
Holds nightly court, and mounts his throne;

But when the morning flaps his wings,
The ruined halls are sad and lone.

New York, 6th Mo., 24th D.

Song.
From the German of Rückert.[1]

Hope tremulous and low,
    All silent now!
Glad voices faded so,
    They're silent now—
    Silent now!

Love evanescent, too?
    All silent now;
Dreams vanished like the dew
    Are silent now—
    Silent now!

Life murmuring sad and low,
    All silent now;
Loved voices faded so,
    They're silent now—
    Silent now!

Joy departeth after grief,
    All silent now;
A soul in its love-light so brief,
    And silent now—
    Silent now!

Death approacheth with the dawn,
    All silent now;
Groan, and sob, and sigh hath gone,
    All silent now—
    Silent now!

---

[1] The original German poem has not been identified.

Our Mother.

Affectionately inscribed to My Sister Annie.

We know full well why ills betide,
　　And disappointments mar our schemes;
We've lost the angel from our side,
　　The spirit-counsel from our dreams.

I never dreamed that soothing tone
　　Again would bless my waking ear;
But ever at th' Eternal throne,
　　I knew it pleaded for me here!

That fervent prayer, averting ill—
　　That earnest love, invoking care,
For husband, child, and sister, still
　　The lone, *lone* heart, but ill could spare.

I hear a sister's lonely wail,
　　I hear the orphan's bitter moan;
And wander down life's dreary vale,
　　Alone, *alone*—O God, how lone!

We may not soothe each other's grief,
　　We may not wipe each other's tear;
Our Father God, bring thou relief,
　　And bind the heart left broken here!

New York. 9th Mo. 11th D.

The Last.

Depart! I cannot call you back;
　　Cold pride shall guard my heart,
And hide the blottings of the grave,
　　Therefore, I say—depart!

I'll teach me soon to scorn such love,
   That idle words can sway;
I give you back your broken vows,
   And now, false one, away!

With careless mein you flung aside
   The garnered trust of years;
At first my spirit felt the wound,
   But now—no woman-tears.

No tears to tell of love's despair,
   This heart is hardened now;
I join the cold and heartless world,
   No shadow dims my brow

Yes, now I laugh at love and truth,
   False names to falser themes!
I tell the trusting to beware,
   That these are fleeting dreams.

Depart! I will not call you back;
   Cold pride now guards my heart,
And hides the blotting of the grave,
   Therefore, I say—depart!

NEW YORK, 10th mo., 9th day.

Passion.
From the Latin of Catullus.[1]

Dicebas quondam,
Ad Lesbiam.[2]

When I believed thee true, my love
   Was pure as virtue could impart —

---

[1]   Catullus, *Poems* 72.
[2]   Once upon a time you would say to Lesbia (Latin). Catullus, *Poems* 72.1-2.

Pure as the feeling parents prove
For the dear nurslings of their heart.

But, though, since all thy ways I know,
Thy heart is worthless in my eyes;
Yet warmer still my passions glow,
I love thee more that I despise.

When I believed thee pure and good,
The high desires that swelled my breast,
The fervent currents of the blood
Were, by that chastening thought, repressed.

But now that all respect is dead,
I bid my pulse unbridled beat;
From me, the soul of love is fled,
And Passion triumphs in its seat.

Conscience.
From the Latin of Buchanani.[1]

"Ad furta qui se comparat
nocturna vitat lumina;
sui furoris consciam."[2]

I.

Far happier is his fate, whose name
Bears the report of guilt and shame,
Who yet his bosom folds within.
Feels not the sting of crime and sin,
Than his who hides from human eye,
His secret guilt of darkest dye—

---

[1] A loose and re-arranged translation of lines 833-862 from George Buchanan's
Baptistes. See *Baptistes* (1577) in *George Buchanan Tragedies,* ed. P. Sharratt and P.G. Walsh
(Edinburgh: Scottish Academic Press, 1983) 120-21.

[2] See *Baptistes*, lines 833-36. Menken's translation of this epigraph appears in lines
9–12 of the poem.

Yet feels his ever-conscious breast
With dire reproach of crime opprest.

II.

The robber, in the midnight hour,
Dreads the bright lamp's betraying power;
The murderer, in his deed of night,
Shrinks from the dawning ray of light;
But let them veil in darkest shade
The rain that their guilt had made—
To light more clear than morning's rays,
That guilt the conscious heart betrays.

III.

Dissemblers! though the brow of pride,
From common view your souls ye hide,
There is within the burning heart
A ceaseless sting—a lasting smart;
And while ye seek, with wild affright,
To hide your pangs from human sight.
Remorse—the sleepless monster—feeds
On the foul memory of your deeds.

Gold.
From the German of Buckhart.[1]

"Aurum—
—potentius
ictu fulmineo"—Horace[2]

I wished to win the smiles of love,
And all its fabled raptures prove;

---

[1] "Buckhart" is not the name of a known German poet. This is probably a typographical mistake for perhaps either "Bürger" (Gottfried August Bürger [1747–94]) or "Rückert" (Friedrich Rückert [1788-1866]). The German text upon which Menken's poem is based has not been identified, a task that is complicated by the fact that Menken's translations are often quite loose and creative.

[2] Gold ... is more powerful than lightning (Latin). Horace, *Odes* 3.16.9-11.

In Hymen's saffron woven bower
To spend my life's love-brightened hour.
I wished on Fame's proud wing to rise—
On Fame's proud wing to reach the skies;
To win the voice of splendid praise,
And leave a name to future days.
I wished to climb Ambition's height,
And dazzle with fictitious light—
To burst the bounds of simple worth,
And leave the low-bent sons of earth.

I loved; but Love, with scornful eye,
Asked *Gold* his purest joys to buy.
I sung; but Fame forbade me sing,
Asked *Gold* to lift her eagle wing.
I toiled; Ambition aid denied—
Asked *Gold* my towering steps to guide.
No treasures in my coffers shine—
No love, no Fame, no power in mine.

New York, Kislev, 2d D., 5621 Y.

Farewell to Fanny.[1]
On Her Departure for Cuba.

Thou wilt go home? then speed thy way,
No sigh of mine shall bid thee stay;
Though years may pass, nor bring a smile
So soft as thine—so free from guile.

The shades of home! what flowers more fair
Can earth display than blossom there?
Say, wilt thou there the mem'ry keep
Of her who has no home to seek?

New York, 11th Mo. 19th D.

---

[1] Fanny has not been identified.

A Wish for Nellie.[1]

Sweet Nellie, may *thy* youthful dreams
    In tempest ne'er be rent,
But fade, if fade they must, as flowers
    When summer-time is spent;
And when life's wintry years have come,
    Thy blood grown oldly chill,
May thoughts of kind deeds thou hast done,
    Thy heart with blessings fill.

Louisiana.

My childhood home! my childhood home!
    Long, dreary years have glided by
Since my young feet first learned to roam
    From underneath thy summer sky!

Yet oft, amid the toil and care
    That aye attend my creeping years,
Thy every scene, so bright and fair,
    In Memory's dream again appears.

And those I loved in childhood's day
    With joy-lit faces round me throng,
As when we joined in sportive play
    To light glad hours that seemed so long.

And feelings that my childhood knew
    Are gushing in my bosom now,
As then, as simple, warm, and true,
    Though woman's cares are on my brow.

Yet oh! these hours when Memory's dews
    Fall gently on the weary breast

---

[1] In its 3 February 1861 issue, the *Sunday Mercury* printed a poem for Menken titled "A Wish" authored by someone writing under the pseudonym "Nellie."

Are like a summer-evening's hues
    Which fade as sinks the sun to rest.

They waft the thoughts from wintry care
    To scenes where fairest spring-flowers bloom,
Then leaves them sweetly musing there,
    And lo! each flower adorns a tomb.

But yet these hours to musing given,
    Though swiftly hurrying to the Past,
Yield more the pure, calm bliss of Heaven
    Than Hope e'er wrecked in Time's chill blast.

Though other ties now bind my heart—
    Though other scenes are dear to me—
My hours of bliss but form a part
    Of the blest days of infancy.

Lake Michigan.

Old Tiber's tawny waters gave
    A glorious theme to Roman song;
The Jew with transport views the wave
    Of sacred Jordan glide along;
For by that stream's obedient flood
Was shown the wondrous power of God.

The superstitious Hindoo views
    The Ganges rolling at his feet;
Joy, fear, and awe his breast infuse
    As his wild gaze the waters meet;
In them he sees the unfailing cure
Of all the ills that men endure.

The Briton's heart exults with pride,
    As on the Thames his eye he turns,
The German stands his Rhine beside,
    And love of country in him burns.

To each beneath the extended sky
No stream more lovely meets the eye.

But not a river, lake, or sea,
    That leaves the strand or flows the plain,
Brings pleasure half so sweet to me
    As Michigan, thy blue-waved main!
There Grandeur ever keeps his throne,
And with bright beauty reigns alone.

Milwaukee, Wis., July 28th.

The Storm.

O the cold and dreary midnight,
    Where the wind goes wailing by
And shrieks through the leafless tree-tops
    With its wild and desolate cry.

There's a sound as of mingled shouting,
    And the shuddering groans of fear—
The voice of the terrible tempest
    Sweeping on in its mad career.

From the heart of the tortured force
    Strong arms are tossing on high,
And struggling, and vainly praying
    For rest to the troubled sky.

The brow of the Night looks fearful,
    With its black funereal pall
So thick not a ray of starlight
    Through the shrouding folds can fall.

The fitful gusts of the tempest
    Drive the cloud-ships to and fro,
As souls in the storms of sorrow
    Drift over a sea of woe.

Ah me! there's a grave in the meadows,
   Far back in the long-ago,
Where the buds of my heart's young Summer
   Lie dead 'neath the Winter's snow.

A L'Outrance![1]

I have faith in thee yet, my destiny's star,
    High hope and a trust that abides evermore;
The crag may be steep, and the eyrie afar,
    The Eagle shall yet to its pinnacle soar!

His plume may be reft, and his heart may be cold,
    For the chain that still chafes, hath galled him full long;
But the spirit is brave, and never of old
    Were his pinions and glance more daring and strong.

Oh! child of the sun, half buried in clay!
    Oh! vision of light, that upward would soar!
Oh! proud bird of Jove, one spring away—
    Thy home it is high, *evermore*, EVERMORE!

Dark, dark lies the shadow on future and past,
    Yet music still sleeps in the harp's latest string;
Æolian tones may be wrung from the blast—
    Oh, *on*, tameless bird of the poor broken wing!

Disaster may crush, *never* conquer the brave!
    The day is not lost while the cry is "ADVANCE!"
And the triumph rings back in loud tones from the grave,
    "I'M VICTOR IN LIFE!" I have warred "A L'OUTRANCE!"

CINCINNATI, April 14, 1859.

My Spirit Love.

Where shines the star of thy destiny,
    Sweet spirit love?

---

[1] To the extreme.

No longer o'er the azure sea
It floateth on in majesty;
Quenched is its light in eternity,
    Dreaming above!

Where sounds the harp of thy minstrelsy,
    Gifted one?
Are æolian strains now sung by thee?
Is spherical music thy harmony?
With seraph souls, oh, canst thou be
    In the world unknown?

Oh, say, in thy clime still dost thou weep,
    Child of song?
Doth holy love thy heart yet steep
In its dreamy waves—as pure, as deep,
As erst did o'er thy spirit sweep
    In joy along?

My soul waits by the boundless sea
    For thy voice, love!
No longer o'er the emerald lea,
The lute-tones swell so light and free;
And the night-bird chants a dirge for thee,
    My stricken dove!

Had earth no ties to bind thee here,
That thou shouldst seek a brighter sphere?
I list, thy answering voice to hear,
    My spirit love.
The boundless sea in silence sleeps,
And with mournful moaning weeps,
    Thou art above!

The Poet[1]

The poet's noblest duty is,
    Whatever theme he sings,
To draw the soul of beauty forth
    From unconsidered things.

That, howso'er despised may be
    The humblest form of earth,
His kindly sympathy may weave
    A halo round its birth.

For deepest in creation's midst
    The rarest treasure lies,
And deeper than all science delves
    May reach the poet's eyes.

And, with poetic instinct fired,
    He finds his greatest art
In raising Nature's hidden gems
    To set them in his art.

Reply to Dora Shaw.[2]
Westminster Palace, London, Aug. 29, 1864.

There comes no change upon my heart,
    Though many a one may cross my brow,
The hopes I nursed ere life grew dark,
    Those very hopes I cherish now!

---

[1] Composed around 1864, Menken copied this poem into Charles Warren Stoddard's album.
[2] The daughter of a minister from Ohio, Dora Shaw was a poet and actress whom Menken had known for years. Like Menken, she was divorced and remarried. Both worked as actresses in New Orleans around 1856-57. In New York in the early 1860s, Shaw associated with the group of bohemian writers that included Menken. See Browne in Appendix D; James R. Newhall, *History of Lynn*, vol. 2 (Lynn, MA, 1897) 130; John S. Kendall, *The Golden Age of the New Orleans Theater* (Baton Rouge: Louisiana State University Press, 1952) 305, 363.

Fashion and Ease in vain may smile,
    Or Wealth his glittering hoard bestow,
Or Love strew flowers with sweeter wile,
    Their charms are bright but all too low.

What though I frequent Folly's Fair,
    Where hands and hearts are often sold?
What if my smile be the lightest there?
    When nearly viewed 'tis something cold.

Ambition! I have sought thy shrine,
    And at thy altar kneel I yet;
For lofty thought and high design
    In recreant heart were never met.

My woman's spirit owns the sway,
    Nor writhes beneath the binding chain,
Nor falters on the toilsome way,
    With truant thought and pining, vain!

The fealty vowed in early youth,
    And kept through all my weary lot,
I pledge again in Woman's Truth;
    I am no changeling—doubt me not!

Prose

The Angel's Whisper.

I have a habit, began in early childhood, of sitting alone and musing, as twilight deepens into night. I always feel the bringing in of lights an intrusion, and keep them away as long as possible. Oh, the lives I have lived! the dreams I have dreamt in those twilight reveries. Like the German sleeper, no matter what the cares or pains of the day, my dream-land life make up, with its gorgeous beauty, exquisite harmonies and noble sentiments, for all or any unpleasant reality.

What great, good, beautiful and pure beings; what noble sentiments, what extatic harmonies, what light filled my glorious ideal land! How my heart has ached for words to describe, for power to portray some of its wavy, graceful, floating pictures, to bring to the ear some of its exquisite harmonies, to write down admirably some of its grand and noble sentiments. And when I have essayed, how bald and mean was the attempt—no more like my beautiful visions than the bone skeleton is to some tropic bird of gorgeous plumage.

As time wore on and the real pressed more heavily on my heart, the glowing light of my dream-land faded from its full noon of gold changed to a rose-hue, which gradually deepened through all its shades of purple, more beautiful, because more mellow, till death came, like Winter's frost, stripping the Autumnal forest of its glory. From that hour the light has been grey, growing colder as the picture contracted its dimensions, until now my twilight musings cover only the space of a cemetery, and my communings are only with the spirits of those lives loved and lost for a season. And the last, which is so new that the grass is not yet on it, encloses a form of truly noble proportions, and covers a heart that was warmed by the quickest pulse. And the air of my dream-land is filled with its graceful motions, and softly on my ear falls a familiar voice that breathes gently the echo of 'Wife,' and my own murmurs 'Husband.' The sound startles me from my spirit-home and I look down. On my bosom rests a little head, covered with golden curls; two large, wistful blue eyes are gazing into mine, while tears are rolling down the dimpled cheeks, and a sob shakes the little form.

"What is it, darling, that grieves you?" I ask with a kiss.

The little mouth whispers, "I am thinking of father."

Alas! must she begin where I have ended?

Shylock.

[...] A strong feeling exists in favor of old things and old times. The old dramatists are regarded as immeasurably superior to the modern, whether read in the closet or viewed on the stage; but whatever opinion we may have of these masterly writings, there can be no question that the Jewish character has received a truer estimate in the present time than in former days.

We now find, when a Jew is introduced by most of authors, he is represented as having the impulses and feelings of a man, and not devoid of higher aims than merely to amass gold or gratify an ignoble spirit of envy or revenge against his Christian fellow men. Formerly the Jew was portrayed as possessing little but a combination of the darkest vices and worst passions that could possibly disgrace or degrade man; pictured as a being without consideration or remorse, to whom no position was too mean to stoop to, the Jew was scarcely brought forth but as a being to be scoffed at, reviled, and despised. It was this ill-prejudiced feeling that called forth Marlow[e]'s play of the "Jew of Malta," and this, we have every reason to believe, caused the production of Shakespeare's "Jew of Venice"—the original title of the "Merchant of Venice"—for even he, with his god-like strength of mighty genius, was not exempt from prejudice. The evidence of this is in the Italian romance, from which Shakespeare took this great play. The Shylock is a Christian, and the victim a Jew.

The character of Shylock is one that has few friends; there is a general detestation toward him and his proceedings. From the play being familiar to all, its result is known; the Christians will triumph, and the consequence is, that he is prejudged—that the end is only looked to, while the causes that have existed to lead to this end are forgotten. The generally adopted conception of

Shylock as represented on the stage is not justice, it does not convey, properly, the varied phases of the character as drawn by the poet. To a careful and discriminating reader of Shakespeare, this must be very evident. If a person had never seen the play represented, yet had studied it carefully, and unprejudiced, should witness it according to the general rendition, he would be greatly disappointed—wonder how and where he had ever sympathized with the Jew. We must acknowledge, however, that the two strong passions—avarice and revenge—are the prominent points in Shylock's character. But let us look at the causes which appear to have engendered these passions, as related by himself. The wrongs of his Christian enemies, inflicted on him and his race, have goaded him almost to madness. Hear how he replies to Antonio, who haughtily demands the loan of three thousand ducats for his friend Bassanio: [*Merchant of Venice* 1.3.105-128].

We may look upon Shylock as being the representative of the whole race of persecuted Jews of the period antecedent to and at the time Shakespeare wrote. He is the embodiment of this idea in several parts of the play. His terrific outburst of passion on hearing that Antonio was bankrupt, gives us an idea how his race was trampled upon at that time, and how every feeling of his heart gasped for revenge: [*Merchant of Venice* 3.1.54-73].

Through many other speeches, as well as in the shrewd and eloquent appeals in the trial scene, we distinctly mark a species of sublimity of character surrounding the Jew that involuntarily claims our sympathy and admiration.

He stands, the unbending, inflexible type of a race, no wrongs nor contumelies can ever overcome.

Midnight in New-Orleans.[1]

Beautiful city of the South! who would dream to gaze upon thy lofty spires, and marble mansions, that mystery and misery were

---

[1]   The original printing included epigraphs, some long, before each section. Those quotations are: *Hamlet* 1.2.189 and *Hamlet* 3.2.393-395; *Henry VI, Part 2* 2.4.88-89 and (within this second section) a perhaps misremembered quotation of Psalm 127.2; *As You Like It* 2.7.179-81; Shakespeare, "The Rape of Lucrece," stanza 31.

dwelling in thy very midst? All is quiet; bustle and confusion have subsided, the cabs and omnibuses have ceased their deaf'ning rattle; the street-stragglers have departed, each his separate way— the beggar to his loathsome hut, the thief to his dram-shop and midnight revel. No sound breaks the stillness, save now and then at weary intervals the *baton* of a watchman ringing hollowly against the stone *banquette*, or the slow heavy footfall of some printer wending his way home from his hard toil. God bless him!

See the soft moonlight, how it rests as a beautiful silver veil fringed with mist, over the magnificent architecture of the Cathedral! Hark, to its deep-toned bell, as it slowly and solemnly tells of the "witching hour of night!" List to the mournful murmur of the mighty "Father of Rivers," as he winds majestically along his crescent course. My heart hears no ballad of gladness from the sparkling waves to-night, only a sorrowful requiem to the Past.

We will walk far out Canal street. Surely where there is so much wealth and beauty, there is certainly something to suggest happy thoughts.

See that cottage in the shadow of the grand edifice, almost buried in trees and creeping vines, that fairly smile in beauty and innocence. Home, seems written all around it.—This, indeed gives me happy thoughts, for in a home like this I first learnt the blessing of a dear mother's love; first knew the sweet influence of an only sister's confidence and affection; first felt the holy spell of a brother's consolation and encouragement. Oh, happy hearts, as mine then was, must now be slumbering beneath that humble roof! I can picture, in frames of love, the wax like faces—curly heads of dear children, weary of their little cares—tired of play, now sleeping a tranquil unbroken sleep of innocence, for which they will yearn in after years, when the world of sorrow has put its impress upon their hearts. And a happy mother, the sweet children's mother, sleeping in glad contentment near the noble heart that asked her girl love, and won a woman's worship! Oh, fond husband, wear her in your heart of hearts, for it is a grand thing this woman love! Who may know its depth and glory!

Yes, yes! There must be a heaven of happiness in this beautiful cot. Hush! what was that? was it the wind? Listen again! Now it comes to my heart, for lo, 'tis the fearful wail of anguish! And from the cottage too. Open the wicket gate, we will enter. Step softly, for behold a little coffin with a wreath of fresh, white flowers upon it, to fade, alas! as did the bud beneath the lid, but not as it to hover around the Almighty Father's throne with golden wings.

Why should we weep and feel sad that there is another angel added to Heaven?

Look upon the drooping form of the young mother as she stands in agony and prayer by the little coffin. She is now all alone in this wide world; well may'st thou wail in heart rending grief, childless mother; our God, in love and mercy, gave thee a gem of peerless, Heaven beauty. [...]

Never more shall it raise its rosy lips to thine in all the fondness of childhood's warm affection: memory tells thee thou art desolate; it tells too, of a thousand soft and winning ways that twine around the mother's bosom; and of the sweet, wild throbbings of unspeakable bliss that were thine when softly soothing and repose. Now the nursery will no more resound with its gladsome mirth: the cradle, in which it so often reposed, is now desolate. Thy ark of refuge is indeed wrecked. Father, mother, brother, sister, and the husband of thy heart, thy only child! All, all gone! Thou hast nothing left to live for; thou canst but lift thy soul above the many graves and pray our God, to take thee home to the loved ones in Heaven! Mortals can not alleviate thy misery— it is of the soul and must abide the time of the Great Jehovah.

Let us hurry on, the wind blows cool, and my heart beats sadly. I trust that we may soon meet with some cheering influence in the shape of a happy, friendly face. Is it possible? A woman, in the street alone, this time of night? What can she be doing here? perhaps she may be a wretched beggar, no home to go to, or, worse still, some miserable wife thrust from the door by a drunken, brutal husband. (What a profanation of that dear title!) As we draw near to her, the rouge upon her hollow cheeks—the sunken eye—the dress of lace and gauze—the unsteady walk, tell us that she is one of those poor abandoned creatures who have lost all that makes life dear! To her, virtue is but a name. Oh, who may tell her mournful story? Roll back the iron gates of time; behold her the pride and sunlight of her Father's household! Hear a fond mother's voice raise in song of life and gladness as she gazes upon this, her first born child! Mark that brother's look of pride as his eye follows her graceful form! See the clinging tenderness of her baby sister, as she asks for just one more kiss. Oh, she indeed weaves figures of light in that happy household! But man, the spoiler man, came with his mask of love, and gentle words, which he so well knows how to assume! and she, so innocent, so confiding, thinks all the world as pure as herself—loves him with all the wild worship of her Southern nature! What return does he make for this gem of priceless worth, woman's love? He basely tears the jewel from its setting, withers the heart's noblest feelings, scorns her affection, pollutes her young life; brings the gray hairs of her parents to the grave, her only brother a suicide; and her sister—her gentle sister is dead. And she, now heart broken and abandoned, seeks forget-fulness in a whirlpool of sin! This, man, is thy work! Thy *boasted* work! Yes, boasted over your gambling tables, and convivial cups at midnight revels! Oh, hang down your heads and blush as you look upon these lost creatures! *You!* whom God made for the grand and noble protector of woman's honor—her virtue and her love! Shame upon you, who can insult her dependence—play off mean jests upon her affections—bandy unclean doubts of her, as a wretched substitute for wit; and whisper vulgar suspi-cions of woman-purity, which, if compared to your own, is like the immaculate whiteness of angels! Remember there is a just God! Bow your head in prayer for her you have slandered and polluted! You alone are answerable at the Great Tribunal for this ghastly spectacle of blasted charity!

Let us turn into *Rue Royale* and see if all there is in sleep and dreams. Ah! I hear a loud laugh. Now, methinks, we will come to the bright side of the picture. I hope so, for my heart in its sympathy has partaken of the slow, heavy throbs of misery around us. What bright light streams through those half open curtains! There must be a ball—no, for as we draw nearer, none but loud, rough voices are heard. Up the marble steps, ring the bell. It is answered directly, and we are cordially invited in, and shown into a large parlor, elegantly furnished. The walls being adorned by pictures of value. On the mantle is a profusion of exquisite filigree ornaments, interspersed with marble statuettes, artistically fashioned. There are small tables of Italian marble, upon which are all the popular periodicals of the day. Many magnificent mirrors that reach the ceiling—and flowers! beautiful flowers!—the rose, the lily and the violet are here, with their delicious perfume that steals o'er my senses, and breathes sweet thoughts to my heart of home!—But I forget,—this is no place for pure home thoughts. The most striking establishment of this spacious and elegant apartment, is a long, low, black table, in the centre of which is a cloth, containing all the cards of the "full deck."—There are about forty or fifty individuals standing close around it; a man sits at one side of the table with a small silver box from which he mysteriously slips a card at a time. There are sundry heaps of ivory chips "some red, some white" lying promiscuously about on the stationary cards. Noiselessly and eagerly the game goes on; beaming and reckless and despairing faces are alike intent upon the movements of the man with the box. Mark that handsome youth with the black curls over his brow, dark eyes, and noble, sad cast of features; he has evidently been taught a higher, grander lesson of truth and purity than this. See how nervously he leans over the table, watching every card as if the destiny of his immortal soul hung upon the issue! Alas, perhaps it does.

Oh, young man! whosoever thou art pause and listen! It is not too late. There is a way, and a sure way, to roll this load of sin and guilt from thy young heart: its humiliation and despair will crush thee to earth.—Perhaps thou hast wasted, not only thine own, but thy employer's money, yet for all that it is not too late. Quit this poisonous den of iniquity, go to your sleepless couch; and when morning breaks see your employer, tell him frankly and calmly all, disguise nothing from him, neither your temptation nor your dreadful fall. If he has the heart of humanity, he will receive and trust you and love you more than ever. Should your reception be harsh, do not despair; you have only one friend less, and you have conquered a powerful demon and gained a priceless lesson, that will guard your heart from sin in after years. Oh, as thou regardest thy soul's peace,—thy mother's pangs, thy father's blessing, and thy future salvation—the forgiveness of an Almighty God, pause and look back—repent and you are saved forever!

Death and Eternity.

"Ten thousand times ten thousand suns describe
The cycle of infinity."[1]

What is death? What is it but the separation of the immortal gold of the soul from the earth-clay of the body? the end of our probation, the frail gateway betwixt time and eternity? What is the import of that word probation? Is the eye of Omniscience upon us? Is the quality of our moral character soon to be determined? Are we to exist somewhere in the universe forever? Is there beyond death woe interminable, as well as perfect bliss? Does exemption from the one, and the attainment of the other, depend entirely upon our conduct here? Are we the architects of our own eternal fortunes? Do everlasting consequences hang upon a moment?

Oh, then, how solicitous should we be to pass the ordeal successfully! What are the personal and relative duties devolving upon us! If we, and our race, are on the very verge of either perdition or Paradise, how zealously should we labor to do good to others and to secure our own eternal happiness!

That our activity may be commensurate with the mighty interest involved, let us place the brief space allotted to us here in just a position with the eternity to which we are hastening. We have seen the almost nothingness of the former: how shall we speak of the latter? Shall we illustrate eternity by the numerous years of a long tiresome, weary life on earth? by the centuries that have rolled down the golden years betwixt the creation and the present? by the countless starry-worlds which revolve in immensity? by the leaves of a thousand autumns? by the drops of water in all the reservoirs, rivers, and oceans of the globe? or by all the particles of matter embraced in the wide domain of glorious and eternal Deity? Shall an immortal mathematician employ himself

---

[1]   Unidentified.

for millions of ages in multiplying and re-multiplying all these together? Even then, the immense aggregate would fall infinitely short of an adequate illustration. The mighty sweep of duration which we have just imagined makes not the slightest approximation to eternity. After the expiration of these supposed myriads of ages, our pleasures or our pains, as our conduct here may have been good or bad, still will we be eternal!

Who, then, can sin in the sight of eternity? It is only when we close our eyes upon the great future that our souls droop to earth and become soiled with the dust of men, that we transgress the laws of eternity. How can we give ourselves to idleness, or to frivolous pursuits? The foregoing view makes life a terrible and solemn reality—clothes every movement with startling significance. If the reward be glorious and imperishable, how can we grow weary in striving and struggling for that higher, purer, heavenly life beyond the gateway of death?

Oh, let the thought of this eternal brightness of true life inspire the believer amid all his toils and conflicts of this dreary, bitter world!

Let the poor think of incorruptible riches! the aged, of immortal youth! the weary, of everlasting rest! the homeless, of the house not made with hands! the persecuted, tempted, forsaken and heart-broken, of the golden crown that fadeth not away!

The Jew in Parliament.

(This article is defiantly inscribed to the narrow-viewed Editor of "THE CHURCHMAN," who thinks that "there is a bitter curse hanging over England, and Queen Victoria is doomed to eternal perdition," in consequence of the admission of Baron Rothschild into the House of Parliament.[1])

It is his *right*! Shame on the narrow souls, who, for so long,

---

[1] Baron Lionel Nathan de Rothschild (1808–79). Although initially elected to the House of Commons in 1847, he did not take his seat until 1858, when he was finally permitted to swear the parliamentary oath in a manner that accommodated his Jewish faith. On 12 August 1858 *The Churchman* (New York) ran an unsigned editorial, "A Jew in the English Parliament," that condemned the British parliament's move. The antisemitic editorial did not mention Queen Victoria or her damnation, but did say "the wrath of God hangs over England."

raised their feeble voices to throw him in the shadow of their great wrong. Rothschild! A Jew! in whose veins flows the golden blood of Kings, of David and Abraham, ancestry before which the proudest shield among the peers of England should be lowered in homage. His race is of that line of crowned monarchs on whose heads the hand of GOD placed the jewelled crown! And England's crowned heads think, doubtless, that they have conferred favor on Israel's race, and that we are thankful to them. No, not to *them*, but to GOD we are thankful! It is He who watches over his children! He will give them their right and their glory! Make room, ye kingdoms! Stand back, ye empires! A JEW would have his *right*! [...]

There is not a kingdom or an empire that has not near the throne one or more of these God-graced JEWS of talent, education and rank. Spain, Austria, France, Russia, Persia, and England have ministers of State, or council, who are JEWS. And there beats in those hearts, prouder, nobler blood than e'er flowed through the veins of Norman or Tudor monarch! In Germany, all the highest walks of literature, music and philosophy are filled with JEWS. And in this country they grace our colleges and schools by their profound learning. In the Congress of the United States are honored the names of Benjamin, Phillips, Florence and others.[1]

This grand race excels, in the fine arts, as composers, painters, sculptors, architects, authors, musicians, actors, men of genius, they are remarkable for having astonished the world with the brilliancy of their talent. They tread the stage as *stars*, or fill the boxes of the Academy as patrons of the Lyric art.—The composers of the most scientific and classical operas are JEWS!

The great strength of the Jewish mind lies in the entire decision and earnestness with which each individual follows his ambition. They have the power of seizing the strongest points of whatever they attempt to do, beyond any other nation, and developing them with unsurpassed energy and firmness of purpose. And these glorious gifts, and God-like strength of mind are theirs in the very face of opposition and tyranny. A nation without a

---

[1]   Judah Philip Benjamin (1811–84), Henry Myer Phillips (1811–84), and Thomas Birch Florence (1812–75).

country! nation without a land! without cities, without a temple, without an altar—without any thing but that Holy Page before them, containing the promise of glory and restoration of all they have lost. And the promise is dawning! The glory is rising as a pillar of fire, o'er the East!

What other race has preserved during two thousand years of dispersion, their language, their laws, their religion, their God? How carefully have they preserved their names, and the blood of their royal time! A nation waiting for its time! an army daily expecting the coming of its Leader for eighteen hundred years, to unfurl the banner of its Restoration, and lead them "by a path through the nations,"[1] until it be planted upon the rocky summit of Mount Zion, to wave forever over the ramparts of Jerusalem! What people so wonderful as this? what miracle so grand as this ever-living and present one, open and patent to all men's eyes?

Let England rather revere and honor the children of Israel, who represent the brightest stars of talent and genius in her crown of intellect! [...]

Swimming Against the Current.

Swimming against the current is hard and dangerous work.

Strong, firm, and iron-bound must be the noble vessel; brave and fearless must be the hearts that stand at the helm. "God and our right" must be the password of those who lift their sails to stem the current.

Individuality of intellect, and an affinity with God—not society—powerful energy, a potent buoyancy, and a strong volition, can and will venture the task. Cowardice is the demonstration of weakness. Strength and valor must exert themselves in valorous actions. Courage is the true demonstration of strength. And whoever is gifted with that mental and moral god-power, to stand like a rock in the midst of a roaring storm, feels the mighty impulse to oppose the impetuous billows of the rushing current—dare the storm—stem the tide, will reach the goal, gain eternal life, for they are God's children of inspiration!

But few, oh! too few, possess these holy attributes, to bear

---

[1] See Deuteronomy 29.16.

them up against wind and wave. Therefore, the vast majority of mankind intrust of themselves with so much ease and convenience to the current of popular sentiments, fashions, weak, driveling notions, idiotic principles; plying, now and then, a little with the useless rudder of their intellect, they swim lazily along with the current; flattering the ambition and passions of the influential and great men, worshiping the idols of the day, to suit prevalent notions; taking every advantage of the timid, the weak, and infirm, they swim down the current of life, and arrive quietly and conveniently into the labor of Death.

Swimming against the current is *hard and dangerous work!* How few are the brave souls that are to-day stemming the tide! Seward, Jefferson Davis, Sumner, Lovejoy, Wendell Phillips, Beecher, Theodore Parker, Garrison, Walter Whitman, Mrs. Hatch, and perhaps some few more.[1] There they stand, in the midst of humanity, few and far apart, like the islands of the ocean, fertile and fresh as the cases of the desert, "their shoulders and upward higher than all the people,"[2] as the mountains range and overtower the plains and valleys below.

There they stand with their spontaneous and generous impulses, the internal ear and eye of humanity, that sees and grasps with instinctive eagerness at the faults and corruptions of men, things, religions, and institutions around them.

They have braved the current, for they hear the divine voice of inspiration calling. "Whom shall I send to the rescue?" And they could not help responding, "Here I am—send me!"

But alas! they swim against the current, and laborious and tiresome is the task. Many a foaming wave rushes at their heads, and

---

[1]   William Henry Seward (1801-72), statesman, Republican Party leader, and secretary of state during the Lincoln administration. Jefferson Davis (1808-89), president of the Confederate States during the Civil War. Charles Sumner (1811-74), U.S. Senator famous for his uncompromising stand against slavery. Elijah Lovejoy (1802-37), abolitionist and newspaper editor. Wendell Phillips (1811-84), abolitionist, social reformer, and orator. Henry Ward Beecher (1813-87) minister, orator, writer, and antislavery and temperance activist. Theodore Parker (1810-60), minister, theologian, abolitionist, and social reformer. William Lloyd Garrison (1805-79), abolitionist and editor of the antislavery newspaper *The Liberator*. Walt Whitman (1819-92), poet. Mrs. Hatch (also known as Cora L.V. Scott Hatch Daniels Tappan [1840-1923]), spirit medium and trance lecturer.

[2]   1 Samuel 9.2, 10.23.

renders them almost helpless for a while; but they recover, and swim on, God bless them!

Sometimes overcome by the strong battle of the waves, a fainting soul pauses for rest; he looks down the stream, and sees thousands of pleasure-boats moving smoothly with the current, and rocking softly the rich, gay, happy, and successful passengers. He hesitates. "Shall I join them? Shall I blot out God's voice that calls me?" he asks. *No*, he *cannot* resist that holy voice. *Onward* is his course—he must swim again.

Look at Walter Whitman,[1] the American philosopher, who is centuries ahead of his contemporaries, who, in smiling carelessness, analyzes the elements of which society is composed, compares them with the history of past events, and ascertains the results which the same causes always produced, and must produce. Thus analyzing, he becomes aware of the errors, faults, and evils now existing and penetrating into the future. He hears the Divine voice calling him to caution mankind against this or that evil; and wields his pen, exerts his energies, for the cause of liberty and humanity!

But he is too far ahead of his contemporaries; they cannot comprehend him yet; he swims against the stream, and finds no company. The passengers, in their floating boats, call him a fanatic, a visionary, a demagogue, a good-natured fool, etc., etc. Still he heeds them not: his mental conviction will not permit him to heed them.

Thousands of philosophers, poets, senators, preachers of God, philanthropists, friends and saviors of liberty, women of inspiration, men of reform, have been drowned in the current of life, because they swam against the stream—died with the deep-seated pain in their breasts, poisoned with disappointment, insult, or ridicule, or starved to death by an ungrateful people—poor Edgar A. Poe, for example. But when in the next century their words and schemes will become understood, because circumstances will take that turn which they predicted, marble statues

---

[1] On 12 June 1860, Whitman wrote to Henry Clapp, Jr.: "Did you see what Mrs. Heenan says about me in last 'Sunday Murcury'—first page?" See Walt Whitman, *The Correspondence*, ed. Edwin Haviland Miller, 6 vols. (New York: New York University Press, 1961-77) 1:55.

will be erected over the remains of him whom they suffered to starve, because he swam against the current.

Suppose all men would yield to the current of the age? None would manfully uncover the rotten spots, expose the errors and prejudices entertained, and the evils practiced. Would not humanity soon be degraded into a reckless pleasure-party, skipping around, and approaching always nearer the yawning whirlpool, until finally the whole boat would rush in.

Yes! those men who have the valor and moral courage to swim against the current, are the noble and generous towers of humanity. Yet we ignore and contradict them; yet they are, nevertheless, the Messiahs of humanity. Mankind is obliged to them for new ideas, periodical regeneration, and the progress of civilization. They combat with the waves, and are frequently buried beneath them; but, after centuries, they are rescued from the aqueous grave, and rise to perpetual glory!

If there is any truth in the above—and close observation of facts proves that there is—it is also morally certain that thus Israel will rise to perpetual glory! So the house of Jacob will be rescued from the grave, and a proud monument assigned us in the history of the world. So Judea will triumph, after darkness and ignorance will be utterly dispelled by the radiant sun of divine truth! For thus Israel has swam against the current for thirty centuries and more! Thus it has struggled and combated against the corruptions of all ages in history; Thus is Israel the savior, the Messiah of the nations!

Israel swam against the current when heathenism reigned supreme, when Grecian philosophy undermined the ancient superstructure of religion, when Epicure's doctrines demoralized Rome, and heathenism gave way before Christianity and the Islam. It swam against the current of popular religions in all periods of history; and does it yet, with the same energy and unabated vigor. Buried under the waves of popular prejudices, it always resurrects again in youthful strength, valor, and glory of eternal life!

"Hail thee, Israel, who is like unto thee? a people saved by God, the shield of thy salvation and the sword of thy pride!"[1]

---

[1]   Deuteronomy 33.29. See also Psalm 18.35 and 2 Samuel 22.36.

Self Defence.[1]

Under the above startling caption I do not propose to expound the theory of the "*manly* art," or I should have solicited your attention through the columns of a "sporting paper," and in "arms" with my pen, barbed with heartless and cruel words to spurn the truth and purity of womanhood. I should have laid down in the dust honor, virtue, love and humanity; I should have shut my eyes to all that is good and beautiful in life; wiped out the sacred impress of a mother's prayers; and boasted of power enough to drive a pure and loving woman to destruction! Yes, *boasted* over gaming tables, and convivial cups at midnight revels! I should have insulted her dependence—jested of her affection; and, as a wretched substitute for wit, laugh unclean doubts of her; whisper vulgar suspicions of her virtue; slander and pollute her character; and, as far as lay in the futile pen of some wicked and unprincipled amanuensis, I should have shut up every avenue by which she could honestly gain her bread, and drive her down the whirlpool of sin through the forgetfulness of ghastly shame and blasted charity!

But, thank God! It is *not* in defence of these "*manly* arts" my poor pen will struggle to-day. This weak little hand will strike its meagre weight against sin and oppression, and lift up the down-trodden colors of *woman's rights!*—her birth-rights—her rights of intellect—her rights of honor—her rights of love—her rights of protection; and the rights of our land of freedom in giving her claims to be heard; and the God-right, giving me power to raise the banner of truth and strike for self-defence!

Men who practice the "*noble* art" have a certain length of time, I believe, to prepare for their contests, and the enemy dare not appear on the field of battle until his opponent has had every opportunity and ample time to go through the process of what

---

[1]   In the wake of her marriage to Heenan, his desertion of her, and the bad publicity that followed, Menken publicly defended herself. She announced a poetry reading at Hope Chapel and presented there on 20 August 1860 this personal essay. "Self Defence" was first printed in *The New-York Times* in 1868, though paraphrased passages appeared earlier in "An Evening with the Poets: The Position of Miss Adah Isaacs Menken," *New-York Tribune* (21 Aug. 1860): 8.

they call "training," to gain strength and power to enable them to stand up unharmed under the weight of blows.

But is this privilege granted to woman?

Do they give her time to gather up her little strength, and shut out her weakness of love and dependence, before they raise their powerful hands and hurl her to destruction?

Do they give her time to call for help?

Do they give her time to clasp her children to her bosom and cry for mercy?

No! for man to woman is merciless. He heeds not her prayers! He hears not the voice of his own children!

Why not give her time and opportunity to even reach the battle-field?

Why seek her in her humble home, amid her sorrows and her desolation, and there try to crush out her life and purity, and trample upon her love, and mock her misfortunes, thus striking blow after blow, until her heart, once fresh with the roses and sunshine of life, becomes cold and dead with pain?

Think not that my imaginative and poetic nature is striving to lay the groundwork of some thrilling romance, to be read by schoolboys and sentimental chambermaids, who revel in the genius of COBB and "Ned Buntline."[1] But a woman, with all a woman's dignity of honor, a woman's meekness and gentleness, her weakness and love, wearing the God-given crown of daughter, sister, wife and mother, humbly comes before you to vindicate truth and reality, and to lift the smiling mask from the dark faces of falsehood and oppression.

I write for the men and women of our land who are not afraid to stand up in their own right of individuality and speak the truth.

Anything tending to the development of truth is an achievement of human freedom! And I would be free—free from reproach—free from the bitter and malicious calumnies of those who would "ruin if they cannot rule,"[2] and who are even now

---

[1]   Joseph Beckham Cobb (1819–58) and Ned Buntline, the pseudonym of Edward Zane Carroll Judson (1823–86), were popular American writers of the mid-nineteenth century.

[2]   Dryden, *Absalom and Achitophel* 1.174.

scattering their venom among the human race, to induce them to laugh at virtue and trample it under foot, and who are industrious to collect the vilest insinuation of slander and blazon them to the world, while they conceal the opposite facts of religion, virtue, toil, endurance and love.

The fruits of this infernal lying and blasphemy are really egotism, sensual madness and wickedness.

If man exerts himself to depict woman as an abject being, artful, inconstant and vain, and denies to her the sacred fire of friendship, the undying flame of love and the right to purity and religion, has she not—supposing her to be a human being—the right to raise her feeble voice in self-defence? "Strike, but hear,"[1] contains a volume of just advice, even in transactions between men; but he who would deliberately strike down a helpless woman, and cover her name with shame, and heap upon her the contumely of the world, without giving her an opportunity of legal defence, deserves not the name of man, but should take his appropriate place with those brutal creatures who have no sense of honor themselves and rejoice in the degradation of superior natures.

I write for those men and women who do not reject religion, that sole sanctifier of man, and who do not turn away from the light of goodness wherever it is found; and for those who honor a woman for her affections and domestic virtues, wherever she may be found. [...]

I do not lay aside womanly dignity and modesty to assume the tattered garb of the amazon; but the language of innocence may be bold, and it has the right to be defiant. I shall use no honeyed words and suppliant tones to those who have wronged me. I will speak the truth in strong—not unwomanly—phrases, and support all I have to say, by referring to undoubted facts and irreproachable evidence.

This defence is called for by my personal friends, and the friends of humanity. It is not of my seeking, but my enemies', who have endeavored to crush me, involving on their side falsehood and corruption, and on the other—I will not say what. Let

---

[1] Plutarch, *Themistocles* 11.3

those who read these pages say where the falsehood lies; I do not fear the result.

The dagger that was sheathed in my unsuspecting heart, by hands that I most trusted, I have wept over in secret and silence, striving to bury my sorrow and desolation in my own soul from the eyes of the prying world; shrinking from exposing one whom I have loved, how dearly wives and mothers alone can tell. But I am hunted to the river brink, and must speak or perish.

Amid the barbarism of the Middle Ages the institution of chivalry was embellished by the influence of devoted and disinterested love and respect to woman. It has been her due through all ages, and never was there a state of society in which woman had a fairer opportunity of being or doing anything that is good or right in her own eyes than the present. If her pride, her freedom, and her courage, and her soul are wrested from her, it is not by the universal spirit of the age, but by individual influence. Then let her rise up and cast it off. This alone marks an advance in common sense and civilization. A woman can be strong and free only as men and nations obtain their freedom, vis.: that of showing herself capable of obtaining and holding it. He who cut the Gordian knot told the whole secret of human success—if the knot will not be unraveled, *cut it!*

I have seen editors who professed an ardent zeal in the cause of humanity, and unparalleled virtue in the columns of their journals, and at the same time busied themselves in scattering obscene and infamous items, blasting the heart and reputation of women of whom they knew *nothing*, and who, if compared to themselves, would appear as the whiteness of immaculate angels! Yet they inwardly rejoiced in their power of feeding the intoxicated senses of the rabble, on their own slimy venom, and in destroying all faith in womanly excellence. [...]

Reject the temptation, ye who wield the battle-ax of pen and ink, to follow in the foot-prints of those who, the son of woman, have looked upon her with disdain. Turn away thy steps from all who do not honor in woman the mother who gave them birth. Trample under foot the public journals that vilify any woman. Render thyself worthy, by a noble esteem for female honor, to protect her to whom thou owest life, to protect thy sister, to protect the being who shall acquire the sacred title of the mother of thy children.

This much I have said to "mitigate the justice of my plea."[1] I owe none but my friends a defence or explanation of my actions. I have always endeavored to do my duty to the best of my knowledge. I need no tutor, and will listen to no rebuke. [...]

Affinity of Poetry and Religion.

Poetry and Religion!

Twin stars, born in heaven, whose magnetism of silver and gold pierces the clay of our bodies and lights souls up to the beautiful! Who can doubt that the hand of God rests on the head of His children of inspiration, and that the divine glory of human love, with all its sublime poetry, is born of religion—of that religion which is in itself the poetry of Heaven? In this originates the grandest conceptions; the most supreme ideal of the Deity.

Poetry and art are indebted to the truth and sublimity of religion for their development, and their purity.

The religion of all ages that have rolled over the globe, and of all nations that have dwelt upon it, has constantly manifested itself in the most sublime and undying poetry.

Human imagination has sought to approach, in its creations, the works of the Deity, and the excellence of the justice, mercy, love and beauty of God, when religion had taught it to comprehend these qualities of the Supreme Creator and His creations.

The poetry of religion does not consist in its external manifestations; but these manifestations are results of the poetry that lies hidden in every wide, glowing human heart.

If these same poetic manifestations in the temples, manners of worship, and religious history of nations, were not so universal, the intimate relations of religion and poetry might be doubted. But wherever we find the first, it has produced the second.

Religion in Rome was attended with an architecture whose

---

[1]   *Merchant of Venice* 4.1.205.

strength and boldness embodied the religious idea of the age. Strong and bold were its gods, that threatened or frowned, or reposed in mighty self-reliance in marble. It was attended with a literature bold, strong, and bright as a diamond, with poetic actions, sentiments, just, great, and powerful. And in Rome, with the growth of religion, its external manifestations, the architecture, art, and poetry of the age increased.

In Greece, where sublime gods loved and lived in beauty, the splendid temples, the lovely statues, the smiling paintings, and the smooth, beautiful poetry, the elegance of manners, the luxury of love and magnificence were evident manifestations of a religion whose chief ideas were beauty and sweetness.

In Asia, at the present time, the religion of Bramah shows us the same results. The beginning of their religious history is: The great God of all, the supreme excellence, lay floating on the water, while Vishnu slept on his bosom. Then a lotus-stalk sprang from Vishnu's body, and reached the surface of the water, bloomed, and was beautiful; and when the flower was fully expanded, Bramah leaped from the petal.

This shows an unnatural poetic beauty.

The religion of their gods, with blue complexions, with double faces, and with thousand-headed snakes, has produced an unequally unnatural state of poetry. Their sculptured figures are adorned with four heads, eight hands, and other members in proportion, or rather in disproportion, to these. Their poetry is full of unnatural images.

The religion of the ancients, Teutons and Gauls,[1] with their dark caves, human sacrifices, and butchering priests, ought to have produced an equally fierce and dark art and literature. But Druidism was tempered by the belief in the Almighty Father, vast, powerful, and good; by their temples in the wild wood and grove—keeping the works of God, and not of man, in their contemplation. Their poetry was wild, bold, and beautiful. The bards, with stringed shells and harps, led them to battle, and by

---

[1] The Teutons were an ancient Germanic or perhaps Celtic people. The Gauls were an ancient Celtic tribe. The Druids were the priests of ancient Celtic Britain, Ireland, and Gaul.

wild, patriotic songs, inflamed their enthusiasm to frenzy. Works of art they had few.

The religion of Christ, containing countless truths, many good maxims (which, indeed, may be said of all religions), is still founded on a history which partakes largely of poetry. The religion is itself poetic and eminently so. As history, they have a God, or offspring of God, coming down from Heaven to save humanity from its sins. They have a woman, patient, loving, mother of the God-child, adoring it as God—loving it as a child. They have the death at the cross, an act of the richest poetry attributable to mortals. This poetic history—this beautiful picture—speaking in every one of its particulars to the imagination and the heart, has had its proper effect upon art and literature.

Churches have been built in a style of architecture that rivaled the beauty of the magnificent forests; and in marble glistened leaves and flowers on their walls, and vaulted ceilings. Their floors inlaid, to resemble the ground covered with gorgeous leaves of autumn. Organs breathed harmony like the wind, wild and unsettled, surging among the trees.

The effects of Christianity upon literature, sculpture, painting, and music are well known. It is, therefore, not necessary to illustrate them.

Now, lastly, how far does Poetry enter into the religion of the children of Israel, and how much of their religious history is mere Poetry, how much Truth?

The religion of the Jews is not an offspring of the heart—not born of the reason, the imagination, or the poetry of the human mind—but is an external revelation; a revelation which speaks to the reason, and only through reason to the poetry of the soul.

The history of Judah's religion is the history of its nation—clear, lucid, and evident—speaking only through the reason to the soul, only through the mind to the heart. The mournful songs by Babel's streams; the groans and cries of the Roman era; the blood and tears of the middle ages—all highly poetic, but too true, too real, too well established to excite our imagination, without burning our hearts. And because the Jewish religion is a religion of reason, which partakes but indirectly poetry, the literature and the art of the Jewish nation were eminently reasonable; and wherever poetry appeared, it was the poetry of reason. Strength of mind and education is necessary to be a true and pious Israelite, to understand fully the religion of Jacob. For mere loving trust, mere childish confidence in God, does not, according to Jewish principles, suffice. It is a revealed religion, with laws and commandments that must be followed rigidly, with rules that must be strictly attended to, and with limits that are well defined, and cannot be slighted.

The Jewish heart is full of poetry, but this poetry is connected in the slightest possible manner with religion. The idea of the One Great Power is so vast, so immense, that the mind cannot grasp it. The love of God is so powerful, that the selfish human soul cannot comprehend it; and all His attributes so infinite, eternal, and immense, that the poetry and art of man is unable to imagine them in any tangible form, except in their effects. Those effects impress us with a mysterious awe, love, and gratitude, but nothing further. They impress us with a vivid desire to imitate, a wish to please this vast, unknown Power. This feeling alone would make but a very incomplete religion. But when the Lord, in His mercy, seeing the wants of men, came down on Mount Sinai and there gave Moses the law, there gave tangible forms to unexpressed feelings, there reduced mysterious impressions to words and acts, suitable to man and human life.

And Israel went forth, bearing these revelations, expressed translations of the highest, most sublime, and God-like feelings of men, and suited to the every day life of this world by the God of creation.

This is the one grand and blazing link of Israel's religion with its poetry.

The love of God and all His creatures is in itself the very refinement of Poetry.

True religion is Poetry, and true Poetry is religion.

Women of the World.

"_____ Fashion makes the law
Your umpire, which you bow to,
Whether it has brains or not."
—SHERIDAN KNOWLES.[1]

Who are the women of the world?

Who are the lost women?

They are your fashionable mothers, wives, sisters, and daughters.

What is God-created woman's mission?

The holy mission of building temples of the Beautiful, the Lofty, the Sublime, to God's children of the earth!

With her is born all that lights up the sunshine of inspiration.

Virtue, Purity, and Love are her gifts—jealously intrusted to her, by the Creator, to glorify rude souls of clay that cling too close to the dust.

Then, who are the women of the world?

Who are the lost women?

Why does she not fill her grand mission?

Why does she not work out the golden threads of her mighty destiny?

Alas! Fashion has bought her soul with its glare and gold.

That unclean thing, called Society, has swallowed her body; and she is eternally lost to her mission of the everlasting!

I am not writing of individual instances.

There are but few untainted lambs in the flock.

But why has the serpent been permitted to enter the garden of woman's soul, and leave his slime upon all the flowers?

Because her glorious birthright of beauty—soul-beauty—is left uncared for, uncultivated, overgrown with bitter poison-weeds of ignorance, indolence, and folly!

"Soiled with the dust of men,"[2] her highborn gifts lie withered at her feet.

---

[1] James Sheridan Knowles, *The Hunchback* (London, 1859) 1.2.70-71.

[2] Menken, "The Autograph on the Soul," line 8.

Charity, gentleness, and love for her sister-woman are all crushed out of her nature, by petty jealousy, envy of face and form, love of senseless admiration.

No music of thought is left to vibrate to the glory of religion—if religion embraces charity to one another.

If a frail child of earth fall into the pit of error, will a woman hold out the helping hand to her?

Will she pour the balm of charity and sympathy into the wounds that perhaps penetrate to the very soul of an erring sister? Never!

If words and sneers could dash a sinking, erring creature to the bottomless pit, it would be a woman's work to do it.

Fortunately, these women of the world can do nothing else than talk and sneer.

A haunting gleam of shapeless light, fitfully flashing at midnight, when she is alone, is all that is left of a fashionable woman's gratitude and charity.

Fashion is the god she bows to.

Wealth is the only distinction she seeks.

Through dress and gold you may woo her, and buy her, but love and intellect weigh nothing in the balance.

I have seen these passive dolls shun, with contempt, a woman great in her grandeur of soul, mighty in her strength of learning and feeling, because she, perhaps, was plainly dressed, or did not belong to "our circle," and scorned to be other than what she was, disdaining fashionable affectation and useless ceremony.

But let us look at the *cause* of this waste of life.

Why are these women of the world lost to the Good and the Beautiful?

It is the evil of education.

Their extreme ignorance is the chief cause of their frivolity.

As girls, they are educated only for display.

Thus brought up, without solid information, they cannot be expected to have any inclination or taste for study, or the practice of those virtues that make woman beautiful.

There are very few virtues that are fashionable

"_____They are legends,
Left us of some good old forgotten time."[1]

In high (?) life, young women are not obliged to devote their time to study; they spend a few hours each day at their needle, merely because they see other women do so (logic!), not knowing that it is a *right* for women to be useful.

This idleness, joined to ignorance, produces a thirst for amusements—frivolous vanity—insatiable curiosity.

Intellectual women, occupied by serious studies and the good of their fellow creatures, possess but a very moderate degree of curiosity.

What they already know of the grander and higher aim of life leads them to despise smaller things of which they are ignorant; and they see the insignificance of the gossiping small-talk and slander with which women of society are so eagerly occupied. But these women are never fashionable.

As girls are educated, they will educate another generation.

Thus the great evil grows.

Gilded moths of Fashion are not in the slightest degree conscious of their duties as mothers.

A daughter is trained to be accomplished, and that the ultimate end of every accomplishment is to please the opposite sex.

To win for herself a wealthy husband is the lesson.

She is taught all the feminine arts that woman is capable of teaching and learning; and every thought is concentrated in this all important event. And the only really serious thought she has on the subject of matrimony is: "Has he money? Can he support me in style?"

Yes, this is woman.

She, whose very nature, as God-given, ought to stimulate her to higher and holier motives for taking upon herself the marriage relation.

But *money*! that all-absorbing thing, has drank out the beauty of her soul, and trailed it o'er its own filthy slime!

---

[1] Henry Hart Milman, *Fazio, A Tragedy* (Oxford, 1815) 4.3.102–103. In New Orleans in 1857, Menken starred in this play in the role of Bianca.

I wonder if these "splendid matches" —as fashionable marriages are termed—ever feel the loneliness of their unwedded hearts?

I wonder if they ever remember dreams?

Their hands may be united by the silver clasp of dollars; but to feel, in silent hours, that in heart you are separated, must be misery indeed. To think of being obliged to associate for life with one who has not a feeling in sympathy with you, and, moreover, in sentiment, taste, and feeling, directly opposed to you! Oh, how revolting the thought!

Alas! *I* remember dreams.

Ah, how many women learn this dark, bitter lesson!

Some, alas! learn it too late, and never know what a sweet thing it is to be loved purely, and truly for herself, for her beauties of soul and thought, her gentleness and her purity.

O mothers! believe me, daughters should be trained with higher and holier motives than that of being fashionable and securing wealthy husbands.

They should not be taught to secure them at all.

There are other missions for woman than that of wife and mother.

Train your daughters to usefulness and religion.

Women of the world cannot be religious.

Cultivate their mental faculties; train their hearts and souls to rise in their majesty of Heaven-created power!

Teach them of the life within, not of the world.

Yet, should they be blessed with the true loyal love of one of God's children of inspiration—should a happiness little less than the angels' be insured to them, through a grand human love— with your prayers let them marry!

Behind the Scenes.

"Divine creature! Magnificent! Glorious! Isn't she?"

So exclaimed a thousand tongues—so felt a thousand hearts— as the star of the night came out, with her princess air and classic beauty, while her light laugh rang its music over the crowded throng, and met its echo in every spell-bound heart.

"Glorious" indeed she was; with her glad, liquid eyes glancing a thousand fetters to the hearts that sent back their smiles. Yes, she was "divine." But could they have seen their petted idol of the comedy, a little hour before, bending in agony beside the death-stricken form of her mother, what then would they have thought of their favorite?[1]

Would they have laughed and clapped their sounding hands to the low moans and sobbings of her heart-rending agony?

Those gleaming eyes, that flashed back the light, were blinded with tears.

Those jeweled hands had wiped off the death-dew from a pale, cold brow—and then, O horror! the painted stage, the gaslight, called her to laugh and sing, whilst under the gold-'broidered vestment that poor, lonely heart was breaking!

This is no imaginary picture! Would to God this heart could not answer for its truth!

The festive hour is past.

The *comédienne* is weeping bitter tears—how bitter none but those who have seen a dear mother die, may know—over the still, white form, with the hands folded over the pulseless breast.

The silver coins sealing the eclipsed eyes; the white-bandaged chin; the cold, rigid outlines of the form, throwing shadows on the shroud—these tell how surely the Angel of Rest had claimed the weary-hearted.

Where is the laugh?

Where the applause? the call before the curtain? the flowers? the jewels? the smile? the good-night?

Where the liveried menial that bore his master's "love" upon a silver salver?

Where the haughty prince that stood uncovered to offer her gold and—his "heart?"

They, too, have "strutted their brief hour on the stage."[2]

The last echo of the last retreating footstep is gone. The long line of carriages, with their prancing steeds and gloved footmen, have rattled away with their living, joyous burdens.

---

[1] Menken's mother had died earlier this year, and a poem on her mother's death, "Our Mother," had appeared just three weeks earlier in the *Sunday Mercury*.

[2] See *Macbeth* 5.5.27.

Pride, envy, malice, shame, guilt, love, hate, and jealousy, have left the pit and boxes, as their interpreters faded from the stage. One solitary light trembles along the line of the old green curtain. The pasteboard palace, and the canvas street; the painted prison, with its huge bars and bolts, and chains of paper; the waterfall, turned by a crank (oh, shades of the Alps, with thy gorgeous, dashing streams!) rest in all their tarnished glory, till to-morrow night's gaslight shall renew their brilliancy.

How hideous seems the gloom! how ghastly the white and gilded cornices that peep under the dim shadows into the darkness!

Look back into the few short moments since, when we were striving to deceive ourselves that all this was real.

But what was the use?

We know that the poor fellow who played the king, with his glittering crown and peacock-train, and his lofty air, came to the theatre supperless, for the want of a shilling.

We know that the "populace" who shouted so exultingly consisted of poor boys anxious to earn a few pence.

The battle-axes were all pasteboard.

The queen, who was so loudly applauded for her speeches of virtuous indignation, and suffered imprisonment and death for loyalty to her husband and king, we knew was the wife of a gambler, and flirted with at least twenty besides.

The ardent, poetical lover wore a false moustache, and knelt to a withered dame of sixty, and swore "by the blessed moon" that she was divine.

A murderer, with a slouched hat and black wig, groped about in the dark for his victim, while the stage was bright as day!

The sheet-iron thunder pealed forth its deafening power; the blue lightning flashed, and the mimic rain poured, while people were floundering about on dry planks, and crying out that they were drenched to the skin!

Innumerable farewells were taken, and departures to foreign lands, beyond the seas, whose boundaries lay in the green-room.

Years passed in a single moment—old Time was fairly annihilated.

Afflicted heroines were shedding imaginary tears over a hero, who was dying so unnaturally from a thrust at his belt with a wooden sword, while the orchestra played "Hail, Columbia!" the curtain fell "mid thunders of applause!"

Well, the mimic scenes are over, and, like the poor, heartbroken actress, whose glad, eager personations brought down the house, I, too, will go home to life's realities. Perhaps, alas! many of us had better been there before.

Lodgings to Let—References Exchanged.

Everybody likes good lodgings.

Americans carry this desire further than any other nation.

Spasmodically they grow wild over the excitement of presenting references, and putting in claims to the best and most desirable lodgings.

Such is the dearth of good houses in the market, that there are many competitors for every vacant tenement.

But there is one house in "my mind's eye," about which there is more wrangling, lying, nonsense, and humbug, than any other building I heard of.

Married and single, old and young, rich and poor, handsome and ugly (the ugly are decidedly in the majority), are all after it; and so long as it stands, there will probably be the same eagerness to occupy it.

This house is not the property of an individual, but belongs to an immense company; and the proprietors are always quarreling, and calling each other names about the tenants.

This dwelling is leased for a term of four years.

The proprietors have been known to renew the lease; but lately they disagree, quarrel, and fight to such an outrageous extent among themselves, that no tenant need entertain the faintest hope of obtaining a renewal of the lease.

I think, to judge from the fighting calendar, that the tenants do well to escape with their lives.

Indeed, I may say (looking through South Carolina spectacles), the gentleman who has succeeded in securing this house for the next term of years will not escape with his life.[1]

---

[1]   Elected to the presidency on 6 November 1860, the month before this article appeared, Lincoln was assassinated in 1865 while still in office.

His references have been examined by the Southern members of the firm, and found to be of a doubtful character. Some of the names attached are not satisfactory. That of "Old Massa Greeley"[1] has thrown the affair into bad odor (no wonder!) with some of the owners of the building. In fact, they are having an awful row about it. [...]

What renders all this row and rage as to who shall dwell in this house the more surprising is, that it is not by any means a convenient building, though a large one, and it stands in a very unhealthy situation.

Indeed, two of the tenants died soon after taking up their quarters there.[2]

The building itself appears to be a cross between a barn and an Oriental palace.

Some of the rooms have Turkey carpets; others, bare floors. Sumptuous sofas, and broken-backed chairs with one and two legs (three altogether); $1,000 looking-glasses in the front room, and broken windows in the back; well heated and ventilated parlors, and leaky roofs and damp beds.

Some years ago, it was my misfortune to be obliged to sleep in this desirable house. Grant Thorburn's "First Night in America" was nothing to it.

But instead of getting up next morning to read the third chapter of Proverbs, as "Laurie Todd" did, I read what the spider said to the fly.[3]

I would advise Mr. Lincoln, the new tenant, to read this entertaining and useful little poem before he removes to this celebrated mansion.

Still, with all its imperfections and disgraceful reputation, there is a perfect army of house-hunters after this particular house of all others, whenever it is in the market—so great are the attractions (?) of the "White House" at Washington.

---

1 Horace Greely (1811-72), politician, abolitionist, and editor of the *New York Tribune*.
2 William Henry Harrison (1773–1841) and Zachary Taylor (1784–1850) each died while serving as U.S. president.
3 See Grant Thorburn, *Lawrie Todd. Life and Writings of Grant Thorburn: Prepared by Himself* (New York, 1852), chap. 2; Mary Howitt, "The Spider and the Fly," *Sketches of Natural History* (London, 1834) 123-28.

The rent is cheap.

I guess that is what all this row is about.

Doesticks says so, and he ought to know.[1]

Well, thank my stars I am not President of the United States!

I never look around my own cozy little room, and think how real comfortable it is, with books and pictures for company, but I exclaim: "What would the poor President of the United States say if he had such a nice room as I have got?"

---

[1]   Q.K. Philander Doesticks, the pen name of journalist Mortimer Neal Thomson (1831-75), author of *Doesticks: What He Says* (New York, 1855).

Appendix A: Biographies

1. Mark Twain, "The Menken—Written Especially for Gentlemen," *Territorial Enterprise* [Virginia City, Nevada] (17 Sept. 1863).

[This piece, which survives as a clipping in one of Twain's scrapbooks, is not so much biography as a comic account of Menken's performance of *Mazeppa* in San Francisco in 1863.]

When I arrived in San Francisco, I found there was no one in town—at least there was no body in town but "the Menken"—or rather, that no one was being talked about except that manly young female. I went to see her play "Mazeppa," of course.[1] They said she was dressed from head to foot in flesh-colored "tights," but I had no opera-glass, and I couldn't see it, to use the language of the inelegant rabble. She appeared to me to have but one garment on—a thin tight white linen one, of unimportant dimensions; I forget the name of the article, but it is indispensable to infants of tender age—I suppose any young mother can tell you what it is, if you have the moral courage to ask the question. With the exception of this superfluous rag, the Menken dresses like the Greek Slave;[2] but some of her postures are not so modest as the suggestive attitude of the latter. She is a finely formed woman down to her knees; if she could be herself that far, and Mrs. H.A. Perry[3] the rest of the way, she would pass for an unexceptionable Venus. Here every tongue sings the praises of her matchless grace, her supple gestures, her charming attitudes. Well, possibly, these tongues are right. In the first act, she rushes on the stage, and goes

---

[1] Henry Milner authored this adaptation of Byron's poem in 1830. A popular melodrama in the nineteenth-century for its spectacle, *Mazeppa* was especially known for a thrilling scene in which Mazeppa is stripped of his clothes and tied to the back of a "wild" horse that ascends an on-stage "mountain." Because of the obvious danger of the stunt, directors often tied a prop or mannequin to the horse's back. Partly because she performed this feat herself and partly because she was the first woman to play this male lead, Mazeppa became Menken's most famous role.

[2] Depicting a nude female slave for sale, Hiriam Power's *The Greek Slave* (1847) was one of the most discussed nineteenth-century American sculptures.

[3] A fellow actress in Menken's company.

cavorting around after "Olinska";[1] she bends herself back like a bow; she pitches headforemost at the atmosphere like a battering-ram; she works her arms, and her legs, and her whole body like a dancing-jack: her every movement is as quick as thought; in a word, without any apparent reason for it, she carries on like a lunatic from the beginning of the act to the end of it. At other times she "whallops" herself down on the stage, and rolls over as does the sportive pack-mule after his burden is removed. If this be grace then the Menken is eminently graceful. After a while they proceed to strip her, and the high chief Pole calls for the "fiery untamed steed"; a subordinate Pole brings in the fierce brute, stirring him up occasionally to make him run away, and then hanging to him like death to keep him from doing it; the monster looks round pensively upon the brilliant audience in the theatre, and seems very willing to stand still—but a lot of those Poles grab him and hold on to him, so as to be prepared for him in case he changes his mind. They are posted as to his fiery untamed nature, you know, and they give him no chance to get loose and eat up the orchestra. They strap Mazeppa on his back, fore and aft, and face upper-most, and the horse goes cantering up-stairs over the painted mountains, through tinted clouds of theatrical mist, in a brisk exciting way, with the wretched victim he bears unconsciously digging her heels into his hams, in the agony of her sufferings, to make him go faster. Then a tempest of applause bursts forth, and the curtain falls. The fierce old circus horse carries his prisoner around through the back part of the theatre, behind the scenery, and although assailed at every step by the savage wolves of the desert, he makes his way at last to his dear old home in Tartary down by the foot-lights, and beholds once more, O, gods! the familiar faces of the fiddlers in the orchestra. The noble old steed is happy, then, but poor Mazeppa is insensible— "ginned out"[2] by his trip, as it were. Before the act closes, however, he is restored to consciousness and his doting old father, the king of Tartary; and the next day, without taking time to dress—without even borrowing a shirt, or stealing a fresh horse—he starts off on the fiery untamed, at the head of the Tartar nation, to exterminate the Poles, and carry off his own sweet Olinska from the Polish court. He succeeds, and the curtain falls upon a bloody combat, in which the Tartars are victorious. "Mazeppa" proved a great card for Maguire

---

[1] Mazeppa's beloved.
[2] Worn out, as if run through a cotton gin.

here;[1] he put it on the boards in first-class style, and crowded houses went crazy over it every night it was played. But Virginians[2] will soon have an opportunity of seeing it themselves, as "the Menken" will go direct from our town there without stopping on the way. The "French Spy"[3] was played last night and the night before, and as this spy is a frisky Frenchman, and as dumb as an oyster, Miss Menken's extravagant gesticulations do not seem so overdone in it as they do in "Mazeppa." She don't talk well, and as she goes on her shape and her acting, the character of a fidgety "dummy" is peculiarly suited to her line of business. She plays the Spy, without words, with more feeling than she does Mazeppa with them.

2. Adah Isaacs Menken, "Some Notes of her life in her own Hand," *The New-York Times* (6 Sept. 1868): 8.

[Menken prepared this inconsistent, fragmentary, and partially fictionalized autobiographical statement in 1862 for Augustin Daly, a playwright and close friend, who planned to transform it into a book. The book never appeared, but Daly published her notes, along with his own introduction, shortly after her death.]

Introductory.

These notes which I print to-day came into my possession six years ago. At that time I was writing some weekly chapters on the drama for the New-York *Courier*, in a vein much more popular than reverential. The impudent style seemed to please, among a good many other people, Miss MENKEN. She was then enjoying the first rosy finish of notoriety, and according to the common penalty for floating a new name above the usual water-mark, everybody was asking, "Who were you before?" The reckless girl was not averse to paying the penalty and gratifying this curiosity, but with a shrewd sense of justice, she was determined the public should pay for this knowledge which it sought. Following up this idea, Miss MENKEN proposed to publish her

---

1   *Mazeppa* played at Tom Maguire's Opera House in San Francisco.
2   The residents of Virginia City, Nevada.
3   John Thomas Haines's *The French Spy* (1837), a military comedy in which Menken starred many times during her career.

"Memoirs," and wrote to request my aid as editor of the book. I was to revise in *Le Pelerin's*[1] saucy way, the notes, which she would furnish me with at intervals during her rests from acting. She worked faithfully at her self-imposed task for just three days, and in that time I received the "Defence,"[2] which I append to her biographical memoranda, and about half of the "Notes." She went to Boston, and I heard nothing more of her book. She returned to New-York, and the tortures of neuralgia, to which she was a rather impatient martyr, conquered any inclination she might have had to write more. Then came her marriage with Mr. NEWELL; then her visit to California. Sometime after, one day the English mail brought me a letter as long as my arm and as heavy as a legitimate tragedy—which upon opening I found to be another installment of "Notes" from this eccentric heroine of her own life, who had reached London in her round-the-world flight, and remembered her biographer in New-York. These were the last I received.

This is the explanation of the origin and purpose of the following disjointed chapters. I do not suppose an apology is needed for offering them for publication at this time. They were designed for the public, and no confidence is violated in printing them. I simply offer them without the elaborations which I was requested to make. If I thought for an instant that I was doing less an act of justice for a poor mistaken woman, who in this manner may be said to lift her voice from the grave, (in explanation sometimes of her own heart,) I should have burned every page, and permitted no eye, other than my own, to read the lines.

Disjointed as the memoranda are, they give for all that, when her excusable vanity permits, an honest revalation [*sic*] of her own feelings. Where the notes refer to these, we may rely upon their truth. Much of the rest, I suspect, being intended for sale, was made as salable as possible by the introduction of some innocent and allowable romancing. The localities are correct—the names may not always be so reliable, I think. As a matter of record, I may state that ADAH's own true name was ADELAIDE MCCORD!

MENKEN's crime was weakness of heart! There never was so weak

---

1 Charles Victor Prévôt, Vicomte d'Arlincourt (1789-1856), who published an account of his travels and social contacts with German and Dutch aristocracy as *Le Pélerin* [The Pilgrim] in 1842.
2 "Self Defence," xx.

a woman. And with this feminine feeling came its attendant fault, reckless generosity! Gentleness and generosity were the qualities she presented to friends; and these distinguished her, when he for whom she wrote the ensuing notes knew her. [...]

Notes of My Life.
I.

In the lovely City of Bordeaux, in France, the year——, dwelt a family whose lineage could be traced to kings and princes. For twelve years had lived AUGUSTE DE VERE LALIETTE, and FRANCINE, his wife, in matrimonial solitude. Wealth and the world's good well they knew, but in all this time the Holy Virgin had not heeded their prayers for the sunshine of young children's faces. The sky brightened, for the Mother of Jesus smiled, and on the 3d of December, year——, was born to those people two lovely girls—twins—who grew up to the loveliest pictures of beauty and grace RAPHAEL ever dreamed. No other children came, but these flowers filled the great hearts of many family relatives. They asked no more.

Both bore the same names. Each were MARIE JOSEPHINE RACHEL DE VERE DE LALIETTE. But they could not be confounded by even the most casual observer. One a delicate blond, the other a Spanish-looking brunette. Both the same form, the same features, voice, gesture, expression and yet so unlike.

Educated in Paris and London.

When seventeen years of age they were on a tour through all Europe.

Rested some months in Ireland.

Scenery so beautiful; life so rich to them.

The family on a pleasure excursion on the banks of the Lake of Killarney.

While sailing on the bosom of the most beautiful lake in the world, many miles from shore, a strong breeze—a struggle against the wind—the boat overturned—MARIE, the brunette, is drowned. A male servant also perished. Grief overwhelmed the family. They decided to visit America—had distant relatives in New-Orleans and Cuba. The only remaining daughter seemed to fade toward the pale gates of death.

But Love, the never-failing messenger of Life, came.

RICHARD IRVING SPENSER, a young American student, whose father so nobly defended Spenser Ford in South Carolina during the Revolutionary war as to hold a place in history, loved and was beloved by the most beautiful, refined and lovable creature God ever blessed—Marie Josephine de Vere Laliette—who in one year after her marriage became my mother.

Oh, adored and sainted mother! I see you only in extreme beauty, tenderness and the grace of a thousand lives bound up in your fragile body! A saint from my very birth. It seems a sacrilege to write to the world of one so pure, so holy in all her life as thou. Forgive me! Let the world know that my heritage was Heaven at last; that in the depths of my wild and wayward soul still lives and breathes the very refinement of God's truest beauty. But the light in the dark fainteth.

Marie was married in New-Orleans, where her first and best beloved child, Marie Rachel Adelaide de Vere Spenser was born, Dec. 11, 1839.

Richard Irving Spenser was a splendid specimen of manhood, strong, healthy, and handsome.

I never knew him. He died, strange to say, of consumption too. I was two years of age. In 1843, my darling mother was again married to Dr. Josiah Campbell. She met him while on a visit to France. He was a graduate of the famed University of Edinburgh, Scotland; had received diplomas for the Latin, Greek, Hebrew and Portuguese studies. At twenty-five years of age he was considered the most thoroughly learned man in Scotland. No one had ever graduated with such high honors. He delivered extempore orations in the Greek and Latin tongues with all ease and facility. His life was in his studies. He loved my mother because she adored him for his learning and talent.

They returned to New-Orleans. Dr. Campbell joined the United States Army as surgeon; was stationed at Baton Rouge, La.; was wealthy and beloved by all. My earliest remembrances are of that old barracks, and the near cottage of Zach. Taylor. Two children were born to my mother in this place, John Auguste Joseph Campbell, and two years later my only and beloved sister Francine Josephine Campbell. Here my education commenced. At six years of age I astonished my stepfather by my eagerness and proficiency in study. About this time we went to Cuba for my mother's health. There my father purchased an estate near Matanzas. His duty to his adopted and beloved country recalled him to his post as United States surgeon.

I now commenced my study in French and German, both of which my mother was perfectly conversant with.

II.

I was always called a wonderful and eccentric child. Never very fond of doing things because other people did them. At an early age I had a determination and will that no force could bend, and yet an affection so deep and true that I could not bear to see my dear mother bend her face down to a book. I wanted Love. The strongest always seemed weak and driveling to me beside my own. And so jealous as to set my soul on fire when my dear little brother and sister seemed to be in the slightest way ascendant in my mother's or father's affection. My extreme individuality manifested itself at the early age of seven and eight in various ways. For days have I—the little child—been wrapped in serious thought, so that scarcely a word could be drawn from me by any cunning strategy. There was an under life that even to this day no human being has fathomed. I have always believed myself to be possessed of *two souls*, one that lives on the surface of life, pleasing and pleased; the other as deep and as unfathomable as the ocean; a mystery to me and all who know me. The one, of the surface, enables me to infuse its very breath into the dance, until I seem to float on the very tide and current of joy, and to play the coarsest farce, and the broadest vulgarisms of comedy and melo-drama, until the whole city may exclaim: "What soul! What earnestness and fire!" Whether it be resting on the bare back of the leaping, dashing steed, and whirled up the mimic mountains of peril and danger, or wielding the combat sword with an energy that causes the strongest man to cower (NUNAN[1]) in dread; in negro songs, or the bone solo,[2] it is always said: "She plays with her very soul." And this intense life does not fail me as I leave the stage. I am as wild and as earnest in my dressing-room, and woe to the unlucky creature who displeases me, or opposes me in look or deed! I always get a clear stage. Everybody strives to please me as slaves do a master. They think I am crazy at night. My attention cannot be turned to any subject but the stage as long as the piece lasts. I see and hear nothing else. I feel nothing but the character I represent. To be so intense requires soul. Can this be the same soul that breathes in my poems the very air of Heaven? I have written these wild soul-poems in the stillness of midnight, and when waking to the world next day, they were to me the deepest mystery. I could not understand them; did not know but what I ought

---

[1]   This may be a reference to a particular male actor of the era, J. Nunan.
[2]   Minstrel performances.

to laugh at them; feared to publish them, and often submitted them privately to literary friends to tell me if they could see a meaning in their wild intensity. They were first received by the New-York *Sunday Mercury*, whose literary editor, Mr. R.H. NEWELL, was pleased to term me the greatest and most original poetess of the day. All poems were widely copied, and many translated into the German and French. They are strange and beautiful to me, for as I read them, I do not see in them a part of myself; they do not seem at all familiar to me. And yet I know that the soul that prompted every word and line is somewhere within me, but not to be called at my bidding—only to wait the inspiration of God. And it is this soul that makes me religious, affectionate, and good in many things.

(I have said this much to illustrate, in a poor way, the proof of a *double life*.)

While in Cuba, I pursued diligently my studies, directed personally by my dear mother. My father concentrated all pride of learning in me because he thought I had *genius*—that mysterious something that surmounts all difficulties. I was very fond of study. Grecian mythology and the classics were my passion. At 10 years of age I had read SALLUST twice, CICERO's *Orations* three times, VIRGIL once, and the poetry of MINORA[1] four times, and the *Annals and History of Tacitus*, and four books of ROBINSON's *Selections from the Iliad*. Had written a volume of two hundred pages of Latin Exercises; had studied philosophy and mathematics, French, Spanish, German and Hebrew, and had written verses on the blank leaves of all books and on walls of my bed-room, much to the disgust of my orderly mother. We lived in elegance and affluence. [...]

III.

ADAH was never taught to be a conventional "lady," but was told that to be happy was to be great, and to be great that she must be studious, truthful, and, above all, just herself. Her own individuality was cultivated. She was indulged, and her slightest whims were gratified. Her father, mother, and her uncle (my maternal great-uncle, MICHAEL DE VERE LALIETTE, who would speak no English) all joined in this, and most especially when her inclinations took the form of precocious command. The first gold doubloon she ever possessed was earned by

---

[1] This is probably a reference to a volume of *Carmina Minora* (minor songs) by a classical author such as Virgil or Homer.

her taking her pony over a gate in a very reckless fashion, nearly breaking her neck and the pony's too. But her father and old uncle were loud in their applause, her uncle especially. She was encouraged to be daring, madcap and domineering. They only laughed when her temper, upon some petty provocation, broke all bounds, and left her storming with passion. This brought great trouble upon her with her youthful companions—the incessant squabbles and difficulties and fights that she was ever in. Her mother, whose health was delicate, left ADAH entirely to her step-father, and they both thought she could not do anything but what was lovely and right. Her mother always believed ADAH to be beautiful and perfect in all things. [...]

ADAH's step-father (a true and loving father in all to her) died in New-Orleans. He had been extravagant, and his creditors managed to consume his entire effects. Her mother and the younger children (two) left ADAH in the care of the old, faithful housekeeper, and went to New-Orleans. The dear mother was not a business woman, and nearly everything was swept away.

IV.

ADAH became tired of waiting in suspense alone in a large house, and begged to be sent to New-Orleans, which the servants refused to do. The old idea of running away presented itself. But the old Spanish servants were very watchful. Some disguise must be resorted to. A visit to the city, and all was well. Dressed as a smart boy, hair cut short, jacket, trousers and cap, she left the homestead. Wandered about the streets in Havana, smoking cigarettes and seeing life, until nightfall, when going into a lodging-house for a bed she met her mother's coachmen, LORENZO, a negro, who at once recognized his mistress, who, of course, desired her to return home; she did not wish to do so, and requested LORENZO to be silent. For the good of his mistress he threatened exposure if she did not immediately return home. ADAH then attempted to horsewhip him into silence, which attempt created some excitement as LORENZO was not accustomed to this sort of proceeding. There was a general row, which ended in Miss ADAH's finding herself in the hands of the Police. She was taken before the Captain-General, who, ascertaining the particulars of her family, sent her home.

Her mother returned and removed her house-hold furniture, servants, &c., to New-Orleans. The family by degrees became very poor. ADAH became thoughtful and set about her life-work. Her entire character seemed to change from the wild, untameable child to the earnest, working woman. Her only brother was 10 years of age. She went from place to place until she procured for him a situation as carrier in the printing-office of the *Enquirer*. D.O. DORLEY and Mr. McMAHON were the editors and proprietors. They were much struck with the energy and earnestness of the beautiful girl, who, be it remembered, was but 12 years of age, and spoke fluently French, Spanish and English, and read Latin, Greek and Hebrew. She must have been indeed beautiful, too, for from a picture now before the writer of these pages, she appears an ideal of loveliness whose amber-tinted hair reaches far below her waist in rich, wavy masses, like a cloak. The features are classic, the eyes large and dark. Who can doubt that the representatives of the *Daily Enquirer* felt interested in her? The brother was engaged at a liberal salary as carrier. Friendship from this arose between the families of ADAH and the editors. By accident ADAH was present at a theatrical performance at the little Olympic Theatre, at the corner of Baronne and Poydras streets. Silently she watched the performance and silently she resolved her future life. The next day she visited the manager, Mr. J.S. CHARLES, then the most elegant light comedian on the stage, (and then the husband of Mrs. HAMBLIN). Alone she went and asked for an engagement for herself and little sister, at that time but 8 years of age. Mr. CHARLES was amused, talked to the little lady, (who was extremely business-like and dignified in her imagined theatrical ability), and finally promised her $7 per week, and that she should appear in the forthcoming spectacle of the "Forty Thieves."[1] With joy she returned with the prospect to her mother, who was perfectly shocked at the idea of a theatre and would not listen to anything on the subject. ADAH cried a good deal at the disappointment and managed to get out the next day and relate the story to Mr. CHARLES, who then promised to see the mother and talk her over to reason if possible.

After many tears over the downfall of her pride and dignity, the loving mother consented to let her darling go on the stage. "Only for a few weeks, until something better can be done." Mr. CHARLES—the true gentleman and elegant actor—promised the greatest care and $7 per week to our little friend. Sent his own daughter's dresses to be used by DOLORES. Without having a very distinct idea of what she

---

[1] Richard Brinsley Sheridan and George Colman, *The Forty Thieves* (first performed 1806, first published 1808).

was supposed to be doing, or ought to do, she found herself one of the good fairies in the spectacle of the "Forty Thieves,"—which ran three weeks. During this time, ADAH attracted the attention of Mr. P. CLISSEY, the most prominent teacher of dancing in New-Orleans, for she was graceful and beautifully formed. He sought an interview with Madame, and proposed to teach ADAH to dance. The lessons commenced. Soon she was the pride of her polite and elegant tutor. During these lessons, which lasted a year or more, ADAH had left the theatre. Her mother had begun to understand the world better, and followed the art of dressmaking; and her brother still carried papers.

After the long and weary course, which in order to bring the limbs and feet to a proper litheness and grace, is indeed a long, weary course, ADAH was brought out with a grand flourish at the opera house, known as the "Theatre Française de Nouvelle Orleans." She made her first appearance in the difficult role of *Helena* in "Robert le Diable."[1] She received $20 per night.

The opera ran four weeks. The success of our young *débutante* was wonderful. Flowers and jewels were showered at her feet by the ardent young Frenchmen. At the age of 14 Dolores was very beautiful. A lithograph made of her the second week after her *début* is indeed lovely. It represents *Helena* luring *Robert* to his terrible doom.

After this piece, ADAH was retained to dance in other operas, and remained the pet of the Crescent City. The Montplaisir troupe came, and ADAH joined them and went to the Tacon Theatre in Havana. There she attracted great attention. This is the most beautiful theatre in the world, and the loveliest women are to be seen there smoking cigarettes between the acts, which, in the dim twilight of the auditorium, look like so many fire-flies. When the prompter's bell is heard all cigarettes are discarded. The women carried their cigarettes and matches in the braids of their hair, put in *ad lib*. Voluminous braids were then in vogue. The men always make their cigarettes as they use them, one at a time. They carry cut tobacco in one vest pocket, and bits of paper in the other. Among the boxes fitted up and used by the nobility, none is half so magnificent as that appropriated to the Captain-General of the island. Sofas covered with pale blue satin, starred with gold; carpets of velvet, curtains of lace and brocade, the walls entirely covered with mirrors; add to this the most voluptuous perfumes, tables

---

[1] A lavish romantic opera written by Giacomo Meyerbeer and Eugène Scribe and first produced in Paris in 1831.

adorned with fruit and wine, and you see the Captain-General's box. He visited the theatre nearly every evening. On one occasion he stopped to dine with some friends and forgot the theatre—of course the curtain could not rise until he had arrived. He did not arrive until after 10 o'clock. Strange to say, the audience never once signified their impatience by stamping or calling out, but smoked and chattered away in the most contented manner. The first noise heard was a round of applause to receive the Captain-General. As he entered, cigarettes were put away; the play began. But where was ADAH? Disgusted with waiting on the Captain-General, who she said she did not care a straw for, she had dressed and gone home. This was a terrible offence in Cuba, where the Captain-General is as supreme as an Eastern Sultan.

The curtain had to descend. The Captain-General sent four of his body-guards to summon ADAH to appear at the theatre forthwith. She had gone to bed! Through the persuasions of her mother, who was very much frightened, ADAH got up, rubbed her eyes, lighted a cigarette, and asked the fierce-looking bodyguards if they had brought a carriage. They had not. Then they must procure one. To avoid further trouble, two of them started in search of one. They were gone an hour. Returned a little the worse for bad Spanish wine.

DOLORES, with talking and smoking, and dressing got on the stage about 1 o'clock. She was received as affectionately as ever. The ballet went on. At the conclusion ADAH was called out to explain herself. She did. On the same day, the Captain-General, who was a great beau, had ordered a dozen wine to be sent to DOLORES. She told the audience how the Captain-General had sent her wine, but that it was bad wine, and had made her ill, and that is why she went home, and if the Captain-General had been drinking his own wine (the same that she had received from him) that he would not have got there any sooner than she did.

That was the explanation. The Captain-General was dumb-founded, thunderstruck. He could not get up and leave the theatre. He could not speak; that would make matters worse. He sat back out of sight of the audience, and looked at ADAH. What would his jealous wife say? What would his daughters think? He quietly determined to arrest her in the morning for publicly insulting him; and he did. But his nephew, the Count JUAN CLEMENTA ZENEA,[1] who was desperately in love with ADAH, and only 17 years of age,

---

[1] See Introduction, 18.

determined to save her from his uncle's fury. In the open court he asked her release. ADAH returned to her home with her mother. At night there were a few hisses with the great round of applause at her entrance as the *Sylphide*.[1] During these times ADAH was in the habit of driving in the evening (on the Grand Plaza) in an open two-wheeled carriage, with only the driver in livery. She dressed finely, wore a tiara of diamonds, and long Spanish vail on her head, smoked cigarettes, (as was the custom,) and attracted universal attention. Even the outraged Captain-General could not refrain from touching his chapeau to one so beautiful, and the nephew never failed to throw a costly bouquet in her carriage as it passed him. On the Grand Plaza ADAH was known as the "Queen of the Plaza." The noble young Spaniard could be seen every night in his uncle's box. Rather small, pale, black hair and eyes, and a faint black moustache, exceedingly small hands and feet, dressed in black; silent, and lazy, rolling up his cigarette, thoughtful and *distingue* appeared the first true and ardent lover of our heroine.

His devotion reached her heart; she, too, looked back the loving glance. The bouquets fell at her feet, laden with tender words and passionate verses and beautiful jewels. Soon a rendezvous in the Plaza, at twilight, near the great fountain. The Captain-General heard of his nephew. The mother heard of her daughter. There was a general earthquake. Amid its most terrible shock, ADAH and her young lover fled to ———, and there in honor and reality became the Countess JUAN CLEMENTA ZENEA.

Alas! that young love's dream must die, and that the Captain-General was supreme. They were arrested and brought back. The Count's father was sent for from Spain, and in a court the marriage of these minors was legally dissolved. A handsome fortune was given to ADAH. The matter was the daily subject of every journal in Havana.

They had been three months married when they parted.

3. G. Lippard Barclay, *The Life and Remarkable Career of Adah Isaacs Menken*, 19-30, 36-37, 39.

[Barclay's biography combines an impressive number of different popular genres to tell the story of Menken's life. Life history, romance, Indian captivity narrative, dime novel western,

---

[1]   Filippo Taglioni's celebrated ballet *La Sylphide* (1822).

correspondence, comic sketch, sensation story, travel narrative, gossip, celebrity biography, and other discourses are all deployed to create this heterogeneous text. The selections below emphasize her early life (about which historians know the least) and Barclay's comments on Menken's character.]

It has been the aim of many biographers in writing the life of a woman, who during her "short allotted hours upon this earth," has been an actress, to "fill in" imaginary incidents, both ungentlemanly in the writer, and insulting to the subject of his remarks. "How little one half the world knows what the other half is doing," *and has done.* There are thousands to-day who look upon the theatre with perfect abhorrence imagining that, "behind the scenes, Satan himself is on the rampage." If these persons were allowed the privilege of a peep into the "greenroom" of any first class theatre, what a change would "come o'er their dreams."

Adah Isaacs Menken was born in the town of Milneburg, north of, and within a few miles of New Orleans, Lousiana. It was, at the time of Adah's birth, known as Chartrain, the lake of that name being in the immediate vicinity. Adah was born in the year 1835, June 15th, and was the eldest of three children, there being a boy and another girl. The sister was named Josephine. At the time of Adah's birth, her father, Mr. James McCord, was a merchant of eminent standing. When she was about seven or eight years of age, her father died, and as he, previous to his death, was in very straightened circumstances, the family were left wholly dependent upon themselves to procure a livelihood; this was by no means an easy thing to accomplish. Mr. McCord had been, during his life, an ardent admirer of the art of dancing, and at an early age the sisters had been placed under the instruction of a French master. Mrs. McCord, after the death of her husband, as a last resource applied to the manager of the opera, then in New Orleans, for a position in the ballet for her little girls; they were accepted and immediately entered upon their new life. They became, in a short time, great favorites with the company. The natures of the sisters were entirely different; that of Adah was naturally lively. She was arch and piquant, much better formed than her sister, and upon the stage seemed as if "native and to the manor born." Josephine did not possess the assurance of her sister. She was of a passive nature—shy and retiring. Adah adopted the name of Bertha Theodore for the stage.

During her career as *danseuse*,[1] she mastered the French and Spanish languages. When about thirteen years of age she devoted considerable time to the translation of "Homer's Illiad," and as remarkable as it may appear, completed her arduous undertaking with triumph. About this time Adah played a very successful engagement as *danseuse* at the Tacon theatre, Havana. She became an immense favorite, and was called by the *habitues*, "Queen of the Plaza." After this she visited Texas and Mexico, and played an engagement at the leading opera house in Mexico, which was a success both pecuniarily and artistically. She then proceeded to Port Lavaca, Texas, and here met with an adventure very stirring in nature, and which nearly deprived the theatrical world of its "Mazeppa." A hunting expedition was proposed, and Adah, with her customary fearlessness, readily consented to accompany the party.

The following is her version of the adventure: "Having got every thing in readiness, and the morning beautifully serene, we started on the hunt. I rode a splendid horse belonging to Captain P. Gonzalez, who kindly loaned it to me. Both the horse and myself were in excellent spirits, as indeed was the whole party, with one exception. A man named Gus Varney accompanied our party, and a more inveterate coward I have never seen. It appears that he had been induced through a wager to join us, the betting party asserting that Varney was afraid to do so. We had scarcely proceeded fifteen miles when this Varney commenced to show evident signs of his noted cowardice, hinting as to the probability of Indians being in the vicinity. Several ladies became greatly alarmed at his suggestions, and I confess that I did not feel quite assured that such was not the case. The men attempted to make sport of Varney's fears, but his cowardice was greatly predominant over his sense of shame, and consequently had not the desired effect. A young man in the party, a practical joker of the worse kind, proposed to his companions to raise a cry of 'Indians are coming,' to frighten Varney, and then ridicule him, and try to convince him that his fears were groundless. Having communicated their plan to us, we consented to act our parts well by screaming and pretending to be greatly alarmed. At a given signal our joker cried: 'Run for your lives, the Indians are coming.' I was about to do as directed, when a sight that I never shall forget was presented me. There over the hill were plainly visible, not mere spectres, but solid and matter of fact bodies; a large number of

---

[1]   Dancer (French, feminine).

Indians. I am not naturally a coward, but the sight of those savages sent a cold chill through me, whilst a perspiration came over me, outwardly; I lost my balance at the same time, my consciousness left me, and I remembered no more until I awoke within a wigwam, with a dusky 'son of the feather' gazing intently upon me.

"'Pretty squaw—make me—good—like to much?' murmured the Indian in broken sentences.

"All the heroines that I had ever read about, upon awakening from unconsciousness, repeated the well-known 'where am I,' consequently I said the same thing. His reply was as follows:—

"'Big woods—my wigwam; you mine now—me big chief.'

"'Was any of my friends captured?' I asked.

"'Little Mole, he big coward, no fight.'

"I understood from this that Varney had been caught as well as myself, and that had I at the time been perfectly conscious, I would have escaped with the rest of the party, as we were all well mounted, and the Indians being afoot, pursuit on their part would have been fruitless.

"'Want see little Mole?' asked my captor.

"At first I was disgusted at the idea, but having thought that Varney might possess a knowledge which would assist us in our escape, I consented to see him.

"The Indian gave a peculiar signal, which was immediately answered in person by a young Indian girl. In appearance she did not possess any refined beauty, but there was something that drew me toward her; there was certainly something grand about her, as with stately step she answered the Indian's summons.

"'Why am I called?' asked she.

"'Laulerack is more proud than ever,' said the Indian. 'Bring hither the white man;' he spoke the Spanish language this time. She glanced toward me with a look of pity, I thought, and then, as if the act was a condescension on her part, obeyed the Indian's command.

"'Is the maiden your wife?' I asked in Spanish. The Indian started as if some immortal power had addressed him, as I heretofore had only spoken English to him.

"'No,' answered he bitterly; 'as each moon passes she grows more proud than ever, and although I am determined that she shall be so, she is if possible more determined not to wed me.'

"'If you would wed her, why do you wish that I too should be your wife.'

"'The white beauty in summer, the red beauty in winter,' replied he.

"I saw that it were useless to try to divert his mind from having two wives at once. As the Indian did not seem inclined to converse further, I sat meditating upon the possibility of my escape, when Varney entered. Here was a caricature, if J.S. Clarke[1] had been there at the time he would have learned that his low comedy motions were not perfection. His eyes reminded me of a case of 'stage fright' I had once seen. His body was doubled up like Quilp's[2] in one of Dickens' novels. He possessed great facial expression, and at the time it was suggestive of Clarke's 'Bob Acres duel scene in the Rivals,' whilst his legs would put to shame that comedian's 'bend' in Toodles. In spite of my position I laughed heartily, and even on the Indian's face there lingered a smile, mingled with contempt for the cowardly being before him.

"'Oh, Miss Theodore,' cried Varney, in piteous accents, 'we're gone up, as good as dead and buried. I shall be burned at the stake, I know I shall. Even the little devils and their inhuman mothers delight in torturing me. They hunt for pins in my coat, and then when the barbarians find them, they stick me most unmercifully.' The last five words were uttered with groans, and rolling eyes like a calf about to be slaughtered.

"I perceived that it were useless to attempt to concoct a plan, and expect any assistance from Varney in regard to what means we should adopt to escape. My thoughts naturally turned toward the plausiblility of asking the assistance of the Indian maiden. I resolved that it should be so, as this was my last and only hope.

"'Oh, Miss Theodore,' said Varney, 'if there be any chance of getting away, name it. I'll do any thing but fight these darned heathens.' This was all spoken in a whisper, with timid glances toward our guard, who stood with the natural stoicism of his race, saying nothing, but endeavoring to catch each word. 'Think of some means whereby *I* can escape,' added Varney, 'and then if I get to Lavaca,[3] I'll send out armed men to rescue you.'

"The natural selfish nature of the man was predominant, and I

---

1   John Sleeper Clarke (1833-99), actor best known for his physical humor and eccentric comic roles such as Timothy Toodle in William E. Burton's *The Toodles* (1840) and Bob Acres in Richard Brinsley Sheridan's *The Rivals* (1775).

2   Daniel Quilp is an evil dwarf in Charles Dickens's *The Old Curiosity Shop* (1840-41).

3   Port Lavaca, Texas, on the gulf coast, southeast of San Antonio and southwest of Houston.

made up my mind that before I would assist, in any way, a being so incapable to all the true requisite feelings of a man, I would rather remain in captivity. I did not speak my mind to Varney, but at the time felt very much like doing so. Varney, finding me in no mood to converse with him, retired. And I shortly afterwards expressed a desire to speak with Laulerack, which my dusky captor consented to comply with. She entered, and at the same time the Indian, understanding that we would be alone, stationed himself outside of the wigwam.

"'What does my pale sister wish,' asked Laulerack, in a much more pleasant voice than she had used in addressing her Indian admirer.

"'Thy sister's name is Bertha,' said I in Spanish, 'and although I have seen you but once before, I already love you.'

"'My white sister has my pity.'

"'And pity in a woman,' I quickly added, 'amounts to, or soon turns to love.'

"'My sister is right,' Laulerack answered, 'and my pity has thus soon become a love.'

"'Thanks, thanks,' I muttered.

"'No thanks to me, but to the *Great Spirit who has willed it so.*'

"'Yes, but if my sister had not a pure and loving nature, belonging more to the other world than this, the Great Spirit would not influence her to love her pale face sister, or be instrumental in causing her to harbor within her heart, a feeling of pity for the maiden torn from her friends and home, to be held captive in a wilderness, where each visible thing strikes terror, as the thrust of an enemy's bayonet does to the fallen and wounded warrior.'

"'The Great Spirit,' said Laulerack, 'has given thee the power of speaking in winning speech, and thy words have much import to the red maiden.'

"I perceived the advantage gained, and immediately followed it up. 'Then will you not, my sister, help me in my escape? Think of what I suffer in thus being retained. My friends perhaps mourn me as dead.' Laulerack's eyes shone with unusual brilliance, as she made answer and said:

"'What are the pale sister's sufferings, when compared with mine? As the child's troubles are to those of their parents. Listen, and you shall hear my story. As thirteen moons are counted the year, so have four times that many moons passed since I have lost a father's protection, a mother's care. My father was then the chief of a powerful tribe; one cursed day he was prevailed upon to go to battle with another tribe equally as powerful. My father's tribe was victorious, and many captives were taken. A guard was appointed to watch, but being so worn out, and moreover thinking of the glory they had but just achieved, they fell to dreaming. In the meantime, the enemy, although fairly beaten, were not entirely subdued, and their chief warrior, a man of wise thought, resolved upon an attack, well knowing the condition of his opponents. His tribe were also much worn out, but stimulated by the hopes of regaining their lost honors, gladly consented to assist and stand by their leader. The canopy of darkness was chosen as the time of attack. In the stillness of night they moved on, and can you guess? Were successful. My father did all in his power to repulse the enemy, but they were completely mastered. An horrible massacre followed; my father was scalped upon the spot, and my mother tomahawked. Such a fate would surely have been mine, but for the young warrior who stands outside of the wigwam, Eagle Eye by name. He saw me, and claimed me as his captive, brought me to his tribe, wished to wed me, but I have resisted his attempts, and as I have since become a favorite with the other warriors, he dare not force me. But if I had a home elsewhere not one moon would see me here.'

"I was touched by the plaintive manner in which the Indian maiden told her story, and said to her, 'If we could but escape together, you should always be my dear sister, and share with me my home.'

"'We can but try,' said she. 'With the darkness to-night, we will wend our way towards your home, and ere the moon rises shall be far on the wilderness' winding path.' Bidding me prepare, she quitted the wigwam, having first placed her finger upon her lips as a warning to act silently. Night came at last, but oh, how long seemed the time. Although but a few hours, it seemed as if days had passed. I could feel my heart beat as a footstep sounded near the wigwam. It was now nearer than ever. I was sure it was she, and with a bound I sprang to meet her. A cold chill came over me as I beheld not Laulerack but my captor, Eagle Eye.

"'The pale face maiden seems anxious to meet me,' said he.

"'I thought it was Laulerack come to converse with me, as I am so lonely.'

"'Eagle Eye would gladly stay with you,' the Indian answered.

"'I love Laulerack and have not yet learned to love you.' I said this in order to get rid of him.

"'Does the pale face maiden wish for any thing?' asked he.

"'Nothing.'

"He then, with a smile, which he intended for a loving one, but which in my eyes appeared hideous, left the wigwam. A long time elapsed ere Laulerack made her appearance, and I had almost given up all hopes of escape, for that night at least, when chancing to look up I was startled, for there directly in front of me stood Laulerack.

"'Listen. I have kept my word; follow me quickly but quietly,' was all she said, and I followed her out into the open air. I felt as if I were free indeed, and with joyous feelings went with the bounding step usual to one who has realized their greatest vision of success. But oh, how little we know what one short hour may bring forth. We had proceeded quite a distance when sounds of pursuit followed us.

"'Keep behind me and run,' said Laulerack.

"I did as directed, but found myself scarcely equal to keep up to the Indian maiden, who ran more like a deer than a human being. I was consequently far behind, when she stumbled over a stone, directly before her. As I came up I was about to stoop and assist her to her feet, but she said:

"'Do not stop for me, but run for your life.' She was not so badly hurt as I supposed, and presently came within hailing distance.

"'On, on,' she cried, and I with a dreadful pain in my side endeavored to quicken my pace, but found it impossible to scarcely run at all. By this time we could hear guns firing, and I, expecting to be shot down, expressed my fears to Laulerack, who only laughed, as she said, between breath:

"'They would not fire *at* us, but up in the air. It is merely to intimidate us.'

"Explicitly believing all she said I ran for dear life. Laulerack, owing to a sprain received in falling, was unable to catch up to me, and remained quite a distance behind. I know not how long we had been running, when we suddenly came in view of an encampment, and had scarcely come near enough to distinguish if it were our friends, when a voice shouted, 'The Indians! They come!' and then dashed towards the encampment. The alarm was echoed as if by a hundred voices. I knew that these were white men, and shouted, 'A white maiden seek your protection,' but had scarcely got one word out when a volley of musket shots were fired in our path, and Laulerack, who had by this time got in front of me, was shot, and I at the time thought fatally. I really believe that had I been foremost that I would have received the shot. Laulerack, in a faint voice, called out to me to drop, which I did accordingly. The Rangers, (for such they afterwards proved to be,) finding all quiet advanced cautiously, and speaking in a loud, clear voice, I said, 'There are no enemies, but a white woman, and an Indian maiden, whom I fear you have killed.'

"'Wall now I am gollderned if I wouldent 'eve sworn as how there was Ingins in ambush,' said a rough voice, and presently he was joined by others, who came towards us, and lifting Laulerack carefully from the ground, carried her to the encampment.

"'How did this 'ere happen,' said one who seemed to be leader.

"'There is no time for explanation now, the enemy are in pursuit.'

"'Wall I guess as how we'll revarse the action and make ourselves in pursuit of the derned red skins,' said the same man who had spoken before.

"'Their village is but a short distance from here, and they hold a white man prisoner, who will soon be burned at the stake,' I said, forgetting that Varney did not deserve the blood that might be spilled by these brave men.

"'By the living Austin,' said the leader, 'he shall be rescued, or not a man of us will go home to tell of the failure. Ain't I right, boys?'

"'In course you is,' answered the men.

"'Here, Bill Johnson, Ike Winsor, and Guy Gillingham, you remain and perteckt the wimmen.'

"'If you please, I'd rather go and fight the Ingins,' said the last named individual.

"'So would I,' said each of the others.

"'Well, dern it, you've got to be martyrs this ere time.'

"All being ready to follow their leader they immediately set out to meet the Indians.

"'My white sister,' said Laulerack, 'my life is fast ebbing away.'

"'Say not so,' I muttered. 'You will get well and then we will never leave each other.'

"'No! It cannot be so, the Great Spirit has willed it otherwise.'

"'And this was all my fault, had I not asked you to endanger your life by assisting me to escape, all would have been well.'

"'No! No! fair maiden, it was no fault of yours, for I, may the Great Spirit forgive, had resolved to take my own life. But I will soon be with my father and mother in the great Hunting Ground, far, far beyond. Farewell, sister. May the Great Spirit watch over and protect you.'

"'Oh, you cannot, must not die,' I cried, for I had learned to love this red maiden. The three men left to protect us from danger, now came near, and bending down, raised their hats, and looking up to heaven I said—'To thee we consign her soul,' and the men in solemn voices repeated it after me. Here was a living picture, true to the nature and yet more vivid than the imagination could conceive and paint upon canvas. Three stalwart sons of the forest kneeling with hats in hand, and uplifted faces. I sat motionless as a statue, but tears were coursing down my cheek; within the circle lay the now inanimate body of Laulerack. The moon shone through the trees, and God seemed to say: 'I have only taken her from earth—She is not dead.'

"I know not how long we sat thus, and probably it would have been much longer had we not been startled by the sound of many voices, which told us that our friends had returned.

"'Heigho, Gilly, what's the matter?' said the one whom I have mentioned as the leader.

"'Sam, less noise' said Gillingham, 'the Indian maiden has been shot as you know, and you also know in mistake, but the murder lies between us. I hope to God it was no bullet from my musket that did the deed, and may God have mercy on the man who fired the shot that killed her.' 'Amen,' responded the men, as each and every one uncovered his head and looked up towards heaven.

"After my grief had somewhat subsided, I listened to the plan of the attack, and capture of some four or five Indians, and rescue of Varney, whom I saw conversing with the rangers, relating his wonderful experience. Having discovered me in conversation with the leader, he came forward and expressed his immense gratification at seeing me safe and sound. Amongst the captives was 'Eagle Eye,' who was deeply affected at the death of Laulerack, and upon hearing Varney, came toward me, and in Spanish said:

"'White man lie. Says he is glad to see you. He it was who gave the alarm when you escaped, in hopes of gaining his own liberty.'

"I did not dare to translate this to the rangers, who seemed anxious that I should do so, as I knew their tempers were of a violent nature, and that Varney would swing for it. After a weary march of many miles we arrived at Austin, where I was kindly taken care of by General Harney, who was stationed there for three months."

Here ends her story, as given to my friend Mr. Wm. Wallis[1] of the Arch Street Theatre, whilst he was on a visit to Paris. To him I am also indebted for many incidents occurring during her sojourn in

---

[1] William H. Wallis, a London-born actor who became a noted performer in Philadelphia, including work at the Arch Street Theatre.

Paris, of these, anon.

Adah soon left Austin, and returned to New Orleans, determined to give up the stage, and turn her attention to Literature. She commenced by studying assiduously the German language, and reading the Classic Authors.

One day she conceived the idea of collecting some of her poetic writings, and publishing them. She carried out her plans to perfection, and shortly afterwards they appeared in one volume, under the title of "Memories."[1] These Poems gained for her considerable popularity throughout the South. [...]

Adah Isaacs Menken was not a perfect woman; far from it; but where can you direct me to one that is. To me such a woman would indeed be a curiosity, and yet the press of this country have vied with each other in seeking after all her little faults, and converting them into errors of the greatest magnitude. During her life she was continually the object of articles appearing in the different New York journals, "bearing slander written in each and every line." What did these writers know of her? Ah! they have a great deal to answer for. One to my certain knowledge has gone to "that immortal bourne." May God have mercy on his soul, for any man that will relentlessly slander a woman, upon no other authority than empty rumor, has certainly no place among honest men, either in this world or the one to come. That she had faults, and many, perhaps, I will not dispute. Who has not? [...]

The friends and personal acquaintances of Adah Menken, are well aware of the falsity of the many indiscretions attributed to her. She was kind to a fault, but her biographers never classified this as among the rest. Churches or hospitals might have profited in the disposal of her estate, had not her heart told her that to give to those at the time of need, was a greater blessing, than leaving her money to public institutions after her death, and thereby having it recorded in the columns of the newspapers throughout the world that, Adah Isaacs Menken, the actress, had bequeathed to this institution, so many thousand dollars, and to that one, so much. She assisted many a poor and needy sister and brother professional, who sought her aid, either in this country, or Europe. She was a lady of great intellectual endowments, and high literary attainments. Her prose and poetry were alike redolent of bright and beautiful thoughts. She also

---

[1]   No copy of this volume of poems has ever been located, and most Menken biographers doubt its existence.

possessed a keen sense of the ridiculous, and would often copy down laughable incidents occurring under her observation! [...]

Adah Menken was as gentle a woman as ever lived, and, as "old mother Stanton" remarked in a number of the Revolution, of which she is editress, "she *might* have been an honor to her sex."[1] Let me ask, is "mother Stanton" an honor to her sex? If so in what way? Adah Menken was the constant recipient of notes begging an interview. But listen and mark my words—"*She kept virtuous.*" [...]

4. Ed James, *Biography of Adah Isaacs Menken*, 3–12.

[Ed James was Menken's close friend, and this biography benefits from his intimate knowledge of her. His story emphasizes her courage as a performer, her generosity while a celebrity, and her poverty at death.]

Early Life.

Over thirteen years have passed since poor Menken died—died penniless in an ill-furnished room in a by-street in Paris. Letters by the score and items by the hundred have been kept floating around, ever and anon, some writer bringing new and startling facts (?) to light. We have been frequently personally assailed by correspondents of American journalists residing abroad. Some of the writers doing so maliciously, knowing their statements to be untrue; others unacquainted with the circumstances have but added to the thousand and one stories in circulation.

Menken was not born a Jewess, and there was nothing about her features except, perhaps, her large lustrous eyes to lead any one to suppose so. Her real name was Adelaide McCord, and she was born at Milneburg, near New Orleans, on June 15, 1835. She had one sister named Josephine, also a brother, who worked at the case as a compositor in Cincinnati. Their father died in 1842, and her mother subsequently married Dr. J.C. Campbell, an army surgeon connected with the barracks at Baton Rouge, Louisiana. Upon the death of the stepfather, in 1855, necessity drove the two sisters, Adelaide and Josephine, to adopt the stage, and they appeared conjointly at the French Opera-

---

[1]   See Elizabeth Cady Stanton, "Adah Isaacs Menken," in Appendix C.

house, New Orleans, as dancers. In this capacity they filled numerous engagements in Texas, Cuba, Mexico and elsewhere. Menken becoming ambitious, however, studied in her leisure hours for a tragedienne, and as such made her first appearance at the Varieties Theatre in New Orleans, as "Bianca," in *Fazio*,[1] in the spring of 1858, afterward making a tour of the South and South-west. While engaged as leading lady for Manager Crisp,[2] of Memphis and Nashville, she became enamored of Mr. Menken, an Israelite. She was married to that gentleman under the name of Adah Bertha Theodore in 1859, and his full name she informed us was Alexander Isaacs Menken, which, with a slight alteration, retaining the initials, she adopted as her stage name and retained it till death. Adah was divorced from Menken in Nashville, but Mr. M. still lives and is a wealthy merchant. She and the late John C. Heenan, the celebrated pugilist, and as handsome a looking man as she was a woman, were brought together by chance, and so fond was she of the "Boy," as Heenan was called, being about her own age, over six feet high, and built in proportion, as to induce him to marry her, the ceremony taking place at a New York road-house known as Rock Cottage, kept by a well known sporting character named Jim Hughes, by the Rev. J. S. Baldwin, on April 3, 1859, and Jack Herman, the Ethiopian Minstrel, informed us that he was witness to the papers. She was as fond of Heenan as was possible, and bore him a male child. Shortly afterward they quarreled, Heenan left her, she was taken sick, and but for one solitary friend still living might have followed her child to the grave. About this time news reached Adah that her mother, too, had passed away, and for some months in her little room on Third Avenue she lay almost at death's door. Being very courageous, however, she pulled through. It was with emotion of the keenest pleasure that she ever afterward spoke of her solitary, disinterested friend, which, lest it may be supposed refers to the writer, we will state was not.

The First Live Mazeppa.

When the late J.B. Smith,[3] the speculative bill-poster, had the

---

[1] Henry Hart Milman, *Fazio* (1815).
[2] William H. Crisp, manager of the Gaiety Theatre in New Orleans and an important figure in mid-nineteenth-century theatre in the South.
[3] Captain John B. Smith of the Green Street Theatre in Albany, New York. According to his own account (*Albany Mirror* [25 Oct. 1879]), Smith—not Menken—proposed that she play Mazeppa.

Albany (N.Y.) Theatre, Menken came along for an engagement, and there being big opposition at a rival house, she and Smith put their heads together to at least get a fair share of the people's coin. Menken proposed playing Mazeppa, and instead of a dummy being used to go up on the runs, as previously by every male impersonator, offered to be lashed to the horse's back and take chances of saving the house from loss or breaking her own neck. Smith looking into her expressive face, with gratitude, said, "No, no, Adah, it is too dangerous." "I'll take all chances, so have my horse ready for rehearsal this very morning!" Her orders were obeyed, and with trembling hands the attaches fastened her on the horse, which had been used to starting off at full speed with the dummy, but not with a living Mazeppa, and was therefore sent up slowly. The horse and its beautiful rider had nearly reached the top, when some noise startled the animal, and missing his footing both came down with a crash to the ground. The people in attendance rushed to the scene, expecting to see both killed outright, but, marvelous to relate, the horse was scarcely injured, while the daring equestrienne came off with a few slight cuts and bruises. Manager Smith ordered a carriage to take her to the hotel, and was thunderstruck when she said, "I will ride up those runs before I leave this theatre!" Every effort to dissuade her failed, she insisted upon again being lashed to the animal's back, and gave the word when to start him, and the well-trained steed dashed up the frail structure at his usual gait and reached the top platform in safety, as well as coming down therefrom to the stage again. "Now," said Adah, "have everything ready to-night and I will be on hand." The announcement of the daring undertaking, and news of the accident, secured a packed house the first and every succeeding night, while the opposition was left almost in the cold. Menken's nerve astonished the nerviest, and she was received with the wildest enthusiasm. She attributed her safety in after life during these risky performances to a little charm worn round her neck, and that charm afterwards came into our possession.

Remarkable Success in American Cities.

The first really brilliant or sensational move made was fulfilling a successful engagement at the old Bowery Theatre, New York, under the name of Mrs. John C. Heenan, during the great excitement here over the International prize fight between Heenan and Tom Sayers.[1] A son of the latter is now in this country singing serio-comic songs. Heenan felt annoyed, but could not prevent her using his name.

She subsequently traveled over the country as Mrs. John C. Heenan, and during the war frequently got in hot water by express-ing herself a little too freely as a Secessionist. She was very fond of decorating her rooms with Confederate flags everywhere she went. While playing in Baltimore, then under military rule, she was arrested and placed under guard during the reign of Provost-Marshall Fish,[2] but was treated with great consideration on account of her manifold charms of manner and person.

During Heenan's absence in England she obtained a divorce from him in order to marry a distinguished New York journalist, with whom (her third husband) she sailed for California in 1863. In her union with Mr. Newell it was stipulated that Adah should give up the stage forever. Such tempting offers, however, were made for her to break this resolution that, womanlike, she changed her mind, and signed a contract with Tom Maguire to appear sixty nights in San Francisco and Sacramento at $500 a performance. *Mazeppa* and the *French Spy* set the miners and sporting men wild.

Unprecedented Triumphs In England.

During the years 1861 and 1862 the writer made a pleasure tour of Europe, and, as a friend of the poet-actress, lost no opportunity towards paving the way for her proposed transatlantic professional trip. The first newspaper engraving of Adah appeared in the *Illustrated Sporting and Dramatic News*, which journal we contributed to both in London and afterwards as special American correspondent; occasionally writing for the London *Era*, the *European News*, Dublin *Freeman's Journal*, etc., so that when she did appear in London, on October 3, 1864, it was not surprising to find her about the best known lady in the city. It happened our lot to be there then also as the *New York Clipper* special reporter for the Coburn-Mace match, fixed for the same month and

---

[1]   English heavyweight boxing champion.
[2]   While this might be A.M. Fish of Michigan, who eventually became a brigadier-general in the Union army, Fish is not mentioned in the standard reference books on the U.S. Civil War.

year, when it was necessary to have representatives at the Court of St. James,[1] for the Atlantic Cable[2] was not perfected, or rather had broken and been left to amuse the inhabitants of the vasty deep, until our "cruel war" was over.

Adah had started from California with "Orpheus C. Kerr,"[3] her husband, in the Spring of 1864, but her *companion de voyage* from the Isthmus to Liverpool, England, was James Barkley, the first named party having returned to New York. Her Californian engagements netted her over $30,000, and Barkley having lots of cash, they took up their quarters at the Westminster Palace Hotel, London, then the *bon ton* house of the metropolis of the world, and gave breakfasts, dinners, and reunions there that would break a Belmont's heart or purse, or in fact almost any one else but Menken's, if continued long. She never really valued money, and in spite of our efforts to induce her to make some provision for a rainy day, she laughing put it off with, "Ed., when I get so that I have to *borrow* money I want to die." At the Westminster we frequently met such men as Charles Dickens, Charles Reade, Watts Phillips, the Duke of Edinburgh, Charles Fechter, the Duke of Hamilton, John Oxenford, Algernon Swinburne, Prince Baerto, Wm. J. Thompson, Howard Paul, Captain Webster, Thomas Purnell, the Duke of Wellington, Geo. H. Parker, Frank L. Downing, Henry Moir Feist, George Maddick, Fred. Ledger, Lieutenant Wylde Hardynge and his wife, Belle Boyd (the Confederate Spy), together with Mad. George Sand, Jenny Lind (Mrs. Goldschmidt), and many others of note whom we can not at present call to mind.[4]

She had her team, with liveried coachman and footman, and a horse's head surmounting four aces for a crest, while, when she drove out in her brougham, little silver bells announced the approach of the Royal Bengal Tiger, as she humorously called herself. Of course she had imitators, one of which with the grandiloquent assumed name of Adah Inez Montclain was a regular New York guy, but the "London Adah Isaacs" traveled pretty successfully on her name, principally in music halls.

Menken had previously been well advertised in London, her

---

1 The name of the English court, a metonym for England.
2 The first trans-Atlantic telegraph message was sent in 1858, but the cable failed. New cables weren't laid until 1865 and 1866.
3 The pen name of Robert Henry Newell (1836-1901), Menken's husband at the time.
4 This long list of celebrities includes writers, critics, actors and performers, aristocrats, famous military figures, and politicians.

portraits published and photographs meeting with a ready sale. She, therefore, soon became a lion. Some of the papers spoke kindly of her; others heaped up abuse, particularly the London *Orchestra*. That journal said her performance had been vile, little less than a model artiste exhibition, etc., and wound up by suggesting the authorities prohibit her playing in *Mazeppa*. Menken replied to this by asking that journal and the public to at least withhold their abuse until she had given them cause, as an act of courtesy due to a stranger. She assured them that her performance was as decent as *Ixion*,[1] *La Sylphide* and other undressed burlesques going on at the time in that very city. The excitement was kept up through the press, and Menken's *suite* made a grand splurge at the Westminster Palace Hotel, adjacent to the House of Parliament, Westminster Abbey and the Queen's Palaces.

October 3, '64, was the opening night at Astley's, and the ferment was at its highest. Rumors were current that John C. Heenan, then in England, was opposed to Menken, and that his hirelings might make trouble at the theatre, which only served to more excite the cockneys, usually rather phlegmatic. To say that this engagement was a success is very tame. So great was the rush that Manager E. T. Smith (at one time a Special Constable in London, when Napoleon III. was also a Constable) made new arrangements for Menken to appear twice a day.

Lucy Rushton, afterward lessee of what is now known as Harrigan and Hart's, 728 and 730 Broadway, played "Orlinska" to Menken's "Mazeppa," and her straining for effects as a rival were quite amusing to the critics, and those better acquainted with both ladies. Miss Rushton's success in this country was not equal to Menken's in England.

From London Menken visited the Provinces with great success. In the winter of '65 the late John Brougham's piece, *The Child of the Sun*,[2] was produced by her in England, but met with a signal failure—whether the fault of the play or the player does not transpire.

Adah revisited this city in the fall of 1865 for the purpose of procuring a divorce from R.H. Newell, to whom she was married in 1863, in company with an English lady, whom her fondness for titles caused her to designate as Lady Stewart, substituting Lady for Mrs. But upon

---

[1] F.C. Burnand's musical burlesque, *Ixion, or The Man at the Wheel* (1863).

[2] John Brougham (1810–80), an Irish-born actor and theatre manager, wrote over 126 plays, including *The Child of the Sun* (1865), in which Menken played four different characters.

procuring the divorce in Allen Co., Ind., in October, her stay here was very brief, as she longed for aristocratic London and gay Paris, finding New York too dirty and democratic to suit her changed notions.

Returning to England she fulfilled a few engagements there, but her restless disposition and desire to see Captain Barkley once more led her to retrace her steps to her native land, which she did in March of 1866, accompanied by Miss Susette Ellington.[1] The Menken appeared at what was originally opened as Brougham's Lyceum, in Broadway, near Broome street, which was then run by George Wood as the Broadway Theatre, playing in April and May, and afterwards making a tour of the West and South, none of which were particularly successful. About this time she induced the writer to collect all her poems together which he could, for publication in England, but "Infelicia" was not produced until after her death, and therefore neither Menken nor any one else so entitled but the booksellers realized a nickle out of the same. It is almost needless to say that "Infelicia" went through numerous editions, and was reprinted in this country.

While residing in New York, at the brown-stone mansion on Seventh avenue, the upper house of the only two on that block, between Thirty-eighth and Thirty-ninth streets, west side, which called "Bleak House," in honor of her friend and admirer Charles Dickens, she was married to James Barkley, of California. "Bleak House" was presented to Menken by her last husband, but through some misunderstanding between them she sought consolation in foreign lands. She was so ill from an overdose of poison, whether taken to sooth her nerves or for self-destruction was never perfectly ascertained, we had to carry her from the tender to her stateroom on board the Cunard steamer Java, on August 22, 1866, and the last we saw of this strange genius was when she could recognize nobody. Soon afterwards "Bleak House" was sold. Barkley eventually returned to California, where he died about the year 1878.

Brilliant Successes in Paris and Vienna.

Adah's first great engagement in Paris, at the Theatre de la Gaietie, in *Les Pirates de la Savane*,[2] commenced on Sunday night, December 30,

---

[1] Menken's secretary.

[2] A thrilling melodrama by Anicet Bourgeois and Ferdinand Dugué and re-written in 1866 specifically for Menken.

1866, upon which occasion the Princes Jerome and Lucian,[1] with their suites, were present. She was called before the curtain nine times her first night. The receipts of the first eight nights were 346,000f. She continued to play at the same theatre for one hundred nights, to immense houses, and upon the hundredth and last night Napoleon III, the Prince Imperial, King of Greece and Duke of Edinburgh graced the theatre with their presence, and she was the recipient of many costly presents. In June of the following year she went to Vienna and appeared in the same play at the Theater der Wien.

Menken reappeared for the second time at Astley's in October, 1867, and for the third time in January, 1868. Her last appearance was at her own benefit at Sadler's Wells Theatre on May 30, 1868.

Last Illness and Sad End.

Arrangements had been made by Messrs. Dumaine and La Roche to produce *Les Pirates de la Savane* at the Theatre Chatelet, in July, 1868, on the grandest scale ever attempted, with the great American *artiste* as the heroine, and although known to be fast losing her figure and being generally broken down, she started for Paris, in company with George H. Parker, editor of the London *Orchestra* as business manager, and Susette Ellington. The air of the city was too strong, and she was removed to Bougeval, in the South of France, but disease had fastened itself upon her, and she had to take to her bed, dropsy, inflammation of the lungs and a complication of disorders giving fearful warning to her companions that the KING OF TERRORS had decreed that she, the once beautiful, fascinating, talented and generous child of genius, must go.

The engagement was postponed for a month, and, hoping against hope, whenever the managers called they were told that Adah needed no rehearsal, but would do her best to be at the theatre in good season. Being put off every time and unable to see her, Dumaine and La Roche appealed to the law, and finally took with them two *gendarmes* to compel her to go to the last rehearsal. Demanding admittance to her chamber, her maid, opening the door, said, "There she lies—it is too late now." Poor Menken had passed

---

[1] Jerome Patterson Bonaparte (1830-93), who was not a prince but was often called Prince Jerome, and Prince Lucien Murat (1803-78): relatives of Napoleon III, Emperor of France.

away that very day, Aug. 10, 1868, attended to the last by a Jewish Rabbi, and dying with a Hebrew testament under her pillow, which she requested might be given to "her brother Ed.," as she was wont to call us. The terror and horror which overspread the faces of the officers and managers as they beheld the lifeless body of the one they had come to take by force will never be fully realized or forgotten.

The piece was produced with a French actress, Mlle. Sarah Dowe, as the star, but proved a ruinous failure to all concerned. The funeral took place on August 13, the remains being temporarily placed in the strangers' part of the Irsaelitish section of the Cemeterie Pere la Chaise, provision only being made for two years at that, and a rough piece of black wood with her name, etc., on was all any one cared to place to mark the spot. There were but fourteen followers, and not an actress among them—Dumaine, Charles Lemaitre, Pauline Maurier, George Parker, Susette Ellington, and a few others.[1] Her stage horse was led through the streets of the gay Capital to the cemetery gates. We will venture to say that fewer people attended Menken's funeral than had she been some unknown grisette. It was a sad end to so grand a career, the short nine years of her stage life. With the almost fabulous wealth she made and spent or gave away or squandered, Adah Isaacs Menken died penniless. [...]

---

[1]   The brevity of this list and the relative obscurity of the people named stands in stark contrast to the long list of celebrities and statesmen on page 224.

Appendix B: Correspondence

1. "To the Public," 29 Dec. 1860, HTC.

[Although it is not clear if she actually attempted to take her own life, the following is a suicide note Menken wrote in the wake of the public scandal surrounding the break up of her marriage to heavyweight boxing champion John Carmel Heenan.]

To the Public.

I feel called upon to make an explanation of the rash step I have taken in defiance of all law, human or divine, because I know that many things will be said of me, some good and very many bad; and perhaps blame attached to those who are innocent. *God* forgive those who *hate* me, and bless all who have one kind thought left for a poor reckless, *loving* woman, who cast her *soul* out on the broad ocean of a human love, where it was the sport of the happy waves for a few short hours, and then was left to drift helpless against the cold rocks, until she learned to love *death*, better than *life*.

Because I am homeless, poor and friendless, and so *unloved*, I leave this world.

Because I have forgotten to look up to the *God* of my childhood prayers, and ceased to remember the good counsel of my dear old mother—and because one of God's grandest handiworks—one of His glorious creatures lifted up my poor weary soul to see the light of his love, and the greatness of his brave heart, until his sweet words of truth and promise, drank out *all* my life—absorbed all of good and beauty, and left me alone, desolate to *die*. I am not afraid to die. I have suffered so much, that there can not be any more for me.

I go prayerless, therefore *pity* and not condemn me.

My worthless life has long since left me and gone to dwell in the breast of the man, who by foul suspicion of my love and truth for him, has thus ushered me up to the bar of the Almighty, where I shall pray his forgiveness for the cruel wrong he has done the weak and defenseless being whose sin is her love for him, as my death proves. *God bless him*, and pity me.

Adah Isaacs Menken
Jersey City
12 Mo. 29th D.

2. To Thomas Allston Brown, 2 May 1861, HTC.

[In the spring of 1861 Menken was working with Brown as her theatrical agent, and they were collaborating on a biographical sketch for publicity purposes. Brown later incorporated his knowledge of Menken's life into his *History of the American Stage*.]

New York, N.Y.

May 2^d 1861

My dear Colonel:

Do not be electrified with the secrets of the "prison house" enclosed herein. Use what you like of them. I will send you the two notices referred to as soon as I reach Utica, where I have forwarded my trunks with my books &c., to play next week. When you send the sketch of me ask Mr. Queen to give it precedence of some others that he has, and to bring out as early as possible. All contained in the notes is strictly *true*, of course I have left out a great many of my adventures in Cuba and Texas, but as it is I fear you will find more matter than you can work up for a short sketch. However, I have sent you all that can be of any importance, and if you do not use all the items now you may wish to do at some future time. I shall really feel under many obligations to you, my dear Colonel, for this step so greatly calculated to benefit me. I shall not forget it.

With kindest regards, believe me

Yours truly

A. I. M. Heenan

3. To Hattie Tyng, 21 July 1861, from photograph of the manuscript letter in Davis, 162-172.

[In this fan letter to a fellow poet (author of *Apple Blossoms*), Menken makes a passionate, erotic disclosure of her romantic attraction to women. René Sentilles has noted that portions of this letter are plagiarized from Margaret J.M. Sweat's *Ethel's Love-Life* (1859), a novel that candidly depicts Ethel's bisexual orientation and her love for Ernest and Leonora. Menken wrote again in 1862, but Tyng never responded.]

Racine, Wis.

7-Mo 21 D. 1861

Miss Hattie Tynge

Dear Lady:

I feel that in thus obtruding myself upon your notice that none but the most sympathetic nature can pardon the offense, and look kindly upon the humble offender.

Could I believe you narrow and cold in your heart forces, no soul would shrink more closely to its own confines of weeds and shadows than mine. But today, the low murmurings of the white-bannered waves of Lake Michigan tempt me out into the sunshine, and lo! I find myself at your side. Do not ask *why* I am here, or how I have thrown off the habitual coldness and reserve of my surface-character, to meet you thus unhooded and unannounced in the sacred precincts of your own heart-life, for this I can not answer. I only know that for weeks and months I have read, not what you have written for the world, but what an uncontrollable magnetism of affinity told me that you had written for *me*, and that your heart bided some response. I waited and reasoned with this great magnetic influence, talked of the world, or society and its iron laws, tried to put you away among *others*, but you did not heed me, only came back more lovingly and seemed to put your arms around me in my most bitter hours of loneliness, and whisper of patience and peace. This morning the little Jude-faced flowers that hedge my window with their sweetness, seemed to lend their sympathy with me as I read of the lost hope, patience and reward under the "Apple Blossoms" of your heart.

Do you believe in the deepest and tenderest love between women? Do you believe that women often love each other with as much fervor and excitement as they do men? I have loved them so intensile [intensely] that the daily and nightly communion I have held with my beloved ones has not sufficed to slake my thirst for them, nor all the lavishness of their love for me been enough to satisfy the demands of my exacting, jealous nature. I have turned from them unsatisfied, and then in my loneliness I learned to shame myself as a foolish spendthrift of love, until their forgetfulness showed me they were as "cisterns too shallow for the depth of water." Still from out of all disappointments of response, do I believe their [sic] waits in this broad land of ours, hearts full and wide enough to grasp, in their sympathy, and love, a nature as jealous and broad in its demands as mine. We find the rarest and most perfect beauty in the affections of one woman for another. There is a delicacy in its manifestations, generosity in its intuitions, an unveiling of inner life in its intercourse, marked by charming undulations of feeling and expression, not to be met with in the opposite sex. Freed from all the grosser elements of passion, it retains its energy, its abandonment, its flush, its eagerness, its palpitation, and its rapture—but all so refined, so glorified, and made delicious and continuous by an ever-recurring giving and receiving from each to each. The electricity of the one flashes and gleams through the other, to be returned not only in *degree* as between man and women, but in *kind* as between precisely similar organizations. And these passions are of the more frequent ocurrence [*sic*] than the world is aware of—generally they are unknown to all but the hearts concerned, and are jealously guarded by them from intrusive comment. "There is a gloom in deep love as in deep water," and silence and mystery help to guard the sacred spot where we meet alone our best beloved.

I have had my passionate attachments among women, which swept like whirlwinds over me, sometimes, alas! scorching me with a furnace-blast, but generally only changing and renewing my capabilities for love. I would "have drunk their souls as it were a ray from Heaven"—have lost myself and lived in them, but for their non-absorption. I have absorbed them, yet their narrowness of magnetism failed to absorb me. I have yearned to leave off for a little while this burden of individuality which cuts into the very soul of me as a sackcloth grates upon the shrinking flesh. Oh, how I at times wish to lie down and fall asleep in another consciousness, and give my panting, quivering vitality a little rest. But the world so curbs in a woman's inner being to its shadows, that few can be reached at all, and even then it so imperfectly that we must go back to the steeps of our own individuality, disappointed and alone.

We can learn but little of any one from the external life they lead; but we learn much, if even for a moment the veil is lifted which covers and conceals the workings of motives, the springs of feeling, the sources of inspiration and the result to be labored for. I think, dear lady, just in proportion as others impart and we attain a true knowledge of the interior nature which lies behind all their visible life, just so much are they really *ours*. If the capabilities of this understanding be mutual and spontaneous, we see the most holy and beautiful friendships that can exist. Its very rarity makes it seem more lovely. Its superiority to all low obstacles and clogging earthliness, makes us recognize its inherent immortality.

It seems to me, dear friend, that between us two it may exist in perfection, that we can each infuse into the other, in a wonderful degree, those influences which modify or control each of our minds, that we, to an unusual extent, find ourselves swayed by similar emotions at the same moment, that the natural current of our psychological forces flow without effort in the same direction, governed by the same impulses, and responding to the same magnetic vibrations. Write to me a letter full of *yourself*, unveil the inmost heart to me, or do not write at all. I have read your writings until I feel that I know you, if I am mistaken let silence tell me so, do not wake me rudely with coldness. Let me fall back into myself slowly and quietly, to regret that I was ever so rash as to gather up my purposes, and step out into the light of love and sympathy.

In the dumb pages of this poor, vague letter, you have the inner and most sacred folds of my heart. I wanted to give you some excuse f[or] thus lifting to your strange[r] a veil so closely shrouded down to the rest of the world, but I fear that I have failed, and must only wait your gentle answer to the bare, bleeding nerves of a lonely heart.

If you speak to me through your facile and loving pen, do not delay, but write *all* the very hour you are prompted. Direct your letter to the Walker House, Milwaukee, where I shall be next week.

Let us hope that God is near to both of us, and in Him we may be near to each other. To Him I speak of you, unto Him I trust my heart to you, and through Him I bless you.

Yours faithfully,
A. I. Menken

Miss Hattie Tynge
    Watertown,
      Wis.

4. To Ed James, n.d. [March 1863], HTC.

[In the midst of the Civil War, in a somewhat confusing move that perhaps had more to do with publicity than political principles, Menken professed her sympathy for the South. In this letter to her close friend and press agent, Ed James, Menken describes the trouble these allegiances created for her in Union-controlled Baltimore. This letter stands in stark contrast to her patriotic poem in support of the North, "Pro Patria" in *Infelicia*.]

My dear Ed:

Your letters and papers all came safe to hand. You are too good to me. The last picture of yourself is the very best of all. It is splendid. But they all look well to me. I shall keep them always. The last one is now in the edge of my large looking-glass, in company with Jeff Davis, Gen. Van Dorn,[1] and Gen. Bragg. How will that do? I must tell you something that happened this week. On Monday I was arrested and brought before the Provost-Marshall for being a Secessionist. Of course I did not deny that charge; but I denied having aided the C.S.A. They wanted to send me to "Dixie," but would not permit me to take but one hundred pounds of luggage. Of course I could not see that. So after a great deal of talk they concluded if I would take "the oath" to let me off. This I refused most decidedly. After all they left me off under "parole." I am to report myself to Provost Marshall Fish in *30 days*. If I have continued my unlawful ways, I can take my choice between the "oath," or going across the lines without any clothes. I tell you, Ed, I gave them "particular fits," and all in good argument, too. Although, for the sake of my business, the matter was kept out of the papers, it has done me a great deal of good, and helped me to knock Mr & Mrs Barney Williams[2] "higher than a kite." I am now playing to crowded houses; and that in "Mazeppa," too, which you know had an awful big run here before. But there seems to be more excitement about the piece than ever.

You are too late, my good brother, about F.Q.'s picture,[3] he has already sent me one. And a splendid one, too. I am obliged to you for your thoughtfulness. God bless your big heart!

I had another letter from F.Q. this morning, enclosing one he received from California. They seem crazy to have me out there, but they dont [*sic*] want to pay any money. How is that? I dont [*sic*] see it.

Write just when you feel like it, and take good care of yourself. I have a severe cold, but will be all right in a day or two.

Yours affectionately,

Adah

---

[1]   Like the more well-known General Braxton Bragg and President Jefferson Davis, General Earl Van Dorn was a hero within the Confederate States of America (C.S.A.).
[2]   Popular American actors who specialized in comic Irish and Yankee character roles.
[3]   Frank Queen, editor of the *New York Clipper* and Menken's close friend.

5. To Ed James, 12 & 19 Dec. 1864, HTC.

[In these two excerpts from letters written from London, Menken asks James to locate the work she had published in New York a few years earlier; she was evidently starting to plan the collection published about three and half years later as *Infelicia*.]

Dear Ed, *do see about getting me that file of "Mercury's."* Go at once to *Cauldwell* or to *Whitney*,[1] and say that you must have a complete file since I wrote my first article. *I* do not remember the date, but you may calculate it. I commenced for that paper just a few days after *J. C. H.*[2] sailed for England. I am willing to pay a good price for the papers. Do see to it immediately, dear Ed. I have the advice and patronage of the greatest literary man of England, who will revise my poems for me. Such a blessing may never occur again. Help me all you can about getting the *Mercury's.* And please write me immediately. If I only had my poems *now*, they could be "out" for the holidays—the book season of England. [12 Dec. 1864]

Dear Ed, do try to get those "Mercury's" for me. I wrote you about them in my last. So I will not enlarge upon the great advantages I should derive from the complete possession of my articles. *Do not undertake to copy them.* It would be madness. I wrote two and three articles every week for over three years. Don't *think of it.* [19 Dec. 1864]

6. To Augustin Daly, 6 Feb. 1865, HTC.

[Daly was a drama critic, theatre manager, and playwright working in New York in the early-1860s when Menken met and socialized with him. In this letter she not only talks about the London theatre scene but also remembers fondly their Bohemian life in New York, including loafing, following newspapers, and smoking hashish.]

2d Mo 6th D '65

My dear Gus,

To be truthful,—which you are aware, is one of my most glaring follies,—I am not in the proper condition to be at all brilliant,

---

[1] Cauldwell and Whitney are presumably employees of the New York *Sunday Mercury.*
[2] John Carmel Heenan, Menken's ex-husband.

elegant or amusing. I am angry, disappointed, restless and annoyed. You wonder why? At this moment—12 A. M.—there is a dense fog (according to the approved rules [of] Daly's intense English I should have spelt "Dense Fog" with caps), is hanging darkly over all London. I am obliged to write my interesting effusions by gas-light. I had an engagement to ride on horseback in the Park today at 12. And you know the Prince[1] is again on Rotten Row,[2] and what woman of spirit or taste would keep away if she could possibly get out, and more especially if Poole[3] had just sent home her new and beautiful riding-habit?—dark blue embroidery with silver, *a-la-militario*, long white plumes, &c., &c. It is too bad! There is one comfort, I know my horse is as angry as I am. He likes his Park gallop.

But enough, and too much, of my trials and ills of life.

I feel, dear Gus, that I ought, by all rules of regard, love, friendship, and that sort of thing—"draw out." You have not treated me any too well. My eyes have starved for *Couriers*.[4] My heart has yearned for photographs. I have thirsted for "hasheesh." I am jealous of you, Gus. You have forgotten, or progressed out of, our once charming flights of vagabondism.

Poor me! I am just as foolish as ever; I long for those jolly careless loafings again. I have no "chum" like you in London. I only go round with *old men*. They are generally "slow." But all the Bohemians, critics and authors are old here. However they are quite jolly. John Oxenford[5] of the *Times* [is] my sole beau fo[r] Theatres and Operas. Of course we are always joined by the best and loveliest of the Press. But he only likes "opening nights." Apropos. We were present at Miss Bateman's debut in "Julia."[6] There were about seven of the leading "papers" in my box, and we did all we could for her. We all stood up in the front of the box to receive her at the end of the play. The critiques were the best possible of her. But "The

---

1   Prince Edward (1841-1910), Queen Victoria's second child and first son and later King Edward VII of Great Britain.

2   A famous horseback riding track in London's Hyde Park.

3   Henry Poole & Co., fashionable tailors on Savile Row, London.

4   Issues of the *New York Sunday Courier*, the newspaper for which Daly worked early in his career.

5   John Oxenford (1812-77), playwright, critic for the London *Times*, translator, and song-writer.

6   Kate Bateman (1842-1917) was an American actress working in London during the Civil War. She was well-known for her roles as Julia in Sheridan Knowles's *The Hunchback* (1832) and Leah in Augustin Daly's *Leah, The Forsaken* (1863).

Public" [could] not see it. She played two nights and got "sick." The houses after the first night was fearful. But she did not look so pretty! Just like a *lilly*. I admire her much more than in your "Leah." She was charming. I hear she is to have a new piece soon.

As for my insignificant self, I am to reappear at Astley's March 6th in "Child of the Sun," written by John Brougham for me. Write soon, old fellow, and tell me the news. With much love, believe me, yours as ever,

Dolores.

7. To Robert Reece, n.d. [1866?], BPL.

[In this letter to a friend, a stage writer, Menken explains a few of her more controversial opinions about women and marriage.]

Cataldi's
42 Dover St.
Friday A.M.

Today, Roberto, I should like to see you if you are good tempered, and think you could be bored with me and my ghosts. They will be harmless to you, these ghosts of mine[.] They are sad, soft-footed things that wear my brain and live on my heart—that is the fragment I have left to be called *heart.*

Apropos of that, I hear you are married. I am glad of that. I believe all good men should be married. Yet I dont [sic] believe in women being married. Somehow they all sink into nonentities after this epoch in their existence. That is the fault of female education. They are taught from their cradles to look upon marriage as the one event of their lives. That accomplished nothing remains. However Byron might have been right after all: "Man's love is of his life a thing apart— it is a woman's whole existence."[1] If this is true we do not wonder to find so many stupid wives—they are simply doing the "whole existence" sort of thing. Good women are rarely clever, and clever women are rarely good.

I am digressing in to mere twaddle, from what I started out to say to you.

Come when you can get time, and tell me of our friends the gentle souls of air. Mine fly from me, only to fill my being with

---

[1]   *Don Juan*, 1.194.1-2.

painful remembrance of their lost love for me—*even me*! Once the blest and chosen.

Now a royal Tigress waits in her lonely jungle the coming of the King of forests.

Brown gaiters not excluded.

Yours (through all stages of local degradation)
    Infelix
      Menken

8. To Charles Warren Stoddard, n.d. [1867], from Stoddard, 486–87.

[In this encouraging letter to a young writer, Menken represents herself as a melancholic, Bohemian artist and poet. According to one of Menken's biographers, Wolf Mankowitz, the letter below is Stoddard's editing and recombination of two separate letters.]

My Poet—

Your letter and poems came just today, when kind and beautiful things were so much needed in my heart. That letter and your thrilling poems have fulfilled their mission: I am lifted out of my sad, lonely self, and reach my heart up to the affinity of the true, which is always the beautiful.

I am not in the condition to tell you all the impressions your poems have made upon me. I have today fallen into the bitterness of a sad, reflective and desolate mood. You know I am alone, and that I work, and without sympathy; and that the unshrined ghosts of wasted hours and of lost loves are always tugging at my heart.

I know your soul! It has met mine somewhere in the starry highway of thought. You must often meet me, for I am a vagabond of fancy without name or aim. I was born a dweller in tents; a reveler in the "tented habitation of war"; consequently, dear poet, my views of life and things are rather disreputable in the eyes of the "just." I am always in bad odor with people who don't know me, and startle those who do. Alas!

I am a fair classical scholar, not a bad linguist, can paint a respectable portrait of a good head and face, can write a little and have made successes in sculpture; but for all these blind instincts for art, I am still a vagabond, of no use to anyone in the world—and never shall be. People always find me out and then find fault with God because I have gifts denied to them. I cannot help that. The body and the soul don't fit each other; they are always in a "scramble." I have long since ceased to contend with the world; it bores me horribly; nothing but hard work saves me from myself.

I send you a treasure: the portrait and autograph of my friend, Alexander Dumas. Value it for his sake, as well as for the sake of the poor girl he honors with his love. O! how I wish that you could know him! You could understand his great soul so well—the King of Romance, the Child of Gentleness and Love: take him to your heart forever!

In a few days I shall see him, and then a pleasant hour shall be made by reading in my weak translation what I like best in your poems. We always read and analyze our dearest friends—but Alexander is too generous to be critical.

I shall not remain here long. Vienna is detestable beyond expression. Ah! my comrade; Paris is, after all, the heart of the world. Know Paris and die.

And now, farewell! Let me try to help you with my encouragement and the best feelings of my heart. Think of me. I am with you in spirit. Your future is to be glorious. Heaven bless you. Infelex [*sic*],

MENKEN.

9. From Charles Dickens, 21 Oct. 1867, from facsimile in *Infelicia* (Philadelphia, 1869), frontispiece.

[This is the letter in which Dickens accepts Menken's dedication of the volume. It was not included in the first printing of *Infelicia* but added to later ones.]

Monday Twenty-first October 1867
Dear Miss Menken
I shall have great pleasure in accepting your Dedication, and I thank you for your portrait is a highly remarkable specimen of Photography.
I also thank you for the verses enclosed in your note. Many such enclosures come to me, but few so pathetically written, and fewer still so modestly sent.
Faithfully yours
Charles Dickens

10. To John Camden Hotten, n.d. [1868?], from Swinburne, *Adah Isaacs Menken*, **vii–viii.**

[In a flirtatious letter to the publisher of *Infelicia*, Menken asks about the inclusion of certain poems and the publication schedule.]

Dear Mr. Hotten,—I am glad we have found another copy of "Answer me." I hope you will get it a good place in the book. It is a poem that *I* like, and I believe you will. If you believe in my idea of omitting the "Karazah" to "Karl," you might put "Answer me" there. However, I am sure you will do the best you can for it. Can you get "Aspiration" in? I am so anxious to get the book out. I fear you put others out before me. In that case we shall certainly quarrel, and that would be vastly disagreeable *to me*. Do hurry those printers, and I shall like you better than I do now. When you have an idle day let me come and see more of your wonderful old books.—Yours faithfully, A. Menken.

11. To John Camden Hotten, 17 March 1868, AJHS.

[In this second letter to her publisher, Menken worries that the volume's portrait of her looks "affected."]

Dear Mr. Hotten,

How long to wait for the "proofs." You do not forget?

When am I to see you?

When will you advertise the book?

Remember I ask these questions merely from curiosity. The affair is all decidedly yours. I am satisfied with all you have done except the portrait. I do not find it to be in character with the volume. It looks *affected*. Perhaps I am a little vain—all women are—but the picture is certainly not beautiful. I have portraits I think are beautiful. I dare say they are not like me, but I posed for them.

Do tell me, mon ami, can we not possibly have another made?

Your friend,

A.I. Menken

12. To John Camden Hotten, n.d. [1868], from Northcutt, 40.

[Although a meeting seems to have answered most of her questions and allayed some of her anxiety about the forthcoming publication of *Infelicia*, Menken continued to express uneasiness about proofreading and the portrait.]

Dear Mr. Hotten,—I am much pleased with the interview between yourself and Mr. Ellington[1] yesterday. Your ideas are all excellent, and I am confident that we will have a grand success. I will call at your office to-morrow about two o'clock, if you will be so kind as to be at home to me. I am anxious to see the designs that are to be engraved; also I would be glad if I might look over the later proofs again, as I was very ill when they were corrected for me.

You know I never really liked the idea of my portrait being printed, but I am willing to submit to your judgment in all pertaining to our mutual interest. The proofs of the portrait you sent me are wonderfully well engraved.

Believe me, dear Sir, yours truly, MENKEN.
There is no "A" and no "I."

---

[1]   Susette Ellington, Menken's personal secretary and companion. "Mr." is probably Northcutt's mistranscription of Menken's handwriting.

Appendix C: Critical Reception

1. "New Poetry," *The Athenæum* (29 Aug. 1868): 268.

[Although apparently interested in the melancholy and intensity of the book, this British review ridicules *Infelicia* for its irregular style and affected emotion.]

A little book, which is ostentatiously anonymous as to its publishers, and bears on its title-page *Infelicia*, by Adah Isaacs Menken, may be next taken from the pile before us, and, by any one who does the like, found to contain verses which, if they were really written by the person whose name they bear, show much uncultivated pathos in sentiment and sense-ful love of nature to have existed in the author's mind; also a wilderness of rubbish and affected agonies of yearning after the unspeakable, which achieve the nonsensical. As it is, blue fire and red fire of the theatre are nearer the eternal glories than the author's rhapsodies and crudities of psuedo-imagination—we cannot say imagination unrestrained, which is vented in such nonsense as this: [extract from "Resurgam," section II, lines 3-10]. And so on, to the termination of a work which, in its conception, is marked with intense beauty and grandeur. "Miserimus" is in this strain, but dull. A torrent of force appears in the poem "Judith"; much tender and delicate beauty of diction and thought in "Dreams of Beauty" and "In Vain." In its utter incoherency and peculiar style, "Genius" reminds us of Mr. Martin Farquhar Tupper,[1] and of what a friend irreverently described as the "jagged prose" of that inimitable bard. Poe, recovering from *delirium tremens*,—a maudlin Pythoness, over-drunk, not with the god, and still poetic, but rapt by an intrusive demon,—were no unapt antitypes of the woman whose deepest unhap-piness is in the half-conscious "acting" of this book.

2. "Miss Menken's Poems," *The London Review*. Rpt. in *Every Saturday* (12 Sept. 1868): 332-33.

[Placing Menken in "the wild school of poetizers," this review—typical of the critical response to Menken's work—

---

[1] Martin Farquhar Tupper (1810-89), British writer known for his pop philosophical works and their loosely rhythmical form.

blends a disapproving evaluation of the poetry with comments on Menken's scandalous life.]

The somewhat sudden and certainly unexpected death of Miss Adah Isaacs Menken has formed the text for a number of more or less gushing articles, and may form the text for more. If Menken had lived another week, she would have made her appearance as the living authoress of a volume of half-sad, half-biblical poems, which will now be published and received in many quarters with a tenderness they may not deserve. There is something calculated to tickle certain imaginations in the career of a woman who made herself notorious as an equestrian actress, married two, if not more, prize-fighters, one or two journalists, besides several private individuals, and then burst upon a world, which is always willing to be astonished, with a volume of semi-religious poems. The poems, in themselves, may be valueless, but the mere fact of such a woman having her name attached to anything in the shape of verse is a new literary "sensation." There have been instances within the memory of young journalists in which female notorieties have had books written for them and published as their own, and this fashion has been peculiarly popular in Paris. Rigolboche, Finette,[1] and other heroines of the casinos, have all published their *mémoires*, written in a style that suggests the autobiography of the once famous "Harriet Wilson,"[2] but Menken takes a far higher flight in the book that will be given to the public in the course of next week. Under the title of "Infelicia," about thirty short poems and prose fragments will appear, plentifully larded with quotations from Scripture. Luxuriously printed, artistically illustrated, and dedicated, by permission, to Mr. Charles Dickens, the volume will doubtless find a sale far above the average of poetical ventures. The dedication to Mr. Dickens will probably have something to do with this, particularly when the public learns that [his] letter is handsomely printed in *facsimile* as a preface to the book. [...]

The poems thus bowed into the world by this distinguished

---

1 Rigolboche and Finette were famous cancan dancers. Rigolboche was said to have invented the dance, which was popular in Parisian casinos and night spots. Both published autobiographies in the mid-nineteenth century: *Mémoires de Rigolboche* (1860) and *Les mémoires de Finette* (n.d.).

2 Harriet E. Wilson (1828?–1863?), African American author of an autobiographical novel titled *Our Nig* (1859).

author are of various degrees of merit, the weakest being certainly those which are written in rhymed verse. The strongest, or apparently the strongest, are those in which the Whitman style of rhapsody is copied, and language is thrown about wildly, with here and there a few happy combinations. People who have the English vocabulary to deal with, who never seem to pause to think, and who stick at nothing that will produce an effect, would be very unlucky if they always failed to "strike oil." A cat running over the keys of a piano will sometimes produce harmonies that have escaped the great composers; and in the same way the wild school of poetizers, to which Menken belonged, are often the parents of a few happy phrases. Menken is as bold in poetry as she was on the stage. [...]

Some of the poems have a sadness and genuine force which prove them to be the outpourings of a heart ill at ease, and some have a grace of expression far removed from the wild rhapsody we have alluded to. The poem called "Drifts that Bar my Door" is worthy of full quotation for this quality. [...]

Menken was evidently an impressionable woman, as plastic as wax, on whom the last influence had the strongest effect. The animalism of the prize-fighter affected her one moment, the philosophy of the poet at another. There are thousands of such women in the world, and always have been.

3. "Adah Isaacs Menken's Poems," *New-York Tribune* (29 Sept. 1868): 6.

[This review attacks Menken by associating her with Whitman and the theatre. Like many critical responses, it preferred a more traditional poem like "Infelix" over the free verse pieces but, unlike other critics, would not commend Menken for her sincerity or generosity.]

The notoriety of the author's life will awaken a degree of interest in this volume to which it is not entitled by any poetical merit. It is little more than an echo of Walt Whitman, Ossian,[1] and other suspicious models, with no assuring proof of originality or even of sincerity. As a

---

[1] Very popular during the nineteenth century, the rhapsodic poems of Ossian were allegedly translations of ancient Scottish epics. It was later discovered that most of the work was fabricated by Scottish schoolteacher and poet James Macpherson (1736-96).

record of personal feeling, it might challenge curiosity, did not the melodramatic character of the writer prevent any reliance on the truthfulness of its effusions. She unvails the secrets of her experience as unscrupulously as she went through the displays of the theater, but in both cases, one will detect a morbid love of publicity, inflamed by a passion for admiration and a thirst for gain. Hence her disclosures have no value as studies in human nature, or as illustrations of abnormal passion. The tone of the volume is for the most part sad, often cynical, even desperate, but the smell of foot-lights and burnt rosin pervades the whole composition, leaving the impression that stage-effect rather than sorrow is the source of her inspiration. The expression of tender or lofty sentiment by such a jovial, rollicking adventuress, has only a ludicrous aspect, even in the eyes of those who have the most faith in man,—or fast-riding Mazeppa women. There are perhaps occasional revelations of the self-conscious soul, that give transient glimpses of "the angel in the devil," like the closing piece in the volume, in which a charitable father-confessor might discern the accents of unhoping penitence, though he would not venture to describe a face that wears a perpetual mask. ["Infelix" quoted.] This is better both in rhyme and reason than most of the contents of the volume, which is made up of sonorous rhapsodies in which prose takes the form of poetry without its spirit.

4. Elizabeth Cady Stanton, "Adah Isaacs Menken," *The Revolution* (1 Oct. 1868): 201-02.

[Although she treats Menken as a fallen woman, "a victim of society," this famous feminist thinker discovers in Menken's poetry a kind of inspiring virtue that stands apart from the moralities of the comfortable or complacent.]

Poor Adah! when she died she left the world a book of poems that reveals an inner life of love for the true, the pure, the beautiful, that none could have imagined possible in the actress, whose public and private life were alike sensual and scandalous. Who can read the following verses from her pen, without feeling that this unfortunate girl, a victim of society, was full of genius and tenderness, and that under more fortunate circumstances, she might have been an honor to her sex. How sad and touching is this confession of the failure of her life. ["Infelix" quoted.]

We who have lived and loved in comfort and satisfaction, need a new evangel to teach us that nobler virtues than we shall ere possess are found to-day among the poor children of want and temptation. Let those women who wrap their mantles of complacency about them, and thank God that they are not such as these, consider if they had been subject to like temptations might they not have suffered like infirmities. In death, poor Adah speaks sweet words of love and purity that will help to ennoble the life of many a girl that might have followed in the paths she led. They who have seen life in its worst phases, know its needs and temptations; and none so mighty to save as they who have tasted the bitterness of death. Says Victor Hugo: "As the debris of sewers have been found to possess those chemical elements that can alone restore the worn-out lands in the old world, so from the very dregs of society, through poverty and suffering, shall come forth the grandest virtues of self-sacrifice and heroism that can alone redeem the race."

5. "New Publications," *The New-York Times* (21 Oct. 1868): 4.

[This review strongly disliked the Whitman-inspired prosody, preferring instead the more traditional "Infelix." Nonetheless, the critic admires the emotional sincerity of Menken's work and notes her attempt to live and think apart from dominant social conventions.]

The interest of this little volume of poems arises chiefly, to say solely would be hardly too strong, from their association in the reader's mind with the character of the author. Unpolished, crude in matter and in form, most of them would have been consigned to speedy oblivion had they emanated from the mind of any one less known, in the peculiar manner in which her notoriety was obtained, than ADAH ISAACS MENKEN. Though one of the most common experiences in the world, people were really astonished to learn that the most notorious representative of the "nude drama," a woman who in her own person cast aside all the conventionalities and most of the moralities of society, had moments of serious thought, of poignant mental suffering, of regret, of yearning after better things, of aspirations for a higher life. The evident sincerity of her writings, as well as the contrast between these moods and her actual life, goes far to win our sympathy and disarm criticism. We need not spare the character of Miss MENKEN in judging of these poems. She never spared herself, was never modest for herself, nor asked others to be shame-faced for her. Her whole life was passed in violation of social law, yet these poems show that there was left in her this grace of virtue, that she never set up her life as a protest against society, nor claimed to be anything other than what she was; that she was conscious of the better way, and oftentimes, in the wildest delirium of her career, had thoughts "too deep for tears" and inexpressible in words.

Few of her poems display the finish of an artist. Most of them are hardly more than prose out in lengths of varying measure, in the manner rendered familiar by WALT WHITMAN, whose style she admired and imitated. We quote a few lines from the poem called "Resurgam:" [...]

Though disfigured by extravagant and incoherent phraseology, there is a great deal of genuine pathos in these lines, and the imagery is original and poetic. Here is an extract from another poem, called "Into the Depths:" [...]

Still more pathetic is the poem called "Drifts that Bar my Door," from which we take the opening lines: [...]

The most beautiful, most touching, most highly finished poem in the volume is the one with which it closes, and with which we take leave of it. The verses ought to be engraved on the author's tombstone, as the appropriate epitaph of a wasted life. They are called "Infelix" [...]

6. "Table-Talk," *Putnam's Magazine* (Nov. 1868): 638-39.

[Comparing her work to Blake's, Whitman's, and Tennyson's, this brief review casts doubt on the rumors and public accounts of Menken's life and yearns for the truth about it, attempting to discover this truth in the poems themselves.]

The above remarks are apropos of the publication of the prettiest little book we have seen for a long time in this age of the Macmillians, the Leypold-&-Holts, and the Bell-and-Daldys:[1] the poems, namely, of the late notorious Adah Isaacs Menken, whose recent death, in Paris, seems likely to draw the veil from what must have been a curious character. For several years her name has been associated, in the public mind, only with theatrical performances in

---

[1] Publishing houses.

which the limit of shamelessness was reached and overleaped, and with rumors of a private life that was popularly believed to have matched in lawlessness and dissoluteness all that was known of her in public. Claiming, at one time, to be the wife of Heenan the prize-fighter, but disclaimed by him, she was disclaimed by other men whose name she from time to time assumed. Of late, she had lived in Paris, and photographs representing her sitting on the knee of the elder Dumas, he in his shirt and trousers, and she in the simple dress of an acrobat when that is simplest,—the couple looking very much like the male and female gorilla—have been freely circulated all over Europe, and in this country. As is well known, her wide-spread noto-riety was gained chiefly by her performance of the character of Mazeppa, in the melodrama of that name, in which she made all the display of her person that the law allows, and by that display amassed a considerable fortune. As for her acting, it is said to have been beneath contempt, and, indeed, she never associated her name with any part that did not admit of the indecent displays she was so ready to make. Such being all that the public had ever known or heard of this woman up to the time of her death, it is not a little surprising to be told, that she was a woman of genius, that she wrote religious poetry of a high order, and that she had many excellent virtues! Her poems have been published, and, as we have said, in a very attractive form, but we do not know by whom. Before our copy reached us we read somewhere that they were to be issued by that refuge of the Bohemians, John Camden Hotten of London. But the English edition bears no publisher's name. It is printed on the most delicate toned paper, in the clearest print, and is illustrated with a number of small wood cuts, some of which are very pretty, and with a well engraved head—a steel vignette—of the author. There is also a photo-lithograph copy of a note from Mr. Dickens in which he accepts the Dedication of the volume offered him by Miss Menken herself. We presume that Mr. Dickens would not have written just the note that this is, unless he knew more of the person he addressed than the world has been permitted to know. Indeed, we have it from one who knew her that she was a woman extremely amiable, quick at repartee, and so soft-hearted to suffering fellow-mortals, that she gave away her money in charity as fast [as] she earned it. We dare say that, in one way or another, we shall soon learn enough to enable us to judge fairly of this remarkable phenomenon. We wish it may be possible to get from some one a statement that shall depend for its value and interest on the plain unvarnished truth of it, and into which as little as possible of the "sensation" element may be allowed to enter. As for her book of poems, it is but fair to say that while the greater number of them are allied in their structure to the rhapsodical, fragmentary, and often incoherent verses of Ossian, and Walt Whitman, and the so-called "Prophetic Books" of William Blake, they do often show the possession of the poetical sense, and are interesting not only from their origin, but in themselves. [...]

But there are not many quotable, nay, to speak frankly, there are not many readable, poems in this little volume. Two, we should like to quote, "One Year Ago" and "Working and Waiting;" this last suggested by our townsman, Carl Muller's, statue of the Seamstress, at the Dusseldorf Gallery.[1] "Working and Waiting" is a little poem on the same subject as Hood's "Song of the Shirt,"[2] and though not so striking in form and expression, as that famous lyric, it seems to us far fuller of feeling, more touching in its sincerity. In truth, these poems have left a far deeper impression on our mind, as we have read them, than any thing in their literary execution, or even in the ideas that the writer labors, in vain for the most part, to express with clearness, would make appear reasonable, if we had room for pages of extracts. We feel that this woman carried about with her a suffering heart, that she aspired after a better life than the one she led, that she was conscious of powers misused, and that she struggled vainly in the meshes of a net woven by her want of early training, by passions she was never taught to control, and by circumstances that finally became too strong for her. If we read her verses aright, she was a mother, and she had deeply loved some one who had betrayed and abandoned her. Such a story must move any human heart to pity, and it is with the sincerest pity that we have closed this book.

7. Dante Gabriel Rossetti, to William Michael Rossetti, 3 July 1871 and 16 July 1871, from *Dante Gabriel Rossetti: His Family-Letters* (London, 1895) 2:232-233.

[The sometimes morbid and melancholic English poet and painter, Dante Gabriel Rossetti, found Menken's sometimes

---

[1] See "Working and Waiting," 52-54.
[2] Well-known in the nineteenth-century, "The Song of the Shirt" by Thomas Hood (1799-1845) treated the poverty and toil of seamstresses.

morbid and melancholic poetry "remarkable" and encouraged his brother to include her work in his anthology of *American Poems*.]

I forgot till this moment that your American Selection ought certainly, I think, to contain some specimens of poor Menken. I have her book, which is really remarkable. If there is still time to introduce them, I would mark the copy for extract, and write some short notice to precede them, to save you trouble, as I know the book. [3 July 1871]

To my surprise I cannot find my Menken's Poems anywhere. So I send you on a letter and notice received from Purnell, and am writing to him to get a copy sent to you.

My own impression is that much the best piece in the book is one called (I think) *Answer Me*; though I remember finding that some points of it were much better than others, and should have been inclined only to print the good stanzas, which make a fine poem enough by themselves; but I don't know if such plan would suit you. There is also a short rhymed poem which is remarkable, called I think *Ambition*, or something of that sort, but it is defective of a line somewhere—accidental omission, I suppose. These two, I remember, are clearly the best. However, there are one or two others I had marked, but my copy seems nowhere. One of the most characteristic is that about "Angels, sweep the leaves from my door." [16 July 1871]

8. William Michael Rossetti, "Adah Isaacs Menken," *American Poems*, ed. William Michael Rossetti (London, 1872) 444-45.

[William Michael Rossetti apparently listened to his more famous brother's advice, included Menken in the anthology, and wrote this headnote, which emphasizes her "intense melancholy" and compares her to Poe.]

Born in New Orleans, 1839; died of consumption in Paris, August 1868. She was the daughter of a merchant, a Spanish Jew, and her maiden name was Dolores Adios Fuertos. Her father dying when she was only two years of age, she was taken by her mother to Cuba, and brought up in the family of a rich planter. This gentleman also died when she was but thirteen—her mother's death had occurred previously. He left her the bulk of his property: but the will was set aside,[1] and the girl of fourteen came out on the stage as a dancer,—afterwards playing various parts in tragedy and drama. She next married a Mr. John Isaacs Menken [*sic*]; and changing her proper name of Adios to Adah, made up the married name by which she thereafter continued to be known. Towards 1860 she married again—Mr. Robert H. Newell, author of the *Orpheus C. Kerr Papers*: this alliance was terminated by a divorce. The impetuous actress made her southern sympathies, during the war of secession, rather perilously prominent; and in 1864 crossed over to England, where her performances—chiefly as "the female Mazeppa"—are fresh in many memories. Of the numbers who admired her lavish graces of face and form, few indeed would have thought that she was predestined the victim of consumption within four years. "She expressed a wish to be buried in accordance with the rites of her religion (the Jewish), with nothing to mark her resting-place but a plain piece of wood bearing the words 'Thou knowest:'" an inscription as sublime and profound as it is majestically simple.

Living a turbid and irregular life, with uncommon versatility of talent (though she showed no great gift for her professional calling as an actress), Adah Menken had a vein of intense melancholy in her character: it predominates throughout her verses with a wearisome iteration of emphasis, and was by no means vamped up for mere purposes of effect. The poems contained in her single published volume are mostly unformed rhapsodies—windy and nebulous; perhaps only half intelligible to herself, and certainly more than half unintelligible to the reader. Yet there are touches of genius which place them in a very different category from many so-called poems of more regular construction and more definable deservings. They really express a life of much passion, and not a little aspiration; a life deeply sensible of loss, self-baffled, and mixing the wail of humiliation with that of indignation—like the remnants of a defeated army, hotly pursued. It is this life that cries out in the disordered verses, and these have a responsive cry of their own.

---

[1] In some of the incidents—not to speak of the general tenour—of Adah Menken's career, the reader may observe a curious parallelism to that of Edgar Poe: and indeed (allowing for a great difference in poetic merit) the tone of mind and inspiration of the two writers were not without some analogy. Poe was a man and an artist in a direction of faculty wherein Adah Menken was a woman and a votary. [Rossetti's note.]

9. "Introduction," *Infelicia* (London, 1888), xiii–xiv.

[Sympathetic to her life and writings, this introduction to the 1888 edition of *Infelicia* provides some impressionistic commentary on Menken's poetry.]

Adah Isaacs Menken's faults lay on the surface, and it is idle to attempt any concealment of them. But, with all her faults, she was a noble creature. Her generosity was unparalleled. She squandered money recklessly, but seldom upon herself. The attachés at the theatre, men, women, and children, were her beneficiaries, and even in the streets she would thrust handfuls of silver or rolls of bills in the hands of strangers who attracted her pity or liking. "No one cared less for money than Adah Isaacs Menken," said a writer in the Boston *Courier*, "and, had her income been a thousand dollars a minute, she would have been poor at the end of an hour." While she loved a man she would cling to him with doglike fidelity, giving up everything, and exacting the same self-abandonment in return with a jealousy that was not only unreasonable, but unbearable. Sometimes, when her fiery temper was enraged by some real or fancied slight, she would go into a cataleptic fit that is described as terrible to witness. But she never said an ill word behind another's back, no matter how brutally he might have injured her, and she never forgot a kindness.

Her poems are as erratic, as impulsive, as faulty, as herself. They may not have the true lyric form. The true lyric cry wails through them in defiance of form, and goes straight to the reader's heart. "C'est magnifique, mais ce n'est pas la guerre,"[1] might be the martinet's criticism. But the martinet does not win all the battles.

Never was the anguish of a broken spirit put into more potent words than in such poems as "One Year Ago," "My Heritage," and "Infelix." Even in her brightest poems there is no joy—nothing but a maddened sense of the impossibility of joy which has a sort of delirious ecstasy of its own. It is like the wail of a lost soul that has had a glimpse of heaven, and it appeals with sudden and blinding force to us poor creatures who, grossly hemmed in by our earthly senses, know neither hell nor heaven.

---

[1]   It's magnificent, but it's not the war (French).

10. Reviews of the 1888 edition. *The Literary World* (24 Nov. 1888): 421; *The Dial* (Dec. 1888): 210; *The Atlantic Monthly* (Jan. 1889): 139–140.

[*Infelicia* remained in print throughout the nineteenth century, though later reviewers often greeted new editions with superficial but disparaging criticism.]

Just why the hysterical outpourings of that brilliant adventuress, Adah Menken, should continue to be offered to the public is one of those literary problems which one cannot easily solve. However, here they are, with a remarkably frank biographical sketch of the author, with a number of undesirable illustrations, with broad margins, and with red lines around every page. It is a morbid, undisciplined, erratic nature that finds utterance in *Infelicia*, and we cannot conceive of any one deriving profit from its perusal. [*The Literary World*]

Adah Isaacs Menken's erratic career—which was not without a tinge of genuine pathos—lends an interest to her verse which it would not otherwise possess. A handsome new edition of her "Infelicia," with a sketch of the author by W. S. Walsh, is issued by Lippincott. The poem is appropriately illustrated by F. O. C. Darley, F. S. Church, and others. [*The Dial*]

The pictures, the red rule round the page, and the binding all pronounce this a holiday book. The frontispiece, which is a slice of chaos, excellently symbolizes the poetry, which despairs of the incoherence of verse, and settles into the incoherence of prose. [*The Atlantic Monthly*]

11. Joaquin Miller, *Adah Isaacs Menken*, **n.p.**

[A writer and editor from the American West and Menken's contemporary, Miller praises her poetry in this excerpt from a piece first published in San Francisco's *The Morning Call* in 1892. He calls it "the best that America has yet to offer in the line of sublime thought."]

Born in a small town[1] and at a time the least poetical of all times and

---

[1] According to Miller, Menken's hometown was Cincinnati.

places this woman, so far as I am able to say, was the most entirely poetical of all women that have yet found expression in America. [...]

Little is known about her except lies. Like Lord Byron, as Sir Walter Scott says of him in his recently published journal, she was always trying to make believe she was dreadful bad;[1] that is, in her intercourse with the world about her. But with her soul and her soul's friends she was very much another woman. She was sincere there; earnest; sad, piteously sad; though her outer life, as all know who came only superficially near her, was one continuous ripple of laughter. [...]

She loved California ardently, and had she lived she surely would have made this her home. How do I know? Why, she told me that this was the only place in America where she could write, and to write was her one ambition and ability. And I know she told the truth about this being the only place where she could write—as she did about everything else, of course—for the book 'Infelicia,' published in London and dedicated to Charles Dickens, was written almost entirely in San Francisco. I doubt if there are ten pages in that most remarkable book not to be found out in *Golden Era*.

If you care for poetry, grand, sublime, majestic, get this one little book of Adah Isaacs Menken and read it from lid to lid. It is the best that America has yet to offer in the line of sublime thought. You will bear me witness that I never criticize or commend books, or mention them at all as a rule. There are better things than books for a man who can afford to live in the woods, as I do. And so I have not one book in the world, except the Bible. But if I did not know this little book of hers by heart I would surely buy it.

12. Charles Warren Stoddard, "La Belle Menken," 482–83.

[Composed 37 years after her death, Stoddard's magazine article remembers Menken and her writing with affection.]

That Adah Isaacs Menken was a woman of unusual talent is beyond question. She may not have been a genius, but her nature was of that difficult sort that is near allied to the madness of genius. She proved this in everything she said or wrote or did. Her chirography advertises the fact; and if the handwriting of a person is the index to his

---

[1] See journal entry for 23 Nov. 1825, *The Journal of Sir Walter Scott*, ed. W.E.K. Anderson (Oxford: Oxford University Press, 1972) 8–10.

character, hers was one to call forth the sympathy of all Christian souls. It has been thus interpreted by a friend, at my request:—Nature gave her the joy of sensations; to all the senses she responded easily, and each thrilled her; a creature of real refinement; possessed of much natural delicacy—yet with moments when the physical got the better of the spiritual; tactful, sincere, witty, with an appreciation of the ludicrous, and liking to chaff a little; not without a touch of coquetry; of quick perception, sometimes arriving at profound truths as by a short cut—intuitively; kind, generous, simple, unaffected, but with profound and lofty emotions and at times almost mystical; unaffected, yet occasionally having an air of affectation. A natural capacity for taking pains; fond of detail, all her impersonations showing clever conceptions carefully carried out. Prone to melancholy; not easily hopeful; possessing a grace in repose as satisfying to the eye as a chef-d'-oeuvre in sculpture. One seer pronounced her the victim of a deeply religious and spiritual nature perpetually at war with the flesh that overwhelmed it. [...]

[S]he stormed high heaven, or bewailed her fate in rhapsodies that sometimes verge upon frenzy and sometimes seem the despairing cry of a lost and loving soul.

Her imagination was of a lurid cast; it had feasted upon and echoed the wild and wayward rhythm of the Psalms of David and Walt Whitman's "Leaves of Grass." In her little book of verses "Infelicia," there are few lines that are not more or less inflated, some that are truly noble, and some that are poor enough. This volume of one hundred and twenty-four pages was dedicated to Charles Dickens "by permission"; the permission gracefully granted in an autograph letter was reproduced in facsimile as a frontispiece to the first edition of the poems. [...]

That Adah Menken could write simply and sweetly is evidenced by the following lines ["The Poet"] which she very kindly wrote for me in an old-fashioned album, the pride of my youth. They are written in a hand that is highly characteristic: a free hand of large swinging curves flowing bravely from a stubby quill; the i's dotted with bullets, the t's crossed with javelins, the flourish after her signature as long and elaborately curlicued as the whip-lash of a Wild West cow-boy.

Appendix D: Cultural Contexts

1. Rev. Dr. A. Guinzburg, "The Mortara Abduction Case Illustrated," *The Israelite* (14 Jan. 1859): 221.

[On 23 June 1858, using the pretext that Edgardo Mortara had been baptized by his Catholic nurse, Pope Pius IX directed police to kidnap the six-year-old boy from his Jewish family so that he might be raised Catholic. The incident incited large public protests in Europe and the United States, which contributed to the ongoing erosion of church power during the nineteenth century. The controversy continued into the twenty-first century, as Jews (and many Catholics) worldwide denounced the beatification of Pius IX in September 2000. In 1858-59 the Mortara story received a great deal of attention in *The Israelite*, including this piece by Guinzburg. This event and its coverage in *The Israelite* inspired Menken to add her voice to the chorus of public protest with "To the Sons of Israel," a poem that shares in Guinzburg's outrage and his anti-Catholic rhetoric.]

Watchman, watchman, what of the night?[1] In what state of civilization do we live?—Have we, after so many struggles for the emancipation of the mind, at last overcome that malignant and evil spirit of church government, when the church of Rome could, unpunished, commit crimes of all kinds, even of the most horrible nature; when the *Holy* (?) office of the inquisition stretched out her gigantic arms over the world, and year by year, amid shouting of joy plundered and robbed, broke the hearts and buried alive thousands of innocent human beings in *Sanctam Ecclesiam Catholicam*;[2] or do we live in a century of humanity and justice, in a century of reason and enlightenment?

Watchman, watchman, what of the night? Oh, ye enlightened rulers over nations, and ye philosophers and philanthropists, why are ye not on the alert when you see that this once so formidable power of Rome tries anew under tricks of all kinds to serpentine the whole world! Watchmen, watchmen, where is your watchfulness, where your

---

[1] Isaiah 21:11.

[2] Holy Catholic Church (Latin).

vigilance, where are your cares for mankind, and where your deeds and actions, to protect yourselves and your fellow beings against the dangerous monster called Papism, or Roman Catholic church government; that, that is the echo that reverberates from land to land, from country to country; yes, even over lakes and seas and oceans, from one part of the civilized world to the other, emanating from the doom of those dumb and unhappy parents who live in a country of shudder and horror.

Surely, I need not tell you, kind reader, that I speak of the unhappy Mortara family, that had the great misfortune to live in the Papal dominion, a land where not only "foxes walk about,"[1] but where there is the hotbed of an idle and cunning priestcraft, where not only wolves are clothed in sheepskins, but where tigers, with human faces, tigers decorated and adorned with purple do govern, and in their tyranny do not even allow those who become a bloody sacrifice of their arbitrary power, publicly to complain about the injury that was inflicted upon them; do not allow them to lament aloud the darling child that, with heartless cruelty and tyrannic force, was snatched away from their hearts to be buried alive, and to be educated in principles contrary to theirs, to be alienated from them and their God, to be trained to contemn, despise, and curse those who gave him birth, nursed and fed him, who toiled and struggled for him during the day and watched his cradle in the night.

Truly, in the face of such an event, we must exclaim, with the prophet: Watchman, what of the night; Watchman, what of the night! or, with the old Roman orator:[2] *O tempora, O mores!!!*[3] If this principle, so subversive to all natural rights, so dangerous to all mankind, should be submitted to—for *qui tacet consentit*[4]—where is there any security for the welfare of families, or even of States? The same violence that has now been committed against an Israelite boy, would it not also be committed against any Protestant child—German, English or American—under a similar pretext, that some hireling, affected with a proselyting mania, has brought him into the "only and exclusive beatific Roman Catholic church," in order to save his soul from eternal damnation, for, "*extra ecclesiam Catholica nulla salus,*"[5] for

---

[1] See Lamentations 5:18.
[2] Cicero.
[3] O time, O customs (Latin).
[4] one who is silent consents (Latin).
[5] outside the Catholic church there is no salvation (Latin).

this is also the doctrine of that institution, and the Holy Father of Rome, who keeps in his hand the key of St. Peter, even in our days, most solemnly curses from the Vatican, *all heretics, all who differ from the Catholic dogmas, all, without exception, to eternal damnation*, would this careful janitor of heaven allow that a soul that was saved by his "alma church"[1] should be lost again? Surely, if the pope should triumph in this case, he would in defiance of all the world, resist in all other kidnapping cases too. Therefore has the liberal press of all countries and all denominations, even Catholic not excepted, protested against the assumption of such power on the part of the Roman government, and most emphatically condemned this act of tyranny. Yes, even Catholic powers have protested against the further detention of the kidnapped Mortara boy. But the court of Rome adheres to the Jesuitic principle, that "the end sanctifies the means," and the members of the Inquisition, as worthy disciples of their master Torquemada, have, in spite of all demonstrations, decided, "not to restore the child to his parents," but rather morally and bodily to kill them and him altogether; the parents by breaking their hearts, as they never shall enjoy the presence of their child, and him, by burying him alive in some cloister, depriving him of all worldly enjoyments, and to raise him—if he should live so long—to a life against God's laws, which He has planted in human nature, to become a morally corrupted, flagrant and vicious Roman Catholic monk. Still, in order to palliate their crime, they have circulated false reports and lies of all kind, and argued upon this case in a most sophistical and ridiculous manner.— Thus, for instance, they pretend that the boy, Edgar Mortara, was *thirteen* years old, whereas it is a fact that he is at present only *six* years; and the dipping of a drop of water upon him, by a deluded hired girl of *fourteen* years, took place (?) *five* years ago, when he was sick, and neither of his parents nor the babe had the least knowledge of the act.—"*Risum teneatis, amici.*"[2]

Another such foul report was, that the parents have consented to his becoming a Roman Catholic, whereas all the world knows that they followed the vehicle of the inquisition through the streets of Bologna, screaming vehemently, "give us back our child, give us back our child, the child is ours, you have no claim on him." When all the world knows that since that sad night, when they were robbed of

---

[1] Fostering or nourishing church.
[2] that should keep you laughing, friends (Latin).

their dearest jewel, they did not cease to weep and mourn, and that the unhappy mother fell into an agony of despair, and the father had applied to the authorities of Rome to restore him his child, but, alas, in vain, for even admission was refused to him.

A still more ridiculous, or rather infamous lie was communicated in an official letter from Rome, "that the boy, Mortara, has declared himself to be a Catholic in heart, and that he intends to enter the ecclesiastical state."

Churchman of Rome! Is there such a depravity of all moral sense, such a degeneration among you that you do not blush for shame to publish such an *open, stupid and ridiculous lie!* as that a child of *six* years old has declared himself to be a Catholic in heart? Does this little boy of six years know what Catholicism is, that he should have a predilection for it? Has he attained the age of discretion? Or has your cruel act of robbing him at midnight—of snatching him away from the bosom of his beloved parents; does this act fill him with so much love and attachment to you, as to have become a Catholic at heart? Churchmen! when was a child of six years ever asked about a matrimonial affair? and ye dare officially report that this child has declared *himself* not only to be one of your church, but also to desire to become *a monk*? Does this little child know the destiny of man? has he any idea of the instinct of man? is he of the age to judge for himself whether he would be able to govern his natural passions as a man, and therefore honestly fulfil the duties connected with celibacy? and you have ruined the moral character of such an innocent boy of six years old! "*O, shame! shame!!*" but, as there is no shame with you, as you, in your hypocrisy, are not able to blush, I say: "*Wo! wo!! wo!!!*" unto you.

2. Dinah Maria Mulock [Craik], *Woman's Thoughts About Women* (London, 1858) 50–51, 54–61, 63, 220–22, 262–63, 265–67, 270–71.

[Although she avoided aligning herself with "bluestockings" or feminists, Mulock Craik defended the rights of single and working women and treated seriously a variety of women's issues, including work, independence, female friendships, depression, and sexuality. Mulock Craik's moralistic and advice-driven views do not often agree with Menken's own perspectives on women in society. Still they share similar concerns, and a comparison reveals the radicalness *and* Victorianness of Menken's work. The first selection presents Mulock Craik's thoughts about women in the arts; the second deals with fashionable women, or "women of the world," the subject (and title) of an essay by Menken; the final selection discusses women's melancholy, the most important theme in Menken's poetry.]

Chapter III. Female Professions.

[I]n literature [...] we meet men on level ground—and, shall I say it?—we do often beat them in their own field. We are acute and accurate historians, clear explanators of science, especially successful in imaginative works, and within the last year *Aurora Leigh*,[1] has proved that we can write as great a poem as any man among them all. Any publisher's list, any handful of weekly or monthly periodicals, can testify to our power of entering boldly on the literary profession, and pursuing it wholly, self-devotedly, and self-reliantly, thwarted by no hardships, and content with no height short of the highest. [...]

[H]igh as the calling is, it is not always, in the human sense, a happy one; it often results in, if it does not spring from, great sacrifices; and is full of a thousand misconstructions, annoyances, and temptations. Nay, since ambition is a quality far oftener deficient in us than in the other sex, its very successes are less sweet to women than to men. [...] [I]t remains yet doubtful whether the maiden-aunt who goes from house to house, perpetually busy and useful—the maiden house-mother, who keeps together an orphan family, having all the cares, and only half the joys of maternity or mistress-ship—even the active, bustling "old maid," determined on setting everybody to rights, and having a finger in every pie that needs her, and a few that don't—I question whether each of these women has not a more natural, and therefore, probably, a happier existence, than any "woman of genius" that ever enlightened the world.

But happiness is not the first nor the only thing on earth. Whosoever has entered upon this vocation in the right spirit, let her keep to it, neither afraid nor ashamed. The days of blue-stockings are over: it is a notable fact, that the best housekeepers, the neatest needlewomen, the most discreet managers of their own and others' affairs, are ladies whose names the world cons over in library lists and exhibition catalogues. [...]

---

[1]   Elizabeth Barrett Browning, *Aurora Leigh* (1857).

This fame, as gained in art or literature, is certainly of a purer and safer kind than that which falls to the lot of the female *artiste*.

Most people will grant that no great gift is given to be hid under a bushel; that a Sarah Siddons, a Rachel, or a Jenny Lind,[1] being created, was certainly not created for nothing. There seems no reason why a great actress or vocalist should not exercise her talents to the utmost for the world's benefit, and her own; nor that any genius, boiling and bursting up to find expression, should be pent down, cruelly and dangerously, because it refuses to run in the ordinary channel of feminine development. But the last profession of the four [governess, painter, author, *artiste* or performer] which I have enumerated as the only paths at present open to women, is the one which is the most full of perils and difficulties, on account of the personality involved in its exercise.

We may paint scores of pictures, write shelvesful of books—the errant children of our brain may be familiar half over the known world, and yet we ourselves sit as quiet by our chimney-corner, live a life as simple and peaceful as any happy "common woman" of them all. But with the *artiste* it is very different; she needs to be constantly before the public, not only mentally, but physically: the general eye becomes familiar, not merely with her genius, but her corporeality; and every comment of admiration or blame awarded to her, is necessarily an immediate personal criticism. This of itself is a position contrary to the instinctive something—call it reticence, modesty, shyness, what you will—which is inherent in every one of Eve's daughters. [...]

But that is by no means the chief objection; for the feeling of personal shyness dies out, and in the true *artiste* becomes altogether merged in the love and inspiration of her art—the inexplicable fascination of which turns the many-eyed gazing mass into a mere "public," of whose individuality the performer is no more conscious than was the Pythoness of her curled and scented Greek audience, when she felt on her tripod the afflatus of the unconquerable, inevitable god. The saddest phase of *artiste*-life—which is, doubtless, the natural result of this constant appearance before the public eye, this incessant struggle for the public's personal verdict—is its intense involuntary egotism. [...]

---

[1] Renowned actresses/performers: Sarah Siddons (1755-1831), British tragedienne; Rachel [née Elisa Felix] (1820-58), French tragedienne; Jenny Lind (1820-87), Swedish soprano.

And for this reason the profession of public entertainment, in all its graduation, from the inspired *tragédienne* to the poor chorus-singer, is, above any profession I know, to be marked with a spiritual Humane Society's pole, "*Dangerous.*" Not after the vulgar notion: we have among us too many chaste, matronly actresses, and charming maiden-vocalists, to enter now in the old question about the "respectability" of the stage; but on account of the great danger to temperament, character, and mode of thought, to which such a life peculiarly exposes its followers.

But if a woman has chosen it—I repeat in this as in any other—let her not forego it; for in every occupation the worthiness, like the "readiness," "is all." Never let her be moulded by her calling, but mould her calling to herself; being, as every woman ought to be, the woman first, the *artiste* afterwards. [...]

Conning over again this desultory chapter, it seems to me it all comes to neither more nor less than this: that since a woman, by choosing a definite profession, must necessarily quit the kindly shelter and safe negativeness of a private life, and assume a substantive position, it is her duty not hastily to decide, and before deciding, in every way to count the cost. But having chosen, let her fulfil her lot. Let there be no hesitations, no regrets, no compromises—they are at once cowardly and vain. She may have missed or foregone much;—I repeat, our natural and happiest life is when we lose ourselves in the exquisite absorption of home, the delicious retirement of dependent love; but what she has, she has, and nothing can ever take it from her.

Chapter IX. Women of the World.

"A woman of the world"—"Quite a woman of the world"—"A mere woman of the world"—with how many modifications of tone and emphasis do we hear the phrase; which seems inherently to imply a contradiction. Nature herself has apparently decided for women, physically as well as mentally, that their natural destiny should be *not* of the world. In the earlier ages of Judaism and Islamism, nobody ever seems to have ventured a doubt of this. Christianity alone raised the woman to her rightful and original place, as man's one help-meet, bone of his bone and flesh of his flesh, his equal in all points of vital moment, yet made suited to him by an harmonious something which is less inferiority than difference. And this difference will for ever exist. Volumes written on female progress; speeches interminable, delivered from the public rostrum in female treble, which from that very publicity and bravado would convert the most obvious "rights" into something very like a wrong; biographies numberless of great women—aye, and good—who, stepping out of their natural sphere, have done service in courts, camps, or diplomatic bureaus: all these exceptional cases will never set aside the universal law, that woman's proper place is home. [...]

Thus, to be a "woman of the world," though not essentially a criminal accusation, implies a state of being not natural, and therefore not happy. Without any sentimental heroics against the hollowness of such an existence, and putting aside the religious view of it altogether, I believe most people will admit that no woman living entirely in and for the world ever was, ever could be, a happy woman; that is, according to the definition of happiness, which supposes it to consist in having our highest faculties most highly developed, and in use to their fullest extent.

Chapter X. Happy and Unhappy Women.

Infinite, past human counting or judging, are the causes of mental unhappiness. Many of them spring from a real foundation, of sorrows varied beyond all measuring or reasoning upon: of these, I do not attempt to speak, for words would be idle and presumptuous; I only speak of that frame of mind—sometimes left behind by a great trouble, sometimes arising from troubles purely imaginary—which is called "an unhappy disposition."

Its root of pain is manifold; but, with women, undoubtedly can be oftenest traced to something connected with the affections: not merely the passion called *par excellence* love, but the entire range of personal sympathies and attachments, out of which we draw the sweetness and bitterness of the best part of our lives. If otherwise—if, as the phrase goes, an individual happens to have "more head than heart," she may be a very clever, agreeable personage, but she is not properly *a woman*—not the creature who, with all her imperfections, is nearer to heaven than man, in one particular—she "loves much." And loving is so frequently, nay, inevitably, identical with suffering, either with, or for, or from, the object beloved, that we need not go further to find the cause of the many anxious, soured faces, and irritable tempers, that we meet with among women. [...]

Naming the affections as the chief source of unhappiness among our sex, it would be wrong to pass over one phase of them, which must nevertheless be touched tenderly and delicately, as one that women instinctively hide out of sight and comment. I mean what is usually termed "a disappointment." Alas!—as if there were disappointments but those of love! and yet, until men and women are made differently from what God made them, it must always be, from its very secretness and inwardness, the sharpest of all pangs, save that of conscience.

A lost love. Deny it who will, ridicule it, treat it as mere imagination and sentiment, the thing is and will be; and women do suffer therefrom, in all its infinite varieties: loss by death, by faithlessness or unworthiness, and by mistaken or unrequited affection. Of these, the second is beyond all question the worst. There is in death a consecration which lulls the sharpest personal anguish into comparative calm; and in time there comes, to all pure and religious natures, that sense of total possession of the objects beloved, which death alone gives—that faith, which is content to see them safe landed out of the troubles of this changeful life, into the life everlasting. And an attachment which has always been on one side only, has a certain incompleteness which prevents its ever knowing the full agony of having and losing, while at the same time it preserves to the last a dreamy sanctity which sweetens half its pain. But to have loved and lost, either by that total disenchantment which leaves compassion as the sole substitute for love which can exist no more, or by the slow torment which is obliged to let go day by day all that constitutes the diviner part of love—namely, reverence, belief, and trust, yet clings desperately to the only thing left it, a long-suffering apologetic tenderness— this lot is probably the hardest any woman can have to bear. [...]

As many a man sits wearying his soul out by trying to remedy some grand flaw in the plan of society, or the problem of the universe, when perhaps the chief thing wrong is his own liver, or overtasked brain; so many a woman will pine away to the brink of the grave with an imaginary broken heart, or sour to the very essence of vinegar on account of everybody's supposed ill-usage of her, when it is her own restless, dissatisfied, selfish heart, which makes her at war with everybody.

Would that women—and men, too, but that their busier and more active lives save most of them from it—could be taught from their childhood to recognise as an evil spirit this spirit of causeless melancholy—this demon which dwells among the tombs, and yet, which first shows itself in such a charming and picturesque form, that we hug it to our innocent breasts, and never suspect that it may enter in and dwell there till we are actually "possessed;" cease almost to be accountable beings, and are fitter for a lunatic asylum than for the home-circle.

3. Lillie Devereux Blake, "The Social Condition of Woman," *The Knickerbocker* 51 (May 1863): 381-88.

[Blake was an active social reformer, women's rights advocate, and a prolific author of fiction and cultural criticism. She was far more active in the women's rights movement than Menken and, as the essay below reveals, more focused on specific legal and political reforms. Nonetheless, both examine "the cruel wrongs of which woman has to complain" (Blake) and "lift up the down-trodden colors of *woman's rights*" (Menken). They both criticize marriage, fashion, and the sexual double standard, while emphasizing the importance of women's independence and women's intellectual pursuits.]

That woman is entitled to entire equality on every point—politically, legally, and socially—with man, is a proposition so evidently true that only the wilful blindness of man, and his jealous assumption of superiority, has so long prevented it from being acknowledged. [...] It is as absurd to withhold from any portion of the human race certain prerogatives, on the mere ground of sex, as it would be to make height or grace a requisite for obtaining them. The true qualification for securing any position should be mental capacity, not the physical accident of sex. Every one must agree in the cruel wrongs of which woman has to complain, in her exclusion from the many honorable callings she might fill with advantage, and in the low rate of pay she has to receive for her labors, whereas it is manifest that it should be the quality of the work, not the sex of the worker, that should govern, the compensation.

Now, what is the cause of this state of affairs, and where lies the remedy? All talk of the inequality of the sexes is utterly idle; their minds like their bodies differ in kind, but each are equally excellent in their way. As woman physically is certainly equal in beauty and harmony of proportions to man, so mentally would she be his glorious counterpart and compeer, were she ever permitted full development:—No more to be despised than is the poet by the statesman. Whatever inferiority there is apparent in her at the present day is the result of the humiliations of her position, and the wretchedness of her education. Man is no doubt the stronger animal, and from the earliest ages of the world he has too often made use of this superiority of brute force to oppress the weaker being at his side. He has decreed that she shall only be of consequence in so far as she is pleasing to him; that she shall therefore be early taught that youth and beauty are the two most to be desired gifts; that she shall have no higher aim that the cares of the nursery; that having lived through a few years, as a belle and a young mother, she shall be content to sink into the utter insignificance which makes the very words "old woman" a term of contempt. Thus having assigned her to this subordinate position, and having made stern rules to keep her there, he has educated and treated her as an inferior, till only in a few rare instances has she been able to rise sufficiently above the restraints of her positions to assert her equality. That all this is bitterly true, a brief analysis of society will clearly prove.

Who has made the laws that govern the world? Certainly man; it cannot be pretended that woman has had any voice even on those points that most nearly concern her; and I take it as one of the surest evidences of her inherent equality that, despite all the disadvantages under which she has labored, she has struggled from her first position of absolute slavery, to her present tolerably respectable rank. Man, without a thought that she has an immortal soul, has insisted that she shall perpetually be regarded as a *woman*, and her whole training has been such as will best fit her to be merely attractive. Thus, lest, even under this deteriorating system, she should attempt to contend for the great prizes of life with man, he has made laws that effectually exclude her from all hopes of equality. [...]

[A]s society is at present constituted, the fact of her sex is so perpetually thrust upon woman, that no greater curse can fall on a human soul than to be imprisoned in a female form. Early in childhood she may probably show a superior intelligence, a greater quickness than a boy at the same age, but from the moment that the iron shackles of custom fall around her, from the time she is checked in some healthful exercise because, "it is not proper in a little lady," or hears the young tyrant man sneer at what is "only fit for girls," she must, if of a nature too lofty to submit tamely to control, chafe fiercely against the restraints around her. If she have independence, she must revolt desperately against perpetual subservience to man— as for him she must wait, and upon him depend for every pleasure or comfort. If she have honor and truth, she must bitterly loathe the system of deception that society requires of her. [...]

Enough cannot be said against the present terrible defects of woman's education. [...] Their souls, their minds, too often even their hearts, are so thwarted by the falsities of their training that by the time they are grown up it is almost useless to expect of them any thing but vanity and frivolity. In the first place, the higher branches of study are too seldom taught even where wealth enables parents to give their daughters those advantages. Thus almost invariably the instruction, faulty as it is, is stopped just at its most important point, and the young woman is thrown into idleness, and the temptations of society, at eighteen or nineteen, often earlier. A boy at that age is rightly considered only fit for the schoolroom; and the girl, although a forcing process may sometimes have developed an unnatural precocity, is really but a child, wholly unequal to coping with the dangers that beset the first entrance on life. Upon this point there should be no inequality between the sexes—the studies of both should continue at least up to twenty. Although I would by no means exclude either young men or women from some social pleasures, there is no reason why a young girl more than a boy should be plunged into society merely because she has at eighteen the first bloom of youth in her appearance. Then the endless sewing that fills up all the leisure of woman's life is a fearful degenerator. I know of nothing more cramping to the mind than this perpetual setting of minute stitches. [...] Another point, and a most important one: women are not expected to understand certain things considered essential to every man's respectability. Business, the great rules of trade, even the regulations governing investment, are rarely, almost never, explained to them, yet very few women, married or single, go through life without suffering from the effects of this ignorance. Even the laws of the land under which they live are rarely taught them, yet is it not essential that they should know as well as men what are the legislative enactments that affect their persons and property? Then, again, politics are utterly forbidden; we all know how a "politician in petticoats" is condemned, even by the poor deluded women themselves, who do not see that their weak masters are helping to rivet the chains that bind them.

And in the insensible but none the less influential education of precept and example, how much has woman to suffer from the injustice of man? From childhood she is never permitted to form opinions of her own, on any important question, outside the circumscribed sphere to which man has restricted her. If in the family a young girl ventures to say on any great theme, "I think so-and-so," with what amused smiles or manly sneers her father and brothers receive the novel idea that she should be capable of any opinion on a subject requiring depth of thought. Thus she is forced to lean upon some man, even for mental support, until she becomes after a while the incapable he has made her. [...]

[I]t still remains only too true that the whole aim and object of a woman's education is not to fit her to do her duty in life, whether as a maid or wife, but to "get" a husband—to be admired by the opposite sex. A girl's parents and teachers may try to inculcate higher hopes, but every thing that she sees and hears among her young companions, or in society, instills the lesson that sinks deep in the young heart. Her friends speak of the belle as one to be envied, of the old maid as one to be pitied; and what result can follow but that at eighteen she is eager only for ball room triumphs? Now, I ask, what is to be expected from this false system of training and education? What would be the effect on a dozen men of various characters, who should be reared like women—taught to regard their beauty as their chief desire, and fancy-work as their highest aim? [...]

Mr. Trollope, in his own clever way, discusses the subject of "Woman's Rights" in one of the chapters in his recent book on "North-America," and seems to consider that women are entirely compensated for any evils of their position, by the luxurious idleness in which their fathers and husbands combine to support them.[1] He does not pause to consider how many women are not thus protected and supported, nor how often those condemned to an existence of indolence suffer from the lack of stimulus in their lives. Indeed, I find this mistake in all writers on this theme—that they do not make sufficient allowances for those faults of education of which I have spoken, and that they are too arbitrary in the rules they lay down as guidelines for discussion; generally jumping to the conclusion that certain characteristics, now often seen in woman, are the result of nature, not realizing how frequently they are already due to training. [...]

To come now to one of the gravest aspects of man's injustice to woman. It cannot be pretended that she has had any voice in arranging her position, socially, in ordering her education, or making the

---

[1] Anthony Trollope, *North America* (1862), vol. 1, chap. 18.

rules that govern society; and on this last point, man's position is not only cruelly unjust, but glaringly absurd. Woman, he loudly proclaims, is his inferior in firmness, in nobility, in strength, and generally in high mental qualities; and yet, at the same time, he places in her frail keeping the most sacred virtues that guard society from anarchy. Women, men seem to say, were born to be the subjects of us, lords of creation; let them, then, take the troublesome duties we cannot fulfil. We weary of the perpetual care of young children; we will make it their business, ignorant and petulant though they be, to wear out their lives in the nursery: we are passionate by nature, impatient of control; the virtues of temperance and chastity are not to be expected of us; yet should they be wholly disregarded, society would fall into chaos. Some one must uphold them; let it be the feeble woman who must do as we say, or be condemned to eternal infamy. The principle of these sentiments would not be objectionable; it shows a certain confidence to place such trust in woman's hands. But having issued these decrees, what do men do? Do they assist their subjects to keep them? No, having placed the sacred pearl of purity in the keeping of these beings whom they have themselves educated to be weak and yielding, instead of aiding them in the task for which they profess to regard them as unfit, they at once use every argument and every art to steal from their trembling grasp the jewel that is their life. If success ensues, as it does but too often, who bears the punishment? Man, who has been the tempter? No, he escapes unhurt, to inflict on his victim the terrible retribution; and the poor wretch, whom the faults of temperament and education, perhaps a strong love, have led to ruin, is cast out utterly, and made a thing to be scoffed at—the pariah of society. Let woman, I demand indignantly on this point, have equal rights with man, not that I would have her less virtuous, GOD forbid! but I would have man more so. [...]

Now what can be done to remedy these evils? First, let the whole education of our women be directed on a more enlarged basis than in the past. Instead of sending all girls through a set form of study, having no reference whatever to the constitution of different minds—a system under which all are crammed with music, French, drawing, and fancy-work, whether they exhibit any taste for them or not—let each woman's education be directed by the bent of her mind; and, above all, let every woman, as well as every man, be taught, before her education be considered complete, some mode of earning her living. If a girl has an evident faculty towards languages, let her be educated so as to be able to teach them; if music be her talent, let her be taught that practically; if she has no higher capacity than for embroidery, let her be made a proficient in that humble art. Again, if her mind takes a wider range, let her be taught medicine, or finance; or perhaps, in certain exceptional cases, law. But let *all* women, even of wealthy families, be given a livelihood in this country, where, even among the higher classes, riches so often take wing; and where nine tenths of the women of all ranks have at least to assist in earning their own living, it is great injustice not to have them taught how to obtain it, and not to have open to them all callings and professions. Under this system, I am sure a far healthier state of society would exist than at present; a father would not then regard his daughters as so many dead-weights, to be decked out to catch husbands; nor would any freeborn American girl ever be reduced to the degrading necessity of marrying for a support— that is, selling her self because she sees with despair that, as society is at present constituted, and from the defects of her education, there is no hope of her earning an honest livelihood. Nor would there, were all women taught independence, be any forced marriages; but on the contrary, unions would take place on a far better basis than now, since then there need be no inducement to them but only the pure motive of love. The whole tone of society would, I firmly believe, be elevated by these reforms, since, by strengthening the minds of our women, we would strengthen them in purity; and were they permitted self-assertion, they would, for their own dignity, correct the present evil usurpations of men, that permit some of the sex of notoriously licentious life to be the companions of refined ladies, while contact with a fallen sister is shunned as contamination. Women of real elevation would insist upon equal virtue in men, or refuse them admission to their presence. [...]

Of man, then, I ask equal rights, in holding property and making wills, and admission to all occupations for women. Whatever may be thought of their power in higher pursuits, certainly clerkships and many editorial positions can be admirably filled by women: let them be open to their endeavors. I am convinced that great gain to the employers, as well as to the employed, would result from the use of the delicate female mind in much work now more clumsily executed by men. But if allowed practical operation, of course all these questions would speedily settle themselves on the hard basis of dollars and cents. No one would employ a female book-keeper or physician, unless she proved her superiority over male rivals. Why, then, refuse a fair trial of these much-needed reforms? [...]

And of you, women, I ask courage and persistent endeavor towards the equality you deserve. Teach your daughters not to consider themselves inferior; to be self-reliant and brave; and above all, educate them to independence, and a higher aim than "getting married." Teach your sons to make equals and companions of their sisters, and to grow up ready and willing to aid the reforms you advocate. Never, by any silly sneers at "Woman's Rights," or "strong-minded females," aid man in detracting from the efforts of woman to elevate herself; rather use your influence on the men around you, to induce them to view these great questions in their true light.

4. Junius Henri Browne, "The Bohemians," *The Great Metropolis* (Hartford, 1869) 150–158.

[Though she often preferred the term "vagabond," Menken identified herself with the artsy subculture that acquired the label "bohemian." Browne's affectionate defense of America's "original" bohemians mentions Menken and a number of her friends and acquaintances, including Ada Clare. This piece of pop culture history also provides a contemporary perspective on the literary and social circle Menken most enjoyed.]

The term Bohemian, in its modern sense, has been erroneously applied to gipsies—the wandering, vagabond, aimless, homeless class, who, coming originally from India, it is believed, entered Europe in the fourteenth and fifteenth centuries and scattered themselves through Russia, Hungary, Spain and England.

In Paris, more than a quarter of a century ago, the name was given to the literary and artistic people, who were as clever as careless; who lived in to-day, and despised to-morrow; who preferred the pleasure and the triumph of the hour to the ease of prosperity and the assurance of abiding fame. Henri Murger, in his *Vie de Bohème*,[1] first gave a succinct and clear account of the peculiarities, habits and opinions of the true Zingara;[2] lived the life, and died the death, he had so eloquently described as the disposition and destiny of his class.

---

[1]   Henri Murger, *Scènes de la vie de Bohème* (1848).
[2]   Gypsy.

Since then, all persons of literary or artistic proclivities, regardless of conventionality, believing in the sovereignty of the individual, and indifferent to the most solemn tone of Mrs. Grundy, have received the Bohemian baptism. Journalists generally, especially since the War correspondents during the Rebellion received the title, have been called Bohemians all the country over, and will be, no doubt, until the end of the century.

Bohemian, particularly in New-York, has indeed come to be a sort of synonym for a newspaper writer, and not without reason, as he is usually no favorite of fortune, and his gifts, whatever they may be, rarely include that of practicality. His profession, enabling him to see the shams of the World and the hollowness of reputation, renders him indifferent to fame, distrustful of appearances, and skeptical of humanity. He sinks into a drudge, relieved by spasms of brilliancy and cynicism; rails at his condition, and clings to it tenaciously. Bohemians, however, are older than Henri Murger, or the fourteenth century, or the Christian era. Alexander of Macedon, Alcibiades, Aspasia, Hypathia,[1] Cleopatra, Mark Antony and Julius Caesar, were all Bohemians—splendid and dazzling Bohemians, the best of their kind, the highest exponents of the antique school, of magnificent powers, and melancholy, but picturesque endings.

The Bohemian now-a-days is popularly supposed to be a man of some culture and capacity, who ignores law and order; who is entirely indifferent to public opinion; who disregards clean linen, his word or his debts; who would borrow the last dollar of his best friend, never intending to repay it, and glory in dishonoring his friend's wife or sister.

That is the common idea; but I am glad no such class exists, however many individuals there may be of the kind. It certainly is not true of journalists, who are quite as honest and honorable as members of any other profession, and who continue poor enough to prevent any suspicion to the contrary.

The Metropolis does contain a number of wretched men, ill-paid—mostly foreigners—who act occasionally as reporters for the daily and weekly papers, and who are driven to every shift, and out of every shirt, by press of poverty and the exigency of circumstance. They are not journalists, however, any more than stage-sweepers are

---

[1] Hypatia (370?-415), Egyptian philosopher and mathematician, first celebrated woman in the field of mathematics.

dramatic artists. They are to be pitied, though, in spite of their faults, for which society and temperament are in the main responsible.

The original Bohemians, in this City and country were fifteen or twenty journalists, the greater part of them young men of ability and culture, who desired, particularly in regard to musical and dramatic criticism, to give tone and color to, if not to control, the public press, not from any mercenary consideration, but from an earnest intellectual egotism. They had their rise and association about twelve years ago, and flourished up to the commencement of the War, which broke up the Bohemian fraternity, not only here, but in other cities.

At their head, as well by age as experience and a certain kind of domineering dogmatism, was Henry Clapp, Jr., who had been connected with a dozen papers, and who was one of the first to introduce the personal style of Paris feuilleton into the literary weeklies. He was nearly twice as old as most of his companions; was witty, skeptical, cynical, daring, and had a certain kind of magnetism that drew and held men, though he was neither in person nor in manner, what would be called attractive.

Soon after the inception of the informal society, he established the *Saturday Press*, to which the brotherhood contributed for money when they could get it, and for love when money could not be had. The *Saturday Press* was really the raciest and brightest weekly ever published here. It often sparkled with wit, and always shocked the orthodox with its irreverence and "dangerous" opinions.

Clapp kept up the paper for a year, when it was suspended. After its death he twice revived it; but its brilliancy would not keep it alive without business management, and it was too independent and iconoclastic to incur the favor of any large portion of the community.

The third attempt to establish the *Press* failed about three years since; and Clapp, bitter from his many failures, now lives a careless life; writes epigrammatic paragraphs and does the dramatic for one of the weeklies. He is stated to be over fifty; but his mind is vigorous as ever, his tongue as fluent, and his pen as sharp.

E.G.P. ("Ned") Wilkins, of the *Herald*, was another prominent member of the fraternity, and one of the few attachés of that journal who have ever gained much individual reputation. He was a pungent and strong writer, at the same time correct and graceful, and had the requisite amount of dogmatism and self-consciousness to render him acceptable to his guild and satisfactory to himself. When he promised far better things than he had ever performed, he died, leaving no other record than the file of newspapers—the silent history of countless unremembered men of genius.

William Winter, who came here from Boston, after graduating at Harvard, because he believed New York offered the best field for writers, was a contributor to the *Saturday Press* and other weeklies; composed many clever poems, and did whatever literary work he could find at hand; supporting himself comfortably by his pen, and gaining considerable reputation, particularly as a poet. A few years ago he married a literary woman and has not since been much of a Bohemian; for Hymen is an enemy to the character, and domesticity its ultimate destroyer. He is now dramatic critic of the *Tribune*, and a very hard worker; deeming it a duty to perform whatever labor comes to him without seeking.

Edward H. House, for years connected with the *Tribune*, was a fourth friend of Clapp and also a *Saturday Press* contributor. He has quitted journalism, at least for the time, and made a good deal of money, it is said, by sharing the authorship of some, and being the agent in this country of all of Boucicault's plays.[1] House is a good fellow, handsome, well-bred, winning in manners; is still a bachelor; does little work and gets a good deal for it; and enjoys himself as a man of the World ought.

Fitz James O'Brien, who made his début in the literary world, as the author of *Diamond Lens* in the *Atlantic Monthly* ten years ago, and who was a generous, gifted, rollicking Irishman, was one of the cardinals in the high church of Bohemia, until the breaking out of the War. He entered the field and distinguished himself for desperate courage until he was killed in Virginia and forgotten. O'Brien had a warm heart, a fine mind and a liberal hand; but he was impulsive to excess and too careless of his future for his own good.

Charles F. Browne, having been made famous through his "Artemus Ward" articles while local editor of the *Cleveland Plaindealer*, and come to the Metropolis, where clever men naturally tend, worked to advantage his droll vein for the *Saturday Press*, *Vanity Fair* and *Mrs. Grundy*. He was a pure Bohemian, thoroughly good-natured, incapable of malice toward any one, with a capacity for gentleness and tenderness, like a woman's, open-handed, imprudent, seeing everything at a queer

---

[1] Dion Boucicault (1820?-90), Irish-born actor and dramatist, the most successful playwright of the era.

angle, and always wondering at his own success. He drew about him in New-York a number of the knights of the quill; gained their esteem and affection, and left a vacancy in the circle and their sympathies when his kindly soul went out across the sea.

George Arnold was a very clever writer in prose and verse, a regular contributor to the *Saturday Press*, and remarkable for his versatility. He had many gifts; was good-looking, graceful, brilliant. His easy, almost impromptu poems, full of sweetness and suggestive sadness, have been published since his death, which took place three years ago, and been widely admired. He sang in a careless way the pleasures and pains of love, the joys of wine, the charm of indolence, the gayety and worthlessness of existence in the true Anacreontic vein. From such a temperament as his, earnest and continued exertion was not to be expected. Like Voiture,[1] he trifled life away in pointed phrases and tuneful numbers; but gained a large circle of devoted friends. At three and thirty he slipped out of the World which had been much and little to him, and left behind him many sincere mourners who speak of him still with words of love and moistened eyes.

William North, a young Englishman,—he had quarreled with his parents who were wealthy, and come to this country to live by his pen,—was also of the Bohemian tribe. He found the struggle harder than he had anticipated; for, though a man of talent and culture, he lacked directness of purpose and capacity for continuous work. His disappointment soured him, and poverty so embittered his sensitive nature that he destroyed himself, leaving a sixpence, all the money he had, and the "Slave of the Lamp," a manuscript novel, which he had not been able to sell, but for which the notoriety of the mournful tragedy secured a publisher.

Mortimer Thompson, who had become a popular humorist under the sobriquet of "Doesticks," and who was at the height of his popularity, was a Bohemian in those days, and consorted with the clever crew. He was then a member of the *Tribune* staff. Since that time he has been a war correspondent; had various changes of fortune, and no longer enjoys his old fame. He still lives in New-York, however, and does the drollery for some of the weekly papers over his old *nom de plume*.

Charles Dawson Shanly, a well-known littérateur, Harry Neal

---

[1] Vincent Voiture (1598-1648), French poet whose work is characteristically witty, charming, and subtle.

(deceased), Frank Wood (deceased), contributors to *Vanity Fair* and other publications of the time, Charles B. Seymour, now dramatic critic of the *Times*, Franklin J. Ottarson, for five and twenty years a city journalist, nearly all of which he had spent in the service of the *Tribune*; Charles Gayler, a playwright; John S. Dusolle of the Sunday *Times*, and others were members of the fraternity. They met frequently at Pfaff's restaurant, No. 653 Broadway; had late suppers, and were brilliant with talk over beer and pipes for several years. Those were merry and famous nights, and many bright conceits and witticisms were discharged over the festive board.

The Bohemians had feminine companions at Pfaff's frequently. There was Ada Clare, known here then as the Queen of Bohemia, and of course a writer for the *Saturday Press*. She was of Irish extraction; a large-hearted eccentric woman who had property in the South, but lost it during the War. She afterward published a novel, "Only a Woman's Heart," said to have been a transcript of some of her own experiences, and went upon the stage. The last heard of her she was playing in a Galveston (Texas) theatre, and had been married to the manager. There was a pretty little creature, known as Getty Gay, probably an assumed name, and Mary Fox, both actresses; Jennie Danforth, a writer for the weekly journals; Annie Deland, still on the boards, and Dora Shaw, who was the best Camille on the American stage. The ill-fated Adah Menken, also went to Pfaff's occasionally; and altogether the coterie enjoyed itself intellectually and socially as no coterie has since. But all that has passed now.

The War, as I have said, interfered with Bohemian progress. Many have become apostates now, and others deny all connection with the fraternity. The order in its old form is practically extinct; but without the distinguishing name or any organization, but better, and higher, and freer, and purer, it exists, and does good, though it may be invisible, work.

I might give a long list of city writers and journalists well known throughout the country, who are Bohemians in the best sense, but who dislike the title because so many unworthy persons have made the name repulsive by claiming it as theirs.

Certain reporters are largely of the psuedo-Bohemian class, and do more to degrade journalism than all the worthy members of the profession to elevate and purify it. And for the reason that the former are impudent, sycophantic and unprincipled, while the latter are modest, independent and honorable. If newspaper proprietors would adopt the wise policy of employing good men at good salaries, the disreputable class would find their level and cease to be a nuisance, at least in the vicinity of Printing-House Square.

The true disciples are men and women who are charitable where the World condemns; who protect where society attacks; who have the capacity and courage to think for themselves; the earnestness and truthfulness to unmask shams; the faith to believe sin the result of ignorance, and love and culture eternal undoers of evil and of wrong. They honestly discharge every duty and every debt. Their ways are pleasant and their manners sweet. They are understood because they are in advance of the time, and have comprehensive views the great mass cannot take.

Such Bohemians are found in the pulpit, on the bench, on the tripod; and every day they are increasing the area of Thought, the breadth of Charity, the depth of Love. Children of Nature, they go not about with solemn faces, declaring after the common fashion, the degeneracy of the age and the wickedness of humanity. They have a hope and creed born of reason and spiritual insight; believing that God and Good are identically the same; that Progress is onward and upward forever and ever.

5. Marie Louise Hankins, "Lillie Bell: The Female Writer," *Women of New York* (New York, 1861) 171-74.

[In the 1850s and 60s, women writers such as Harriet Beecher Stowe and Louisa May Alcott were becoming among the most popular and celebrated authors in the world. Yet, as a group or type, women writers continued to face cruel, sexist reproach and often hostile opposition to their endeavors. Though she was of course a "female writer" herself, Hankins portrays literary woman as bitter, unattractive, and pseudo-intellectual in this fictional sketch that draws on stereotypes prevalent in nineteenth-century American culture.]

Lillie Bell's *real* name is plain Ruth Flatfoot. She resides in the city of New York, and inflicts her presence upon the family of her married sister. She is an old maid, whose human kindness seems to have turned to gall. She hates every one who is happy or good looking, and especially pretty girls, because their beauty attracts the attention of those masculine eyes, which she has so long and so vainly endeavored to draw upon her own charms. She hates young mothers, because they are married, and she has never been. She hates old ladies, because they seem to rejoice in the affection of their sons and daughters. She hates little girls, because they may eventually grow up to be pleasing women. She hates men, because they disregard her merits. Ruth is seldom seen at home without a pen between her fingers, and various ink stains upon the bony knuckles of her right hand. She writes articles for the papers, and is very bitter on the faults of poor human nature. Sometimes, in her more tender moods, she attempts sentimental poetry, and introduces love and a tombstone. Her heroes are in perpetual despair, and her heroines all die. Her chamber would strike terror to the heart of any good housekeeper. Old ink bottles cover the tables, quires of scribbled foolscap lay upon the carpet, and magazines and pamphlets without number, are tumbling out of place, and sticking between the hinges of half shut closet doors. Her wardrobe appears to have been tossed into the drawers of her bureau with a pitch fork, and every article of her attire is stained with ink. Her cloak, hanging on a peg behind the door, still bears the label which the shop man placed upon it to attract attention. The label reads thus:— "Very fashionable—only five dollars!"

It is her chief boast that people are afraid of her. She glories in making sharp speeches, and hitting people in the tenderest points; and after inflicting a mental stab, always closes her thin lips, with an air which plainly says, "See what it is to be a smart woman!"

When any lady is spoken of in her presence as being pretty, she assumes a scornful glance, and remarks, "Pretty enough, but, dear me, not at all *intellectual*;" or, "She may have fine eyes, but, then her mind— good gracious!—give me a woman with a *mind*." As for the gentlemen, she has a list of dreadful anecdotes to relate about them.

Mr. Sykes drinks too much. Mr. Bingham flirts with young ladies. Mr. Trotters neglects his wife for a designing widow, and Mr. Harrowbones had cheated all his creditors. In short, her heart is as ill favored as her face, and her actions invariably correspond. No one will ever love her, or feel friendship for her, and she cares for no creature save herself. While living she will never be esteemed, and she will not be regretted when she dies.

Our business necessarily brings us into contact with many female writers who figure in the periodicals, and we must say, that with half a dozen exceptions, Ruth Flatfoot, *alias* "Lillie Bell," is a very fair type of the most of them.

Some are ridiculous in manners, dress, and speech. A few are down-right repulsive. There is one in particular, whose complexion is suggestive of buttermilk and sour cards. She does all kinds of "pieces," for any body who will *pay* her for them, and undertake the trouble and labor of preparing them for type. Her literary forte seems to be in the use and arrangement of dyspeptic adjectives, and asthmatical adverbs. Her principal characters are school girls, old women, and cats. She claims to have studied grammar at the seminary, but being now a widow, its use is totally unnecessary. She is addicted to cold cream externally, and hates soap and water. We always feel qualmish when she approaches. She is forever boring you to *read* her stories, and asks you what you think they are worth. If you reject them, or allude to any of their countless defects, she flounts out, and goes away to hate you forever.

6. Ada Clare, "The Man's Sphere and Influence," *The Golden Era* (3 April 1864): 4; "The 'Blue Stocking,'" *The Golden Era* (3 July 1864): 5.

[Menken's friend Ada Clare rejected the misogynist denigration of women authors. Using humor to expose the ridiculousness of these self-righteous, contradictory, and always personal attacks on women writers, Clare counters the stereotypes circulated by Marie Louise Hankins and others with feminist irony.]

The Man's Sphere and Influence.

I noticed one thing that grieved and annoyed me. That is, seeing so many gentlemen out without any body to take care of them, expressing their opinions without asking any lady's leave, and enjoying the music without begging any lady's pardon. But is it strictly proper that a man should take care of himself, mind his own business, and act like a rational, sincere, and responsible human being. All this might do very well if it would end here; but alas! may it not lead the man into the rostrum, the pulpit, the auctioneer's desk and finally into the editor's sanctum.

I confess that though I often admire the writings of men, it always pains me to see a man exposing himself to public remark and to the gaze of women, by coming publicly forward in print. The sacred precinct of home is the real sphere of man. Modesty, obedience, sobriety are the true male virtues.

We love to see the sweet male violets hidden under domestic greens.

I don't mean to say that men have never succeeded in writing, but compare them with the great pen-women of the present, past and future, and where are they? Echo answers "gone out for a hour; in case of fire, keys may be found next door."

There is something effeminate in the literary or artist man, that our sex repudiates. We do not want man to be too highly educated; we want him sweet, gentle, and incontestibly stupid.

There are many things he can learn with impunity—the multiplication table for instance. He should learn to read, also; because the works of T.S. Arthur[1] and the publications of the American Tract Society[2] should sometimes beguile his weary hours. But, above all things in his education, let not the sacred dumpling be neglected.

But why puzzle his brain, built for the cultivation of moral sense and the adaptation of virtue, with such abstruse sciences as geography, history, grammar, spelling, guaging, etc.

It must not be supposed that we despise men; in their proper sphere we are willing to love, cherish and protect them. But we do not want them as rivals; we wish them low, in order that we may be able to come down from our dignity and stoop to them. Their strength must lie in their weakness. When we draw them under the wings of our protection, let them not take to crowing.

Let no profane women suggest that men have a right to enter the arena of the arts in proportion as they exhibit a capacity for them.

I will indignantly ask what capacity has to do with sphere? I will brand her as a dangerous radical if she say whatever nature has fitted him to do, that she exacts of him. I will ask her if she means to say that these things are to be managed on so low a scale as that of nature and truth? No, no; whenever nature interferes with the exactions of propriety and custom, the best thing you can do with nature is to decently smother and strangle her. [...]

Once for all, we women want men to be all exactly alike to the least atom, and above every thing let them be versed in the heavenly lore of the kitchen.

---

[1] Timothy Shay Arthur (1809-85), author of popular temperance novels, including the hugely successful *Ten Nights in a Bar-Room* (1854).

[2] Publisher of evangelical Christian moral reading.

Let puddings be made though the heavens fall!

We don't want intelligent men, our only choice is the angelic dunce.

On the other hand, we wish their moral and social virtues to be developed to the utmost. The moral sense of the man, the perception of the man, is too sweet and sensitive a thing to be trusted to the companionship of mental ability.

The question is not what the man is or can be, but what we women wish him to be. [...]

If there's any one thing that shocks me above another, it is to see a great strong-minded man going about, thinking for himself; having something to say and saying it; smiling when he is merry; and sighing when he is sad; eating what he likes and not hurrying; wearing warm clothes in cold weather and thin ones in warm; charitable to the unfortunate; ready to succor the oppressed; having no taste for scandal; and, in fact, embodying the qualities gentle, generous, reverent, honest and brave.

I do not envy the moral turpitude of that reader who will not be appalled by such a picture of a man as I have drawn, and who will not shrink with horror from the sight.

My sermon is done, my text is dissipated, I come down from my pulpit, and hereafter will preach no more.

But if through means of my discourse one intellectual man becomes an idiot; if one truthful mind turns to cant and nonsense; if one incipient Isaac Newton leaves of studying the profound philosophical meaning of apple-dropping, and learns to make the apples into pies instead; if one large mind renounces its mental sphere, and devotes itself to fabricating the noble home-made shirt, that discourse will have accomplished its prayerful work, and the writer will not have lived in vain!

The "Blue Stocking."

Once upon a time, I'm told the Blue Stocking was a living fact; now she exists only in the minds of the fogy-men old enough to remember her. Some of these curious old fossil fellows are still extant, and through means of these eye-witnesses and the copious analyses of various male writers, I am thus taught to conceive of her exact picture. For both the minds and works of such male beings kindly retain an unfailing fund of the noxious scales from this fish, in order that we may know how the horrid creature sported herself in the slimy waters of her existence.

Thus to my eye she is painted. The Blue Stocking is an intellectual woman. She is a female who possesseth mental gifts. These mental gifts, of whatever nature they be, she weareth in the manner the porcupine doth his quills and with the same intention. She hath wrenched the curves from her form and her body is thus bounded with square lines, with the occasional diversity of a wildly acute angle. Her hair calleth the brush and comb its direst foe. A threatening pen gapes at each ear. Her claw-like hands are long, scraggy and immortally ink-spotted. Her feet are clothed in maimed stockings, and forlorn slippers flap their wings about her heels as she walketh. Such is the seediness of her attire, that the scavenger claimeth her for his own, the sympathetic ash-barrel singeth to her "come rest in this bosom," and the scare-crow waggeth at her the corn-stalk of scorn as she passeth.

Doubly an Amazon, she hath seared her two breasts, in order to plant upon them the iron muskets of literature; yea, and lest the blueness of their veins should draw to her the softening influence of the blue-eyed angel of love.

She hath been known to bear children, but there is no record that she hath known the maternal sentiment. She cannot rank so high as the weazel in the treatment of her offspring. She feedeth them on sour meal and musty bread, for the pen has dried up the sources of milk in her breasts, ere they were seared.

She delivereth them over to the devouring elements. Naked are they thrust forth to the cruel winds. Hungry dogs attack them before her eyes, and she waiteth to close her sentence, ere she rescueth them from the canine clutches. She seeth them creep into the fire and crisp themselves into carbon before her eyes, but her only emotion venteth itself in a "hum," and a nib of the impatient pen.

She feedeth on strange flesh and mysterious bread. Her food cannot attract caloric; it is cold and clammy even during the process of cooking. A needle causeth her to foam at the mouth. All that is hard and harsh, and graceless in nature clustereth around her. Even the blue-bottle-fly she calleth a coquette and crusheth with ireful heel. Her eyes are optical Gorgons whose glance turneth the heart into stone.

But with the male sex lies the chief terror of her coming. When she beholdeth the male, she mocketh at him in her wrath. Her mane is erect, her eyes vomit flames, her feet are pawing the ground, and her mouth snorting tempest-making words. Tall, thundreth and terrible, she driveth the male shrieking before her.

Now, alas! how painful the contrast. The male sex has ceased to fear her entirely, not a sign of retreat at her coming, and nothing like swooning if she speaks to him. Nay, there is a fact still more astonishing, they are beginning to accuse the literary woman of over susceptibility, and of vanity, of a love of finery and luxury.

How painful indeed is the contrast between these literary women as we now see them, and the glorious picture of the bluestocking of the past as the male has portrayed her.

As far as genius is concerned it is so much above and beyond us that we cannot legislate for it. What it will do we know not, any more than we can predicate what riot an earthquake or a whirlwind may run, but as far as *talent* is concerned, if a literary woman does not show a little more common-sense, forbearance, patience and dexterity in life than the majority of her sex not literary, then she is not fit for her profession. For the habit of thinking and of going through the mechanical effort of arranging such thoughts into writing, should discipline the whole mental force of the woman, and in fact should teach her to make the best use of all materials whether mental or physical.

Now-a-days the woman of brains is generally the woman of specially acute emotional nature. Thus have the mighty fallen, and the literary woman is no longer to be distinguished from the rest of her sex.

Alas, me! how degenerate hath the age become, for in these modern days, the truly great woman hath her heart so fused into her head, that all the fires of hate, and envy, and calumny, and persecution, cannot unlock that God-sealed embrace.

Archives and Collections: Abbreviations

AJA = American Jewish Archives: Papers of Allen Lesser, the American Jewish Archives, Hebrew Union College, Cincinnati, Ohio.

AJHS = American Jewish Historical Society: Adah Isaacs Menken Collection, American Jewish Historical Society, New York, New York.

BPL = Boston Public Library: Adah Isaacs Menken Collection, Department of Rare Books and Manuscripts, Boston Public Library, Boston, Massachusetts.

HTC = Harvard Theatre Collection: Harvard Theatre Collection, Houghton Library, Harvard University, Cambridge, Massachusetts.

Bibliography

Barclay, G. Lippard. *The Life and Remarkable Career of Adah Isaacs Menken.* Philadelphia, 1868.

Barnes-McLain, Noreen. "Bohemian of Horseback: Adah Isaacs Menken." *Passing Performances: Queer Readings of Leading Players in American Theater History.* Ed. Robert A. Schanke and Kim Marra. Ann Arbor: University of Michigan Press, 1998. 63-79.

Brooks, Daphne A. "Lady Menken's Secret: Adah Isaacs Menken, Actress Biographies, and the Race for Sensation." *Legacy* 15 (1998): 68-77.

Brown, T. Allston. *History of the American Stage.* New York, 1870.

Cofran, John. "The Identity of Adah Isaacs Menken: A Theatrical Mystery Solved." *Theatre Survey* 31 (1990): 47-54.

Davis, Kate Wilson. "Adah Isaacs Menken—Her Life and Poetry in America." M.A. thesis, Southern Methodist University, 1944.

Dollard, Peter. "Six New Poems by Adah Isaacs Menken." *Louisiana Literature* 17 (2000): 97-118.

Falk, Bernard. *The Naked Lady: A Biography of Adah Isaacs Menken.* Rev. ed. London: Hutchinson, 1952.

Foster, Barbara, and Michael Foster. "Adah Isaacs Menken: An American Original." *North Dakota Quarterly* 61 (1993): 52-62.

Gates, Henry Louis, Jr., gen. ed., and Joan R. Sherman, ed. *Collected Black Women's Poetry.* 4 vols. New York and Oxford: Oxford University Press, 1988. Vol. 1.

James, Ed. *Biography of Adah Isaacs Menken.* New York, [1881].

Lesser, Allen. *Enchanting Rebel: The Secret of Adah Isaacs Menken.* New York: The Beechhurst Press, 1947.

Lewis, Paul. *Queen of the Plaza: A Biography of Adah Isaacs Menken.* New York: Funk & Wagnalls, 1964.

Mankowitz, Wolf. *Mazeppa: The Lives, Loves, and Legends of Adah Isaacs Menken.* New York: Stein and Day, 1982.

Miller, Joaquin. *Adah Isaacs Menken.* Ysleta, Texas: Edwin B. Hill, 1934.

Northcutt, Richard. *Adah Isaacs Menken: An Illustrated Biography.* 2nd ed. London: The Press Printers, 1921.

Scharnhorst, Gary. "Adah Isaacs Menken." *Nineteenth-Century American Women Writers: A Bio-Bibliographical Critical Sourcebook.* Ed. Denise D. Knight. Westport: Greenwood Press, 1997. 310-13.

Sentilles, Renée. "Performing Menken: Adah Isaacs Menken's American Odyssey." Ph.D. diss., The College of William and Mary, 1997.

Sherman, Joan R., ed. *African-American Poetry of the Nineteenth Century.* Urbana and Chicago: University of Illinois Press, 1992.

Stoddard, Charles Warren. "La Belle Menken." *National Magazine* Feb. 1905: 477–88.

Swinburne, Algernon Charles. *Adah Isaacs Menken: A Fragment of Autobiography.* London: [privately printed], 1917.